New

Rhiannon

by Vicki Grove

G. P. Putnam's Sons

G. P. PUTNAM'S SONS
A division of Penguin Young Readers Group.
Published by The Penguin Group.
Penguin Group (USA) Inc., 375 Hudson Street, New York, NY 10014, U.S.A. • Penguin Group
(Canada), 90 Eglinton Avenue East, Suite 700, Toronto, Ontario, Canada M4P 2Y3 (a division
of Pearson Penguin Canada Inc.). • Penguin Books Ltd, 80 Strand, London WC2R 0RL, England.
• Penguin Ireland, 25 St. Stephen's Green, Dublin 2, Ireland (a division of Penguin Books Ltd.). •
Penguin Group (Australia), 250 Camberwell Road, Camberwell, Victoria 3124, Australia
(a division of Pearson Australia Group Pty Ltd). • Penguin Books India Pvt Ltd, 11 Community
Centre, Panchsheel Park, New Delhi—110 017, India. • Penguin Group (NZ), 67 Apollo Drive,
Mairangi Bay, Auckland 1311, New Zealand (a division of Pearson New Zealand Ltd.). •
Penguin Books (South Africa) (Pty) Ltd, 24 Sturdee Avenue, Rosebank, Johannesburg 2196,
South Africa. Penguin Books Ltd, Registered Offices: 80 Strand, London WC2R 0RL, England.

Library of Congress Cataloging-in-Publication Data available upon request.
ISBN 978-0-399-23633-4
1 3 5 7 9 10 8 6 4 2
First Impression

for Mike, always

25 November, 1120
The White Ship

"The Prince went aboard the *White Ship* with one hundred and forty youthful nobles and ladies of the highest rank. All this gay company with their servants and the sailors made three hundred souls aboard the fair *White Ship*. 'Give three casks of wine, Fitz-Stephen,' said the Prince, 'to the fifty sailors of renown. My father the King has sailed. What time is there to make merry here and yet reach England with the rest?' 'Prince,' said Fitz-Stephen, 'if we sail at midnight, my fifty and the *White Ship* shall overtake the swiftest vessel in your father's fleet by morning.'

"The Prince commanded them to make merry; and the sailors drank the three casks of wine; and the Prince and all the noble company danced in the moonlight on the deck of the *White Ship*. When at last she left the harbour there was not a sober seaman on board. But the sails were set, Fitz-Stephen at the helm. The gay young nobles and the beautiful ladies, wrapped in mantles of bright colours, laughed and sang. The Prince encouraged the fifty sailors to row harder, for the honour of the *White Ship*. Crash! A cry broke from three hundred hearts. It was the cry the people in the vessels of the King heard faintly on the water. The *White Ship* had struck a rock. Fitz-Stephen hurried the Prince into a boat. 'Push off,' he whispered, 'and row to the land. The rest of us must die.'

"But as they rowed away from the sinking ship the Prince heard the voice of his half-sister calling to him. He cried, 'Row back, I cannot leave her!' As the Prince held out his arms to catch her, such numbers

1

leaped in that the boat was overset. In that same instant the *White Ship* went down.

"Only one man survived to tell the tale—a butcher from Rouen. For three days no one dared to carry the news to the King; at length they sent into his presence a little boy who, weeping bitterly and kneeling at his feet, told him that the *White Ship* was lost with all on board. The King fell to the ground like a dead man, and never afterwards was seen to smile."

Charles Dickens, *A Child's History of England*
from William of Malmesbury (1085–1143)

A Wayfarer Meets a Dire End

Everyone knows that even the sunniest forest on the mildest of after-noons is filled with poison-toothed wild pig and ferocious packs of wolf. And some say that when one nears Wales there are other things lurking in the shadows as well, enchantments and the like left from faery days. Yet naturally some folk will venture the forest paths anyhow.

The young wayfarer was such a one. He was on a noble quest, and though after many days he'd found no trace of what he sought, neither had he come upon especial mischance. Until, that is, one nightfall found him fogged completely, adrift upon his steed as a sailor in a tossed boat, caught in that swirling brew that oft sneaks from the Welsh Sea and crawls up over the beachy land, right into the northern Wessex forests.

He soon enough lost the woodland track and could discern no stars for direction.

The last to talk to him, at least in *this* world, was a stout woman gathering firewood in that part of the forest. His horse reared at the sight of her rump as it suddenly loomed from the foggy swirl like some broad and not easily skirted boulder. She was bent over picking up branches, and for her part, she noted not the wayfarer's approach and was some startled herself, as fog tends to mute sound, especially com-ing from behind.

"Sirrah!" the woman scolded when she'd heaved herself upright and turned to face him with her knuckles upon her substantial hips.

"Have a care, if ye please! I'm some lame these days and would not be toppled to the ground by your stampeding mount!"

Well, his steed was picking the way, never stampeding, but the wayfarer was too relieved to see a human face to quibble with the rude manners of this common woman.

He dismounted and addressed her quite courteously in her own Saxon tongue.

"I beg you pardon me, madame, as I'm some lost." He smiled sheepishly as he took a coin from his pouch. "Pray, can you direct me to the nearest settlement?"

The dame's eyes widened and she reached for the coin, bit it, found it solid, and pocketed it. "You're in luck, young sir, as Woethersly's just some short distance," she said coyly, holding forth her palm and leaving the direction open unless he'd buy it with a second coin. Her eyes then hit upon a small sparkle there upon his bosom. "I'd take that charm of yours for the information," she suggested, reaching toward it.

He stepped quickly back, covering with two fingers the tiny silver pin that held his cloak together at the throat. "Good lady, I could never part with this shell, as it is a sacred token of my pilgrimage to the crypt where Saint James himself sleeps eternal."

She raised her eyebrows, pulled in her lip, and crossed herself, some impressed.

"Go some twenty paces back the way ye've come and you'll find the trail," the stout dame instructed, jerking a thumb in that direction. "Go left on it. There's only one fork from here to town. Go *left* at that fork to reach Woethersly, see? The *right* fork ye never want, as it crosses the common barley field outside the town, then goes through the river, then takes ye to the beach and straight up the invalid trail of Clodaghcombe Bluff!"

4

She knit her brow and clucked her tongue, but the wayfarer's heart had taken a quick leap at that word *invalid*.

"Clodaghcombe Bluff, you say? And pray, what might be this . . . *invalid* trail?"

And now she looked at him as though he were a true dunce, as this is how some provincial folk view the stranger to their realm. "Surely ye know that just beyond Woethersly a great bluff rises straight up from the sea, nigh piercing the ivory floor of heaven itself? Oh, sir, surely everyone's heard of high and steep Clodaghcombe Bluff!"

"I've never," he said softly. "Tell me more."

"Well, see, there's a small stone church up there in those clouds," she began. " 'Twas built by some ancient hermit, hundreds of years past. And there's some few cottages built in a circle close around that hermitage. And there's three women what lives up there atop the bluff in one of those cottages. In fact, the eldest up there is a friend of mine from girlhood, Moira's her name. The others are her daughter and granddaughter. They three are Welsh by descent, see. Moira tells it that she and her family's first great-granddames were seabirds flown across the bay from Wales!"

"If you please," he prodded softly, "I'd hear now of why you called the path up the bluff an *invalid* trail. Why that word, *invalid*?"

The dame threw up her hands. "Ha! And who else would take that blasted trail, I ask ye? None would for *pleasure* climb up the bluff." She took time for a large sigh, then added, "Of course, if you've a helpless *invalid* or *idiot* on your hands, someone born witless or become crippled by injury or otherwise smitten by mischance or dire brainpox, well then, it alters the situation. In such conditions it's well worth the risk of the hike to lug that poor soul up to them three women atop the bluff. The red-haired daughter's the one what nurses, with the others to help. Moira, Aigneis, and dark-eyed Rhia. They three nest atop that crag and care for all hard cases handed off to them. The place is for dying, see, not for healing. What can be healed sweats it out here below. Why, I myself am gouty in the leg, with many blisters upon me as well, and when the heat comes, I—"

The wayfarer quickly remounted. "Good dame, I thank you again for your trouble, and now I must ride. But first I'd escort you safely home, if you'd like."

With a pleased smile for the flattering offer, she waved that away. "Ach, and my own son is right here, working alongside me! He would not hear of me coming into such weathers alone, would ye, Arnold?" As she'd got no answer, she turned to peer into the fog behind her. "Arnold, show yourself!" she right out bellowed.

Some moments later a young man with muddy britches and a feathered hat came into view, scratching his stomach and dragging his heels.

Nodding coolly to the son, then more deeply and courteously to the mother, the wayfarer took his leave.

"Mind you stay left at the fork!" the dame called after him. Then she stooped to pick up the pile of sticks she'd gathered and thrust them roughly into her son's limp arms.

"Would that *you* had such a care for your mother's aches and miseries as that well-speaking stranger had," she grumbled as she began the trudge back to their cottage.

"What'd he want?" the son asked, yawning large. "He looked rich to me."

"He wanted a friendly chat," she answered. "And direction to the town."

"He better have paid you," groused Arnold. "He better have paid, and well."

The wayfarer took the right fork and crossed the common barley field in good order. There upon its far edge was some watermeadow, and then the River Woether flowed across the trail, just as the dame had told him it would. His horse easily stepped through, as the river's ford was well marked by many centuries of crossings. Cold mist rose and curled thick above the fast-flowing river, joining with the fog from the choppy sea, which was quite nearby now. In fact, looking to the right, he perceived, at just a little distance, the eery glowing torchlight that marked the town's quay. He could make out several boats moored there, and some movement upon the dock that sent the mist spiraling. At this time of night and on the edge of such wilderness, it was likely pirates were afoot.

The breeze brought a putrid smell from the beach that made him grimace.

He pulled his cloak closer and set his face toward the unknown forest ahead of him, as his destination was neither the sea on his right nor the town on his left. He was after the bluff trail, the *invalid* trail, and he tried to perceive the entrance to it through the murk.

He was all concentration, leaning forward in his saddle and squinting into the darkness, when he sensed a disturbance in the fog behind him. Tightening the reins of his steed, he clucked to his mount, meaning to turn and see what approached.

But he felt a sudden astonishing pain, and all before his eyes went red, then black.

Reeve Almund Clap, chief overseer of Lord Claredemont's lands, had taken up the habit of making rounds right at first dawn after foggy nights. And so it was he who first came upon the body of a young stranger lying in the shallows of the River Woether not far from the quay. The pale corpse moved its limbs in mimicry of life with the light current, and Almund quietly and respectfully dismounted and knelt in the frigid waters to make a close inspection. He concluded that the unfortunate man had been knifed, seven times all told, and stripped of all he owned. He assumed the wayfarer had been on foot, as there was no sign to inform the good reeve of the steed the man had been riding.

Even the prints of its hooves had been stolen by the sticky-fingered river.

Chapter 1

Most down in Woethersly were still groggy with sleep when the murder bell disturbed the peace at dawn that April morn, but Rhiannon had been wide awake for some time already. Not from Granna's snoring, neither—though it *had* been a night of spectacular blastings. But rather because during the wee hours, the wind had switched south and spring had finally come blustering up high Clodaghcombe Bluff.

When Rhia could not keep still for another moment, she'd crept from the pallet and tiptoed to the corner of the loft where sparrows had last year built a nest, leaving a wide and breezy gap in the roof twigs where you could look down upon the world.

'Twas still dark, but Rhia'd lately discovered she much enjoyed the night look of things. The other five cottages atop their bluff shone in the moonlight, the glistening brook sewing them together with starry stitches. They seemed like faeries from the olden days of magic, dancing with joined hands around the small stone church. The church itself looked completely made of moonglow, or elsewise from the honey of Granna's prized hives, which Rhia could just make out hovering ghost white in the misty distance.

She smiled at a lump of shaggy darkness upon the church roof, clearly visible against the bright stone steeple. It was certainly their groshawke, Gramp, standing vigilant nightwatch on behalf of all up here, they three women in this cottage and the invalids they cared for in the other five. Well, four at this moment. They'd a vacancy in their fifth invalid cot, now the ox-kicked yeoman had died of his dire injuries last month.

The moonlight sparked gold off Gramp's ancient birdy eyes.

"G'd evening to ye, Gramp," Rhia whispered through the darkness.

"Crrrr-awkk!" Gramp flapped his hoary old wings so the mites making their snug bed in his feathers were rudely awakened and went spiraling out into the moonlight like glistening faery dust. "Craaah-*awk!*"

At that alarm, Granna gave an impressive last snore and sat straight up. "Thanks be to ye, God, as I'm still a-breathing!" she said heartily, her usual practice upon waking. Then, missing some warmth, she felt beside her on the pallet and found only the indents of Rhia's body in the wool-covered straw.

"Rhiannon, where've ye got to?" Granna called out.

Rhia grabbed her skirt from the peg. "I'm a-hurrying to bluff's edge to gather whatever seed there be, Granna, ere the wind that brought it this gusty night takes it on along elsewheres!"

"But it be darkish, Rhia," Granna warned predictably. "You must await the dawn afore it be safe to . . ."

But Rhia was by then pulling her rough wool skirt over her long flaxen sleep shift as she hopped down the loft ladder. She figured her distance from Granna far enough so's she could pretend not to hear. "Be back later, Granna!" she sang out as she pulled tight on the waist cord of the skirt and knotted it. She grabbed the rawhide ankle boots that awaited her behind the ladder, finding them nice and toasty from the nearby fire.

Usually Mam would have slept beside the firepit, but just now she nursed poor burned Ona and her twins in their cottage both day and night. So without anyone else to question her, Rhia skittered barefoot and light as a spider across their main room, grabbed her seed bag from the rafter, and hit out quite jauntily into the adventures surely awaiting in the mysterious night world.

Upon the stone stoop she sat long enough to pull on the boots and lace them.

It had been Gramp's main business all Rhia's life to heft off and fly above her each time she traveled to the rough lip of the high stone crag. So here he came, swooping from the chapel roof like some cumbrous stone gargoyle come alive.

"Is the wind not wondrous tonight, Gramp?" Rhia called up to him, bouncing to her feet. He teetered above her, straining to gain his wingy balance upon that same rough night wind she liked so well. Had he words, he might surely have naysayed her opinion, as the bluster of that gale provided *him* with only troubles. But that's oft the way of it— the human has the go of things, and the beast is left with no choice but the go-along.

The gardens and the hives were pinkish as Rhia sailed past them, and by the time she and Gramp were zigzagging through the thicket of wind-bent orchard trees, the fog had mostly loosed its hold and slunk on back down to the sea, fog being a watery thing and completely out of place in the sky. Still, it will oft sneak there in the deep of night, pretending to be its better cousin, the cloud.

"Well, here we are then, Gramp," Rhia announced, dropping to her knees when she'd run clean out of solid ground. Gramp mayhaps thought her comment insulting, him being winged and better fitted to judge from the sky such a thing as when the edge of the sheer crag had indeed been reached. But he merely settled in a dignified way onto the faery rock that overhung the water far below, snugging his hard old talons fast into the hole perfectly in the center of that round stone. From his vantage there, he'd keep Rhia from mischance by a growlish sound deep in his throat if she moved too near the edge or ventured onto rock that had crumbled a new bit with the wind or rain.

Truth was, Gramp's job of vigilance was even harder than usual this April that Rhia was fourteen, fifteen in three months. For Rhiannon was not paying attention to her business like she should have been, or like you might think she *would* have been so close to a dire drop. This darkish morn, for instance, instead of starting right in gathering the night-borne seed she'd spoken to Granna so urgently about, she instead picked up a chrysalis that had been recently breached and went all moody with inspecting it.

"Poor butterfly, gone rashly into the bright blue, but now air-stranded and beyond return!" she cried, shredding the torn chrysalis into tiny strips and tossing each one to the wild breeze. "Still, Gramp, what fine adventure it must surely be to have wings, to fly hither and thither at your own whim! To brave the whole wide world!"

Gramp didn't respond to her moody musings, as he never acknowledged her prattle to him here at the treacherous bluff's edge. And besides, he'd another important job beyond the considerable job of keeping her from falling to a certain death. It's rare they got visitors from the seaside town below come clear up their trail, but when they did, Gramp always warned of them, hearing their approach from Woethersly before Rhia's own ears picked up the grunts of their exertion or the swishing of the high weeds that lined the steep path upward along the seaside edge of Clodaghcombe Forest. At detection of someone coming with evil intent, or even *good* intent, Gramp gave a high squawk and spread his old wings wide so as to make quite a fearful spectacle of himself.

"*Crrawwwwkk!*" Gramp suddenly piped, giving his wings a mighty flap that sent his molting winter feathers sailing like dandelion fuzz. "*Crrrrrrawk, awk!*"

He was facing the bay, craning his head so far forward that his stringy neck seemed like an old frayed rope about to come apart.

"What is it, then, Gramp?" Rhiannon whispered in a rush, the air-stranded butterflies instantly gone from her head at that strong alarm. "What d'you see upon the waters?"

The sun had not yet made his grand appearance, but the sea was in no way dark. Indeed the waves were painted pink by the rose-dappled clouds above them. Rhia sat upon her haunches and squinted hard to survey the chop. There *was* a boat out there, all right! *And* it was leaving the port, not arriving. Really, there was nothing so unusual she could make of that, though. Sometimes as many as a dozen boats arrived or departed on days of fine weather, bringing wine and other outside goods for the town of Woethersly and taking away rye, oats, and the much-prized cheese produced by the manor.

Still, this ship was different from any other Rhia had seen. She watched it sail, some dazzled by the beauty and solemn grace of the strange ship's riggings.

"Well, Gramp, as you say, that ship is certainly no plain-rigged Welsh wine trader's craft, and not a gaudy boat of buccaneers," she pronounced solemnly, as if she were some authority on nautical styles. "Indeed, it's festooned and draped more richly than anything I've seen sailed by the knight of our manor, Lord Claredemont himself!"

And then the absent sun threw his first fistful of bright spangles upward against the pinky clouds and she saw what had been too shadowed for her observance before. Except for a single bright pennant displaying the owner's coat-of-arms, all of that strange ship's elegant riggings and drapes were of one single color—black!

Rhia tapped her chin with one finger and gave a sigh so filled with windy sadness that Gramp could not dare choose to ignore it.

"Well, Gramp, for certain that ship is owned by high nobility. And is it not just unbearably sad that all the nobility are draping themselves and all their belongings in black these days, in mourning for poor King Henry's only son? For indeed, Prince William Aethling has gone to his watery grave aboard his grand *White Ship,* and they say our king has not smiled since, and claims he never will!"

Rhia sighed again and shook her head, imagining it, though Gramp hunched his shoulders and squinted forward, peeved, if you want the truth, as Mam would have been peeved with Rhia about that as well. For Rhia imagined that horrid disaster at least two or three times each day and had a good pathetic sigh about it each and every time. Morbid, Mam pronounced Rhia's constant return to that tragic shipwreck. A shameful use of her thoughts, which might better have been set upon her present business of gathering the seeds ere they blew on along or were eaten by birds. So would have scolded Mam had she heard Rhia sigh so deeply, not once but twice.

But give Rhia slack, because it happens the prince and his large retinue of lords and ladies had all been near her own young age when that grand ship had hit a sea rock and gone so quickly to the murky bottom of the sea last November. To picture such horrors and then to look around with living eyes and see the new buds swelling everywhere, to imagine the cold sea and then to feel the warm wind twining through your hair, to smell the honeysuckle and the rose and know

14

that you lived and were young this first true morn of spring when others were . . . well, alas, simply were *not*.

Well, 'twas doubly sad, imagining that, but made life all the sweeter. And made you grateful you had it—life, that is—which is not completely a bad thing to feel, is it?

And besides, to be fair, Rhia was by no means alone. Most in England were still very much consumed with the details of the *White Ship*'s final tragic sail. A generation of young nobility, gone without a trace, drowned in the cold sea! Oh, yes, most folk in King Henry's lands had it still much in mind, though near six months had passed away.

And nowhere was it spoken of more often or with more gruesome embellishment than here on the western frontier, where court details were sketchy and therefore imaginings plentiful and constantly embroidered.

"All aboard that chilly sail are now lying in the briny deep between Francia and England with their finery and jewels admired only by the fishes, and caressed by the slim fingers of the probing seaweed," Rhia whispered, shivering at the thought.

And right then is when the church bell down in Woethersly broke the dawn quiet.

Bong! Bong! Bong!

Rhia jumped to her feet with her hands to her mouth. "Gramp, did you count three rings?" she demanded, her heart beating as though it would escape her chest. " 'Twas *three*, I'm right sure of it, and that means a murder most foul has been done down in Woethersly!"

Again Vicar Pecksley rang the great bell in the steeple below. *Bong! Bong! Bong!*

"It *is* a murder, then!" Rhia whispered. Murder was far more interesting than four rings for a wedding or a dozen for some old person's death. Murder was something that set all kinds of pictures to spinning in your mind . . .

"Crrrrrr-*awk!*" Gramp gave out, ignoring both the bell and Rhia's reaction to it. He'd turned clear round on his rock to glare at the opening from the woods.

Rhia came to instant attention. Two threats perceived by Gramp at one time, one watery and the other coming right up their trail! This was *exceptional* strange to the point of being never heard of at all. And indeed, she now saw with her own two eyes that the high weeds down the trail a little ways were moving as though in a good wind.

Why, the murderer himself might be the hoodlum a-stirring up those weeds as he progressed to the top of the bluff. Rhia might be plain-out *killed* by him when he arrived! And if she ran and hid, that would leave the way open for him to reach her mother and her granna, which would be even worse, or nearly as bad!

So she cowered inside the shadow of Gramp's spread wings and got her legs ready in case a treacherous, murdering outlaw was indeed coming up the path, as she'd resolved to see which way he turned and to follow him close in order to stab him in his back.

Of course, she hadn't taken the time to consider that she had no knife.

Chapter 2

Luckily for Rhia, the thrashing weeds revealed no murderer whatsoever, but instead the tall shape of Woethersly's good overseer, Reeve
Almund Clap. As he climbed the last stretch of the trail, he was occupied with wiping sweat from his streaming brow with one sleeve of his
wool jerkin and so did not notice Rhia or Gramp. Rhia was glad of
that, as she could shoulder her seed pouch and hightail for home without the delay of giving him courteous greeting. She must tell Mam with
all possible haste!

Gramp launched himself with a grunty heft of his old wings and
flew in such close circles above her that Rhia could scarce keep her
footing as she ran the homeward path.

"No need for such protection, Gramp, as it's only our reeve!" she
finally called up to him. "Mam will go giddy when I inform her that
he's on his way, just *see* if she doesn't."

Rhia sped around the edge of the new-plotted vegetable rows, then
dodged through the crooked orchard trees and picked up speed past the
line of honeyed hives, though she heard a sharp, concerned buzzing in
her wake. Bees will always be curious about what goes on, of course,
and to ignore their concerns invites all sorts of trouble to a place.

So Rhia slowed and turned long enough to call, "Don't fret, bees,
as it's only our reeve come up the trail on some limp excuse to
see Mam!"

Sassy talk, and only part true, as there *had* been a murder, after all.

The reeve would doubtless have thought it his official duty to hike the long path to inform them of it as soon as his other duties permitted him leave.

Still, it must be said, some of the time he *did* come up on limp excuses.

At any rate, the bees were satisfied, that's the thing, and their sharp drone eased back to a mild enough murmur. And so Rhia could run straightaway again until she neared the first of the invalid cottages, the one wherein Ona and her twins rested uneasy in their pain. There Rhia slid to a respectful walk and crept quietly to the window, expecting Mam to be inside.

Ona tossed fitfully upon her pallet, moaning softly, and the little twins lay asleep on a straw-stuffed pad laid near the firepit, their arms around each other.

The fire had been stoked and the water jug filled, but there was no sign of Mam.

She could certainly be found in one of the other cottages, then, and so Rhia ran to take a quick look in each. The Man Who Sleeps was deathly still upon his raised pallet, just as he had been since they'd got him. But no Mam was present to dab his brow or force some gruel down into him as she did each morn and evening. In the third cot, Dull Sal lay sleeping upon her side with her golden hair about her face. She sucked hard upon her thumb, as was her wont. Sally had kicked her blanket off in the night, but Mam was nowhere nearby to throw it back over Sal's long legs. Rhia crept in and quickly did that herself, then hurried to check the fourth cottage.

Mam was not there, and Gimp Jim himself was indeed absent, along with his walking stick. Frowning, Rhiannon turned from the window to scan the nearby grounds, expecting to find Jim hobbling about, mayhaps feeding the ducks where they oft paddled in the brook that ran alongside his cottage.

No Jim, though, which was odd, seeing as how his one-legged state kept him close at all times. But Rhia'd spent enough time searching for lost folk. Soon enough the reeve himself would arrive and spoil her surprise! She ran to tell Granna, at least, of the reeve's approach, splashing across the mossy brook where it curved twice through their toft, then jumping the broken grindstone that formed their stoop, then finally bursting through the front door, all breathless.

"Granna?" she panted. "Reeve Clap comes up our path this very minute!"

The smoky gloom inside the cot made her blind after the bright sun, but Rhia could make out Granna as she sat on her stool, discerning from the morning fire what she could about the coming day. Rhia hurried around the edge of the firepit to stand close behind and join her in her watch. Though she seemed to completely lack Granna's gift of special sight, she figured there was always hope.

"I've already seen our reeve, Rhiannon." Granna chuckled and nodded toward a point in the fire. "There, where the blue flames be. Can you na see a yellow-haired man with green bracca pulled high over his Saxon grasshopper legs?"

As she squinted into the flames, Rhia snuffled a bit at Granna's joke. To Granna, Saxons were too long, too loose-strung, and some laughable in their easy gawkiness, unlike the Welsh, who, bird-made or natural, tend to be close to the ground and quick in step. Though none, neither Saxon nor Welsh, were near as ridiculous in Granna's eyes as the Normans, rulers of all these days. Why, they'd not so much as learned the English speech, but still spoke the chicken cackle of their loved Francia!

19

Granna spit whenever they were so much as mentioned.

Rhia gave up trying to form the blue flames into Reeve Clap. "Should I go find Mam, d'ye suspect?" She shifted her weight from foot to foot, fidgety and impatient.

"Find Mam?" her mother asked, for there she suddenly stood inside the doorway, shaking dew from the greens she'd just been gathering. Her bright hair brought a soft glow to the cottage, as from candleflame.

"Aigneis, are ye about?" Reeve Clap called from a little distance outside.

Mam whirled toward the sound, one hand upon her throat.

"Sounds quite chipper, don't he, Aigy, for someone who's just climbed two miles straight up a rock trail?" Granna murmured. "What is it about the very saying of your name would so refresh him, d'ye think?"

Granna winked at Rhia, and Rhia bit her lips. Granna, with fewer scruples, cackled.

"The reeve elected by the good people of Woethersly to take charge of all the lord's farm dealings has more to do than take a pleasure hike up our bluff and stand grinning like a dunce, I'd venture," Granna called out so the reeve would hear. "Quit dillydallying and state yer business here with us this morning, Almund, will you? We've heard the murder bell. What's afoot below?"

Mam came unfrozen, ducked her head, and, blushing all the harder, came inside to sort her greens, giving Reeve Clap invitation to follow over her threshold.

"G'morn to ye, Moira," Reeve Clap said, squinting toward Granna across the smoky gloom as he ducked through the doorway. "G'morn as well to you, Rhiannon."

Rhiannon stood up straighter, pushed her black hair behind her ears, and nodded polite greeting, but Granna, not so patient nor formal, either, asked again, bluntly, "So, who's got hisself kilt today, then, Almund?"

Almund Clap crouched near the chicken pen, elbows on his knees. He seemed far too big for their cot, like some albatross squeezing small into a bluebird's nest.

"Well, Moira, it's no one local. I made an early patrol on one of Lord Claredemont's horses this morn, as on a murky night much can go awry. And sure enough, I came upon a stranger who'd breathed his last. He lay near the west ford of the river, not so far from the foot of your bluff. Even now my men are combing your bluffy woods for clues."

Rhia looked at Mam, who'd gone pale as milk. The deed was done so close!

"He'd deep cuts to his stomach, so it was a murder, for sure," Almund murmured, frowning as he remembered it. "As for suspects, well, there were several vessels in port last night, traders and fishers, also brigands. I especially noted the slapdash boat of a certain band of freebooters moored at our docks. That pirate crew have all seven of them spent fair amounts of time cooling their heels in local gaols, so my first thought was that they were likely the ones who'd done it. As soon as I'd found men to tend to the body, I galloped to quiz that bunch ere they could sail with the morning tide."

Rhia saw Mam press her lips together at the grim nature of these events.

"As I approached the docks, the torchlight revealed the spindly-legged leader of that brigand pack throwing a bucket of waste over the side of his vessel," Almund continued. " 'Ho, Captain,' I called to him.

'You docked under cover of darkness, not in daylight as those who arrive here to trade. So now I'd know what you were up to in the night!' There was a terrible stench in the air. I covered my nose with my sleeve, and the horse I sat tossed his mane, begging to flee the aroma. But the captain merely showed green teeth and roared a laugh. 'It's rotted goat meat ye smell, Reeve.' He pointed to a sooty mess upon the beach. 'There lies the waste of its carcass, where we cooked it first thing when we arrived. My crew all et bad goat meat in the night, turned sour from when we poached it last week from far shores. We've heaved ever since and lost our sea legs. Can you not hear the groans from down below deck?' "

"*Could* you indeed hear them . . . heaving?" Rhiannon couldn't resist asking.

Almund nodded, scratching his head. "Yes, I *could*. And further, I don't think it likely those poor ne'er-do-wells prowled the night in such condition, let alone had the strength for this sort of bloody murder. Still, I ordered their ship kept in port for now, in case I'm proved wrong when we know more facts. They're to stay shipboard upon it and not to mingle among the folk of the town."

Mam asked quietly, "Will those ruffians truly stay upon their boat when your vigilance is elsewhere, Almund? Or will they . . . skulk about?"

The reeve looked at her. "The captain seemed willing enough to do as told, Aigy. He's escaped the hangman's noose often enough that he knows his reputation alone might hang him if he's seen about on shore with a murder just done. His words to me were, 'We'll stay tight upon this craft as living crew, or skeleton crew, if ye get my drift.' Then he leaned over the ship's rail and retched quite heartily. At that, I gladly turned my mount. 'Captain, you're too stringy tough to die,' I called over my shoulder as I rode on. 'And don't neglect to clean up that mess upon our beach, or I'll send our bailiff out to meet you. And I'll be sure to put in a word to Bertha, who cooks for prisoners in our gaol, just to let her know you enjoy a fine helping of well-aged goat!' "

Granna and Rhia laughed at that, though Mam, the worrier of the three, did not.

"We've raised the hue and cry throughout the manor and will beat the fields all day," Reeve Clap now told them. "My men have talked to those in the forest cottages that lie along the trail to town, but no one seems to have heard or seen a thing. I myself went to Hilda Mopp's house, as her son Arnold is a sulky sort of lad and has had some brushes with the law. Nothing approaching *this* sort of heinous crime, but a hare poached now and then, a cabbage pilfered, each leading to a whipping or other discouragement. Dame Mopp was quick with their alibi. She told that they both had been abed early, it being fogged, though she declared Arnold slept with a heavy club aside himself, always protective of his mother. She claims they saw no stranger pass their way in the night, nor during the previous day, for that matter. Arnold was not at home, but when I come across the boy, I'll see if his story is a match for his mother's."

"And so your interviews have yielded up no felon, and you will beat the fields all this day," Granna mused, chewing hard upon the stem of her pipe. "And I'm certain our vicar will decide there must needs be a laying of hands upon the corpse for the morrow."

Almund nodded wearily. "Vicar Pecksley has declared that the body will indeed be displayed on the wide table before the butcher shop tomorrow noon, and all in the manor will be required to take part in a laying of hands on it, including yourselves up here upon the bluff. Unless the crime's positively solved by then, of course, in which case

23

only the captured murderer will lay his hands upon the corpse as proof positive of his guilt. It seems unlikely we'll have our man by then, so assume it's on if you've not heard otherwise by tomorrow dawn from me or one of my men."

"The dead man's wounds will gush blood when they're touched by the hands of his foul murderer," Granna murmured, staring at the flames.

It was one of those things beyond explaining. A newly dug well won't fill right unless a shoe is hung inside it. Bees will bring misfortune upon a place unless informed of all goings-on. And the wounds of a murder victim will gush blood when the vile murderer lays his, or her, hands upon the body. And so all must take a turn doing it.

Rhia didn't really mind. She'd done it three times before during the other three murder investigations in her lifetime. The touching was bad, but it lasted only a moment, and on the *good* side, it brought an excuse to go down into town, where the sellers and street performers would likely take advantage of such a crowd to make the day merry.

She might even link with her friends to hear the new gossip!

Rhia was instantly ashamed of that thought, for there could be no *good* part in such a dire crime, of course. Still, it wasn't her fault, this bloody murder, and if her friends showed up to gab, how could she courteously refuse? She could not, that's all.

Glossy, the big red hen, suddenly stuck her beak through the willow of the chicken cage and began nibbling at some small thing stuck to the elbow of Reeve Clap's tunic.

"A business such as this murder is why you women had best forsake this high bluff," the reeve quietly observed. He drew his hands across his face, thereby moving his elbow and robbing Glossy of her juicy tidbit.

"Rhia, a cool drink for our guest," Mam ordered from the table near the doorway where she worked sorting greens. Her back was mostly toward them all, though Reeve Clap kept stealing glances her way, and she his.

Rhia hurried to fill him a mug with ale made from their malt.

"You *choose* to exert yourself to such a sweat climbing up here on a hot spring day, Almund Clap," Granna observed, back to teasing now that she had her fill of information. "We've never asked for invite down from you, and never invited you up the bluff to us."

"Aw, Moira," said Reeve Clap, flustered. He took the ale from Rhiannon and gulped it down in one long quaff, then wiped his mouth with his thick fingers and said again, more forcefully, "I *do* worry about you three women up here alone."

"You forget there are others up here, Almund," Mam said quietly. "And what of *them* tomorrow? There be six invalids at the moment in four of our five hospice cots, and not a one of them can walk down the bluff to file by a dead man, as can't my mother with her aged legs, not easily."

To Rhia's surprise, Granna didn't contradict her.

"Only the fit to walk must come tomorrow," Reeve Clap said. "Your invalids and idiots can stay put. But if the murderer's not discovered and Vicar Pecksley orders a second laying of hands for the next day, Lord Claredemont's orders may change in that regard. If it comes to that, we can find strong men to carry down all who dwell up here."

"Har!" Granna roared, throwing back her head. "The day Woethersly calls its forgotten damned back down this bluff is the day the town will sink into the sea!"

Shocked, Rhia looked quickly to Mam, sure she'd give Granna sharp reproof for her heathen language. But Mam was looking down at her hands, stilled in the midst of sorting those greens. Rhia looked then to the reeve, who leaned back against the wattle as before, but now with his head bent so he stared at the floor.

What had there been in Granna's riddling words to cause such a strain to fall upon the house? After some time of that tight silence, the good reeve stood and handed Rhiannon his empty mug. He smiled his thanks, but his eyes then quickly shifted to Rhia's mother.

"Aigneis, I'd like a private word before I go back down, if I might."

Mam stepped out with him. Rhia, breathless, watched from the window as they walked to the edge of the woods, her mother so small with her clouds of red hair flowing in the breeze and the reeve gangly-tall and light, a big old Saxon through and through, but not bad to look at if you like that kind of thing.

For all her sad-eyed agreeing about her legs being old, Granna jumped up and skittered quick as a hare to Rhiannon's side so she could get a good view as well.

Chapter 3

They watched as Mam and Reeve Clap passed through the bracken and then were cloaked from sight by the deep shade of the thick oak trees at the forest's edge. When they could no longer see them, still they stood at the window, trying their best to.

"Granna?" Rhia whispered as they peered. "Why'd you give Ona and her girls and Gimp Jim and Dull Sal such a heathen description, saying they were the town's forgotten damned?"

"You've forgot the Man Who Sleeps," Granna muttered. Then she spit into the rushes that covered their floor. "I was including him as well in my *heathen* description, Rhia. He, too, is one of the forgotten damned, brought up here and left to die." In a low voice she added, "Don't mention this floor-spitting to your mam, if you please. I forgot myself."

Rhia turned to look into her grandmother's eyes. "But their sicknesses and injuries are not their own fault, Granna! So how could God damn them, if He is just? And if He isn't, why do we go to such trouble trying to please Him?"

It was an important question, possibly the most important thing Rhia had ever thought to ask. Granna poked with the toe of her boot at the rushes she'd grimed, hiding them under others that were fresher, then fished in her waist pouch for the fine bone comb she'd inherited from her own granna. She handed it to Rhia and turned her back so's Rhia could braid her hair. Once, Rhia'd found a small bird nested within her grandmother's thick and snarled tresses. Another time she'd uncovered Granna's favorite smoking pipe, which Granna'd feared was lost forever.

"So you'd have it that only the Lord God can dispense damnation, heh, granddaughter?" Granna's head bobbled as she spoke, as Rhia was just then chopping with the comb at a mass of spiderweb. "Oh, human beings can give a person a damning too, and one that may have a sting greater than the merciful Almighty's! Tell me, child, how many would you count have gone back down the trail once they've been brought up to us, each one of them all addled or crippled or, like Ona and her worst-burned twin, singed by house fire crisp as a twig dropped into the firepit?"

Rhia didn't have to think. "No one has gone back down," she answered quietly.

The first of the invalids had come to them six Januarys before, when Rhia had been only eight. He was an old uncle who'd been sleeping on the beach when a freeze set in and ice took hold of his feet and hands, turning them soft and black with rot. They figured he'd made it up their path by accident, just wandering with his wits inflamed. Mam eased him mightily with her salves, and when he died, they three women had buried him inside the largest of the faeries' stone circles, within the sacred heart of the forest.

When word of that got down to the village, it quickly became routine to bring such invalids up their path. They'd had elders who'd lost their reason or use of their limbs, two babies born lacking wits, and several of all ages, men and women, so horribly hurt by animals or mischance that Rhia sometimes could scarce keep from turning her head or covering her nose when Mam sent her to their bedsides with food and drink. Each had been pulled up the trail on a carrying sledge or led by a waist rope, and each slept eternally now within the stone circle.

"But soon enough, I expect Jim may well return to his own home, now that he manages so well with his stick," Rhia quickly pointed out. She added, with a defiant lift to her chin, "In fact, he was out somewheres when I looked into his cot this very morn."

"Oh, yes, of late Jim rambles the woods at night," Granna allowed.

Rhia, who thought she knew everything, had not known that. She blinked in surprise. "But . . . should he not fear walking our woods, and at *night*?" she whispered.

"It's Jim's business where he wanders, Rhia, and none of our own. And I reckon Jim chooses dark night as he wishes no gawkers whilst he practices his hobbled gait."

But had Granna forgot there'd been *murder* done in the woods just last night? Rhia picked at an intricate knot of bristly hairs and mused that Granna was in most ways right—it was not, strictly speaking, her business where Jim rambled. But then again, so *much* was not her business that it ofttimes seemed truly annoying!

She let it go, but with a peevish sigh. "Back to the other then, Granna. Does it not insult my mother for you to say that her patients are damned? Mam's the best healer in all Lord Claredemont's manor, mayhaps in all Wessex. She knows all manner of things about gathering the herbs of the forest for her decoctions and ointments. She can call the birds to herself as well!"

"Exactly so, Rhiannon," Granna soberly agreed. "Being bird-descended, she can, and makes good use of the eggs they give in her calming salves. Mind now that you comb out that little fringe along me neck and catch it in the braid, as it tickles me mightily in my sleep if it's left down to hang."

"She uses the dropped feathers of our sister birds in grave wraps for too-early-born babes," Rhia murmured as she tucked in those neck hairs. "In hard circumstances she's used squabs to make a gruel for someone fevered, and the doves have not seemed to resent such frugal use of their young. *They* gladly help in her work with their sacrifice, and would never think her patients 'damned.'"

Rhia knew she'd pushed it with that last nervy statement. Granna stepped forward so's her hair was jerked from Rhia's grip, then turned to grip Rhia's shoulders.

"Rhiannon, dear, now don't be daft. Your mother's work is not what damns her patients—far from it! Here's the gist of the thing, then. In Woethersly these days they've grown so grand that they take pride in having naught to blemish their view nor cast a pall upon their light-heartedness. And so they send up to us whatever, *whoever*, might get in the way of that. We care for those misfortunates, then we safekeep them in our cemetery, and those below never even have to know when they've passed from this world to the next. Your mother's good medicine is exceeded only by the goodness of her heart, but folks in town now turn away when she walks by as if she does the devil's own work! No, dear girl, proud Woethersly won't welcome back to their midst someone sent up our path, as t'would remind them of much they've decided they will never, ever think about again."

Rhia could only shake her head. "That . . . makes no sense," she whispered.

Spent from her strong riddling, Granna shuffled toward her stool. "No, dear Rhia, like much that humans feel, that makes little sense. Still, I reckon humans will go on feeling nonsense until the Almighty calls an end to time."

She reached her place beside the firepit and eased down to a sit upon her three-legged stool. Rhia regretted seeing Granna's hair so lopsided now, half a braid and half dangling loose. That loose part stuck out bristly and coarse as a donkey's tail. Rhia reached with her arm to sweep under the fall of her own long black hair, bringing it round over her shoulder to make use of the comb she still held. Its teeth went through her thick tresses easily as through water. The small flowers she liked to braid in here and there usually slid right out, so sleek were her locks, but her hair was every bit as thick as Granna's. Could she expect a tail of donkey hair herself one day, ages and ages and ages from now?

The fire popped and blew sparks up toward the rafters, causing Rhia to jump, shamefaced and guilty. Could Granna possibly read her ungracious thoughts?

"Shall I finish your braid for you now?" she asked meekly.

Granna laughed quite heartily. "Nay, Rhia, best start water for the turnips as it grows late for our meal. My donkey hair will wait."

Reeve Clap left directly and they fixed their meal in silence for as long as Granna could stand it, around the time it took the turnip water to come to a bubble.

"Well, Aigneis!" she finally demanded. "What did he talk to you private about?"

Mam sighed. "He brought a sort of warning, Mother, though it made little sense. Almund wanted to let us know that the earl's ship docked last night in Woethersly with cargo for us up here, though Almund knew not what the cargo was."

Rhia looked at Granna, and Granna looked harder at Mam, squinting her eyes. "Well, what sort of a Saxonish half-brained warning is that to be giving, Aigneis?"

Rhia cleared her throat and ventured, "I saw a grand ship leaving the quay while I gathered seeds this morn! It was aristocratic in its draperies, but its cargo couldn't really be for *us*, could it? He must have meant it had come from the earl for them below, in the world. I mean, in Woethersly."

"Strangely, Rhia, I think he meant it *was* for us up here," Mam said quietly. "Almund was at the manor house very early today giving an account of the murder to Lord Claredemont, and as they spoke, a messenger came to inform the lord that the earl's boat was leaving after delivering its cargo *for the bluff*. Almund distinctly heard those three words, but could learn nothing beyond that."

Rhiannon frowned, remembering something else. "Mam, do you recall the day last winter when the earl's son and his friends arrived, the young men now squiring at Lord Claredemont's? You and I were down at market, and everyone stopped their business and went to the docks to see the fine spectacle they made as they left the ship and rode to the manor house with their packhorses and servants."

"The whole town stopped, you say!" Mam played shocked and went wide-eyed. "I remember *your* friends came to fetch *you*, and that Maddy begged me hard to give you leave to go with her and the other girls to gawk and giggle as those fellows left their boat!"

Granna laughed as Rhia blushed and shrugged. "Well, it was only fit that *someone* give them welcome!" she protested weakly. "Anyhow, the boat they came on was much more sprightly than the one I saw this morn, yet *it* was the earl's boat."

"That would have been the earl's *pleasure* boat, Rhia," Mam said. "The one you saw this morn was apt to be the boat the earl keeps for his dirty work. His men use it for hauling oxen and loads of building stone and battle horses and such. It's grand enough, but he'd never have his kith and kin sail in such a filthed contraption."

Mam turned briskly back to her pots. "Turnips smell done, so bring the bread, Rhia, and let's eat," she instructed.

As a rule they ate in silence, chewing good and slow to make sure that what they'd got would stick to their bones and spleens and livers and be of good use to their bodies. But that day they made short work of their meal, having morning chores to catch up.

Mam stood, turned to her medicinal corner, and said, "I'll finish this batch of salve, then go right quick to change Ona's bandages and see about her little girls."

Granna, muttering something softly to herself, moved from the eating bench to Mam's sleep pallet in the nether corner. Almost immediately, she was snoring.

Rhiannon pushed the table to the wall and wiped the bench of crumbs. Lucy sprang eagerly down from the window ledge, and Rhia bent to shake a finger at her. "Crumbs are for the poultry, selfish Lucy, as you well know."

She pulled the latch of the pen and let Glossy and her chicks out to rummage their leftover bits from the floor reeds. Lucy licked her paw and would not look at Rhia, proudly pretending this licking job had been her only intent all along.

Then suddenly, Lucy stopped, her head cocked and her paw motionless in the air. She was onto some smell or small racket under the reeds.

Watching the actions of the cat, Rhia murmured, "As for the murdered man whose wounds we must touch tomorrow, I think someone in town's merely harbored a vagabond, then cut him to death for some coin he told of having."

Mam was crushing feverfew she'd taken from herbs strung on the rafters. "*Merely,* you say? You sound pretty casual about that poor soul's death, Rhiannon."

Mam sounded miffed, and Rhia felt unjustly rebuked. "Well,

it's . . . it's a crime and a sin as well to harbor vagabonds. Or to vagabond yourself. 'You reap what you sow' is what Vicar Pecksley would have to say about it. It's the way of things is all I meant."

Mam said nothing. Lucy dove beneath the rushes and came up with a small mouse. It struggled, jerking and twitching in her jaws.

"Out with that!" Mam cried, shivering her disgust. "There's too much talk of killing in the air today for killing under our own roof!"

Rhia deposited Lucy and her unlucky prey outside, then wandered back to the bluff's edge to finish the morning's job of seed gathering she'd really not started at all. Gramp shook free of the tree roost where he'd been napping and drifted drowsily above her.

When they reached the jutting crag, Rhia quickly made piles of the scattered fennel seed that'd blown from the kerne, then gathered next the tiny purple berry seeds that had separated from the droppings of birds. Today as always there were a few scattered seeds that were strange to her, brought from far lands by the mist, the wind, and the birds.

She glanced at Gramp, settled on his holed rock. "We got our first rye from wind-borne seeds, and our first yellow beans. Also, an ivy that sends itching boils all over you. But bad will come with the good, and good with the bad, Granna always says. Also, you reap what you sow. Why should Mam be cross with me when I mention a heathen vagabond's bloody fate, seeing he brought it down upon himself? It's God's way of dealing with things, wouldn't you say so, Gramp?"

Gramp narrowed his eyes, which Rhiannon took as agreement.

Sighing, she sat back on her heels to search the waters. The fine black boat sent from the earl had long since sailed out of view, and no other craft were in sight. In truth, little of Woethersly could be seen from the bluff because of the thick trees, though you *could* see the shadow of the castle Lord Claredemont kept for the earl, who himself kept it for King Henry. All that "keeping" and not a single person lived there for more than a week or two at a time, to hunt or some such thing. The castle was a deep purple stain stretching far across the blue water. On this clear day, Rhia could also see beautiful Wales floating green in the far distance, touched by the shadow of the castle tower as you might touch a small tuft of grass with your finger.

Shading her eyes, she looked for the place her own da and Mam's da slept beneath the waves. She spotted the small whirlpool of sudsy foam where their tiny fishing boat had capsized, and as always when she spotted it, she whispered a prayer for their souls.

That whirling water opened with the devil's own quickness was how Granna told it, though it was a story she claimed she had barely the heart for, even after these twelve years. *Had it not come on so quick, I might have found a spell to turn my dear Egan and your fine da into mermen ere they sank from sight—*

"Crrrr-*awwk*. Crrrrrrrr."

Startled from her daydreams, Rhia demanded, "Gramp, what do you spy?"

She dropped to her stomach and crawled to the very edge of the crag, then stuck her head out so it was pillowed by thin air. She craned her neck to look to the far right, just as Gramp was doing. And soon enough, she saw it, too.

A cluster of great sea boulders arose on the beach where no such cluster had been before! But no, Rhia finally made out that it was rather a group of people, huddled together on the sand like you'll see oxen huddled of a winter's night. They wore long robes and cloaks the colors of the rocks, all grays and blacks and browns, though a warm spring

35

day like this called for much lighter gear. Even their faces were cov-ered—some by hoods, some by bits of cloth. Some of them had walk-ing sticks like Jim's thrust up under their armpits. But it was the *way* they stood that sent a shiver down her spine. Yes, like oxen, not like hu-mans, who shift and reposition as they stand, thrusting out a hip or hik-ing up a shoulder, too impatient to freeze in place so completely.

"Gramp, they stand so *still*," she breathed, and a shiver went down her spine. "They seem like an ancient group of standing stones. How very strange."

She pushed back from the edge, and there was a little tremble to her hands as she went to quickly pouching her seeds. Who *were* they, those stone people?

What were they?

Gramp continued his silent gawk at the beach with his old round head stretched so far forward that Rhia feared it might pop right off his stringy neck and go bouncing down the cliff like a befeathered ball. Mankind or monsters—even Gramp couldn't seem to decide what the stone folk on the beach might be.

Chapter 4

Mam didn't come back from nursing poor burned Ona till it was nigh dark, and when she came she brought Daisy, the less burned of Ona's six-year-old twins, along with her. Daisy settled on a pallet Rhia spread near the firepit, sucking her fingers for comfort.

Granna squatted to stroke the child's forehead, murmuring, "It's a miracle she's healed so, when her sister and mother languish."

"She's grown much better these last days, it's true," Mam whispered back, then she touched Granna on the shoulder and gestured for her to follow to a more private corner of the room. She gave Rhia a look telling her to do the same.

"She's not been willing to leave her mother's side," Mam told them both when they were out of Daisy's hearing. "But this evening, she gave Ona a kiss, whispered into her sleeping sister's ear, then slipped her hand inside mine. I believe Ona and Primrose may well die very soon, and the child somehow feels this."

Granna frowned and murmured darkly, "The banshee will come howling up our bluff at the smell of their souls. You must stay close to them tonight, Aigy, and shoo her away, else she'll try to trick their heaven-bound spirits into taking the devil's fiery path downward instead!"

The banshee, a terrible shrieking ghost that was drawn to the dying, was one of Granna's ancient faery notions. Most times Mam fiercely objected to Granna's pagan thinking on such matters. Rhia braced for

Mam to say that it was indeed dire blasphemy to go on about the banshee, and that certainly even *if* the banshee had once existed, she was without doubt burning with the devil in these modern Christian days.

But Mam merely sighed. "I *will* be staying the night with them, Mother, but only because they'll need the nursing." She rubbed her forehead with her fingertips, as she oft did when she was tired out. "Daisy will stay with the two of you."

Lucy, out of some catly sense of sympathy, ran to the pallet and began licking the wounds on the little girl's arm and foot. Daisy smiled, then giggled at the touch. When Mam did not stop the cat, Rhiannon knew that Daisy was surely well healed. Mam held with animal spittle being of good use and soothing when a wound was almost mended, though dangerous when a festered place was still open or fiery-looking.

"I'll keep Daisy company down here tonight, Granna," Rhiannon whispered.

And so, with the cat between them, Daisy and Rhiannon slept beside the fire.

Mam had not come home yet when Rhia awoke at dawn the next morning to the summon of the church bell down in Woethersly. The murderer hadn't been found, then, and the laying of hands was indeed on for today. Seeing that Daisy still slumbered with Lucy curled about her feet, Rhia tiptoed outside and splashed her face at the brook, called good morning to Gramp astride the steeple of Bluffkerne Chapel, then hastened to fill a jug of the cold water to take to Ona's cottage.

Gramp followed and waited on the roof of that sad cot as Rhia quietly used her hip to push open the door. Ona and Primrose lay in a deep sleep and Mam was scooping ashes from the burned-out fire. She held up one hand to tell Rhia to put the jug within the door frame but not to come closer, then she finished her job and came out to join Rhia. They quietly closed the door and walked away from the cot and into the cool morning air.

"They've had a bad night and just gone off to merciful sleep," Mam whispered. Her shoulders slumped and her voice was hoarse. "How's Daisy?"

"Sleeping still." Rhia moved behind Mam to rub her neck, then asked, "Shall I stand watch over Ona and Primrose while you get ready to go down the trail?"

"I nay can leave the bluff today with these two in such a state, Rhia," her mother said in a way that brooked no argument. "Take Daisy down with you. The exercise will work the stiffness from the new-grown skin on her little foot. And Jim won't hear of being left behind. He'll hobble along slow, but he may prove some help with Daisy. Also, unless I miss my guess, your grandmother will be eager for going as well. As long as you take your time, you'll make a plenty capable band of four, with you in charge."

Rhia's head nearly spun on her shoulders with all this. Mam couldn't just *ignore* an order from the vicar to come lay hands, could she? And though Granna had spoken of Gimp Jim venturing the woods of late, could he travel on one leg and a stick clear down to Woethersly and then back up? And little Daisy, what of her childish step?

Then she remembered Granna's riddling talk about the "forgotten damned." Would Daisy and Jim even be *welcomed* by the town? And if not, what might happen?

Rhia quickly slammed the door of her mind on that last—too much to think about!

"Crrrrrrrrrrick." Gramp eyed Rhia hard from his perch, telling her to buck up.

Rhia took a deep breath. "Will you tell Granna that I'm to be in charge?"

Mam smiled, but then, from within the cot, Primrose suddenly whimpered in her sleep.

"Forget the seed gathering for today," Mam said quickly, hurrying back to her patients. "But see that Sal gets her breakfast before you leave, will you? And look in on the Man Who Sleeps as well."

When Rhia took Dull Sal her morning gruel, Sally was kneeling on the rushes of her floor, tapping her breastbone with her hand and rocking herself to and fro. This was always her chief activity, though in fine weather Mam and Rhiannon would sometimes lead her by the hand to sit outside upon the stoop in the bright sunshine. Sal seemed mayhaps thirteen years old to Rhia, a beautiful girl whose delicate head was marked above her left ear with fine lines like the cracks in an egg that's been handled too roughly, this from a hard cuff by her brother some months ago.

Sally'd had no living mother when the thing was done. Her father and brothers had fashioned a carrying bed from two oak poles with flax matting stretched between them. The brother who had cuffed her fell to his death carrying one corner of it whilst they brought Sal up the trail. No one mourned him much, as all thought it God's just punishment for the brutal crime he'd done his innocent young sister.

Rhia knelt beside Sal and began her feeding. "Good day to you, Sally," she said.

"I'll have three of those fish," Sal answered, grinning. This was her constant saying since that hard blow to the head, the only bit of talk she would make.

Sal opened her mouth wide like a small babe will, and Rhiannon spooned in the gruel.

"Some of us up here go down to lay hands on a corpse today, Sally," she told in a hushed, suspenseful way. "There's murder afoot in our shire!" Rhia thought it courteous to give Sally all the news, though clearly Sal had not the wits to take it in.

"Three fish," said Sal. "I'll have three of those fish."

Rhia wiped the gruel from Sally's chin and confided, "There's a fine black boat from the earl himself that came and went as well, though I saw it only from afar. Not his pleasure boat what brought those young squires, but still, it seemed quite grand! Reeve Clap came up here yesterday to bring direct word of the murder to Mam, though he'll take any excuse to see her, I'd say, wouldn't you?"

"Three of those fish," answered Sal.

Rhia combed Sal's hair with Granna's bone comb. "I'm glad your brother fell to his death," Rhiannon whispered as she smoothed Dull Sally's beautiful golden locks. She often said this, but that day she added, quite sassily, "I'm sure he burns with the devil."

Feeling both shocked and pleased with herself for that new bit of nervy talk, Rhiannon took her leave of Dull Sal and reluctantly went next door, to the cottage occupied by the Man Who Sleeps. She didn't bother knocking, as he was far past hearing.

He lay there on his bench with his arms crossed upon his chest and his ankles crossed as well, just as the four men arranged him who had carried him up to this cottage a fortnight past. No one knew a single thing about him, as he was found on the beach, but he looked somewhat noble with his strong-angled face and sharp beard. Therefore, they'd crossed his arms and also his ankles, as is done for a knightly Crusader.

Privately, Rhiannon figured him for a pirate.

No one could feed him much, though Mam got a bit of gruel to drip down his throat and oft stopped by to wet his lips from a crock of water they kept beside his bench.

He wasted away, though the wasting was slower than you might expect.

Rhia quickly wet his lips from the crock and left, as he plain gave her the willies.

Gimp Jim was at their place when she got back to it, drinking a mug of ale Granna had given him and all beaming with happiness about that morning's coming expedition.

"Little did I expect to ever see fair Woethersly again when I was carried up here all bloody and one-legged and done for!" he exclaimed, raising his mug in a salute. "Here's to the fine sight the town will make!"

Granna raised her own mug to his, but as Jim quaffed his ale, she jerked her head, signaling Rhia to join her in Mam's medicinal corner.

There, she was solemn. "Best these two, the child and the gimp, have us as friends close beside them and alert for hazards of all sorts today," she whispered.

"You still say they'll not be welcome in Woethersly?" Rhia whispered back. "But Daisy's just a child! And Jim is so funny and good-natured. Why, I myself would have hard feelings if someone's ill-driven oxcart had left the path and run *me* over in my own toft, yet Jim bears no grudge. How could anyone bear hard feelings toward *him*, then?"

Granna just looked for a long moment deep into Rhia's eyes. Then she murmured, "Granddaughter, I hope you're right and I've misjudged the feelings of the town. But we mustn't count upon it, as my misjudgments happen so extremely seldom."

The sun was fair high in the sky when they set off down the trail. Granna led the way, then came Gimp Jim on his one leg and his stick, and Rhiannon bringing up the rear with Daisy's hand tight in hers.

"You dasn't let go my hand for any reason," she told Daisy every few yards, squeezing her small palm all the tighter. "The trail is treacherous if your wits aren't about you at all times, understand?"

Daisy would nod each time, three sharp dips of her head, her eyes wide and serious.

To one side of them was the deep forest, and on the other was the sheer drop down to the sea, with bracken hiding the edge. The trail often changed, new pieces of it having fallen away from the rough kiss of the constant wind. One false step could be the last of you, as it had been the last of Dull Sal's bad brother.

"You look pretty!" Daisy suddenly chirped. "What's *that*?"

She was pointing to the sprig of wild cherry blossom Rhia'd painstakingly worked through the loose weave of her shawl. She'd pulled back her hair as well, knotting it in three places with grapevine so it swung to and fro jauntily as a horsetail, and she'd changed to her other skirt, the one Granna'd dyed deep red with beetroot. She was certain it was neither sinful nor proud to go wearing your best on such a day, since indeed it showed courtesy to the poor dead man. Still, she'd taken pains to avoid Mam's sight once she'd donned this festive garb.

"Jim looks funny!" Daisy noticed then. "He walks with but one leg!"

"Shush, now, with such talk," Rhia whispered, breaking part of the cherry blossom to slip through a small hole in the bodice of Daisy's shift. "You'll hurt Jim's feelings."

Jim had heard, but far from acting low about the childish com-

43

ment, he pulled off his watch cap to reveal his wispy orange hair, did a one-legged bow to his companions, then danced a comical little jiggy hop to make Daisy laugh the more.

To say it plain, though death was almost for certain making its gnarled way up the bluff to Ona and her worse-burned child that day, those going down the bluff began to assume some high spirits, as will happen when you're traveling in good company on a fine clear day under the cool sun in the frolicsome spring. When Rhia came down the trail each month to take their things to market, to do her mother's errands, and to gather town news, she was usually alone. Granna rarely went down these days, her knees ached her so. And Mam hardly as often as Granna anymore, being required at all times by the constant needs of her invalids.

Rhiannon had forgotten how company makes a long, steep trail seem much shorter.

As the path twisted and turned, over this boulder and around that oak, they settled into a companionable picking of the way, though studying to keep footed. Daisy turned out to be sure-stepping as a little goat, so Rhia concerned herself most with the two in front.

They finally got nigh to the last big twist in the path, a zigzag through thick ash trees. Rhiannon hefted Daisy into her arms for safety, knowing that this stretch was especially treacherous but that once by it she could consider them past harm's way. The ground would level out quite a bit then, and they'd be able to see the port and the castle in the distance, with watermeadows and fields stretching from them all the way to the town.

"What was that?" Granna suddenly demanded, stopping in her tracks so quick, Jim ran right into her back, nearly toppling the both of them before he managed to right himself.

"Woman, give a care to signal ere you halt, please!" he complained. He reached his stick to retrieve his watch cap, knocked clean off his head by the force.

Granna seemed not to even notice the small havoc she'd caused. "The woods be strangely changed right here," she said in a quick, tight way, cupping her ear with her hand. "Do ye all not perceive it?"

Rhiannon held her breath, listening. What with taking charge of Daisy last night and then all she'd had to think about this morning, she'd clean forgot about the stone folk she and Gramp had perceived on the beach yesterday. But now they came rushing back to her mind, clothed in their eery stillness. They'd been clustered on the part of sand that stretched just below this ashy part of the trail, hadn't they?

"The wind is all it is," she said quickly, swallowing her feeling of dread. "It's died down so sudden, that's the change. The stillness is all you hear, Granna."

But there *was* something amiss, and Rhia well knew it. She could hear a faint clicking, like locusts, only not really like locusts at all. And she thought she perceived ghostly shadows slipping through the new ash leaves, darting from tree to tree.

"Or it's red deer, mayhaps," she added in a whisper, holding Daisy tighter.

"We'd best move on," Jim said gruffly. "This steep ledge is no safe place to tarry."

Granna didn't argue, but straightaway resumed her downward trudge. She wasn't one to be bullied into speed, so Rhia was all the more certain that Granna suspected something fearsome in those ashy trees and had decided she must hurry them past it.

Shivering, Daisy circled Rhia's neck with her small arms and circled Rhia's waist with her small legs and pressed her face against Rhia's shoulder. The child felt it, too, then. *Breathe in, breathe out, keep watch on your feet, keep your wits,* Rhia cautioned herself.

It seemed endless, that fraught trek through the shadows. But then suddenly as one wakes from a bad dream, they came from the dark shawl of woods into glistening sunlight and the last short stretch of the trail, which was none so steep as before and none so rugged. In the distance you could see the quay with its English boats and also several Welsh coracles, tiny craft made from oiled hide and shaped like tortoise shells. Rhiannon's father had owned one for fishing and carried it to the water snugged onto his back. Rhia remembered laughing at that when she was small.

Daisy lifted her head from Rhia's shoulder and squirmed, eager to take her own feet.

"Not quite yet," Rhia whispered, holding tight.

Before she'd let Daisy go, she scanned the part of the beach now spread on their left and a little below. The endless water lapped at the white sand like the large blue tongue of some huge dog, but where the stone people had stood yesterday, the shore was empty.

"The Lord be thanked," she whispered, putting Daisy to her own feet.

"I saw monsters in the woods," Daisy mentioned in a tiny voice. "I did!"

"You saw red deer and squirrels." Rhia forced a laugh. "Silly thing!"

If only she could convince herself that her *own* imaginings were silly. Because by the time they went back this way, the shadows would be much, much longer . . .

"I can see the castle!" Daisy suddenly cried, clapping her hands.

Rhia squinted into the distance and gratefully focused on that splendid sight.

The motte, as the Normans called the man-made mountain beneath the castle, had been built up on the beach by order of King William just after the Conquest. The local peasants had used the glistening beach rock to construct it, then on top of it they'd built the tower, gatehouse, and stockades with huge burnished oak logs from Clodaghcombe Forest. When the sun shone bright as it shone today, the whole thing, sandy motte and oaken castle, seemed to be crafted from the same big chunk of sparkling gold.

How could ancient haunts thrive in the vicinity of such a modern wonder? Rhiannon felt the phantoms of the woods give up the last of their clinging hold. The power, might, and sheer beauty of the castle could fend against anything!

She crouched and pointed, her arm around the child's waist. "Look how you can see the goings-on inside the castle bailey from way up here, Daisy. What a view! Our own high trail is the only place in the shire to have such a vantage of the country all round, wouldn't you say so, Granna?"

But Granna had no interest in praising their trail.

"I had a *fine* vantage when I was a girl, all right," Granna muttered, resuming her downward trudge. "Afore that *mountain* was built by these *invaders* where God's beach had once stood. And now I hear tell they'll be building all over again in stone! Stone! There'll be the crushing of some workmen's good skulls. Saxon skulls and Welsh skulls and none of them Norman, you can wager on that. Why, if . . ."

Granna raved on quite contentedly as she went, and Jim followed a few good yards behind her, not eager for another of her quick stops to tilt him off-balance. Rhiannon stood up but stayed still a moment longer, clutching Daisy's hand.

She'd just spotted a lone walker on the beach, someone she'd not seen around before.

"Rhiannon, why are the pretty red flags no longer flying from the castle towers?" Daisy asked quietly. "Once my mother brought us to the beach and I saw that the castle flags were red and had yellow lions on them. I liked the lions."

"All King Henry's castles fly black flags just now, Daisy," Rhia murmured, her attention elsewhere. "Prince William Aethling lies drowned beneath the waves."

Not much beyond her own age, she'd have said the walker was, long of limb and graceful in his movements. He wore a coarse black robe snatched up at the bottom and hitched into his rope belt so his legs to the knees were bare for wading. A young priest, then, but with straight and shiny brown hair blowing in the wind, not tonsured, priestly hair at all. His eyes were deep-set above cheekbones so high and sharp they'd purple shadows pooled beneath them. He seemed to be thinking about something, surely something extraordinary and important from the intelligent look upon his face. His feet were skinny and white. She thought them comical and smiled.

"Rhia!" Daisy squealed, jerking her arm.

Rhiannon had nearly stepped right off the trail and into thin air.

Chapter 5

Now they had finally reached the flat land with Woethersly in clear sight, but they'd still the River Woether to ford and then the common barley field beyond to trek through.

"I wonder where upon this riverbank the foul murder was committed," Rhiannon murmured as they waded the shallow crossing. She kept her eyes on little Daisy, who splashed and whirled, laughing with delight as she slip-slid over the smooth river grasses.

Granna put a hand on Jim's shoulder to steady her crossing, then again used him for balance while she turned her wet shoes to pour out the river rocks. Patient Jim grunted and leaned hard on his stick so's not to topple as Granna took a penny from her waist pouch and bit it till it was bent and killed, then threw it over her shoulder into the river. This was a thing she did each time she came to town, for protection from all the evil that had overtaken the place since she was a young girl, back when the Saxons were still in charge and all was well with the world.

Daisy ran to crouch near the small splash of Granna's coin, and Rhia bent beside her. They looked at the glitter of it sinking as Rhia whispered, "In olden times coins were given to rivers for luck, Daisy. Granna still believes a bent coin will guard us from mischance on this journey to town, and who's to say her nay?"

Then something caught Rhia's eye there in the fast water, just a few paces beyond the coin. A clamshell it seemed, though it glittered much as the penny glittered. She waded close, pulled up her sleeve, and fished the little shell from its rocky bed, and the shiny thing *bit* her, just as if it *were* a living clam! She sucked her pricked thumb as she turned it over to explore it close. A tiny pin was fastened to the back of it. How very strange . . .

Then suddenly, the ground was ashake and a group of horsemen was right upon them, bursting from the woods as though summoned from hell itself. Rhia just had time to take in a swirl of bright color and flash as she slipped the clam pin into her waist pouch and sloshed frantically to the bank to grab up Daisy.

The careless riders had kicked up a fine cloud of rocky soil, and by the time Rhiannon had batted the air enough to find herself and Daisy a clear breath, the pack of them had galloped on across the river and disappeared into the copse of ancient willow trees at the south edge of the manor's private grounds.

"Not everyone that can *afford* to ride *deserves* to ride," Rhia complained loudly. She put Daisy to her feet, ripped out the grapevine pieces holding her own painstakingly constructed horse's tail in place, then bent and threw her loosed hair forward to shake out the dust. "The *nerve*," she stated when she'd straightened back up.

"That was King Henry and his knights, riding from King Henry's castle!" Daisy sang.

Jim and Granna laughed, and Rhia recovered her good spirits and smiled along.

"We won't see King Henry way out here," Rhiannon told the child, combing the dust from Daisy's hair with her fingers. "King Henry owns dozens and dozens of castles throughout all of England and much of Francia. The earl holds some three or four castles for King Henry, and Lord Claredemont takes care of this one for the earl. The earl himself comes sometimes to stay awhile in it and hunt in the forest hereabouts, but not often, as his wife dislikes the country life. Anyhow, that's what I've heard."

"I expect those riders be the earl's son and his cronies, the young squires from the manor house," Jim guessed.

"Well, our Rhiannon should know all about *that*," Granna said with a jolly har-har.

Rhia rolled her eyes. "Could be them," she said lightly, her chin in the air. "I've seen them only the once, when they arrived, and I'm sure I was much too busy just now saving Daisy from a deadly trampling to especially notice."

"They've cleared land back of the manor house as a tilt field for them to practice their swordplay and horsemanship," Jim eagerly told them. "Looks like they've also cleared more land in this vicinity since I had my accident and was took to your bluff. Cleared for an archery range, I'll wager. I'd heard talk they'd be needing that as well."

More land *was* being cleared from the bottom edge of Clodagh-combe Forest's bright green skirt. In fact, Rhia could hear the ring of axes this minute as Lord Claredemont's foresters assarted another piece of field from the forest trees for the lord's personal use.

Suddenly, she was itchy with impatience, for the sooner they got to town, the sooner she could link up with her friends, who would certainly have a great variety of details about these reckless young squires.

Her friend Maddy and the others would doubtless know something about the handsome walker on the beach, as well.

Woethersly had no charter from the king to hold a fair, but a murder investigation would be the next best thing. As they reached the outskirts of Woethersly, they joined a steady stream of folk picking their way along the road that led to the center of town, most wearing what most surely was their best attire. The ladies were generally in their light woolens, as she and Granna were, but those able to afford it showed off finer spring linens. The men were in their cleanest tunics, girded at the waist, and their bracca were braided up with woolen strips to keep the bottoms from flapping in the road mud.

Though she saw no one in motley or other outrageous garb at that moment, Rhia knew that traveling entertainers might well be drawn by expectation of such a crowd, and merchants from as far away as the next shire might come to show their wares.

"Druce, good friend!" Jim suddenly called out as they neared the mill.

Rhia turned and saw Druce Hulce, the miller, stepping from his grain-storage shed.

"Well, the devil take me. Is that really you, Jim?" Druce called, hastening in Jim's direction. "We'd expected ye to die, Jimmy, so bloodied up was ye that day ye was run over by them oxen!"

Rhia bounced on her heels, eager to witness the happy reunion of Jim and his friend.

The miller's wife, Ardith, meanwhile had come from the mill house and stood frowning there beside the turning wheel with her hands upon her hips. "Will you waste more time, Druce, when time's been lost already this morn?" she called to her husband.

"Wife, do you not see it's our good friend Jim?" the miller called back.

"I see that well enough." Ardith stood glowering a moment longer, then went back inside, slamming her door so hard, it caused a breeze that sent a spray of water out from the mill wheel.

Druce turned back to Jim, all hangdog. "I'm sorry, old friend. With the murder trial on the square, we've made a late start with our work today." He took Jim by the arm and added, "It's a great shock you've given Ardith, Jim. We'd no expectation ye'd survived that runaway cart! All have took ye for dead, y'see."

Jim squinted his eyes, thinking hard about that, then nodded. "Tell Ardith I regret it," he said. "I'd not meant to give her such a jolt."

Druce nodded too, looking down. "Well, good luck to ye, Jimmy," he said gruffly.

"G'bye then, Dulce." Jim turned away.

Daisy, catching something strange in the sound of his voice, stopped in her play with the ducks and skipped over to take his hand. The four of them moved along.

Rhia could think of nothing to say as they walked, so hard did she feel toward Ardith Hulce at that moment. Granna had *plenty* to say on that same subject, but there was a loud racket now that made it hard to hear. The commotion—hammering and clanking, it was—got louder as they went through the rest of the mill yard and toward the main road.

As they cleared the last of the mill buildings and came in view of the churchyard across the way, Jim gave a low whistle of surprise. Granna, Rhia, and Daisy stopped walking and stood agog.

Stone was piled everywhere around the church, and even in the road! Not merely the chunky stone ballast that was dumped from ships, but big squared slabs of beautiful gray stone. There were lots of men about, many of them dressed in the garb of artisans. Some were kneeling and hammering at that stone. Several folk Rhia recognized from the village were at work as well, doing the less exacting job of hauling cut blocks to parts of the churchyard. All that pounding and shifting of rock!

The line of folk going to the green stepped carefully around, the women holding high their skirts against the pool of stone dust hanging like heavy fog above the road.

"Well, for years I'd heard grand talk that the church was going to be built over in stone, and the castle tower as well, but until this day I'd ne'er seen a sign that it was more'n just gossip!" Jim told Granna, shouting to be heard. "Saints save us, it's certain that things prosper greatly in fair Woethersly of late!"

And more great change progressed across the road. Where there'd been a collection of old sheds when Rhia had last been down here, there now was a cleared lot of ground. A high crucked roof had been raised, and the straight trunks of a great many ash trees made a framework beneath it. The whole thing resembled the bones of a huge and fearsome dragon, just waiting to grow flesh.

Jim gave a long whistle. "Whatever *that's* to be, it'll rival the manor house in size."

Three wives of the town were coming quick down the road, bringing empty buckets for filling from the town's water well. They shared merry talk as they ambled, laughing and poking with their elbows.

Jim beamed when he saw them. "G'day to ye, mistresses!" he called. "How does that good husband of yours, Adda? Say to him that Jim's ready to come back and will be around right soon to see to that ax he wanted fixed!"

The three of them stopped and stared as though Jim were a ghost. The fat one in the middle put her hands over her face and right out sobbed, "Oh, Jimmy, that ax was mended long months ago!"

The other two linked their arms through hers and hurried her over across the street.

"How came ye back in such a state, Jim?" one of them scolded over her shoulder, staring rudely at the stump of Jim's lost leg.

Rhia felt a gorge rise in her throat, and she could not bear to look Jim in the face.

Even Granna, who always had a word or two, seemed stymied for any talk and merely stood there with her arms at her sides.

It was Jim himself who presently rallied them. He pulled his cap back upon his head and squared his shoulders with a heartiness he could surely not have felt.

"Well, let's move along, then," he said. "My own place is near here. My home lies just back from this churchyard, tucked prettily enough beneath two fine, well-grown willows. I've longed to show it to ye, and here's my chance!"

And so they went on along, though Granna looked in the direction of the mill and bit her thumb hard at Jim's false friends.

Past the church, the stone dust that hung in the air cleared a bit, but big patches of black on the ground showed where some burning had been done to clear a big lot.

Jim stopped walking. The wind kicked a bit of blackened grass against Daisy's skirt, and Rhia bent to brush it off.

"Let's hasten past this waste, Jim," Rhia complained, "before we're sooted good."

But Jim was silent and seemed frozen to the spot. Rhia looked up to see him staring at one of those blackened patches. He spoke then, but as if in a dreamy daze.

"There was my cot, where the ground is black ashes in yon corner. Mark how the smoke still wafts? Willow burned green will simmer like that for a good long while."

And then, something just seemed to pass right out of Jim, as if his spirit, so strong through all his torment of healing, now had met its match at seeing his home destroyed. They saw him sway a bit, and it was lucky there was stacked stone just beneath to catch him, for he would otherwise have surely fallen clean to the ground.

"I planted those willow sprigs two springs before my Maizie died." Jim's words were spiritless and heavy. "I thought they'd give over last year with the drought, but no, they came along, they did. Maizie so loved those willows, and I thought of her ever I looked at them. The cottage we lived in was small and nothing special, fit to be burned, some might say, but those willows of Maizie's . . ."

Jim's words petered out, and he just sat slumped upon his hard granite seat.

"Look, Rhia, will you?" Daisy whispered, taking one of Rhiannon's fingers.

Rhia was too gloomed to do aught but give a glance to where Daisy pointed. Three robed men were leaving the church by its coffin door. One of them held a page of vellum with some writ, and they'd stopped to give instruction to four local peasants who were heaving a sledge of stone to the nether side of the building.

"With so many priests at work, no wonder ill play's afoot," Granna muttered.

Rhiannon saw her hard-eye one of them to emphasize her point, but then she looked quick away when he glanced in her direction. Even Granna was scared of a thing or two, such as fire in the roof thatch, brain fever caught from wild pigs, and churchmen.

"Granna, you were right as rain when you spoke yesterday," Rhia forced out, her chest all tight and raw. "Jim is forgotten as well as damned by his so-called friends. And now these churchmen have burned his cot and trees to make room for their fine stone buildings! They seem to have no care that their church will be made grander by the loss of all Jim had left in this whole world!"

Then all of a sudden Rhiannon's legs, with a life of their own, were pounding along hard through the stone dust, heading her right toward those fine clergy like a bull will run full-tilt at a marauder to his field!

The robed priests turned toward her as she got near, seeing the shocked expressions of the local workers who already faced her way. For Rhiannon was flailing her arms like a berserker, though it wasn't really hitting she wanted, unless she could have torn their heads clean off, which, of course, she'd not the strength for.

She began to scream at all of them, clergy and workmen alike. "You fine religious with your stony church, will you be building it upon the bones of a brave man? Because you've kilt Jim's large soul with your burning his cot, so you'd might as well have burnt his whole self while you were about it! He's a just man who deserved not such ill treatment of his willow trees, one-legged though he be! Granna had warned of such a clear damning as this, though I would not believe it, and from God's own clergy yet!"

The dust was churned by her stomping feet and blown about by her whipping arms. She felt it settle on her face, gummed to angry tears she'd begun to spout.

The workmen pretended not to notice any ruckus and fled on about their business, and the three clergy stood and looked at her with a calmness that made her even angrier.

One even smiled in a chilly way and stretched his white hand in Rhia's direction. "Stop, child," he said. "You imperil your soul with such sacrilege, and you haven't the wisdom or understanding to question such matters."

And then they put their backs to her and walked on, looking again at their writ.

Rhiannon watched after them, too dizzy now to know what to do next. She dreaded turning back to Granna and the others, as she'd made such a certain fool of herself. Neither could she rush forward and be a nuisance to those clergy again, as her outlandish nerve for that was spent and she now felt only embarrassed misery.

"Your Lord Claredemont told us that he burned only the useless cots of his tenants who'd died," a quiet voice behind her spoke. "The space was cleared for our abbey garden, you see, as well as for a fish-pond to provide for a meager meal on fasting days."

She whirled toward the speaker and saw the brown-haired young priest she'd seen walking upon the beach, now standing framed inside the coffin door! He looked grave and puzzled, and was not smiling in the least at her foolishness.

He came down the stair, and now stood in the sun. "Your Lord Claredemont's brother was spared while fighting at King Henry's side across the sea in Francia last year. In gratitude to God for his brother's life and for the victory, your lord has become benefactor to a prior and six of us monks, all just this few days past arrived from Glastonbury Abbey. The earl's given generous support, as well. With God's grace we'll expand your church here, taking it from wood to stone and building our priory buildings next to the site with a tithe barn across the road." He leaned closer and whispered, "But say true, lady, were we mistold that this space was free and clear of other use?"

Rhiannon could make no answering speech. She just dropped her eyes.

His voice was troubled when he spoke again. "Our good abbot at Glastonbury saw chance in your lord's largesse to establish a new cell for our order here in these hinterlands. We would bring to this place sustained prayer and hard work to further God's kingdom, as set out in Saint Benedict's Rule. But our brother abbot nor Benedict himself would have had a single man put out from his living."

"Thaddeus! Come straight along, now."

The young priest looked quickly at his elders. "I beg you pardon me," he murmured to Rhiannon. With bent head, he hurried to join his three fellows.

All agog so she could barely think, Rhiannon walked back to her own group.

"Well done, Rhiannon!" Granna said, clapping her on the back.

Mam's reaction would be opposite, Rhia knew. She bent to Daisy and whispered words similar to those Granna oft used. "I lost my wits upon seeing those religious, and figured them liable for Jim's burnt cot. No need to mention this to my mother, all right?"

Daisy solemnly nodded, and Rhia moved close to Jim. "Lord Claredemont thought you'd died, Jim," she said quietly. "He was surely mistold, or he would not have given leave for the vicar to destroy your cot and so besmirch your willowed toft."

Still staring at that smoky patch as though in a trance, Jim answered, "No, Rhiannon, it's just the same by the law as if I *had've* died. I couldn't give the lord his week-work now, and I have no son to take over. How could I stay tenant? I just wasn't studying it right, 'tis all. Now I study it right, I wonder why I had other expectation."

He got up then, leaning hard upon his stick, and turned to hobble on, toward the morbid task awaiting all of them at the butcher shop table on the green.

Rhiannon sadly took Daisy's hand and made to follow close, but Granna clutched at her sleeve, stopping her.

"Jim is now a homeless man," Granna whispered. "He's without a skill, friendless, near vagabond. The shame of that is not something he'll want pressed with talk, so better give him a bit of space, Rhia."

And so they three just stood and sadly watched his halted progress along the muddy road. When finally they lost sight of him among the throng of townspeople moving toward the green, they moved along toward that place themselves.

Chapter 6

Beyond the churchyard, the cottages of Woethersly were strewn along all haphazard, each with its narrow strip of croft behind, leading back to a garden spot. Each also with a small toft in front of it, a patch of yard crowded with animal sheds and the like.

The tofts were alive this day with skittery activity—children playing in the dirt by their stoops and gawking at all the passers, buzzards and gulls scavenging the rubbish heaps where wives had thrown peels and bones and duck innards, goats and cats and geese running into the cottages and back out, all flummoxed at so many people parading by. The milch cows in their byres watched as well, kicking their back feet at the confusion and rolling their large, bulging eyes. Porch dogs yapped and nipped at the skirts of the women, often earning a sharp kick in the ribs, which appeared not to discourage them from instantly resuming the same uncouth behavior.

Rhiannon was edged to the ditch at one point by a packhorse piled high with bright cloths and led by a man with bristly gray whiskers to his waist. Many people walked in gangs and looked too swarthy, or elsewise too pale, to be from Woethersly. Around here folk, being farmers, were somewhat fair complected at winter's end. Rhia's guess was that the swarthy were sailors, and the pale folk had come from some wooded settlement where the sun ne'er got through to them.

"It's fine weather after a bitter winter, giving people itchy feet," Granna remarked, her eyes glistening. "Under such conditions, folk will make a fair of any excuse."

A black goat ran kicking through the street with a tortoise tied to his back. Three boys circled the terrified ride and the hapless rider, laughing and prodding at them with thorny sticks of hedge. An oxcart swerved around the commotion and nearly tipped, and the driver raised his own leather switch to the boys. They hightailed it.

Daisy knelt in the dirt to go eye-to-eye with the poor tortoise, who was all shrunk with fright into his shell. Rhia untied the creature from its similarly terrified ride, and the goat shook his fleece, felt his freedom, and sped away to find his owner's toft.

"I'm keeping her," Daisy whispered, wrapping the tortoise into her skirt. "Her name is . . . King Henry."

"Well, you can't go around with your clothes to your waist," Rhiannon scolded, yanking down Daisy's skirt but catching the tortoise as it unfurled. "Here, I'll make you a carrying pouch."

Rhia pulled off her light woolen shawl, which had become too warm for the bright day anyhow, and bent to work. "Since you say she's a girl, why not name her after our queen instead?" she suggested. "Queen Matilda would make her an elegant name."

Their queen had been dead for over two years, much the pity, and there was rumor the king would soon wed another. Still, the old queen, come partly from Saxon stock, had been dear to most everyone. Even Granna had had a good word or two to spare for her.

Daisy clapped with delight at that idea. "Queen Tildy, for short!"

"Rhiannon! Rhee! Over here!"

Rhia jerked up her head and peered toward her good friend's welcome voice. Maddy was with two of her mates from the lord's dairy. The three were approaching from a distance, laughing as they elbowed through the crowd. Some group of uncouth men, rough cowherds or the like, stood watching them, smiling and nudging one another as they leaned together and drank from a jug.

"Eyeing up young girls, will ye?" Granna said, rushing over to thump one of them on the head. "Off with ye, galloots! G'wan now about your business!" For good measure she added a shoo with her skirts, and they fled, the one rubbing his noggin.

Rhia quickly nestled Queen Matilda into her new sling and draped it over Daisy's shoulder, then stood. "Granna, may I go with my friends for a bit?" She glanced down at Daisy in hopes Granna'd get her meaning, then quietly added, "I mean, alone? To catch up with the news and all?"

Granna took Daisy's hand. "Daisy can come meet my cronies at the ale booth," she said. "And Rhia, you tell Maddy her blouse gapes too low for modesty. I'm surprised Lord Claredemont allows such from his maid-of-all-poultry."

"I will, Granna, and thanks!" Rhiannon waved good-bye to Daisy and set out, easing slowly and carefully through the press of folk, hoping she'd not lose sight of her pals.

Far to her left, rising above the sea of heads and shoulders, she glimpsed the flowing pennant atop Lord Claredemont's colorful pavilion. The lord oft had this fine silken shelter constructed to give himself and his family comfortable viewing when some tournament or race was staged on the manor grounds. But today, he'd lent the pavilion to be set up on the green, where it gave the butcher's table shelter. Rhia supposed it would give shade to the body of the murdered man, and would also lend some privacy to the ritual, which by local custom should be witnessed only by God, the vicar, and the bailiff.

Still, with its orange and green stripes, the pavilion struck Rhia as unseemly bright and cheerful for such grim work. A long line of people moved slowly toward that tent, where each must take a turn putting hands upon the corpse.

Rhiannon shivered and felt no hurry. First, some fun.

"Rhia! Come on, then!" Maddy stretched her arm through a gap in the crowd and grabbed Rhia's wrist, and Rhia was well content to be pulled along.

Maddy was a strong girl, bigger than Rhia and with far more nerve. She had no qualms at all about treading on the feet of others or barking rough orders when making her way, and so she maneuvered them through the roiling crowd, jabbing with her elbows at those who wouldn't move and sometimes giving someone a little kick.

Soon they reached the spot where Maddy'd left the other two to wait, and the four girls linked arms to keep from being separated. Giggling with freedom and good spirits, Nedra, Ginny, and Rhiannon left it to Maddy to blaze them a passage on toward less congested space where they could talk all at once and hear themselves as they were at it.

Sometimes Rhia envied these three. Nedra and Ginny worked within the high-walled manor house complex just as Maddy did. They were two of Lord Claredemont's dairy maids, and, as Granna had noted, though Maddy was only the orphaned daughter of local peasant farmers, she had nevertheless risen to the important job of maid-of-all-poultry. Her strength and bluster were put to good use in the job, as she was boss of the lazy young boys who carried in the firewood and mucked out the chicken yard.

Rhia sometimes thought it hard, meeting your friends only on market days. When they'd all been little girls, Nedra and Ginny and Maddy had worked together as a gang in the fields. As farmers' daughters they'd picked fruit, gathered rocks that might have stopped the plow within the furrows, brought home kindling for the fires, that sort of thing. Rhia'd met them all when she first came down to market with Mam when she was about Daisy's age, and from then on they'd taught her their new games on the fly each time they met. Now, she imagined it would be fine living with your mates in the loft above the manor house kitchen in the center of all the world's activity with no one to supervise you. Well, no mother or grandmother, that is, though these three claimed there were plenty of higher maids and housekeepers to make their lives miserable.

They did not *seem* miserable, though. They seemed lively, always filled with the manor gossip, which they generally knew well before Lord Claredemont himself did. In fact, Nedra said it was not unusual for Lady Claredemont to wangle news from her under pretense of wandering through the manor kitchen to check the condition of the eggs collected of a morning and eve.

"Maddy, where are we *going*?" Rhia called, suddenly realizing they'd left most of the crowd behind. She resisted a little, pulling back her arm, but Maddy showed no signs of slowing the pace she'd set for their little caravan of four.

Rhia's question triggered some alarm in Nedra and Ginny, too, and they came out of their complacent run and put on the brakes, each in her own way.

"Oh no you don't, Madeline Atwater!" Ginny yelled, skidding the heels of her slippers along in a vain attempt to slow things. "I see now what you're about and by all things holy I swear that I am *not* going ever again to that demon-ridden place you fancy so much! Once was plenty too much and then some!"

She withdrew her arm from Rhia's and dropped behind.

"Nor will I go, either!" Nedra screeched, dropping to her knees and yanking her arm from Maddy's. "You've lost your wits, Maddy, to tempt the devil so! And you've no right to take Rhiannon all unsuspecting to share in your dangerous folly! Rhia, get free from this rash and stupid escapade before it's too late!"

Rhia looked back to see both Nedra and Ginny fallen behind, staring at her with fearful faces. But Maddy had Rhia's arm clamped tighter within her own by then, and Rhia suspected she would not now slide free of such a muscled girl.

Besides, she was plenty curious. Demon-ridden? Rash folly?

"Where are we bent to in such a headlong rush, then, Maddy?" she yelled.

"I've a grand surprise for you, that's all!" Maddy called without slowing a whit.

They were on the far side of Woethersly by then, heading into the broad lawns of the north demesne of the manor grounds. That alarmed Rhia, as it was trespassing to enter the lord's private lands—not so much for Maddy, being employed by Lord Claredemont and well able to make up some story should she be caught. But certainly for those with no business whatsoever there, like Rhiannon herself.

Maddy turned them a sharp left when they reached the gated wall of the manor courtyard, and then they were running along a line of handsome yew trees, grown by the manor's foresters for the fine arrows their branches made. Then next they were splashing right through the nether ford of the River Woether without so much as stopping to raise their skirts!

"Maddy, what's got into you to lead us in such a chase?" Rhia yelled, truly peeved by then. "I'm soaked, and I've rocks in my shoes!"

"Would you complain about witnessing a wonder the likes of which the Roman Pope hisself would pay gold to see?" Maddy yelled back, neither stopping nor slowing.

They ran up the rise beyond the ford and then passed close by the small hillock called Gallux Hump, this from the fact that criminals were hanged from a wide black oak that grew there. Should a vile murderer be discovered today, soon enough he or she would struggle and kick their last whilst adangle from that very same old bent tree.

Rhiannon shivered at the thought, but she might better have focused her shivers on the equally dread sight that loomed in the distance straight ahead of them. For in fact they were barreling toward a perfect circle of tall and ancient trees that was ringed clear about by a high and crumbly stone wall. Indeed, 'twas Wythicopse Ring itself!

Rhia'd never in her life come near this close to that eery circle of tree and stone, but like everyone in the manor, she'd *heard* of Wythicopse Ring all her life. Oh yes, *all* knew of it and steered clear of it. When the rest of the forest out here in the marshy land had been assarted, cleared to make the sheep more grazing, this stand of trees and its brambly wall had been left alone. These poplars were the finest in miles and would have built a church or else a stable worthy of the lord's own horses.

Yet none dared touch the trees of Wythicopse with an ax.

Most thought of it as a site of ritual from the olden days, mayhaps marking a place where the land of the dead reached up to meet the sunny world of the living. For sure, it was best left untouched in its broody mystery. A faery site it most likely was, but not like the enchanted places in Clodaghcombe Forest that Rhia knew well. Nay, this place seemed wrapped in a damp gloom that even the brightest sun could not dispel.

Pride stopped Rhia from admitting her fear and digging in her heels to slow them down, but she felt blessed relief when, still some lit-tle distance from the walled grove, Maddy all of a sudden flopped down to the grass and let go Rhia's hand so that Rhia could flop to the blessed grass as well. They both lay on their backs there, gasping for air as their ears rang and the blue sky spun round and round above.

"I've lost . . . my left . . . shoe," Rhia panted, when she could.

"We'll find it," Maddy said with her usual simple confidence, plucking up a stem of daisy to chew.

Rhiannon would have enjoyed having Maddy's sort of breezy con-fidence herself, but you had it or you hadn't, and there were always too many questions in Rhia's mind for her to ever have it. Such as, what were they *doing* in such a fraught place?

Still, she raised up on an elbow, feigning nonchalance. In fact, she plucked her own daisy stem, gave it a chew, then asked, "Well, Maddy, what's this wonder of yours?"

Maddy sat up and smiled mysteriously. "It lies just over the bram-bly stone wall, within the circle of poplars. Don't fret, Rhia, we'll go there in a moment."

So Maddy *did* plan on breaching the forbidden walls of Wythicopse Ring! Rhiannon near choked on the daisy stem she sucked. To climb over the walls of Wythicopse was *not* to be done lightly, and all that Maddy ever did *was* done lightly.

"But Rhia," Maddy continued, breathlessly. "Right now I must tell you something before I burst! Something I've told neither Nedra nor Ginny!"

At that, Rhia eagerly sat up knee-to-knee with Maddy. She oft felt the outsider of the four, and to hear she was picked first to hear a se-cret was welcome. "Tell! Tell!" she urged, as the wind began drying their skirts and lifting their hair.

"Oh, Rhiannon, saints bless me!" Maddy whispered, throwing her apron over her face, then peeking from its edge, all flustered. "I'm fearfully in love! Oh, Rhia!"

Rhiannon's hands flew to her face. "Is it Willard who helps the smith?"

Maddy, giggling, shook her head.

"All right then, Oswald the carpenter's boy? Or Rufus who lives in the mill house with his grandsire?"

Maddy leaned forward and took Rhiannon's hands. "Oh, Rhia, those are merely *town* boys! Good friend, I'm in love with Frederique, a squire visiting at the manor house!"

Rhiannon gasped. The sun had gone under a cloud, and a chill wind suddenly blew up from the marsh. An ill wind, if ever Rhia had felt one.

"Oh, Maddy, the earl's own son? You *can't* love the earl's son, Maddy!"

"Not the earl's son, Rhia. That would be Roderick. Frederique is one of Roderick's bosom friends, come last winter to squire with him! Roderick is paunchy and dull, with limp hair and a pout. But my Fred is so handsome and gallant, I melt upon merely *thinking* of him!"

To tell it plain, Rhiannon felt sick at the thought of Maddy fallen for an aristocrat. Had she forgot that she was only a peasant girl, exalted to do work in the manor house by her strong good looks and neat habits? This was entirely unnatural, and layered with danger upon danger.

Rhiannon swallowed and licked her lips. "Does Frederique . . . does he *know* of the love you hold for him?"

Maddy squeezed her friend's fingers, demanding an oath. "Swear to tell no one what I'm telling you, Rhiannon! Swear it as a vassal swears fealty to his lord."

Rhia squeezed Maddy's fingers back. "I so swear."

"All right," Maddy whispered, shivering with happiness. "He *does* know, Rhia, and he swears he loves me just as well! He *does!*"

Rhia gave Maddy a smile, though a cautious one.

Maddy nodded toward Wythicopse Ring. "We meet right there, inside the stone-clad circle of sacred poplars, where we won't be seen. Frederique says none will *dare* venture into the dragon's chamber! It's spooky—you've *got* to see it, Rhia! Come on!"

Maddy jumped to her feet, hoisted her skirts, then ran straight to the brambly wall and began to scale its stony side. Rhia watched her openmouthed—the *dragon's* chamber?

"Will you come, or will you gape like a fish all day?" Maddy called over her shoulder.

A friend is a friend when all's said and done, especially when a secret's been told that binds you oathlike to the other. Rhia took a breath, then jumped to her own feet, then ran to the copse and climbed the stone wall, trying not to think, nor to imagine. She followed Maddy right to the top, then slid down the mossy stone of the other side and landed upon her knees within that eery, enchanted place.

"What did I tell you?" Maddy asked in a whisper, which seemed the manner of speech called for inside this walled circle of swirling shadow and mist. She turned round slowly with her arms outspread. "Have you ever *felt* such a place in your entire life, Rhiannon?"

"I've . . . not," Rhia whispered.

No leaf rustled within this glade, and no bird sang. It was a frozen place, thick with twisty vines that felt grabbish as fingers clutching at your ankles.

"Maddy, I feel we're being watched," she whispered.

"I know," Maddy whispered back. "I always have that feeling here, though Frederique says that's nonsense. And isn't this place *romantic*, Rhia?"

Rhiannon pondered that as Maddy skipped off a little ways, then settled on her knees before a broad mound of violets. "Here, Rhia, hurry!" she called.

When Rhia'd knelt beside her, Maddy slipped her fingers far as they'd go into the soil and easily lifted that mossy violet mound right off the earth it grew from! She placed it like a huge pudding onto the nearby grass, then knelt to brush away dirt from deep in the soily pit where the violet had been.

"Frederique placed that violet clump atop what I'm about to show you, to conceal it and mark it," she whispered. "He and his mates found what's beneath here when they were riding one day. Their horses scuffed up the ground and exposed a bit of her brow, then they dug out more of her with their swords."

"Her?" Rhia looked into the small pit and saw a face staring right back at her! She cleared more dirt to find a woman made all of tiny colored stones, a picture lady with a leafy crown upon her head and a swallow bird upon her shoulder. And there was a red, red rose grown up along her white sleeve, it being made of those same little stones.

"What magic is this?" Rhiannon breathed.

"You've seen nothing yet." Maddy jumped to her feet and ran along, then knelt and pulled a deep cap of mud and vines from another small section of the ground.

When Rhiannon hastened to look into that second hole, she was peering at a picture of a hare made of those same tiny stones, no single colored stone so large as a silver penny, all put side by side in shades of brown with some pink along the ears and tail and upon the nose, just as a hare would have in life!

"Everywhere we dig within this circle, the ground beneath is covered over with such pictures," Maddy whispered. "Frederique thinks they lie in one great wall beneath the earth within this copse, and Leonard says they're made to form a seal above a great chamber dug to hold the Dragon of Cymrhough. Or perhaps the Dragon of Brynourth. Leonard says the chamber surely holds one or t'other of those two ancient dragons, and that the beast is sleeping under strong command from some great wizard of Arthur's time, mayhaps the great Merlin himself! Leo says he longs for a chance to slay it, but not as it sleeps. He would wait until it awakes so he might have the sport of the chase!"

Rhiannon sat back on her heels, speechless.

"Leonard is as handsome as my Fred, or nearly, and the best at swordplay of the squires. He fears nothing, I tell you, and he has curls to his shoulders, near as light as your own are dark, and a dimple in his left cheek. Roderick the Paunchy Whiner, Frederique the Handsome, and Leonard the Rough and Tumble. I made that up, but it fits them well indeed. The other four squires are younger and of no account, and they ride a bit behind. I tell you, Rhia, that was I not so fearfully in love with Fred, I would most certainly love Leo, as he's strong and fearless as his namesake beast, and he—"

Rhia, still stunned by her surroundings, finally interrupted. "What's over there?" She pointed over Maddy's right shoulder.

Maddy frowned and rolled her eyes. "Have you not been listening about Leo, Rhia?" She sighed and looked over her shoulder. "Well, beneath that hump of moss is a man in a white robe riding a donkey. And beneath that spot where the wild onion sprouts is a man hunting with two dogs, all sinfully naked but for a shawl around his neck."

Maddy giggled, but Rhia was far too dazed to join her in it.

72

"Now, watch," Maddy instructed. "You can hear the great dragon's breathing!"

She held back her hair with one hand and knelt far forward, putting her whole head and shoulders right into the hole! Rhia watched helplessly as Maddy then pressed her ear right upon the colored stones at the bottom that formed the pink-eared hare.

Maddy presently jerked up straight, her face flushed with excitement. "Yes, yes! I heard it plain! Now *you*, Rhiannon!"

She gave Rhia a little push from the shoulders so Rhia's *own* head now ducked near the gaping hole. Rhiannon snatched her dark hair back and dared to bend forward until her own ear rested on the cold stone of the hare's brown eye.

And sure enough, she heard a great and fearful sighing coming from below! The deep, strong whirl of sound beneath that dome of tiny rocks could only be the breath of a fiery dragon! No doubt they *were* tempting the devil here, she and reckless Maddy.

Rhiannon's heart thudded and she pulled up from the hole, trembling all over.

Maddy clapped her hands, eyes wide with excitement. "Want to go again, this time over in the violet hole where the rose-bedecked lady lies?"

Rhiannon nodded. "I do!" she admitted, shocked by her own reckless decision.

Maddy and Rhia sat astride the brambly stone wall a little time later as two knights will sit atop a shared mount. Rhiannon wanted with all her heart to finish the climb over and run back to town. Also with all her heart, she longed to sit forever with one leg inside magical Wythicopse Ring and one leg out in the bright, common world.

What power there was in mysteries! How sharp and alive they made you feel.

"They say the age of the faeries has passed," Rhia whispered. "And yet there really may be . . . *things* still afoot in our modern world that remain beyond any earthly understanding. Mayhaps even enchantments. Who's to say?"

"Who is?" carefree Maddy agreed, laughing into the bright spring wind.

Chapter 7

They were running back to town side-by-side, galloping like colts with their skirts blown above their white knees, when Maddy began to spring her trap, or so Rhiannon later thought of it. Much as a forester will drape a concealed net for the taking of a hapless fox, Maddy had certainly *trapped* her into a plan that could only end in no good!

They were just past Gallux Hump when Maddy turned to her, calling, "You're the only one I've shown who didn't flee the dragon's chamber, Rhia! I knew you wouldn't, and I knew as well you'd be a true friend and meet Frederique's mate Leonard there on Beltane Eve! We'll party gloomy winter away together the evening before May Day brings in the spring—me and Frederique, you and Leo!"

Rhiannon stumbled but kept up her run, gaping now at Maddy.

"Before you say anything, hear more about it!" Maddy rushed on, puffing. She spotted Rhia's lost slipper hanging on a nettle bush, swooped out an arm to retrieve it, and tossed it across to Rhia. "All the young squires will be there! Frederique said to bring the most comely girl I know for Leonard. And of all, you're the very *most* comely, Rhiannon!"

But Rhia was not that easily duped. The others had surely said a firm no to this misthought idea!

"I canna meet you, Maddy," she called back, stopping to gather her wits whilst she pulled her slipper back on. "I must go down the trail with Mam and Granna to Roodmas on Beltane Eve. I've promised them." A tight excuse, and religious to boot.

But she could not look at Maddy as she said it, for 'twas a bald lie—the baldest. They three women held their own services upon Clodaghcombe Bluff, along with whatever invalids were able to attend. Vicar Pecksley sent up an acolyte with the sacraments for Roodmas, just as he did monthly for their regular worship.

"Only the old spend Beltane Eve at Roodmas, Rhia," Maddy teased. She shook her yellow curls back from her face. "The young spend the night a-running the woods and jumping the field fires and flowering up the Maypole for the morrow! Your mother let you come down with us last year to the bonfire on the green, remember? So I'm sure she'll let you come as well this year. When we're bent and prune-faced, there'll be time enough to go to Roodmas and repent our youthful follies!"

She laughed aloud at that picture, and Rhia couldn't help but join her. But Mam had only reluctantly let her come down to the Beltane festivities last year, yielding to longstanding custom that allowed all who'd reached the age of thirteen to attend. And spending last Beltane with other girls laughing around a bonfire was different completely from this party Maddy had in mind. Mam would *never* consider it, not if she knew.

"Wait!" Maddy then exclaimed, clapping her hands. "What an idea I've just had! Since you say your mother and grandmother will be gone to Roodmas, our party will come up through the woods and we'll have our fun atop the bluff whilst they're gone. Roodmas goes on for ages and ages—time enough for a fine frolic. And your chapel is perfect, so dark and private, with the benefit of a ceiling for keeping out the drafts. Wythicopse is romantic for sure, but it lacks a cover excepting the trees and so can get quite dampish if the dew comes thick. Oh, friend, what a fine plan!"

Rhia could find no scrap of anything to say, so preposterous was this notion. Maddy'd been up to the blufftop only once, when they'd both been very young girls, nine or ten. When Rhia'd shown her the ancient hermit's stone chapel, Maddy had swirled in the gloom, dancing with the sunbeams that lit the ancient stones of the floor.

Mam had been scandalized when she passed the window and saw that dire misuse of such a holy place. So just *think* what she'd do if she could so much as *hear* Maddy speak of using the chapel for a "fine frolic" on the bawdy festival night of Beltane Eve!

"It's settled then, Rhia!" Maddy pronounced, taking Rhia's silence for the answer she desired, as such a headstrong girl is wont to do. "Whichever way it goes, the chapel or the ring, will be just dandy with me, now *you're* coming. Your dark good looks will make a moon to Leonard's sun! Oh, Rhia, I'm so relieved, as I couldn't have found the nerve to go all by myself! And I cried at the thought of Frederique finding other company for Beltane Eve! Not that he'd be tempted, as he loves only me."

Rhiannon could only feel agog at how Maddy had cornered her like Lucy would corner a helpless mouse. She could not think of a single way out of Maddy's clutches. Beltane Eve was yet some days away, and in that time she might somehow think of an excuse Maddy could not reject. For now, though, it seemed she was trapped.

At the wall of the manor house courtyard they slowed to a walk and parted ways, as Maddy needed to lay the kitchen fire and get to her other appointed midafternoon chores. Rhiannon watched till her friend had reached the wide gate, then raised an arm in farewell as Maddy saluted her likewise.

And in that moment, right before Rhia turned back around to rejoin the crowd in the green, she glimpsed a small thing she'd remember large on a day to come.

The fine timbered manor house loomed just the other side of the wide wall, and there in an upstairs window, standing with his arms folded, stood Lord Claredemont himself! He stared grimly down at the part-open flap door of the pavilion, where Vicar Pecksley was allowing one person at a time to enter and lay hands upon the dead man. With one gloved thumb, Lord Claredemont tapped his bottom lip. And then he gave one curt movement of his head, side to side, as though denying something said to him by an unseen speaker in the salon behind him.

Rhia caught herself then and looked away, ashamed for disturbing the lord's privacy. It was just so seldom you actually *saw* him! Of course, he hadn't seen *her,* and would have looked right through the likes of her even if he had.

Still, she felt flustered as she hurried on toward the ale-tasters' booth. Several of Granna's close cronies were in charge there, as only those who were female, of some substantial age, and of unsullied integrity were respected enough for the job of brewing the ale sold to the public. It was tempting to water it for added profit, is why.

As Rhia came up close to the thick oak table where the ale was served, a tiny lady in a gray dress was holding forth against a group of rowdies.

"I'll serve no riffraff, nor those acting brash!" she said curtly, closing one eye and pointing a knife-sharp fingernail toward them. She noticed Rhia waiting for her attention and turned to her, letting the chastened rowdies grow thirstier as she spoke in a different, gentler voice. "Moira's just now taken little Daisy and gone on along into the line for touching the poor dead body, dear. She told me when I saw you to instruct you that you're to do the same."

Rhiannon smiled her thanks and turned back toward the green to join the ragged line snaking toward the grim pavilion. The crowd had lessened a bit from before, which was good. Yet the proceedings moved slowly, slowly. After a while of standing there and barely moving, she sighed, scanning the line ahead for a sight of Granna and little Daisy. The sun at the midday hour was right hot, and she longed for the drink of cool barley water Granna's crony at the stand would have given her, if she'd only thought to ask.

And, too, where was Jim by now? She'd had no sight of him since returning from her sojourn with Maddy. Keeping track of their foursome was like herding chickens!

Suddenly, a commotion started up ahead and traveled quickly back to where Rhia stood. She perked her ears and leaned sideways, trying to see forward. The line was losing its orderly shape and widening out loose as folks edged up quick into a crowd.

Rhia, stretching on tiptoe, perceived that the vicar and the bailiff had stepped together from the pavilion, but this glimpse was all she had before the crush of shoulders before and behind her closed like a wave.

"What's happened, then?" demanded a burly man, speaking to no one in particular as he shoved roughly past. He hefted his small son to his shoulders. "Has the foul murderer been discovered?"

It was the question propelling everyone closer, as all wanted a sight of whatever had occurred to bring the vicar and bailiff out into the open. But all *Rhia* wanted was to go against the stream and get free! She always felt sick in close quarters, but never had she been entrapped as thoroughly as in this sudden surge of bodies. She worried she'd swoon clean away and be trampled underfoot, so before that could happen she took a good gulp of air, closed tight her eyes, and used her slenderness and flexibility to edge and slide her way along, desperately struggling toward the open air.

Presently, she was spat from the mob like a beached fish—though she found herself not back near the ale-tasters' booth, as she'd wanted to be, but just the opposite, arrived mere paces from the gaudy pavilion! She'd gotten turned completely in her panic! She could actually see the swarming flies that coated the inside of the grim tent's newly thrown open flap door like some dark, furred lining.

The lord's chief law officer, their bailiff, Guy Dryer, was a broad-faced man, large and quiet. In fact, he spoke so seldom, some in town wondered if he *could* speak. Today, as usual, he showed no emotion, though the morning's ordeal inside that wretched tent had surely taken its toll. His jaws worked as he clamped his teeth tight, and his face was sheened with sweat. His long, lank hair, entangled with flies, clumped along the soggy neck and shoulders of his shirt.

A step ahead of him, as befit the holiness of his office, stood Vicar Pecksley.

Vicar Pecksley always looked a bit unwell to Rhiannon, so gray-faced and waxy-skinned was he, but now he looked more thin-lipped than usual as he took a step forward and held up the crucifix he usually wore atop his vestments.

The crowd went instantly silent at that gesture, meant to remind all present that God Himself was behind this gory business.

"The Lord will not suffer the wicked to triumph, but by their own hands they will indeed be revealed," the vicar intoned. "The pavilion shall now be opened wide so that all here may confirm what the bailiff and I have just witnessed in private."

A couple of young boys who crouched near hoping for the chance at just such a job scrambled to roll up the front wall of the pavilion. Some in the crowd groaned and looked away at first sight of the corpse, who lay there bluish and naked on the butcher's table except for a cloth covering his private parts.

The vicar turned and held the crucifix toward the pavilion, commanding in a solemn voice, "Come out that all may see ye, James Gatt, in the name of Our Lord!"

A figure who'd been far in the nether corner of the tent began making his way slowly forward through the deep shadows. Those in the crowd whispered together and strained to see, but the concealed accused was in no hurry to present himself to their scrutiny.

"Have patience and give me amblin' time, friends, now would ye?" the foul murderer finally called out from within the tent. "I come slow, as my hurryin' days was lost with my leg, but on t'other hand, there's no chance a'tall I'll be runnin' for escape."

Some folks laughed at that, then looked shamed and stifled their laughter quick.

Rhiannon felt turned to stone, and for the second time that strange afternoon, she thought sure she might swoon. Jim! It was their *Jimmy* in there, accused?

She had the small presence of mind to step behind a nearby stout woman, hiding herself, knowing Jim might find it hard to see her gawking so close. How could this be *happening*? Where was *Granna*? She wanted her granna!

Rhia turned to look for her, and her eyes arrested for a moment on the manor house in its walled seclusion. The lord still stood at that upper window, indistinct at this distance but there nonetheless. Surely, surely, he would not suffer this to happen to one of his villeins, especially one so wronged already by rough fate?

Another party was heard from then, a shrill speaker from deep in the mob.

"Well, and couldn't I have easily *predicted* such an end to Jim if he once ventured off Clodaghcombe Bluff down to grand Woethersly?

But tell us, Vicar. How d'ye imagine he *did* this murder, all one-legged as he be? Mayhaps he *rolled* clear down to the River Woether, knocked the victim to the ground with his rolling, then held the knife between his teeth for the stabbing, is that what ye suppose?"

The mob shifted with a gasp, searching to see who'd the outrageous nerve to speak so boldly. Many tittered with guilty laughter as well at the scene the speaker had just painted with her storyteller's words, though Rhiannon could feel only despair.

The vicar's face went tight as a skull, as meanwhile folk parted, giving Granna ample pathway to charge forward with Daisy by the hand. Rhia could scarce bear to look as the two of them reached the front and stepped right jauntily into direct confrontation with the bailiff, who himself had stepped in front of Vicar Pecksley.

Granna was dwarfed by the bailiff, her nose direct even with the middle of his shirt.

"That's right, Guy, protect the vicar from those two ruffians!" called some wag in the crowd, to laughter.

Several things happened at once, then, so that Rhia only got them straight in her head later. Almund Clap came shouldering through the mob and took Granna's arm and Daisy's shoulder, easing them sure and quick away. The vicar gave a nod and two of the bailiff's assistants came forward, took Jim by the arms, and pulled him up close to the butcher's table, handling him roughly so that his stick fell to the ground. Jim looked once over his shoulder, and his face seemed white beneath the red of his stubbly beard.

And then, darkness ate at the edges of the bright day, and all sound and movement seemed to Rhia to go magically spinning away into nothingness.

And in that eerily becalmed moment, the bailiff's men took Jim's two hands and extended them forward, onto the stomach of the corpse.

"Witness, good people, what the bailiff and I have observed in private," Vicar Pecksley intoned. "See how the wounds open their mouths and bleed afresh! Thou Who perceivest hidden things hath made Your truth manifest to us, Your servants. Your name be praised and Your will be done, O Lord, forever and ever, amen."

Dark blood trailed down the side of the dead man, black against white skin, against white day, against white everything as daylight flared bright before Rhia's eyes, then went out like the flame of a snuffed candle.

For a third time that day Rhia'd felt she might swoon, and this time, she had.

When she came back to herself, she was in a cool and quiet place, with whispery voices swirling above her head. Her surroundings were dim and shadowy, churchlike, though she knew, most from the sweet smell of fermented grain, that this was no church. Indeed, it was the undercroft of the ale-tasters' booth. Long-handled spoons and iron brewing pots, not water fonts and carved saints, crowded the space beneath every high arch that supported the timber building above.

She was stretched on a low stone table with a sack of barley for pillow. And above her head hovered, gentle as heavenly host, several of Granna's white-wimpled and crisply aproned friends, as well as Granna herself. The women's long white fingers were folded beneath their ample bosoms in what looked like concern. For *her*? Had she, then, somehow died and been laid out on this stony bier for viewing?

Well, she'd worry about it later, as it was too much to think about just now with her head aching so. The lavender cloth laid upon her brow felt so soothing. She closed her eyes and slipped again into a place where she was but a tiny child, really still a babe, sleeping on a pallet near the hives as her mother gathered wax and hummed a sadly beautiful tune to the listening bees . . .

"Rhia!" Granna's voice was a jolt, and moreso was the sharp slap she'd given Rhia's cheeks, one and then the other. "Don't ye go drifting away from us again, ye hear, girl?"

Something hard hit her right in the chest then, and she sat up, gasping for breath.

"I've decided to give you Queen Matilda till you grow well, Rhia," Daisy pronounced, all solemnly. "She'll make you feel better, you'll see."

Rhia shook the last fuzzy cobwebs from her head. Queen Tildy—who'd been affrighted herself when she'd been thrust so rudely into Rhia's rib cage, then tumbled all akilter to Rhia's lap—shook her own hide-covered head as though to regain her own wits.

Daisy leaned her elbows sadly and familiarly on Rhia's leg and let her head droop, needing comfort. "I love Jim," she said simply.

Rhia grabbed her in a fierce hug. And then she found herself sobbing along with the child, as some watergate inside her had been breached by Daisy's innocent and heartfelt sentiments. Why, *she* loved Jim, too.

"This is an awful day!" the child suddenly exclaimed in her simple way. And then, she began to shiver so violently that Rhiannon was alarmed and clasped her all the harder, fearing she was fevered.

"The Gwent-Traed-y-Meirw has hold of her for sure." Granna bent to murmur near Rhia's ear. "See yon white dog in the doorway? If we need more proof, there it be."

Granna held that a white dog appeared when death had just come calling, and sure enough—a large, light-furred mongrel now stood in the doorway looking straight at them, his jaws aslobber. Granna also said that a cold gale blew over a new corpse and was immediately felt by closest family members, no matter if they were miles away. The Gwent-Traed-y-Meirw, that deathwind was called.

If Mam were here, she would have instantly berated Granna's belief in such ancient Welsh omens, but Rhia wouldn't. She believed Granna was perfectly right and that Daisy *was* shaking with the wind of death. She herself was somehow sure that Primrose and Ona had just then given their souls to God. Yes, she was sure of it.

She took Daisy's small face in her hands.

"It is a bad day indeed. But you and I are true sisters now, Daisy. You'll bear no sadness alone, not *ever*! I will always be there beside you."

Daisy, pale as milk, nodded fiercely.

"Rhiannon, try your legs," someone ordered, and Rhia saw Almund Clap elbowing closer through the hovering women. "Your grandmother's been too worried about you to worry about herself, but outspoken as she's been on the green today, we'd best take her right quick away from Woethersly. I'll travel as escort, and the moment you are able, we should make fast tracks up the bluff."

Rhia stood, then crouched to place Queen Matilda gently back into the sling still suspended over Daisy's shoulder. She felt great relief that Almund Clap would be escorting them, but then new anguish over the great change in their returning party.

"Jim won't be going back with us, will he?" she whispered. "He's arrested, and will be held in the gaol until they surely . . ."

She stopped herself from finishing, because of Daisy. Though Jim

85

would surely *hang,* out on Gallux Hump! She'd been in charge of their group today—this was *her* fault! Why'd she let Jim come along, especially after Granna's strong misgivings? And why'd she left the lot of them to consort with silly and feckless Maddy?

"We'll talk of it later," the reeve said quickly and quietly. "As for now, let's away. I meant exactly what I said—this is no safe place for your group with Moira's insult still ringing in the ears of the local worthies. We'll take the nether way out of town, back through the newly burned lot beside the churchyard. I'll lead, with Moira. Rhia, you and Daisy follow close, and Thad's agreed to bring up the rear and keep watch behind."

"Thad?" Rhia asked in a small voice, unheard by most in the room, as Granna's friends had gathered close around her and were giving last bits of strident advice.

Someone detached himself from the shadows beneath an arch. He came a few steps closer but stayed on the edge of the crowd, bowing his head slightly to Rhia.

"*Thad,* Rhia!" Daisy, recovering her energy, pointed at him. "Thaddeus! You stared at him down on the beach this morning, remember? He was behind you at the green and caught you when you fell. He *carried* you here, and got word of it to us, as well."

Rhia's face burned as though it were afire. "I wasn't *staring,*" she protested, gulping.

"Yes, you were so!" the child piped, all innocence. "You nigh stepped right off'n the bluff from staring at Brother Thaddeus so hard, don't you remember? You *did!*"

Chapter 8

As they followed Almund's lead and slipped out of town the back way, then trudged along the nether side of the common barley field, then forded the River Woether, Rhiannon couldn't bring herself to so much as glance over her shoulder at the young monk who served as rear guard to their party. He surely regretted saying he'd serve as escort for a group containing such a shameless fool as she! *Twice* fool she must appear to him, one time fool because he'd witnessed her rage at his fellow clergy this morning at the churchyard, and a second time fool because he'd heard Daisy's childish insistence that Rhia'd been *staring* at him this morning from the trail! She almost hoped he had slipped away from their party in stealth, that he had run away and would keep on running clear back to Glastonbury Abbey, thereby freeing her of the need, required by the laws of courtesy, to turn and thank him for his service to her on the green this afternoon.

With only a small grunt for preface, Granna suddenly stopped hiking and sank down upon the lush grasses past the river to rest a bit before the steep trail. Almund Clap bent to show Daisy some little silvery fish, and Rhia, heart beating within her chest like a caged bird, finally took a deep breath and turned to face Thaddeus.

"I thank you for your service to me today when I became unwell," she said in a rush before her nerve could desert her. Her neck felt afire. "How fortunate for me that you happened to be nearby. But what do I call you, sir? Brother Thaddeus?"

He smiled. "Call me only Thaddeus, as I'm a novice and have not yet taken final vows. And if I may, I'll take the liberty of calling you Rhiannon. And, well, I'd better confess that I didn't just *happen* to be there when you fainted. I was waiting behind you, hoping to have a word when you had leisure."

When she looked puzzled, he quickly added, "Not that I'd go tailing you about! I assure you, Rhiannon, I meant no harm. I'm no vile stalker."

She laughed, put at ease by that unlikely image. "I would hardly take someone like *you* for anything like *that*."

"I'll consider it a compliment," he murmured, laughing a bit at himself.

He pushed back his wide woolen sleeves and crossed his arms. The nails of his long, blunt fingers were stained with several colors, primarily black and beetroot, also a deep yellow and some woad. The bones in his wrists seemed large, and the muscles above them were strong and knotted. Rhia caught herself and dropped her eyes as Thaddeus took a step forward to speak more confidentially.

"When Reeve Clap told me this afternoon that your family is settled atop this high crag, I could scarcely believe it," he murmured, shaking his head. "It *is* an extraordinary place at all times, I'm sure. But I looked for you at the village green to ask . . ."

He stopped, frowning, looking beyond her, over her head, letting his eyes travel the vast expanse of steep wooded slope that was Clodaghcombe Bluff.

"To ask . . . what?" she prodded.

"To ask about a group of folk I came upon last night as I walked the beach. They hastened into the forest at my approach, and though I came out to look for them again this dawn, they'd not come back. Reeve Clap says you and your mother and grandmother know Clodaghcombe

Forest better than anyone else, so I looked for you to ask if you had recently come upon some folk living wild amongst the trees."

Rhia narrowed her eyes. "Well, there did seem to be *something* amiss at one place along the trail, though in these deep woods the wind and the light can oft hoodwink the senses." She lowered her voice to a whisper. "Tell me of these people. Were they standing with very little movement, some of them bent?"

Thaddeus nodded eagerly. "You *did* see them, then. My concern is that they are ill and not provisioned. I've seen their kind before, and know somewhat of their plight."

Rhiannon sighed. "I saw them not today, but on the beach yesterday, as you yourself did. They're not from around here, but mayhaps they live the hike of a day or two away and were come for a spring diversion, as so many others did. This is for sure—*no* one can overnight in this steep forest of Clodaghcombe. There are wild boars and wolves, and pitfalls along the ground, which is very rocky and rough at best."

Not to mention the ancient enchantments, such as the Devil Dogs of Clodagh, said to be held in a cave somewhere within the woods by a wizard's entrapment spell.

Thaddeus looked troubled, but didn't answer. A fog was coming in as evening approached. It hovered like a fist over the sea and extended white fingers ashore, beginning to slowly grope through the trees and up the bluff as if looking for something lost.

"Come then, slackards!" Granna called, and they both jumped a bit, rapt as they'd been. The rest of their party had started up again and they'd not even noticed.

As Rhia'd feared, it was slow and treacherous climbing with the fog so thick that evening, concealing both woods to the left and the drop to the

89

water on the right and seldom allowing a peek farther ahead than a pace or two. All sound was muted as well, except for the howls of the wolves, equally chilling and lonely-sounding in all weathers.

The one good thing about such a perilous hike was the concentration it took, allowing little room for thought about anything except the next footfall. Rhiannon desired *not* to think of poor Jim left behind, nor of the sad situation with Daisy's kin waiting for them at home. And yet it was impossible *not* to think somewhat about those things, as the very effort of not thinking of them proved to bring about the *thinking* of them!

"Queen Matilda is somewhat afeared for her life on this awful trail," Daisy mentioned in a tiny voice. "I've told her to be a good, brave girl like you, Rhiannon."

Rhia sighed. "I'm not so brave, Daisy. You'll find that out, now we're sisters."

"What *do* you fear, Rhiannon?" Thaddeus asked quietly from behind them. It was the first time she'd heard his voice since they'd started up, which seemed an age ago.

She felt all flustered and could not talk.

"Rhia!" demanded Daisy. "The priest asked you *what* you're afeared of!"

Rhia sighed, remembering her jaunt with Maddy. "Well . . . dragons. I'm afeared of *dragons!* How's that?"

Daisy said nothing at first, then quietly asked, "*Are* there dragons?"

Rhia silently considered how to answer that troublesome question.

"Daisy, I'll tell you of Saint George and the very *last* dragon in the whole world," Thaddeus spoke up heartily from the rear. "That fearsome beast lived within a bottomless pond just outside a village, you see, and each day the villagers threw him two sheep for his dinner. Well, that satisfied him for a while. But then, as all beings want some variety in their diet, he decided he required something richer. 'I demand one tender human a year as my Christmas feast!' the ugly beast bellowed. 'Why, I waste away with hunger for young flesh! You can see my very ribs, I grow so gaunt! Youth or maiden, either will do for this meal, by the by, as I'm not particular in my tastes!' "

Daisy looked up at Rhia with her eyes wide, but with a bit of a smile. "Dragons don't talk," she whispered.

Rhia shrugged and bit her lips, rolling her eyes in agreement.

"And so once a year the town cast lots, and one unlucky young person was given as sacrifice on Christmas Day. And I believe that for a great many years this saved the village from destruction by that beast's fiery breath! But then . . ."

Thaddeus paused a moment, just as Granna oft did to build suspense in her storying.

"But then, one year, the lot was drawn by the king's own daughter!"

Daisy gasped and squeezed Rhia's hand. "What was the princess's name?" the child asked. "Was she beautiful? Was her hair long and shiny?"

"Her name was Cleodolinda," Thaddeus said, "and she was beautiful as a princess."

"But she *was* a princess!" Daisy corrected as Rhia snuffled a laugh.

"Yes, well, anyway, the princess was dressed in a white gown and led out to be sacrificed. But Saint George the Dragonslayer came along just as she was waiting there beside the pond for the monster to appear from the briny deep. 'Leave me for your own safety, though you have a noble heart!' Cleodolinda told George quite tearfully. You see, like

91

Rhiannon, Princess Cleodolinda was afeared of dragons, especially ones that were about to eat her for their Christmas treat! Yet she was too polite to link another to her troubles."

"And what did Saint George do then?" Daisy asked in an eager whisper.

"Well, he lifted his great lance, made the sign of the cross, and just at that moment the fearsome dragon *exploded* from the pond with a great spray of steam! 'Fear not, for I will help you!' George called to the princess. Then he charged right at that dragon and plunged his lance right into his great belly!"

"Killed him!" Daisy breathed.

"Oh, no, it would be too commonplace a thing for Saint George to simply *kill* the very last dragon on earth! No, no, no. George *mesmerized* that dragon, is what he did. Shocked him so good that the dragon ne'er could think nor act. Meanwhile, as the dragon stood addled, George whispered to Cleodolinda, 'Throw your belt right over his neck, and he'll be led by you like a dog.' And from that day, the beast followed along behind Cleodolinda everywhere she went, and was to her a gentle pet. I heard she even wove for him a fine red shawl, and tied a silken bow around the tip of his scaly tail."

Daisy giggled, and Rhiannon was filled with gratitude to Thaddeus. A little mirth was a great gift on such a treacherous night, with heartache surely awaiting the child when they finally reached the end of this climb.

But when *would* that be? This did seem like limbo, and the five of them seemed to Rhia like lost souls a-wandering in endless mist, trudging ever upward, upward . . .

"Crrrrrraaahh! Craaaawwwk! Crahhh-awk!"

Rhia's heart sang. "Gramp!" she called out to the others, forgetting in her relief that only when she was by herself or alone with Granna did she make bold to call the great groshawke that familiar name. "It's Gramp! We're almost home!"

"Gramp?" she heard the young monk query softly behind her.

Even at the crag's unwooded and level top, it was hard to tell solid ground from formless sky. Gramp was perched upon the faery rock he always used when chaperoning Rhia at the bluff's edge, but tonight he seemed suspended within the fog, roosting on mere clouds.

"Which way?" Daisy asked as the five of them stood grouped, plotting the next move.

Rhia was wondering the same thing. Though she could normally have found her way home from the bluff's edge blindfolded, there was no telling up from down nor right side from nether side. Even Granna stood undecided, pulling at her ear, and the reeve and the novice merely looked round in complete puzzlement.

"Will you serve as guide to the settlement so's we don't step off the edge?" Rhia asked Gramp, and with a great, honking "Crawk!" that said he'd merely been awaiting polite request, Gramp took off and flew slowly just above them so they merely had to follow the sound of his strong old flapping wings.

Soon enough, the six cottages began to loom ahead, squat shapes in the swirling fog. As they got a bit closer, Rhia noticed tiny points of candleflame in the windows of five of the cots, but only one of them showed the bright light of a true fire.

It was not their own cottage, either, but Ona's.

"Aigy, are ye about?" Granna bellowed toward that best-lit cot.

Mam instantly appeared as a dark silhouette in the doorway, then she hitched her skirt and ran headlong to their group, throwing herself into Granna's arms so's she nearly toppled the both of them.

Rhiannon was surprised to see her proud mother in such a state, and then more surprised yet to behold her crying upon her own mother's shoulder. "I was so worried about all of you," Aigneis sobbed, clutching Granna. "Two dead within, Mother, and the fog came on so! I *needed* you to be here with me, to tell me what to do!"

No one *ever* had to tell Mam what to do, or was allowed to! And Rhia also knew her mother would not have so bluntly mentioned the two dead in front of Daisy if she had not been beside herself with nerves and weariness.

Rhia crouched eye-to-eye with Daisy and whispered, "I'm so sorry for your loss." She pulled her close and felt the child's tears warm upon her shoulder.

"There, there, and you're exhausted with all you've done for Ona and her girls," Granna meanwhile was comforting Mam. "It's all right, Aigy, as we're all here now to help with everything."

She'd been gently easing free of her daughter's grasp while she spoke, and now Granna took Mam by the shoulders and turned her so she faced Reeve Clap. With a little shove, she propelled her direct into the startled reeve's arms.

"*There's* the comfort you're *truly* needing, Aigy," Granna said with a chuckle.

Then Granna turned her face toward the lighted cottage and led stolidly on, with Rhia, Daisy, and Thaddeus following.

When Rhia looked back over her shoulder from the threshold of Ona's cot, Mam and Reeve Clap were still where they'd first come together, their arms about each other.

Thaddeus and Reeve Clap could not have gone safely back down the path with the fog so heavy, and since there were funeral prayers to be said throughout the night, and a double burial to perform upon the morrow, their presence was indeed a godsend.

Mam had already prepared the bodies of Ona and Primrose, washed them and clothed them afresh, and laid them out upon Ona's cot with the child sheltered inside the mother's arm. A fresh white blanket covered them, and four long beeswax tallows had been set burning, one at each corner of their shared bier.

Granna took Daisy's hand. "You and I will sit right beside them throughout this whole night," Granna whispered to the child, who leaned for comfort against her skirt. "You can say anything you'd like to your dear mother, and she'll hear every word and remember it eternally."

At Mam's instructions, the reeve and the monk carried the long bench and the short one over from the main cottage, and Thaddeus placed the long bench at the wall right next to Ona's head. Granna settled herself upon it, with Daisy close. Later in the night, there would be ample room for Daisy to stretch out and sleep with her head in Granna's lap, and Granna would likely sleep some as well, slumped there. The others of them could keep deathwatch from the small bench, or could sit upon the floor reeds and lean back against the wattle to catch a nap.

Mam next sent Thaddeus and Rhia to go collect Dull Sal to join them in their wake for the two dead, as it was too lonely a night for anyone to stay apart in the drear gloom. The two of them walked silently and slowly toward Sal's place, going single file along the worn rock path that linked the cots together.

When they'd stepped past the last bit of strong light that spilled from Ona's cottage, Rhia suddenly stopped in her tracks and turned to him, putting her hands over her face.

"Oh, Thaddeus, no one's mentioned Jim at all," she whispered. "I grow *sick,* so filled am I with guilt and worry for him! When Mam is told, she'll blame me, I know—as well she *should!*" The fog swirled about her shoulders as though even *it* berated her.

"Rest assured, Rhiannon, that your mother *has* been told," Thaddeus said quickly. "As we went for the benches, the reeve mentioned to me that he's spoken to her about what happened, and far from faulting you, she faults herself for placing you in the midst of such a catastrophe. Tonight, we'll mourn these dead. Then on the morrow, the six of us will make what plans we may regarding Jim, and . . . some other things, as well."

"Some other things?" Rhia echoed.

Thaddeus roved his eyes over the dense fog at forest's edge. "Rhiannon, I don't dispute what you said about the forest being inhospitable, yet I believe those people we both saw on the beach last night *did* overnight in these woods, and will again tonight. I think they must live apart by order of church and law, and so have been brought to your rugged bluff from afar. As a matter of fact, I strongly suspect the earl has gathered these unfortunates from all parts of his lands, and has arranged for them to be transported to this most remote wilderness corner of his holdings. In your woods they will live however they may for a little time until they . . . simply live no more."

Rhia's shock and puzzlement showed upon her face even in the moonlight, so that Thaddeus quietly added, "You see, that's how the great barons deal with the thing. It was told us by our good abbot at Glastonbury that many forests in King Henry's realm are quarters to such tragic folk, though rough housing it be."

"I *did* see the earl's boat yesterday," Rhia whispered. "You . . . you sound like you've seen folk like them before."

"Yes, sheltering beneath the almsgate at our monastery in Glastonbury. Most drift away having received a bowl of food, but some few have lingered and found beds at our wayfarers' infirmary. Have you heard of leprosy, Rhiannon?"

She frowned and shook her head, trying to read the expression on his face through the darkness. Was he angry? He sounded it. Yet no one could be angry with the earl—it plain wasn't allowed. If Thaddeus *was* angry, it was like Granna's undying anger at the Normans. Mam was always begging Granna to curtail her spitting when their Norman conquerors were mentioned, as someday it was likely to get them all in trouble.

"Well," Thaddeus continued, "I strongly suspect the veiled faces of those folk hide the ravages of that malady, leprosy, as do their gloved hands and heavy robes. Such folk as these are much despised for their contagion, Rhia. It's also widely thought they bring their ills upon themselves through some sin or other. I think the folk just arrived at your woods were likely given a lepers' mass, had dirt thrown upon their feet, and were officially declared dead to the world. Then they were brought to these hinterlands at the earl's command and left to fend for themselves. They'll stay apart, and if anyone should venture near, they must by law warn of their presence with some sort of bell, or with a clapper or clicker of some kind."

That was the clicking sound she'd heard in the forest this morning! "But . . . how *can* they fend, Thaddeus? Does the earl expect they'll eat the berries and nuts from the trees, as do the foraging goats? And that they'll sleep rough as the red deer?"

Thaddeus, surprised by the heat in her voice, looked at her direct.

97

"'The earl would call it Christian good works, Rhia, to give them leave to exist among these trees and stones of his any such way they can until they make quick exit from this world. It's . . . how he thinks, you see."

Rhia's eyes widened. "You sound as though you *know* the earl," she breathed.

Thad looked down. "I do know the earl a little, Rhia. He and my father are friends, though Father has just three manors, and the earl, of course, has an honor of dozens. My father's father fought with William in 1066, just as did your Lord Claredemont's father."

This young monk, then, was aristocracy! He was indeed the son of a lord, though he wore the rough robe of Benedict.

He shrugged and gave her a weak smile. "I was given by my father as oblate to the church when I was eleven, six years ago. It's often done with second sons."

Rhia crossed her arms and looked into the darkness. "How can so much be amiss, when near as yesterday all seemed well?" she whispered, her chest tight and hot. "Two dead, one orphaned too young, one jailed and likely to hang. And now this group you speak of, surely suffering worst of all."

Thaddeus made her no answer, and indeed seemed elsewhere in his thoughts. He'd lowered his hood and now cocked his head to better hear the night. A raspy sound had started up in the stew of fog. It had been low at first, but now was swelling.

"It's only the bees," Rhiannon reassured him with a sigh. "Silly bees. They've sensed these deaths and will not be stilled until they're given the respect of being informed directly. Wait here. This will only take me a few moments."

She veered quickly off the path, bound toward the hives.

"Please, don't!" Thaddeus caught her wrist. "What I mean is, your . . . your mother will worry if we aren't back directly, with Sally."

This was true enough. Rhiannon stopped, looking at his hand upon her arm. Thaddeus's eyes rested a moment upon the same spot, then he thought to release her.

"I'm sorry," he said. "It's just that, well, I'd be afraid for you to go outside the circle of these lit cottages alone, and I confess I'm not anxious to escort you, though I will, of course, if you insist upon going. It's just that the night is . . . unknowable."

Unknowable. She still felt his hand, though it was gone, and now she found she couldn't get a good breath. Well, the night was dark and the fog was like milk, a thing to swim in, but not to breathe. The thing to do was to turn and go forward, to lead Thaddeus directly to Sally's cot, so she nodded that she agreed with his thinking on the subject of something, something she'd forgotten exactly what the subject had been, to be honest—and she turned, too quickly, nearly tripping over her own wooden feet.

A few steps on, she managed a sentence over her shoulder, one meant to be joking, but made quavery and uncertain by the milky air. "I'll wager someone like you, nearly a monk, would think the telling of the bees is but a pagan notion anyhow."

"Some of my brothers at Glastonbury call such practices superstition," he answered. "But what could be the harm of showing such courtesy to one of God's small creatures?"

She heard the goodwill in his voice. "You showed great courtesy to another of his small creatures this evening. I'm grateful to you for easing Daisy with your dragon tale."

" 'Twas you that opened the way for that, Rhia, by feigning fear of the beasts."

Feigning. "Just so," Rhia murmured, thinking of the great, sighing breath beneath the stone pictures in mysterious Wythicopse Ring.

They reached Dull Sal's cottage, and Rhia knocked upon the door, then pushed it open. She'd expected to find Sally lying at rest or asleep, but Sal was sitting cross-legged on her sleeping pallet, rocking herself with some agitation and staring wide-eyed at the single window where the candle feebly burned. What was she looking at?

"Three fish, three fish!" Sal exclaimed, rocking all the harder.

"It's all right, Sally, as we've come to fetch you," Rhia said gently, slipping her hands beneath Sal's arms and bringing her to her feet. But when Sal *still* gawked at the window, Rhia dared a glance over her own shoulder and saw a thing that froze her blood.

Thaddeus had seen it as well. He rushed to the open doorway. "Wait, don't flee!" he called toward the woods. Then he plunged outside into the swirling darkness.

Rhia rushed to the window, where moments before a phantom had stood looking in upon Sal, *reaching* in with ghostly fingers. The fog was now moving as smoke will move when a breeze has stirred. Rhia peered harder, and near the brook she glimpsed long tendrils of floating hair and a shroudlike garment, all quickly dissolving into mist.

She turned back to Sal, then rushed to put her arms around the poor frightened girl with her cheek to Sal's cheek. "I don't believe in the banshee, Sal, do you?" Rhia whispered. "Though if she's real, tonight would be the night for her, that's certain."

Chapter 9

Thaddeus finally came stumbling back over Sal's threshold.

"Nothing," he panted, bending forward with his hands upon his knees. "I searched to the edge of the trees and then beyond, but whoever she was, she . . . wouldn't be found."

Without looking in his direction, Rhia took Sally's hand and led her right smartly out the door and onto the foggy stoop. There Thaddeus joined them, taking Sal's other arm.

Near tears, Rhia turned to him and blurted, "Why'd you run away into the darkness like that, Thaddeus? The night is unknowable, as you yourself said!"

She instantly regretted such sharp words, but she'd been scared nigh to death, left alone with Sal after glimpsing such a phantom just outside their very window!

"Truly, I'm sorry," he answered, all contrite. "It's just that, well, I saw someone outside, and as she seemed much too young to be venturing in such weather, I didn't think except that I must pursue her before she misstepped. She was just a child, Rhiannon, much the age of Daisy, I'd say. Do you have some idea who she might be?"

Oh, Rhia knew right well! The spectre at the window *had* been too young to be the hideous banshee, so she could only have been the ghost of Primrose, Daisy's twin. If a child died unbaptized, her spirit would become a ghostly will-o'-wisp, wandering through the fog and marshy places until a great many strong prayers blew her finally safe to God's arms! Even Mam believed that, and had been careful to have Rhia baptized while she was still but a babe.

Still, Thaddeus might consider that mere superstition, so she'd keep it to herself. "I'm sure the fog presented some shape you took to be a girl. The mists and clouds oft trick the eyes of strangers who first venture here." Then, "Let's hurry some, Sal," she ordered briskly, pulling her along.

"Wait," Thaddeus protested, "what about the other cottage? Isn't there someone to be brought from that place as well? A light burns in the window."

Rhiannon glanced toward that drear cot and felt the hairs prickle atop her head. It was bad enough venturing near the Man Who Sleeps in broad daylight.

"Mam has put a candle in that cottage out of courtesy and habit. We need not bring the man who dwells there, as he's past fearing darkness and would not know the difference if he was placed in the midst of a rollicking festival."

Rhia knew that all her life she would remember that night. As they seven sat wake for Ona and Primrose, the fog remained a swirling white sea outside and the firelight danced shadows upon their walls. They seemed to her the only people on earth, with all *outside* become a churning void holding nothing much at all, as before Creation.

It was a sad and fearful night—but also, to tell it true, an exciting one.

She'd remember the look of Granna and Daisy seated there together close, candleglow lighting their pale faces, the one deeply lined and the other angel smooth. She'd remember how the reeve oft got to his feet to tend the fire, then returned to sit close beside Mam on the short bench, finally daring to slip an arm around her shoulders. She'd remember Mam leaning against him, sighing as though home from a journey.

As the night wore on, and with Mam asleep who might have tried to stop her, Granna told an ancient story or two. She told of Sir Gareth burying a nail from the True Cross somewhere in Clodaghcombe Forest, then finding that same nail in his soup seven months later. Then she told of Sir Gawain falling in love with a mermaid princess and disappearing under the waves beneath the high crag of Clodaghcombe until finally Mistress Moon, right jealous of the mermaid's siren charms, pulled that knight to shore a year and three days later.

"Handsome Sir Gawain was half-drowned, of course, and crazy as well with longing for his lost fishy love," Granna told it. "In fact, he stayed nitwit for a good while, until every single part of him had dried out, including his beating heart."

And then, her mood shifted, and she launched into telling of the long sleep of King Arthur, ending with the favorite hope among all Welsh Brits that soon he'd rise from the grave to punish their various invaders. This was the most sacred of all the stories Granna safekept as an official Welsh teller, and she got more and more worked up as she told it.

"Ah, yes, the great king lies asleep in a hidden cave across the bay in fair Wales, see? And his knights sleep as well, nigh ready to jump to their likewise sleeping steeds at some close time. Oh, and then you'll see these present marauders scramble! Doubtless very soon now these Normans shall be given the boot! Aye, their days for sure be numbered, these haughty mountain-makers brought to these shores by thieving William!"

Right here she spit upon the floor, and Rhia burned with humiliation. She glanced at Thaddeus, sure he'd be angry at this description of his own Norman kin, followed close by such a gobbish and putrid sign of disrespect. Yet what could possibly stop Granna except Mam? And Mam was there asleep against the reeve's broad shoulder!

But Thaddeus merely leaned toward Granna, his elbows upon his knees and his eyes alight with pleasure. "Good lady, never have I been in the company of such a fine teller. Now, pray, is there a story behind the name Rhiannon calls your resident groshawke?"

He turned to Rhia and smiled a teasing smile.

"Hee, hee!" Granna responded, slapping her knee. "That name would for certain be Gramp, and your request is welcome, monk, as you've asked to hear my favorite tale. Though I'd never tell it whilst Rhia's mother was awake, and neither, if you notice, will Rhia call that bird Gramp in her mother's hearing. Still, as Aigneis appears to soundly sleep, I *could* bring myself to transgress a bit. Granddaughter, would you have me tell the tale of your great-grandfather's birding upon the field of Senlach?"

Rhia bit her lip and dropped her eyes, discombobulated by the monk's requesting this most personal and pagan of all Granna's stories. Her mother's voice scolded hard against it in her head. *Rhiannon, you're not to listen when your granna talks of spells and incants done for the changing of folk to birds or bird to folk, or for the moving of stones or the making of trees to speak the human language, you understand? Such ancient storying borders on dire sacrilege in these modern Christian days!*

"All righty then, since you insist," Granna spoke, giving up a wait for Rhia to decide. She cleared her throat with a large flourish of sound. "Well, young monk, 'twas in the Year of Our Lord 1066 and I was but a small girl. My da was far away in a place called Senlach, serving our brave Saxon ruler, King Harold himself. And when he'd been gone a good little while, I chanced to look into the fire one morning and there in the flames I saw him clear as could be, going hard with his battleax against a soldier with strangely cut hair and seated upon a gray horse." Granna leaned toward Thaddeus and spoke confidentially. "By the by, *that's* when I found out I had the special sight, see? When in the firepit right in our cottage but so many years ago I watched my own dear da upon a distant battlefield, struggling with all his might to fight off that horsed . . . *invader.*"

Granna paused here to spit another gob, her faithful practice at any mention of the foe come across the sea with William. Then, leaning back against the wattle, she pitched her voice lower and grew dreamy-eyed and somber, as here started the grim part of the tale.

"Later that morn, I felt a jab to my own neck. And didn't I know it for the phantom wound it was? Ah, sure enough, I peered again into the firepit and this time saw my dear da bleeding fierce with an arrow clean through his poor neck. And I saw as well a great groshawke rising from an apple tree nearby the carnage, and what could I think but that it was meant to carry my da's great spirit, since his own flesh and blood was about to give out? And so I said into the firepit the words of a spell I'd heard my own granna say a time or two. I said it at the very moment my dear da's body fell and was trampled by a horse, and his soul rose into that fine bird, it did. Timing's the thing with any good spell and much else in life. Remember that, monk, as it may come in handy."

This was ever Granna's favorite piece of advice, but Rhia dared not look to see the monk's reaction. He'd surely not hold with spells, whether done at the right time or not.

"And three days later, that same great groshawke came flying straight into our woods, sped clear across Wessex to our high bluff!" Granna concluded. "And it's my fine da guarding us still, Rhiannon's great-grandda.

Rhia will tell you that we never so much as doubt it. Go ahead, grand-daughter—*tell* the monk that we do not doubt it in the least."

Rhia's ears rang at this challenge. For truly, she did not doubt it, not much, which is why she called their groshawke Gramp, though not in Mam's hearing. After all, Granna was a member of the venerable Welsh filidh, and those respected storytellers might exaggerate some, but everyone knew they did not lie. At least not so very often.

But what could be less Christian than believing the spirit of a man might take the feathered form of a hawky bird?

"Well, I . . . I believe, well . . ." Rhia stopped, flummoxed and flustered.

"Hee, hee!" said Granna, who was always amused by Rhia's thick tongue when she was put betwixt and between. Then, spent from her telling, Granna found her still-warm pipe there upon the lap of her skirt, clamped it fast between her teeth, closed her eyes, and was very soon snoring.

Daisy sank her bright head to Granna's comfortable lap and dozed as well, just like her own namesake flower will go withered for the day when the sun is gone.

Sal had slept deeply for some time on the pallet Mam had made for her near the firepit.

The young monk said not a word but got to his feet and walked to the foot of the deathbed of Ona and Primrose, kneeling there to pray. He raised the hood of his robe, and Rhia could not see the expression on his face. The colors around his fingernails made him look a bit like a painted church-wall saint. Above him, in the thatch of the ceiling, a family of swallows watched down, their thoughts their own, their bead eyes reflecting the flame.

She determined to pray as unceasingly as Thaddeus did, partly to direct the souls of Ona and Primrose, and partly for the poor stranded lepers, and partly to petition God about Jim, who was much on her mind. But mostly, truth be told, to show the monk that she, too, was pious and righteous and could kneel through the night.

But presently, she sank down to her side and sleep took her in its arms. The flesh must yield when the day has held a long vertical hike in the fog as well as a jaunt to a dragon's den and then also the unthinkable arrest of a hobbled friend.

And other things equally exhausting, feelings and such.

When Rhiannon next opened her eyes, it was past dawn, and everyone seemed gone from the dim cottage excepting Daisy and Granna. Granna looked awake enough, though pinned to her place on the long bench by the deeply sleeping child.

"Where is everyone?" Rhia whispered across to her, scrambling to stand while jerking round her twisted skirt and batting the unruly hair from her eyes.

Granna nodded toward the door with a smile that clearly said, *About their business, sleepyhead, wherever do you think with the morning half gone?*

Rhia spotted her shawl upon the floor and retrieved it, scooping Queen Matilda out and placing her upon the floor reeds near the bench where Daisy slept.

"I'm sorry to disturb your royal majesty's royal sleep, but I *need* this piece of clothing," Rhia mumbled to the insulted-looking tortoise. She then gave a quick sign of the cross before the peaceful dead, bent to kiss Granna's cheek, wrapped her shawl around herself, and headed outside, still groggy.

The sun was shining so astonishingly that she raised a hand to shelter her eyes as she stumbled to the brook. She splashed her face, then sat back upon her heels. With golden breath the sunny wind had blown the fog completely back to sea. Everything up here sparkled and shone like the Garden of Eden.

In fact, the buds had finally begun opening this morning. The orchard was blotched with pink and white blossoms, fragrant even at this distance, and the green collar of the woods was fringed in the fine jewel-like purples and yellows of crocus and forsythia.

"Where *is* everybody?" she called. No answer. "Gramp, where are *you*?"

Gramp came swooping from the woods to settle upon the crucked top of the chapel roof. He then looked down between his own splayed feet at the chapel door below.

So, the others were inside the church, gathering the things they'd need for the funeral.

"Thanks, kind sir." She gave her face another hard splash or two, then pulled her long hair back into a quick knot, ran to the chapel, and burst through its open door.

The chapel was so dim and gloomy after the brightness outside that she could not see a thing at first. There were two small, slitted east windows up near the altar, and golden light poured through them like honey. It would be hours till the sunshine reached through the thick, stone casements of the side windows, though, so all else was cold, shadowy stone, dark and ancient timbers, and soot-grimed daub. The shovel kept in here was gone, as well as the cup and plate for the sacraments. The people she'd come looking for were gone as well.

With a quick sigh, she turned to leave, figuring the others must be already preparing the grave and that she'd join them at the stone circle in the woods.

"Rhiannon? Have you seen the remarkable pictures above these windows?"

She whirled back around and this time noticed Thaddeus standing alone near the altar, looking up. Surrounded by the thick light that fell upon that little area and that alone, he seemed transparent, his pale hands and face washed nearly invisible.

"For all fifteen years of my life, I've *had* to see those horrible things!" She hurried toward him, happy for the chance to say her age, though she'd given herself a few months she'd not earned as yet. "They're said to be the Devil Dogs of Clodagh, painted there long ago to remind all of the perils of hell. Half-dog, half-dragon they are, with their long serpents' tails double-hooked like the devil's own pitchfork. The painter must have heard the local stories of such animals being trapped in a cave within our wood. When I was little, those awful pictures were all I could think about throughout the sacraments."

"That's exactly the intent of paintings such as these," Thaddeus murmured, moving closer to the wall and looking up at the gruesome dogs in fascination. "They're meant to frighten children into staying quiet yet wakeful, no matter how the vicar drones on and on. The painter was really very good. See how the eyes shine with counterfeit life? I aspire to such truthful embellishments myself, though on gentler themes."

Rhia looked from the paintings to the monk, her eyes wide. "You're a painter! *That's* why your hands are stained as they are!" She was so impressed, she lacked words to tell it, though it surely showed upon her face.

He shrugged and looked some abashed. "Painting is my great love, but please don't think I'm master of it! I've been allowed to apprentice in the great scriptorium at Glastonbury. I'm to illustrate the walls of our church and priory in Woethersly, once they're ready and limed for a smooth surface. It will be my first opportunity to do such a thing—a test of sorts. I'm nervous about how I may please, or *displease*, to tell it true."

Gramp, still upon the roof, chose that moment to give his wings a series of great stretching flaps. They were both startled by the sound, much magnified inside the empty church, then smiled at each other sheepishly.

After a moment, Rhia ventured, "Thaddeus, did you consider that Granna's story about our groshawke might indeed be . . . truth?"

Thaddeus looked raptly and silently at the paintings to dodge an answer, obviously not wishing to offend her.

Still, Rhia could not leave the subject without a further prod. In truth, she liked not the monk being certain of such things when she herself was not.

"And . . . and Granna also says that I myself, as well as she and Mam, came down from feathered granddames. You must admit, it would explain how we three came to be atop this bluff when everyone else has had their start upon the ground so far below us."

To tell it true, she expected he would dispatch that with a laugh. It *did* seem far-fetched, though there *was* oft a longing for flight that came to her in her dreams.

Thaddeus clasped his hands behind him, his eyes still lifted and taking in the art.

"I suspect your grandmother must have once been a great hooded owl," he said quietly. "And your mother might well have been a pure white dove with a tuft of orange feathers upon her fair head. And you, Rhiannon, I believe have come down from a shiny winged rook. You are dark of hair and eye, and like that bird, you have a rogue nature."

She was not sure whether to protest or laugh. "I declare that I have no such thing!"

He looked at her and grinned in a teasing way. "Then how are you capable of giving a blistering scold to important clergymen come clear from the court at Winchester to give advice on the church expansion?"

"They *deserved* it," Rhiannon insisted, her knuckles upon her hips. "You must admit, Thaddeus, that they did. They *did*."

Thaddeus smiled in a different, sadder way. "Yes, they deserved it, Rhia, though God forgive me for speaking thus of my superiors. Jim had a right to his cottage. They might have checked if the owner still lived, but it didn't suit their purposes. They were too willing to trust your lord and your vicar, who themselves acted hastily and selfishly regarding poor luckless Jim."

At this sad mention of Jim, Thaddeus turned with a sigh to crouch with his back against the damp wall, then tucked his hands into his sleeves, shaking his head.

Rhia paced before him, agitated and restless. "All saw the blood flowing from the murdered man's wounds at Jim's touch, but I'll *never* believe Jim could, or would, do such a thing as murder." Her eyes filled with angry tears. "Mam's always giving me private instructions regarding Granna's stories. She'll say, 'Now, Rhiannon, you're not to be listening close to your grandmother's tales of mermen or young women become willow trees and the like, as these things border upon the heathen lie. Well, I'll allow Granna colors things up a bit, as any official Welsh storyteller will do! But exaggeration, hearing it or speaking it either one, just doesn't seem very sinful to me, especially compared to awful things some . . . some fine *Christians* do all the time!"

Thaddeus made no comment that might have stopped her blasphemy, so she went on.

"All those *fine* priests, hired to give those poor lepers a gruesome mass so's they could be abandoned to a horrid and lonely fate. And those churchmen burning Jim's only thing he loved in the world, his willowed toft! And there was such . . . well, such a *haughty* look on Vicar Pecksley's face as the bailiff's men pressed Jim's hands to the corpse of that murdered man yesterday! I was close enough to see it quite clear, Thaddeus, and I believe the vicar took prideful pleasure in the whole thing!"

Thaddeus said nothing, but out the corner of her eye Rhiannon saw him look at her.

"Rhia?" he whispered after a moment. "Are you certain that you saw *exactly* what you've just described? Exactly, in every detail?"

She stopped her angry pacing to look down at where he crouched. "I saw a haughty look upon the vicar's face. I'm *sure* of it."

"Not that." Thaddeus slowly came to a stand, his eyes glistening. "I mean, are you certain that you saw—"

"Rhiannon?" Mam called. "Thaddeus, are you in there? It's time we started!"

"Just so, Mam!" Rhia called. A dizzy wave of guilt went through her head to toe, for what if Mam had heard what she'd been saying about their vicar?

But her mother and Reeve Clap merely stood looking puzzled and sun-blinded in the back doorway. Granna walked up behind them, bringing Daisy along.

Rhia hurried back to them, and Thaddeus came along behind her.

Over her shoulder and against her will, she glanced up at the Devil Dogs. She could have *sworn* they stared back at her with glowing eyes.

Chapter 10

They took Sal back to her own cottage, then carried Ona and Primrose to the stone circle and buried them together in a pretty spot newly covered with wildflowers. As they said prayers over their grave, Rhia saw quick movements from the corners of her eyes and knew that they six weren't alone. Those brought to this place by the earl's false charity were watching from some distance, surely afraid to reveal themselves.

When all turned to trudge with respectful step back up the slope, Mam stayed behind. At first not one of their party noticed her absence, as all eyes were downcast and all thoughts subdued. But then they heard her voice behind them as she called toward the deeper woods, gently but firmly demanding, "Who are you?"

Rhia and the others stopped in their tracks and looked back in surprise. Even Reeve Clap had gone on along, figuring Mam was just behind him on the single-file path.

But there she stood, still inside the stone circle, her dark green cloak billowing in the breeze. "Don't be afraid," she said a bit more loudly, walking down even deeper into the woods. "Whoever you are, come out so that we may meet you and see to your needs."

Rhia should have known Mam would sense the presence of these new folk. She was ever sensitive to the weak and disabled, though they be hidden in a vast crowd. This forest, known so well to her, would be far easier for her intuition to penetrate.

"Now see, and this is exactly what I might have thunk," Granna muttered, planting her hands upon her hips. "Almund, when you said that a ship had arrived what held cargo for us up here upon the bluff, I figured there might be *some* choice in our accepting the cargo or no. But I should've known there'd be no choice a'tall when it came down to it, as there'd be no stopping my Aigy when suffering was involved. And *that's* what cargo *always* turns out to be when pointed toward us. Never a load of beet sugar nor pipe fill nor rawhide for the mending of our frayed shoes! No, not ever some *nice* surprise, I'm saying, but always someone or t'other carrying us up more suffering."

Daisy jerked on Granna's skirt. "What about *me?*" she demanded sternly. "Did I not come up to you as carried cargo, and do you call *me* suffering?"

Rhia ducked her head, biting her lips. Daisy would be one to give Granna back as good as Granna could give, that was becoming certain.

"Well," Granna allowed, taking Daisy's hand and swinging her small arm. "There's *some* cargo does bring a nice surprise with it, that's true enough. I'm corrected."

Meanwhile, Mam walked steadily deeper down the slope. As always happened when she walked beneath the canopy of oaks, the birds from all directions fluttered down to form a colorful train behind her. That sight was always amazing, but nothing new.

There *was* a new thing happening, though. Certain of the forest animals were now revealing themselves, as though they'd understood her call to come forth. Two red deer and a badger had emerged from their hidey-holes, as well as a family of raccoons.

And deeper in the trees Rhia saw something that took her breath away. A horse, it was! A white horse dappled with silvery gray had come now from the shadows, pulled into the sun by Mam's gentle voice. Rhiannon tugged at Thaddeus's sleeve and pointed, and together they watched with held breath, hoping for its closer approach. But as if sensing their too-eager inspection, the handsome horse threw back its head and pawed the ground, then turned to canter into the dense wood, beyond their sight.

Meanwhile, the people Rhia'd seen on the beach had shuffled from behind their tree cover, stopping in a loose semicircle some few paces in front of Mam. They clicked and clacked with little sticks upon small bowls they held.

"Have a care, Aigneis!" Thaddeus called down the slope. " 'Tis not a good idea to approach them close. They're alerting you with their clapper bowls that they carry dire contagion."

"Save yer breath," Granna advised him, shaking her head. "Aigy will not leave a creature in distress. There's but one thing you can count on, and that's it."

But Mam surprised them all by turning and meekly coming back up the slope. At first they thought Thaddeus had prevailed upon her thinking, but she moved right past as though he and the others were invisible, giving fast instructions over her shoulder as she hastened along.

"I'll need my biggest basket to take what bread we have down to them! Rhia, you'll first gather more honey from the hives, then find what butter might be still in the cooling shed. Mother, you can please pour watered ale into the carrying pouch, and you two men can gather what extra blankets we have and get fires lit in the three spare cottages we've got, now that Jim's in town and Daisy's living with us. They've a starved look, but may need medicinals beyond that, so I'll have to replenish my—"

"Aigneis?"

Reeve Clap's steady voice finally got through to her. She turned back around to face him, though she'd an entranced look upon her face, a look which Granna and Rhia well knew. Her whole spirit was now with those below as surely as if she were bewitched.

"Yes, Almund?"

"You must have a care for what the churchman has just told you, Aigy," Almund said, gently taking her arms. "There's contagion among those people. We need to plan how to best fend. You'd not have Rhia and Daisy endangered."

Mam blinked hard, blinked again, then took in a breath and shuddered. "Of course not," she whispered, bringing her hands to her face.

"I will straightaway take bread and drink down where they can find it easily," Thaddeus quickly assured her. "Food's surely their immediate need, as God has given them fair weather, at least for the time being."

Mam nodded at his offer, and Rhiannon wondered at the power of the reeve to break through Mam's strong-willed nature in a way she and Granna were never able to.

As for the small community of lepers, they remained in clear sight at a far distance, all standing as quietly as they'd stood on the beach, as though they truly *were* walking dead.

Rhia squinted, looking past them in hopes of glimpsing the steed one more time. But he was truly gone, surely returned to the manor stables where he must have belonged.

Rhiannon would have liked to help Thaddeus carry bread and drink to the forest folk, but Mam had other plans.

"This morning has passed all pell-mell!" she exclaimed when they were back at the cottage. "Almund, if you will, please retrieve our benches from Ona's cottage. Mother, if it please you, stoke the fire. Sal must soon have her gruel, and the Man Who Sleeps must be fed as well. We're late with *all* that! I need to prepare our own meal as soon as the fire's going good, so it's your job seeing to the invalids, Rhia."

Rhia sighed, but did not argue, as Mam appeared so harried.

She went to feed Sal first and made a slow job of it, as usual putting off the Man Who Sleeps for as long as she could.

"We've now buried the two we watched over last night, Sal," she confided as she spooned gruel into Sal's mouth. Sally had missed her breakfast, and opened her mouth wide as a baby bird will do. "Oh, and the churchman who came up the trail with us last night is very interested in the paintings upon the walls within the hermit's chapel. You know, those hideous dogs above the window slits."

Sally smiled wide, smacking her lips and rocking to and fro upon the rushes.

"It's a beautiful day, Sally, and I think I'll take you to sit upon the stoop." Rhia put aside the empty bowl, then stood and circled Sally's waist from behind with her own arms, thus pulling Sally upright. She held her by the hand and led her from the dim cot so that they stood together upon the warm stoop, under the bright and friendly sun.

Rhia sat down, hoping Sal would copy and let her own legs collapse. When she didn't, Rhia stood again and walked behind her, using her knees to push Sal's knees forward so's Sally went to her bottom, eased down by Rhia's hands under her arms.

Rhia sat again and smiled at Sally, and Sally smiled back. She was so beautiful, so shiny in the sun.

"Three fish!" said Sally. "I'll have three of those fish!"

"Know what, Sal? I so wish I'd kept better watch on Jim yesterday.

I know not what I might have done to keep him from what happened. Still, I spent an hour in selfish dillydallying with my mates when I was *expected* to be in charge at all times."

Rhiannon sighed, filled with remorse for her constant selfishness. "To say it true, Sally, I *often* mean to do worthy things I end up not doing. Such as paring Granna's toenails, for instance. Mam does it, but I should assume the job. I just canna bring myself to the act, as Granna's large toes grow nails that much resemble horses' hooves."

Or going cheerfully over to the Man Who Sleeps and giving his hands and face a good bathing. Mam did that at least once a day. But when *she* was left to take care of him, like now, at the most she'd just hasten into his cot, shove a bit of gruel into his mouth without checking if it went down, wet his lips with a drink, and jump back out.

"Sal," she confided, "I'd like to be more kindly to the bestilled pirate in the cot next door to yours, but he just plain gives me the willies, worse than Granna's toenails do! Life all bestilled is a thing I ne'er can handle easily."

Still, she determined to make a better effort, starting this moment.

"Good Sally, fair as spring." She gave Sal's shoulders a farewell squeeze. "You sit out here awhile. When you grow cold, I'll take you inside."

Rhia then stood, all business, and walked right briskly to the pirate's cot. *Knock knock*, quick. But there was no answer, of course, he being so limp, so she pushed open the door, then blocked it from closing with her heel. She'd balance on one leg to have it open for as long as it took to put the bucket of gruel upon the floor and to spoon his portion into the bowl she'd brought tucked into her waist sash. The door would slam closed when she walked on in, but any moments with it open seemed an advantage.

She decided a good start in being more kindly to the pirate would be to talk to him, just as she talked to Sal. It might some calm her nerves, to boot.

She straightened her shoulders and walked to the raised wood plank that served as his sleep pallet.

"Here's your gruel," she said, prying at his lips with the wooden spoon. She felt a drip of cold sweat roll down her forehead as she pried harder, bent on making a space between his teeth large enough to let some portion of gruel slip through. At last, she had a spoonful down, and then a second spoonful, and then a third. Pleased with herself, she tried for a fourth, and was frightened nearly witless when the pirate's fine white teeth suddenly clamped closed right upon Mam's spoon!

"Let *go!*" she railed. "Cease your biting! You should be right ashamed!"

Rhia was beside herself. If he bit it clean in half, they would be down to two spoons, whereas she was sure Mam would scrimp to save up coin to buy a fourth from the wood turner in town, now that they had Daisy!

"You *must* desist!" she cried, thunking the top of his head with her knuckles, hard, as she'd seen Granna do with young rowdies. It worked. The pirate's jaw came open. The spoon, though its maple wood bore the marks of his teeth, was whole and usable still.

She was too rattled to do naught more but pour some water into the pirate's mouth, and she didn't care a whit whether he opened his fine teeth to swallow it good or whether it dribbled right down into the pointed beard that covered his chin. Enough was enough!

She grabbed up bucket, bowl, and spoon and, trembling, headed swift out the door without so much as a small look back.

Their group of six picnicked that day, it being good weather for it, and whilst they ate on the grassy lawn nearby the chapel, they got down to discussion of the problems at hand. Almund Clap led their talk. As he'd been chosen reeve of Lord Claredemont's manor by agreement of his peers and the lord himself, he was in on meetings with groups from peasants to merchants to artisans. He was a good one to organize the thoughts of others, as he had a naturally organized way of thinking himself.

"We'd best consider first the plight of our friend Jim Gatt," the good reeve began. "We all know he's in the town gaol, under custody of the bailiff. Most here saw how blood flowed from the dead man when Jim touched his wounds, which is the ordeal customarily prescribed by the church for rooting out a murder suspect. Jim will now stand civil trial in the manor court. Unless, of course, he confesses to the crime."

"He *won't* confess!" Daisy objected hotly. "Jim's nice! He didn't *do* it!"

Mam sighed. "You state what we all truly feel, Daisy, but there's need to prove his innocence, which is not an easy thing once the ordeal has firmly pointed to his guilt."

"And therein may lie a catch," the young monk murmured mysteriously.

The others looked at him. "Well, *what* catch?" Granna demanded brusquely.

Thaddeus blushed, then leaned forward and cleared his throat. "Well, here it is, then. This morning, Rhiannon made mention of your bailiff's men *pressing* Jim's hands to the corpse. And that made me remember how our good abbot at Glastonbury once gave a talk in our

120

chapter house about certain ancient murder tests that could be much . . . much *manipulated*. Almund just stated that the laying of hands is customarily used by the church in murder ordeals here. Well, our abbot talked of this very kind of thing being used broadly in Wessex a generation or two ago, but he went on to say that in modern days the laying of hands upon a corpse is thought in many shires to be . . ."

When he hesitated, searching for the right word, Granna jumped in, some insulted. "Lamewit thinking, as you'd expect from frontier bumpkins such as we?"

Thaddeus protested, even more flustered. "No, no! I beg pardon, as that's not what I was going to say at all! It's not used in many shires because, well, again I hesitate to say this clear, as to do so will sound like I'm questioning the integrity of your vicar."

They all looked at one another. Though Mam wouldn't have it spoken out loud, nobody up here was thrilled with Vicar Pecksley, and they knew no one below who admired him much, either. He ministered from sourness, and held his congregation to the straight and narrow by preaching hellfire, never neighborly love. As for integrity, they'd not ordinarily judge him lacking, but if what the young monk was about to say proved incriminating, they'd not rush outraged to the sour vicar's defense, either.

"All right then." Thaddeus took a breath. "With your leave, I'll just say it out plain. It was told us novices by our good abbot that sometimes, back when this particular ordeal was much used here in Wessex, an unscrupulous vicar would pick a likely scapegoat, and would then instruct the bailiff to press his own hands over the scapegoat's hands on a very specific place upon the corpse. And when that place was pressured just so, with the brunt of the bailiff's hand, the large vessel leading direct from the heart would spout, sending blood right out the corpse's wounds. It can be made to appear that the bailiff is merely guiding the hands of the scapegoat, not pressuring them nor putting them on a specific spot. It can look natural, or so said our good abbot."

No one spoke, but all were thinking plenty.

Finally, Mam asked softly, "But . . . why?"

Rhia's heart was racing. "Why pick Jim? He would be the *perfect* scapegoat, Mam! If you'd *seen* how they treated him down in Woethersly. It was just horrible! He was not one whit welcome to come live among them again, so what a sure way to be rid of him!"

"But . . . I meant, why would they *need* a scapegoat?" Mam asked, again softly. "What would it profit them to find a murderer in this case? Many murders go unsolved."

"She's exactly right," Thaddeus rushed to say. "Our abbot told us that usually there was some *known* murderer being hidden and given protection by such scapegoating, elsewise it was too complicated to attempt. It does seem a right lot of trouble, and a risk to the reputations of both vicar and bailiff. They could get rid of Jim in a thousand easier ways, him being landless and without kin. They could trump up some excuse to order him out of town, or they could break his head in some dark alley, or engage some oxcart to run him down and crush his *other* leg." He noticed Daisy staring and covered his mouth with three fingers. "Again, I beg pardon," he said meekly. "I've got too wound up in my talk, as I've been running this through my head for hours."

"Well," Reeve Clap summarized, slapping his knees. "Here's what we have, then. Jim's *possibly* been scapegoated as murderer by the vicar, enlisting the bailiff and his men as help in getting the wounds to bleed when Jim's hands were upon the corpse. And let us assume for argument's sake that this has been done because the true murderer is known but must not be discovered. Then our question must be, who is the real murderer, and why so protected? We've no place to begin in our thinking about that, no hint of a suspect. And without a suspect, all this is only far-fetched speculation."

"All saints above, will ye please keep us from idjits!" Granna howled. She immediately remembered herself, pulled in her lips, and looked apologetic. "No offense, Reeve, as you're no idjit, of course. I meant no disrespect with such an outburst, but how can you not have thought how there's but one house and one house alone round here that could have the money and power to swing such an expensive thing as bribing the vicar! Lord protect us all, as hell's surely just around the corner a short walk when the nobility of the manor commits the most mortal of sins and can pin it on the local peasantry without so much as rippling the pond!"

"Bribery?" Mam sounded shocked. "Oh, Mother, you cannot believe our vicar could be *bribed* to do this thing?"

"Daughter, surely you don't believe it's prayer that's turning the vicar's humble church into a grandee's stone palace? A dog will not bite the hand that feeds it, that's all I say. And always and forever that golden hand is attached to the arm of the gentry."

Granna's hot words brought a memory to the surface of Rhia's churning thoughts. *Tap! Tap, tap, tap.* Lord Claredemont had tapped his chin in measured rhythm when she'd glimpsed him yesterday, as though considering some matter of import. She'd seen him at that window twice, in point of fact—once after coming back with Maddy, then a second time when Jim had just been exposed as murder suspect.

Rhia sprang to her feet. "Oh!" she cried, her hands flown to her cheeks. "I've just remembered that I . . . I saw Lord Claredemont up in his salon, looking out upon the crowd. And as someone stepped to lay hands, he shook his head! And . . . and then later, when Jim was brought from the tent, I glanced in the direction of the manor house again, by accident, as I was seeking Granna in the crowd. And there was Lord Claredemont at the same salon window still, only now, he . . . he *nodded*! Oh! He . . . nodded his head, just slightly! Was he . . . was he nodding as signal to . . . to the bailiff and the vicar to proceed in making Jim appear the murderer?"

Rhiannon must have looked alarming, as Mam stood and came right round behind her. Rhia turned gratefully into her mother's arms, trembling all over and weak in the knees.

And though the last thing she wanted was to be taken back to the cottage, Mam had led her most of the way there before Rhia noticed it was happening.

"I won't go home, Mam!" she protested, though she could not dig in her heels or lift her head from Mam's shoulder for the weakness she felt.

"Too much responsibility has clean worn you out, daughter," Mam pronounced.

And before Rhia was able to find a way to stop her, Mam had gotten her up the ladder of the sleep loft and into bed, where still Rhia determined to protest in the strongest fashion that she was no child now but indeed fourteen and fifteen in three months and therefore would *not* be left out of the meeting.

But she could only whisper, "Mind that Sal's out upon the stoop." Then, she slept.

Chapter 11

When Rhia awoke, it was more dark than light. She kicked the blanket from her legs and cast aside the lavender cloth Mam had placed upon her forehead. Her wits were cobwebby from the long sleep, and she staggered a bit as she hurried to the corner to see out the twiggy sparrow's hole in the roof.

No one seemed about. Most likely Thaddeus and Almund had left some time ago, as it was twilight now. She'd wasted so much of this important day sleeping! Mam then appeared in her line of vision, walking brisk along the stone path that connected the cottages. Rhia was surprised to see her pass the two cots that were occupied without going in to check the invalids. She walked right past the two newly empty cots, as well. When she reached the outermost of the cottages, Mam pushed her shoulder against the heavy door and went inside.

Rhia snatched at her sleep-tumbled hair and worked it into a knot, preparing to hurry down the ladder to quiz whoever she might—meaning Granna. Through the twiggy hole, she now perceived Daisy running from behind the beehives with Queen Matilda nearby. A skirt and apron showed beneath the hives as well, which meant Granna was working at the big stump they used as a chore table there.

Rhiannon hustled down the ladder, but was stopped for a moment downstairs by the surprise of finding Mam's small charcoal brazier set up in the medicinal corner. The wood table and stone grinding slabs were covered with fresh greens as well, and a large quantity of Mam's dried herbs had been untied from the rafters and spread loose.

What decoctions could she be thinking of making in such quantity, with Ona and Primrose past needing salves and remedials and even Jim gone beyond her nursing?

And then the last shreds of sluggish sleep cleared from Rhia's brains and she remembered the lepers. So it'd been decided as she slept that the lepers were to be housed in that nether cottage Mam was just now inspecting! What all *else* had been decided without her? Rhia ran straightaway from the cottage to complain to Granna.

"There is *nothing* so upsetting as *not* being included when a thing is decided, as though I be a child and not fourteen, fifteen in three months!" Rhia hotly informed Granna when she had hard-rounded the hives and come to a rocking stop. She stood breathing hard and glaring, waiting for an explanation and certainly an apology.

"There ye be, sleepyhead!" Granna greeted her mildly. She had the bread trencher upon the stump and was kneading a big quantity of dough, which Rhia'd come close to knocking clean over. "As this is your usual job, I'll yield it to you, granddaughter." Granna stood straight and pushed her doughy knuckles into her back. "And when you've finished, I'll enlist your help in turning the hives back right round. As you see, I had Almund turn them early this morning so's they faced away from the forest, as the bees must face away from a funeral and not be made upset by it."

"Granna!" Rhia huffed, throwing up her arms. "You have such an abundance of sympathy for the bees, but can you not see that *I*, your own closest kin, am *much* upset?"

Granna reached out and amiably patted Rhia's cheek, chuckling a bit. "Yes, girl, and kneading is a very good cure for upset, whate'er the reason for it."

With this, she walked away. And Rhia, seeing naught else to do, rinsed her own hands in the stream with much angry splashing, then set to the job at hand.

As Granna had predicted, kneading that big dough finally got the bile worked from Rhia's spleen, or most of it at least. Good thing, too, because Mam was surely too tired to have to deal with Rhia's foul mood when she finally came back from the nether cottage. It was so late that the bread was not only risen but baked and cooled on the kitchen slab. The chickens were even asleep, as were Granna and Daisy, who now shared the pallet up in the loft whilst Rhia'd been changed to sleeping with Mam, below.

"I'm weary to my bones," Mam admitted, pulling off her apron, which was plain filthy. "I'd meant to just eye the nether cottage, to see what shape it might be in. But here I went to cleaning it after I'd gave it an eyeing. Are Granna and Daisy above?"

Rhia nodded. She'd been set to quiz Mam about the afternoon's decisions, but from the look of her she decided she'd wait. "I'll put that to soak," she offered, taking the apron from Mam with two fingers and walking it quickly over to the washtub.

She could imagine the job Mam had had, as they'd housed their two pigs and the milch goat in that cottage throughout the part of winter it had stood unoccupied.

And even if she'd not been able to imagine, she could have gone by smell.

"I'll go wash myself at the brook before starting in on this," Mam said, looking toward the big job awaiting her in the medicinal corner. She sighed and blew upward to move her hair from her sweated face. "I wish I hadn't got it all laid out to do, as now I'm stuck with doing it still tonight." Her voice was ragged with exhaustion.

127

While Mam was washing at the stream, Rhia looked for the pestle in the mess of greens covering everything in the medicinal corner. She'd found it and had already started crushing some of the feverfew lying upon the mortar slab when Mam walked back, drying her arms and neck with a flaxen rag.

"Thank you, Rhiannon," Mam said, looking a bit surprised and truly grateful.

Rhia stayed beside her for all the hours of that big job, crushing what herbs Mam put by the mortar for her to crush, whilst Mam blended and cooked and portioned things out. It was necessary to make good use of the charcoal while the brazier burned, not waste it in cooking part portions, though this meant working late into the night.

Rhia was a bit surprised at herself for hanging in and helping like that without so much as being asked. She was in the habit of waiting to be nagged some when Mam decided she required help, to tell it true.

But tonight Mam had looked so tired, and there was something else. She'd seemed downhearted. It was upon her face, and in the set of her neck and shoulders. It was a fumbling of her fingers as she worked, when she was never a fumbler at all. Strange for a mother to be downhearted, but there it was, upon her.

Rhia wondered as she crushed the herbs: When had Mam developed such a range of humors—this one of downheartedness, for instance? Rhia herself sometimes felt downhearted, ofttimes when she was lonely, or when she was worried or confused. But she'd never much thought about a mother feeling such a thing.

"Well, now, that's been some job, but we're down to stoppering the bottles," Mam finally whispered. "Thank you again for helping with all this, Rhiannon."

Rhia cleared her own throat and said quietly, "I didn't mind."

For a moment she considered bringing up the afternoon's decisions now. But Mam was so clearly tuckered Rhia decided to let her peevish questions go, though it rankled.

"I know you wonder how everything was left today, Rhia," Mam all of a sudden told on her own. "Not much more was said after you'd gone. Almund will let us know what's happening in regards to Jim." She stretched on tiptoe to return the small onion braid to its hook. "He or Thaddeus, one or the other, will be back with word in two or three days. But one thing—I did get to talk with Thaddeus a bit alone, right before they left. I wanted to learn more about the . . . the contagion carried by the folk."

Mam moved to the window and looked out into the darkness, crossing her arms. "Everyone fears leprosy," she said quietly. "You hear so many rumors, and it is such a dreadful ailment." She frowned, then added in a whisper, "They've a lazarhouse, a hospice for them, near Glastonbury Abbey, so Thaddeus has *seen* some of it, firsthand."

She pushed her bright hair from her face and turned from the window to face Rhiannon more direct. "Rumor is the hardest thing, daughter. It can be deadly enemy to those least able to fend against its poison, like the poor souls left stranded out there in our woods." She'd recovered some pep, and her green eyes flashed her indignation.

Rhiannon swallowed. "What'd . . . Thaddeus have to say about it?"

Mam moved to begin stoppering her filled potions with wax from the hives. "Well," she answered carefully, "he said many who care for the lepers never catch the disease at all. Others do, and some quickly enough. But most often those who catch it have spent years working close around them. It's not like true plague in its contagion, then. Still, it's an awful thing, and can for certain be caught."

"We're bringing them to the nether cottage," Rhiannon said flatly, unable to wait longer for this to be out. "Aren't we? You and the others decided it, without me."

Mam turned quick and looked at her direct. "No, Rhia, I'd never let something like that be decided without you! The two men would have it that we leave those people in the woods, is my thinking. But we didn't really discuss it because I didn't want them . . . intruding. This is . . . *ours*. This is for us, up here, to decide! Just as those years ago we decided together that we'd use the ancient cottages and our own hands to offer care to all who were brought to us."

Then, without warning, Mam just came apart. She covered her face with her hands and bent far forward like a willow branch. Her white elbows supported her against the wood table, else Rhia thought she would have collapsed to the floor.

Rhia had never, ever seen this from her before and she knew not what to do.

"Mam?" she whispered, rushing to steady Mam's shoulders, alarmed at how much she felt her mother's trembling through her own palms, up her arms.

Mam raised up a little, but her hands were fisted and her knuckles bone white. "I know not what to *do,* daughter!" She pounded the table hard with one fist. "I don't know how to . . . to *think* about this!" She pounded a second time. "It's *stumped* me! Nothing's stumped me that I can ever remember, but this *has!*"

Suddenly, then, she stood straight and took Rhiannon's face in her hands. "Tell me, daughter, what would *you* have us do?" Mam brought her anguished face close to Rhia's own and searched Rhia's eyes. "Truly, this is a decision that much involves you, and I'd be grateful to have your considered advice. We *could* take these salves to the woods and merely leave them there in a basket to be found. We could take food as well and let those people live rough under the trees! We could go that way, though halfway it would be."

Rhia could not think at all. But suddenly, she had the strange feeling that she was floating upward, rising and rising until she hung high above their roof thatch. She hovered in a place so far above the ground that she could see *all* below, not just some.

For a moment, she possessed the clear viewpoint of a bird, or of an angel.

"It doesn't seem enough to do, not with that biggest of the cots standing empty."

"Oh." Mam made that one little sound, then covered her face with her slim white hands again. She stood that way, facing Rhia and shaking her head. Was she crying?

"I'm sorry, Mam," Rhia whispered, helpless, her throat aching. "I did not mean to cause you more trouble in your mind! I just said that from picturing how it all might seem from high above, as then it all looked so much simpler."

Mam grabbed round Rhia's neck and hugged her then, burying her face in Rhia's hair.

"I know, and I feel both joy and pity at your answer," she whispered. "Sometimes you seem so much your granna's, so little my own. But daughter, what you've just described is how I've come to every decision of my life."

They stayed hugging like that for a while, neither anxious to give up such comfort on the midnight of what had been such a fraught and anxious day.

It was Mam who finally pulled away, slapping her forehead and laughing a little. "I forgot to put candles in the two invalid cottages tonight! I must be more tired than I realized. Quench the tallow near you, Rhia. I'll finish damping this brazier, then I'll quick take the candles so's we may finally get a bit of sleep."

"*I'll* take the candles," Rhia said quickly, which was surprising, seeing as how she always resisted going after dark into the cot of the Man Who Sleeps. And surely she'd forgot for a moment his bite upon the spoon that afternoon or she'd never have made that bold offer. But there you have it—she hadn't thought of the spoon in hours, and now she lifted the tallow there beside her and found the two others to be lit from it and was off into the midnight darkness, propelled by how Mam had just made her feel of such value.

Leaving Sally's candle was easy. Going next to the other's abode was not.

Knock, knock, then quick, expecting and receiving no call to enter, she pushed open the pirate's door. With blood rushing in her ears, she hurried to the window. She'd not look in his direction, no need for that. No need at all, and besides, she'd remembered the bite by then and her fingers had gone all atremble so if she didn't pay attention she might let the light go out from fumbling it.

She let a bit of wax drip upon the sill to hold the tallow, then . . .

"Halt!" he called from the deep shadows behind her.

It was more a plea than a demand, made by one who'd recently been more dead, you might say, than alive. The command came out all hollow and filled with wind, more a whisper, really, than a call.

But 'twas enough to give Rhiannon the biggest scare she'd ever have, so that her heart was then a hare inside her chest, clamoring to climb right out and run to the woods.

She whirled around, though she'd not meant to look at him, and clearly saw the pirate sitting up on the raised pallet where he'd lately looked so much a corpse that they'd crossed his arms and legs, as for a killed Crusader! Sitting right up straight, he was!

She could not see him well, as the candle had fallen from her shaking hands and was extinguished. She could just make out his head and shoulders, dark against the lighter daub of the wall behind him. He was facing her direct, his legs adangle from the bed.

"Tell me, Adela, is this . . . Francia?" he asked.

"No," she pushed out, then gulped down a breath. "You're in England, sir, near as far from Francia as you can get and still be upon the world and not fallen off. You're in the hinterlands of Wessex, atop a bluff and across the bay from Wales."

To that, he made no response. After a few moments, he lay back down, sighing a monstrous sigh, more a moan, really. A moan of some anguish, one might say.

Rhiannon made for the door, then blundered out, twisting her left foot upon the stoop and falling to the sharp stones.

She bloodied both knees, though she'd not even notice that until morn.

Mam was asleep when she limped in, soft closing the door so's to wake no one. She didn't want to talk of this yet. She just hoped Mam wouldn't open an eye to check for two lights in the invalid windows, as there would be only the one of Sal's.

She pulled off her skirt and in her shift crawled to the nether side of the pallet, wincing as she went, though still not wondering *why* she winced. And then for quite some time she lay curled on her side there beside Mam, awake and wide-eyed, her mind now too bedazzled for easy sleep.

This was a mystery as astonishing in its details as any other they'd come upon this week of mysteries! Not just that the sleeper had woke, but that he'd asked such a question upon waking. And why had he called her Adela, as though he knew her quite well? He'd mistook her for someone, but who? And if he thought he was in Francia, why had he not spoken the *language* of Francia?

And why'd he sighed that awful sigh, so heartbreaking in tone? In fact, so heartbreaking that Rhiannon's last thought before sleep was that she'd not be easily afeared of anyone with a heart so clearly broken, be he French or English, saintly Crusader or merely wretched, bloodthirsty pirate.

Chapter 12

Rhiannon's sore knees woke her in the morning before even Mam was up. She lay for a moment pondering that it had been only one day since they'd buried Ona and Primrose, though it seemed a month's worth of happenings had gone on! She wanted another private peek at the French gentleman pirate before Gramp began summoning her to gather the seeds at bluff's edge, as most surely by the time she and Gramp had finished and got back to the settlement, the man's changed state would have been discovered and he'd have become *everybody's* thing to gawk at and fuss over.

She scooted off the pallet with her legs held stiff, then limped outside. At the brook she got good springy moss to pack her hurts, tying it upon them with long watergrasses.

"Crrrr—awkk?" Gramp asked, having swooped from the chapel roof to observe close. He teetered on a flimsy branch of the yew tree she leaned against.

"The Man Who Sleeps has woken, Gramp!" she informed him. "He no longer seems quite so much a pirate. Now, he seems somewhat a gentleman, as he talks of Francia!" She winced, standing and moving stiff-legged in the direction of the man's cot. "Of course, pirates may talk of Francia as well, I guess, but he speaks gentle, is what I mean."

"Rhiannon!" Mam called from outside their cottage. "You've forgotten your seed pouch, daughter. And . . . why do you hobble along like that, and in the wrong direction?"

The jig was up, and Rhia called back, "I've skinned my knees is all, and Mam? You must come quick! The Man Who Sleeps sleeps no longer!"

Rhia and Mam soon enough stood together near the raised pallet, looking him over. There was nothing to show that he'd moved in the night. Even his ankles and wrists were crossed as they'd been before! Rhia, frustrated beyond easy endurance by this, lit into a description to Mam of how he'd sat up in the night, what he'd said, and how his moan had been so filled with heart's anguish.

"Well," said Mam, sighing. "I know not *what* to think."

Mayhaps she thought Rhia'd dreamed it, is what Rhia figured. That, along with the throb of her roughened knees, made Rhia downright angry. When they'd left that cot and were on along the walk a little way, Rhia turned and ran back to look in his window, hoping to catch him in a move. But there he lay, as much as ever like some stone effigy.

"Here." Mam took the seed pouch from under her shawl and threw it across to Rhia. "If the job hurts your knees too much this morning, you may give it up, Rhiannon."

But Mam's eyes held mirth as she turned to go on along, as if to say, *If you can run to stubbornly prove a thing you dreamed is true, you can kneel to gather as well.*

"Fly slow, please, as I'm some disabled," Rhia grumbled to Gramp. She went slow and hobbling, then, especially back past their own cot and also past the bees, who stopped their raucous morning buzzing. *They* got a good notice of her injury, at least, though it was hard to tell how much sympathy they felt.

Once she and Gramp were arrived at bluff's edge, Rhia could not manage to hold on to her peevish mood. It was such a perfect day, with the breeze from the south and all kinds of seeds for the taking. There were already several small boats out upon the water, pleasure boats and fishing boats, some coracles as well. You saw big boats bringing trade all year long, but small boats were only usual in fine weathers. They made a good sign that spring had really come to stay.

Her knees *did* hurt when she knelt for long, so she took breaks to lollygag. As usual, she falsely assumed Gramp was lollygagging because *she* was, when in fact he was hard at work at all times they were near the bluff's edge, protecting her from mischance.

In fact, during one of her own rests that morning, she went so far as to enlist Gramp in a game she'd just then dreamt up, feeling he had leisure for it because *she* did.

"You be tallystick like Reeve Clap carries to count the crops each farmer owes as tax to Lord Claredemont, will you, Gramp? I'll mention a thing we must puzzle out, and you dip your great beak and make a scratch upon your holed rock perch as Reeve Clap makes a cut upon his stick. When I've said all the mysteries I can think of, we'll count the scratches and have our tally of important things that must be untangled."

Gramp hard-eyed her and raised his shoulders a bit. It was actually a register of the insult he was feeling at being considered a tallystick, but Rhia took it as a go.

She lay clear back to look up at the sky, folding her arms to make a pillow for her head. "All right, first scratch is, we must watch that heartbroken French pirate and find out why he played as he did when Mam was present. Why'd he deceive her into thinking he still slept exactly as before?"

That seemed quite interesting, as she'd not realized he was purposely deceiving Mam until she'd heard herself list it. There was also some small chance, of course, that Mam's hunch had been right and Rhia had merely *dreamed* him waking.

So after a moment's consideration, she added, "And Gramp, if it please, you must somehow contrive to take that scratch away tomorrow if it turns out I've mistook his wakefulness, though I'm *sure* I've not."

She squinted hard. "Here's another scratch. We must make such preparations as necessary for the new folk in the wood, but first we must *know* their needs and we must plan, as much as we're able, our own safe practices." She sighed. "Most of that'll be left to Mam." Thanks be to God, as it made *her* head hurt just thinking of it.

"Yet another scratch would be what must be figured and done about Jim Gatt and his predicament. In fact, this is the most urgent and important task at hand, Gramp. And add a scratch for finding if there is indeed an ancient dragon trapped beneath the grove of colored stones. Wait, that scratch should be for figuring some way out of joining in Maddy's party on Beltane Eve with the earl's son and his cronies."

Every time she thought about that, her stomach flopped and she got hiccoughs.

She sat up. "Give 'em each a scratch, Gramp, the dragon and the party, too."

But Gramp wasn't even turned in her direction, let alone playing this silly game. He was peering out at the bay, and suddenly he started flapping his wings something fierce.

"Crrrrawk! Craaaaa-awk-awk-*awk*!"

Rhia scrambled to her feet. "Gramp, what threat do you perceive?"

Soon she spotted the cause of Gramp's concern. In one of the small boats were two monks, one rowing and the other standing. The one upon his legs was jigging a bit to stay balanced, and also looking straight up at their spot on the bluff with one hand shielding his eyes. He pushed back his cowl and his long brown hair blew wild.

"It's Thaddeus, Gramp!" Rhia moved close as she dared to the edge of the bluff and began waving big-armed waves toward the little boat.

Soon enough, Thaddeus caught that and waved back. He brought his two hands to cup his mouth, and called, "Rhiannon, can you hear me?"

She bounced on her heels with excitement. "Yes!" she called. "I mean, no!"

With this she gave a large-armed gesture toward a place below where Thaddeus's rower might safely bring the little boat in closer to the bluff. When the monk nodded that he understood, she ran and dove into the bracken at the trail's start, slip-sliding down the path until she reached the place in the trail that was directly above that small secret harbor. She watched them drift closer until they were just beneath her perch. She might have jumped right into their boat, though it would have been a long and daring leap.

Thaddeus looked over both his shoulders then to see that others weren't likely to receive the news he was about to give. Their detour had put them well out of range of other likely ears, yet he checked again.

"Rhiannon," he called up, "there's much afoot regarding Jim Gatt! He's now sought and received sanctuary within the church. Have your mother come down if she can!"

Rhia cupped her own hands and called back, "But . . . aren't you coming up to give us the whole news of it? Or is the reeve?"

Again, Thaddeus checked uneasily over his shoulder. "We neither one dare leave town while this churns. In fact, Brother Silas and I have just rowed out to give you this news and must now hasten back to the church. You see, Jim Gatt has confessed to the murder!"

Rhiannon felt turned to stone at this impossible news.

"Tell your mother to come quickly, Rhia!" Thaddeus called again. "And if she can't, ask her if you may come in her stead! You must hear the whole of it!" He sat back down, taking the oars from his fellow and turning the boat back toward the open water.

Rhiannon shook her head. "Oh, Gramp," she breathed, as Gramp now sat nearby her. "Let's get home fast, as a confession from Jim was the *last* thing we expected!"

They four—Granna, Mam, Rhia, and Daisy—tried with all their combined brains to puzzle it out, sitting glumly around the firepit not much later.

"I don't understand how he could have reached sanctuary to begin with, seeing as how he was already in prison and Guy Dryer guarding him," Mam murmured. She was leaned forward, her skirt hitched up and her elbows on her white knees. She stared into the fire hard with her eyes squinted, frowning.

Granna took her pipe from her teeth and shrugged. "Well, Guy's been known to purposely let a pickpocket or two slip through his fingers, as he has to feed his prisoners from his own pocket."

The small wooden gaol where common prisoners were kept was very near the ale-tasters' establishment, thus Granna knew such details from her cronies, though the average citizen would have probably assumed the law was more airtight than that.

"Well, if he *did* escape the gaol, he'd have only had to get as far as the iron latch upon the church door," Mam mused, tapping her chin as though she were seeing these things in the fire, which, of course, was Granna's territory. "Once he had ahold of that church latch, none could lay hands to take him back to prison. Still, the church is halfway through town, and Jim could not go fast."

"And he could not pass unnoticed," Rhia added sadly. "Not with his missing leg so apparent, setting him apart."

"Know what *I* say?" Daisy piped, all straight-backed and sassy. "I say he got *help*!"

The other three looked at her.

"Why not?" she insisted, raising her thin arms. "*I* would have helped him reach the church, had I been nearby! Queen Tildy and I would have garbed him in a costume what covered up his bottom half so's he'd not be recognized as he went!"

Queen Matilda was herself costumed just then, wrapped in rags and flowers.

Mam smiled at Daisy and bent to reach her hand, giving it a squeeze. "Well," she said to them all, "this is only guesswork until we hear it straight from Almund. At least Jim *has* somehow got sanctuary, so now he'll have forty days to ready his soul with prayer before he goes to God. Had he languished at the gaol, his punishment would likely be . . . near immediate."

Rhia gulped and felt her fingers go cold at the idea of Jim hanging on Gallux Hump. "I just can't believe he confessed to doing any such a thing," she whispered.

None of them could, she could see it on their faces.

"Do you see anything bearing on this in the flames, Mother?" Mam asked quietly.

Rhiannon was shocked, as Mam scolded Granna constantly for her heathen habit of flame-watching.

Mam played casual. "Do you, Mother?" she repeated.

"Well, it's hard to say, daughter." Granna peered into the fire in the same way she had been peering all through this discussion, no harder and no easier, as the sights came or they didn't. "I see nothing at the moment, but when I rose this morn I followed my usual routine and looked into the flames to see what the day might hold. And at that time, I saw churchmen opening the door for a fellow churchman who knocked with the iron petitioner's ring. I figured the fellow clutching that latch to be some cowled brother here with the new bunch. But I suppose it might have been Jim I saw."

"I *told* you!" Daisy squealed. "It was Jim in the *costume* of a churchman!"

Rhiannon stood and turned to her mother, throwing up her arms in exasperation. "You have to go *down*, Mam! We have to know and not just guess! I can't *bear* it!"

Mam dropped her head. "I just cannot, Rhia. There are the new folk to think of now. They must have bread and drink and medicinals, and I must see if I can talk with one of them today, regarding some sort of . . . arrangements."

"What *is* rangents?" Daisy piped. When no one answered, she picked up Queen Matilda and started dancing that gaudily bedecked reptile about on the reeds.

Rhiannon, meanwhile, paced, trying to work up the nerve to ask if she herself might go down in Mam's stead. She'd gone alone to market many times, but just to take some seed packets and their honey to be sold.

When Mam had given her charge over the group that went down to the laying of hands, the dire result had been *sure* proof that she was not up to anything beyond selling a little honey and buying a bit of salt.

She'd lost Jim! No, Rhia felt sure Mam thought she was the *last* person to be trusted with this further mission regarding their friend.

"Rhia, you go down in my place," Mam suddenly said. "Tomorrow is weekly market day. Go then and you'll not so likely be deemed suspicious as you seek to find some answers. The crowd will be roiling, and everyone bent upon their own business."

Rhiannon went plain speechless, so grateful did she feel for this second chance.

"Once more we've let the morn slip away, so now to our work." Mam slapped her knees and stood, all business. "Mother, will you help me fix our meal? Daisy, you go to the bees and see what honeyed comb is ready for Rhiannon to take to market on the morrow. Rhiannon, fetch the gruel pot, as the invalids surely grow hungry."

Very soon all were bustling about, doing as she'd ordered. Rhia crouched beside the firepit, tilting the large gruel kettle upon its firehook while she carefully poured a steaming portion into the smaller pot so she could feed the invalids. But then all of a sudden she felt Mam standing behind her, waiting for her to finish her task.

Rhia reluctantly stood and turned to her, dreading what Mam had to say. Surely she'd thought more and decided against entrusting Rhia to venture down tomorrow.

"Daughter," Mam said quietly, and the next thing Rhia knew, Mam had taken the small elmwood cross she always wore about her own neck and slipped its leather thong over Rhia's head. The cross felt light and cool upon Rhia's skin, and when she looked down upon her chest, it glowed as though it were golden. She looked up, beaming, to give Mam thanks for such a precious thing, but Mam was back at work as though it had not happened.

Rhia dropped gingerly to her sore knees beside Dull Sal in her little cot. She stirred the steaming gruel she'd brought, then spooned a large portion to Sal's bowl.

"Sally, tomorrow I go to town alone, to find what I may about Jim!" she confided. "And Mam has given me her own cross." She held the graceful little cross out from herself by its cord, so's Sal might better see it.

Sally looked at her and smiled. "Three fish," she said. "I'll have three of those fish."

And right then Rhiannon had a sudden thought she'd not had before about Sally. It just came to her out of the blue, as will happen sometimes when you're thinking of something else, and it made her feel queasy with its awfulness.

She put down the bowl and placed her hands on Sally's shoulders.

"Sally, is that the last thing your bad brother said to you before the cuffing?" she asked, her mouth gone dry. "Did he want three fish to eat, and did he think you were slow bringing them and deserved such foul treatment as to have your head smashed?"

"Three fish," said Sally, her blue eyes wide and empty. "I'll have three of those fish."

That had been it, then. Rhia would've sworn it. And she could scarce see her way to Sally's mouth with spoonfuls of gruel for the sick feeling she had. The cost of beautiful Sally's good life had been so little! It was even sadder than if Sally had stolen coin, or taken some other thing valued high by her horrible brother.

This was positively the worst thing Rhiannon had ever heard of. She had been light-heeled with excitement coming to Sal's cot, but she was dragging her heels as she went to the other one, her heart awash with grief for Sally, valued so low. In truth she was so upset by it that she forgot to brace herself as she pushed open the pirate's door, slouched across the threshold, and went to ladling gruel into his bowl.

She carried the bowl to the raised pallet, so teared up over Sal's so lightly ruined life that she barely noticed that the man was still a frozen effigy, his ankles neatly crossed.

"Mam's right and I've merely dreamt you awake," she murmured, moving beside him with a deep sigh and prying at the man's lips with the maplewood spoon he'd nearly spoilt the day before. "Yet, Sir Pirate? Even your constant stillness canna rattle me on a day when I've considered a brother bashing in a sister's brains for three stupid fish."

His eyes came open and he grabbed her wrist and swirled to a sit so's the bowl was knocked to the floor and clattered there.

"Adela, are we finally given privacy?" he demanded in a hoarse whisper.

Chapter 13

Rhia stifled a scream at this shock, but once she'd had a cat's whisker of time to get back her wits, she decided it was flattering, really. Most folk wanted Mam, never her.

And as for him calling her that false name, Adela? Well, she'd seen dim-brained misrecognizing before among the invalids. For instance, an old grandfather had been brought to them with his hands and knees constantly ashake, and he'd called Rhiannon his good wife's name, Bertha, the whole two months they'd had him, though his Bertha'd died of ague some forty years before.

"Yes, for certain we are alone," Rhia answered, swallowing down the dregs of her fear. "Calm yourself," she bent to whisper, "as any commotion may bring the others."

He nodded quite readily and loosed her wrist. "Where are we, Adela? Pray tell me we've caught the tide and are all safe returned to Francia again. It seems we're lodged for the night in some fisherman's sheds, yes?"

Last night she'd told him plain and clear that he was come to England. But she'd not mention it again if she could avoid it, as it had occasioned such a heartbreaking outburst.

"Well, sir, if you so say." That wasn't lying, was it?

"I don't mind a night's stay in such rough lodgings all that much," he allowed, wrinkling his nose as he looked around the cottage. "This is crude and dank, of course, but it smells a bit better than some such places. And, well, a soldier's up for anything."

Rhiannon considered that a right stingy description of their nice, clean cot, but she tried not to show her feelings. Instead, she cleared her throat, and said, "Sir, I hear you are a soldier, but now I'd hear you speak your name."

He smiled, though his smile was wan. "Quit your jesting, Adela, and tell now of the others. Are all the knights put up in these lodgings? I'd prefer you ladies were taken to lusher halls, but if these are the best in the vicinity, tell your gentle maids to take heart, as God willing we can try for England again upon the morrow."

And then, his faced pinched up and he turned strange. He reached out like a blind man and gripped Rhia's shoulders with both hands, squeezing tight. "Adela, good sister, all of a sudden I have pictures in my head I cannot account for!" he cried. "Nightmare sights, Adela! My head fair *splits* with the pain and sickness of such hellish visions!"

"Lie down now," Rhiannon said firmly, using the nursing authority Mam had taught her. She took his shoulders and pushed him down, then lay her palm upon his eyes to close the lids. "I'll find you a draft to ease your head, but you *must* lie still."

He caught her wrist as she turned. "Don't leave me, Adela! I'm lost and afraid!"

Rhiannon bent close again. "I'll be back straightaway with the draft, I promise you."

"I . . . know not what my name is." He was whimpering now, like a small boy who's lost from his mother. "I know not how I've come to overnight in this place!"

"Sir, you've been here some time, and came with some injury. You'd a hard blow to your forehead that raised a knot the size of a hen's egg and kept you sleeping for weeks. In fact, we'd not figured you'd ever awake, so now that you have, give thanks to God."

He looked at her with a misery in his eyes worse than any she'd ever seen, and she'd seen plenty of misery among those brought up to the bluff.

"Lady, I'd that God had left me sleeping until I slept eternal," he whispered.

Then he closed his eyes and slowly crossed his wrists and ankles, his limbs going back to their contrary places all natural, as they'd got used to such positions.

And just like that, he was a stone effigy again, with no need for headache draft.

Rhia stood looking at him. He was young when awake, much younger than he seemed when he was so gravely sleeping. Why, he seemed not much older than Thaddeus, hardly a grown man at all. He was to grown man what she was to grown woman, about that.

Whatever his story and whatever his true Christian name, he surely had times when he felt at least half child still, as she so often did. That had showed in the fit he threw.

But what could possess him to say he'd sleep eternal if he could? Mam, who had such sympathy for the invalids, would not countenance *that* dark wish from anyone.

Rhiannon felt itchy and restless back inside the cottage, taking a casual meal with the others. She had this large important secret filling her up right to her tongue, and here they talked willy-nilly of this and that, none of it mattering one sparrow's breath.

Daisy giggled at some standoff between the uppity tortoise and their six chickens. Granna watched her, greasing her bread, then pointed out, "It's that quick laugh made you heal fast, Daisy. When God Almighty opened wide your mouth to put your soul into you, he was laughing at some good joke. That blessed laughter still circles around your innards and healed them right up, whilst Aigy's good salves worked on your outsides."

A small subject, Daisy's laughter-made soul, whilst Rhia had such a huge thing to talk about that had to go unspoken! Well, didn't *have* to go unspoken, but Mam had not believed her one whit this morn about the man, so why speak again of something that would only be met with smiles? The man had chosen *her* as confidant—her alone!

One of the chickens gave Queen Matilda a smart peck, which sent her bald head into her shell. She stayed in there, all asulk, till Daisy bent to try and lure her out with bread.

"Child, don't waste that, as your pet finds greens aplenty outside," Mam said quickly. "The bread we make will have to go further now, with the folk in the woods to feed. We'll likely need more rye and barley than we can manage to grow."

"We'll have to pad with acorns," Granna allowed, nodding. "Else I'll send down some wax effigies to be traded in town tomorrow for more flour."

Everyone looked at Mam. Granna made tiny figures from the beeswax, wax effigies that folk said had healing powers. But Mam, who had *real* healing powers, was doubly critical of this notion. It was false medicine, for one. And heathen practice, for two.

But Mam had been peering out the window, and now jumped to her feet so quick, she nigh turned over the bench they sat upon. "It's someone come from the group in the woods!" she cried out.

They all turned to the window. A lone figure stood at the edge of the bracken, slender and tall, clothed in rough wool layers. A rag veil was across the figure's face so's only the eyes could be seen. In a gloved hand it held a bowl and was tapping it with a clapper.

Mam was by then rushing outside without a thought.

"Aigneis!" Granna called after her. "Mind you don't—"

"Our guest will let me know how close I may safely come!" Mam called back.

And sure enough, as Rhia and Granna and Daisy watched, Mam ran forward until the figure in the bracken held up one gloved palm, telling her to stop.

Granna sighed and shook her head, then took Daisy's hand. "Well, Aigy will for sure stay longer with that poor soul than my old eyes will keep open. Come up to the loft, child, and I'll show you how to make wax figures afore I nap."

Rhiannon eyed out the window as she cleared up from the meal. As Granna had predicted, Mam and the woman stood for a good long while. Lucy the cat sidled on outside and lay on her back in the dandelions near the stoop, boxing at mites she saw in the sunlight. Queen Matilda kept her head in and was much underfoot, so's Rhia had to pay constant attention not to think her some useless stone and kick her from the path.

Above, Granna and Daisy talked in drowsy voices that made a sort of choristers' song, the high and the low of it. And by that lulling sound Rhiannon went to lollygagging, to thinking that if only she knew her letters, she would put a sign upon the door of the troubled young pirate who wished he slept eternal. Her letters would be quite large and would read PRIVACY so's by them Mam and all about would know that only Rhia herself was allowed to go in under any circumstances. He was hers, after all. *Her* big secret . . .

"Rhiannon, *come*, daughter! Come!" How long had Mam been calling her to come out and meet the other? Rhia shivered off her daydreams and ran quick to the bracken.

"Mistress Todd, this is my daughter, Rhiannon," Mam said, taking Rhia's arm when she drew up close. "Rhiannon, this is Mistress Todd."

"How d'ye do, Mistress Todd?" Rhiannon tried hard not to stare, for even at quick glance Mistress Todd's face seemed made of scaly lye and ashes.

Mistress Todd cast down her large eyes and made no reply.

Mam extended a hand, by instinct seeking to take Mistress Todd by the arm, though there was the space of two men's height between them. "There's more bread than we can eat in the house, and some good goat cheese. I'll send Rhiannon with those things."

Again the woman dropped her head in a sort of nod. Then she turned and began a trudge back into the woods. She'd brought back Mam's bread basket and the ale pouch, and Mam picked them up and handed them to Rhia to be refilled once they were home.

"Say nothing," Mam whispered through closed teeth as they walked back.

Rhiannon rolled her eyes, some insulted that Mam would think she'd babble about Mistress Todd's poor face within her hearing, like some child the years of Daisy.

No, she waited till they were good and inside the cottage with the door closed, and even then she spoke in a whisper. "Are they . . . all like that, do you think? Her *skin*."

Mam put her hands upon her hips and frowned, staring at nothing. "She would hear no plan for their comfort," she whispered, sounding mystified. "She would only say, 'We are dead,' as though she thought them truly buried in the ground and beyond all need for shelter or medicinals. Only a little food would she consider."

Rhia swallowed. "Did Thaddeus tell you about the funerals they're

151

given? How the priests declare them dead before sending them to a place like our woods to fend for themselves? That's why she'd say such a thing as 'We are dead,' I'll wager."

Mam looked at her, instantly angry. "That explains as well why she said they are all 'unclean,' and 'under a curse for vast sins.' She's so battered of mind that she can't be reasoned with!" Mam's green eyes shot daggers. "There are two children among them. I ask of God Almighty, what sins could two spotless little lambs commit?"

This was not a question likely to be answered anytime soon by the One it was addressed to, so Mam turned to the medicinal corner and began slamming pots and jars around. She'd have to be left alone to work out her bile in making salves, as Rhiannon had worked hers out in kneading dough yesterday.

Rhiannon knew her own best course was to fill the bread basket and the ale pouch and to take them straightaway back to the place in the bracken where she'd picked them up empty.

After this small task was accomplished, she began preparing for the morrow.

Rhia quietly moved around Mam as she gathered up what goods were supposed to be taken down the trail to be sold at market, and when she had them, she was plenty glad to escape the cottage altogether, a place made steamier by Mam's rage. She carried the things to the work stump to load them into two pack slings, one for each shoulder.

Mam had not said a straight-out nay to the wax effigies, so they were going, along with beeswax candles and clover honey, some loaves of bread and also some braided herbs and leaf-packets of sorted seeds. Right now was the time seeds could fetch their best price, as in April housewives would be hard at work grubbing up garden spaces within their crofts. The rarer the seeds, the better for bragging later as the gardens sprouted, so Rhiannon had hopes of a good profit tomorrow. The seeds she gathered at bluff's edge were known throughout the town to be ofttimes highly unusual.

Granna ambled out and dropped a few more just-made wax figures onto Rhia's pile.

"Now, granddaughter, I've thunk up three things you'd best find out about Jim tomorrow," she instructed. "And here they are. Ask what was said by the bailiff or the vicar just before Jim's confession. Ask who was witness to such a misthought confession. And then, most important, find out who profits from it."

"Granna, the only profiteer would be the murderer!" Rhia protested. "I'll for certain not be able to find that out, not even from your savvy friends at the ale-tasters' booth."

She put the first pack onto the ground and sat on it, then bounced a few times to try and make it some flatter and less cumbrous.

"Others may profit as well from a confession," Granna insisted. "And Rhia, mind you put those wax figures deeper in the sack, lest near the top they trigger some especial notice by your mother."

Rhia sighed, dumped the pack, and started over, this time putting the effigies in first.

"I'll take the candles to the cottages," Rhia said the moment the sky was dark enough that night for her offer not to appear suspicious. "In fact, that'll be my doings from now on, Mam. I'll see to the two invalids in the cots, morn and night, as you've much to think about with the ones in the forest. Your care will go to the forest folk, and I will attend to the folk in the cots. Understand?"

Mam looked at her round-eyed, undoubtedly perplexed.

"All right then?" Rhiannon asked, pocketing two tallows. "Just believe that those two cots are as empty as the others and pay no mind to them." She took a lit tallow and kissed Mam's cheek. "Never, ever look in upon the folk inside."

Granna was smoking her pipe and watching squint-eyed as Rhia left. As Rhia hopped the stoop and walked back past the window from the path outside, she saw Granna and Mam exchange a look and a shrug.

Well, they'd not objected, just been puzzled. Rhia took that as a go-along.

Yet, oddly, now that it was time to check the pirate, and some dark outside, she felt a bit nervous about it and was glad to linger at Sal's a bit before going. She'd brought bread in her waist pouch and honey on two folded leaves. Dull Sal would not eat a piece of honeyed bread direct, but she'd suck it, as a babe will suck a milky rag.

"Are you awake?" Rhiannon whispered as she secured Sal's tallow on her sill.

Sally was on her side on her pallet, her knees pulled up nigh her chin. "Fish," she mentioned, and yawned large.

Rhiannon sat down beside her, opened a honeyed leaf to drip it over a piece of the bread, then opened Sal's clenched hand and put the honeyed bread into her grasp. Sal clamped it in a tight fist. She'd suck it off and on throughout the night. It would give her comfort and help fill her belly, though in the morning Sally's hair would be matted with honey, and oft as not stuck fast to the pallet as well. Mayhaps a beetle-bug or two would have been entrapped in all that sticky mess of hair and pallet straw, which was why Mam lacked enthusiasm for Sal's honey treat. But Rhiannon believed what real harm was it for the pleasure it gave? It all came clean in the brook, where she'd give Sal and the bugs a good washing in the morning.

"Sally, here's a puzzle. Some sleep in the woods who think they are dead. And one who sleeps up here *wishes* he were. Dead, that is. Pray tell, who is the luckier, the ones who are alive and know it not or the one alive who knows it and likes it not?"

Sally smiled around the bread she sucked and closed her eyes. *Suck, suck, suck.*

What mother had Sally had? No living mother on the day her bad brother cuffed her, and *that* was a blessing. No mother should have to know of such a thing. Still, mayhaps a living mother would have stopped his hand. Rhia, sighing at all the wrong things in the world that might have stayed aright with one small nudge, hugged Sally good night.

She determined not to look at the sleeping or waking French or English soldier until she'd secured his candle good in the window. She'd have to play this right. Earlier he'd been skittish and fitful and determined in his dim-brained state to call her by his sister's name, Adela. If he'd been all that in the daytime, he might be worse in the dark. She wanted a good light for it, anyhow.

The candle flickered, then flamed bright. Rhiannon turned toward the pallet, fear and anticipation running apace within her. He lay there, but his ankles had come uncrossed, and his hands were folded on his stomach with his thumbs diddling round and round.

"I've waited all day," he said crossly.

She took a breath. "For what, sir?"

He sat up. "For what? For . . . for service! I *starve*! I *thirst*!"

She hastened to pull his portion of the bread from her waist pouch, slathering it with honey from the folded leaf. Six quick steps put her close enough for him to reach it with urgent hands. He gobbled it in four huge bites, then licked his fingers. Honey ran through the little beard on his chin and dribbled to the sleeveless jacket he wore over his shirt. Rhia hurried to the water jug Mam kept in the corner. She got him a dipperful, and again he grabbed and guzzled, wiping his mouth with his sleeve when he'd finished.

"You've water just over there." She pointed. "You may find your legs poor support at first, as you've not used them in weeks. I'll set the water bucket closer, but you'd best start in on walking a bit. Come the morrow, we should—"

"And what of heartier fare, meat for starters?" he demanded. "And stronger drink?"

She began to feel flustered by his rough manner. "We . . . we've some milk from our goat, though Daisy needs the most of it. As for meat, we've fish sometimes, and a little rabbit on certain holy days."

Most common people would be hanged as poachers for eating from the lord's woods, and as this soldier was seeming now like an uppity aristocrat of the most spoiled and bossy type, Rhiannon thought she'd better quick explain.

"Lord Claredemont looks the other way with us a bit on eating some rabbit, because of Mam's service to him as . . . as a healer. I'll try to get you a little dried fish in the morning, all right? And a cup of milk."

"I puke to think of milk! Powerful ale is what I need for my splitting head!"

He leaned forward with his elbows on his knees, holding his head as illustration.

Well, now Rhiannon was in a quandary. Granna brewed some ale, of course, but she didn't like it known about, as her cronies at the official ale-tasters' booth were meant to have the lock on ale brewing, with no one else allowed to do it.

"I think," she ventured, then cleared her throat and started afresh. "I think, sir, that you're too young for strong drink. You look to be the age of a monk friend of mine, say, seventeen? Or mayhaps eighteen? I'm allowed a bit of well-watered ale if the rain's stirred up our stream water so's we dare not drink it for a day. Elsewise, Mam won't hold with strong drink for, as I said, the young, like . . . like us."

"Who's this Mam you speak of? Hey Nonny, she sounds a right prissy old prune!" The man threw back his head and laughed aloud, slapping his thighs with the great joke.

Well, Rhiannon had been patience itself with this rude soldier, but at that, she flamed. She marched smack to the water bucket and threw the dipper back into it, letting the splash express her outrage. Then she got so nervy as to march to the candle, thinking to just plumb blow it out and leave him in the dark to make merry alone.

But he'd not be able to see her anger with no flame, and she wished him to have a good look, so she left the candle alone and walked back close to glare at him with her knuckles upon her hips. She stood before him with daggers flying from her eyes.

"You're not . . . Adela, are you?" he said quietly, cowering back a bit.

She shook her head very slowly. "I am *not*." She crossed her arms. "I'm Rhiannon, whose backdames come from Wales, called Cymru by us *true* Brits. We have lived upon this bluff since the ancient days of Arthur and before, that is, long before *your* kind so much as arrived. And neither is Mam a . . . a *prune*. She's *beautiful*, if you'd like to know. She's an angel as well, and has saved your life many times over!"

He dropped his chin to his chest as that awful misery of earlier in the day fell upon him again like a gray cloak. "And more's the pity she did," he whispered. "For I know not who I am, but I fear that I'd sooner sleep forever than come full awake and find out."

Well. Rhiannon had been certain that after the dire insult to Mam there was *nothing* he could say or do that would make her have one oat's weight of sympathetic feeling for him ever again. Nor would she even be courteous to such a wag and drear scoundrel as would order her around like some kitchen wench. *I hunger! I thirst! I puke!* Well, let him puke and see how she cared! Let him live on gruel and keep his limbs crossed forever, and she'd not take any of it away from him by offering bread and honey and polite answers to his queries! He could shrivel to dust for all she cared!

But now, this. Of all he could say, *this* saying was an arrow that hit her right in that big part of her that craved first the hearing of a mystery and then the knowing of how it might finally come unraveled.

"Sir, I cannot imagine anything you could have done so horrible in another time and place that you'd so fear knowing yourself the doer of it in *this* one. I can think of no action whatsoever that would qualify."

But the man either did not understand or did not want her to know that he did. He closed his eyes and crossed his limbs to feign lasting sleep again, only did it not so sprightly as before, when they'd locked back in place right quick from long practice.

Rhiannon could see that whether he liked it or no, this haughty soldier was inching back to the sunshiny world, losing his hidey-hole in the shadowy realm of dreams.

Chapter 14

It was some cold in the brook when Rhiannon bathed Sal's hair the next morning, but she felt she couldn't tarry for the sun to shine hotter. The earlier she got down the trail, the more apt she was to get the scoop on Jim. She made a few splashes do, then finished with a light scrubbing over Sal's ear with river weeds.

"Good enough. A lick and a promise for now, Sally, with more to come later."

Sally brought her elbows close to her body and shivered, her teeth clacking and her hands all aflail. Though her wet flaxen nightshift must have felt clammy, she smiled wide and happy. In Sal's world, shivering was as good an adventure as any other.

"What d'ye think I should do about the high and bossy soldier in the house next to yours, Sal?" Rhia queried as she toweled her hair. "I might leave him a fish on the sill of his window and let him try and walk for it, then laugh if he stumbles. Or I might take him in a fish and then refuse to give it, all haughty myself as he *himself* was to me last night. I might even eat it in front of him with great lip-smacking and finger-licking! How's that? Give him a dose of his own aristocratic spleen and spit, huh?"

Nervy talk, and not a whit of it in Rhia's power to do, as she had no fish.

"Fish! Fish!" Sally was delighted to hear her word on another's tongue. "Three!"

Rhia stayed upon her knees and bent far forward to see her own reflection in the waters of the brook. With a willow stick she made part after part in her glossy hair, until she'd braided a dozen small braids throughout it. She shook her head and watched the water approvingly as they jumped and danced about her head, then she washed her face, scrubbing it and then her arms and then her legs until she felt tingly all over, chilled, too.

"Crawwwk!" said Gramp disapprovingly from the yew tree.

"Yes, I know the seeds must be gathered, Gramp, but we'll make short work of it. You wouldn't have me go to town all dusty and bedraggled, would you?"

So much to do! She needed to change into her other shift with her red skirt for over it. And there was also the soldier to be handled. She dreaded it, her nervy talk about the fish having been a ruse to cover how off-balance and fearful she felt around him now. She figured, truth be told, that mayhaps he was too much for her. Deep waters over her head, best left to Mam, much as she'd have liked to keep the mysteries of him for herself.

She sat back upon her heels and sighed, shivering as she fiddled with the waist pouch that hung from her sash. She felt a hard acornlike knob in the bottom of it and remembered the clamshell, pocketed on the last trip to town but forgotten in all the mess of Jim's arrest.

"Sal, looky here." Rhia loosed the pouch string and pulled out the gleaming little shell. "Pretty, see? It shines in the sun as though it be silver. It's a pin, Sally, made to seem a fishy clam."

Sally's eyes grew very wide indeed as she beheld the glittering thing.

Rhiannon pinned it upon the bodice of Sally's shift and Sal looked down at it, enchanted.

"Now you look like a princess," Rhia told her, grinning.

"Daughter!"

Rhia quickly stood and turned toward their cot, where Mam was upon the stoop with the gruel pot hung about her arm and bread in a cloth.

"Bring Sal in so's I may give her breakfast!"

"But . . ."

"I know, Rhiannon, you've said you'll do the caring for the two in the cots. But I'll feed them just this morn as you'd best gather some seeds right quick, then get to town!"

Some relieved that the decision of whether to hand the soldier over to Mam was taken from her hands, Rhiannon lifted Sal beneath the arms. Though Sal pulled to walk straight toward her home, Rhia edged her zigzag to meet Mam along the stone path.

"Crawwwk." Gramp sounded as if his patience was at an end, but he nevertheless began an activity of picking lice from his wing with his strong beak, biding his time.

As they neared Mam, Rhia blurted, "I must warn you that the man has been awake for me of late when I've checked him. I doubt you believe me, Mam, but you should! He may play at sleeping, but he's as awake as you or I!"

Mam sighed, smiling patiently at Rhia's folly. "I long to see him wake, daughter, though I fear it be the stuff of dreamy imaginings if it happens after all this time."

Mam patted Rhia's cheek, then walked on, leading Sal.

Rhia faced Gramp, shaking her head. "Me? *Dreamy?*"

Gramp was all akimbo, balanced on one foot with opposing wing outstretched and the feathers crimped where he beaked. Though he might have given support against this false judgment, he went on with his lice hunt, neither agreeing nor disagreeing.

"Well, let's get the seeds done, then," Rhia murmured, her feelings a large bit hurt.

She began a dull tramp toward the bluff's edge and Gramp had no choice but to give up his quest for lice and follow her. That's the way of it oft enough. The animal awaits the human for long hours, but the human does not give a single care to the animal's present business when the tables are turned.

At least Gramp was soon able to resume his *toilet*, as they say in Francia, because Rhiannon made short work of gathering the seeds, scooping up what was easy and not taking time to find others. Arriving back at the cottage, she added the seeds she carried in a fold of her skirt to the others she was taking, then hurried up the ladder to get into her other shift, the clean one. She shook out the trail dust from her red skirt, pulling it carefully over her head so's her braids didn't tangle, then lacing it tight at her waist with a jerk of its rawhide string. She slid down the ladder, shouldered her two heavy carrying packs with a small grunt, and appeared before Granna draped like a packhorse.

"I start off then, Granna. Here's your questions, so check if they're right. What was said by the bailiff or vicar just before Jim confessed? Who was witness? Who profits?"

Granna nodded, pleased. "Good, Rhiannon. Find answers to those and we'll be on our way to fetching up the true felon."

Mam came in from giving breakfast to the invalids and hung the empty gruel pot on its peg. "Ready to leave then, daughter? Now mind, you *must* start back up before the sun goes past the nether side of the steeple tower, understand? We'll be sick with fretting if you're not back by twilight."

"I know," Rhiannon said, watching Mam close. Since she

wasn't going to volunteer information, Rhia had no choice but to ask. "How . . . did you find the man?"

Mam shrugged lightly. "He sleeps, as he has e'er we've had him with us."

Rhia could think of no way to convince her that he was *not* "dreamy imaginings," so she took her farewell. But it rankled. She went some paces toward the trail, trying to shut the sneaky soldier from her mind, but she couldn't manage it. Slipping off the packs, she ran to his cottage and threw her weight against the door so it opened with a slam against the wattle.

Sure enough—there he lay, stone effigy.

The door rebounded hard to slam closed again, and at that commotion he turned his head and looked at her, having the fine nerve to smile a little at his own deception.

She stomped close. "Why would you fiddle with Mam and me like this?" she demanded. "She thinks I *dream* you awake! What a fool that makes me seem!"

He rose to an elbow and pulled his face straight, though his eyes twinkled. "Maybe you *do* but dream me."

"And *still* you'd fiddle whilst I'm late getting down to town!"

"Nay, I'm very serious. Everything may be but a dream. We mortals may only be doing a play in the mind of God, so what do you think of that?"

She rolled her eyes. "Not much is what I think of it. And you'd do well to drop your ruse and let Mam attend you, as you need the nursing only she can give."

"Ours lives may be but a dream," he whispered. "Mere . . . candle smoke."

Shaking her head, Rhia turned and proceeded toward the door. "I go to town now," she threw over her shoulder, "since you'll not so much as listen to one word I say!"

"Wait!" he implored. "I'm sorry! Truly, I am. Last night, I teased you, I think, though I've only a fogged memory. These ways of being, of speaking . . . they flicker across me as lamplight flickers upon the wall. Here's a way I might act, then it's gone, and another one's taken me over. I feel I'm trying on myself as one might try on cloaks, discarding them in a pile as none are a *fit*. I know not which voice is mine when I hear it! I only know I have need of a friend while I find myself. Not a nurse, kind Rhiannon—a *friend*."

She stopped in her tracks. Not because of his speech, though it had been pretty enough, but because he'd called her by her own name and not that other—Adela.

She turned back around. "All right. But . . . I'll be gone till twilight."

"I'll gladly wait," he answered with a genuine enough smile.

If you'd asked Rhiannon later how the trail had been, whether sunshine prevailed or mist made the footing treacherous that morn, she'd have had no idea how to answer, as her mind had been aswirl with so much else as she traveled down. She might have said, "What trail?" Gramp stayed above her nearly clear down to the river crossing, too, a thing he disliked doing, as hunters abound on the common grounds just past the river. Of course, if Gramp had not been so proud in his own birdy way, he might have realized no hunter would waste so much as one moldy arrow on such a stringy old bag of feathers as himself. Still, Gramp clearly perceived that Rhiannon needed to be watched over that particular market day even more than most, as she was sure to be spinning all the week's mysteries in her head and letting her feet fall where they would.

By the time she'd crossed the barley field and was up even with the watermill, the temptation grew large within her to knock upon the church door to find immediate news of Jim. But she knew she dasn't go that way. No, first the trade, then the news, lest the trade get neglected as she spent too much time hearing the news from he who opened the church door—meaning, she hoped, Thaddeus.

Still, what harm to walk the side of the street the church was on? So she checked with her hands to be certain her braids were in some sort of order, then crossed.

The stonework progressed at an astonishing pace, with the accompanying noise and dust very much progressed as well. Rhiannon saw no clergy about, just stonemasons and pullers of sledges. In the church was surely Jim, but the dust that hung everywhere blotted any chance she might have seen him through a window. Would they even let him near a window, lest he might escape and break sanctuary? Well, he'd be declared outside the law if he did, and must be killed on sight like a ravening wolf. Wolf's head and first target to all law-abiders, they'd call him—a strong reason for him not to budge.

She coughed some dust from her throat and walked to the grassy lot just beyond the church. There she dropped her heavy packs to the ground for a few moments' relief to her shoulders, noting that black ashes still marked several small squares of ground in the nether corner where cots had recently stood, including Jim's.

Some digging had been started near the middle of the lot for the prior's fishpond, and a young woman sat upon a tree stump near those diggings. A babe was at her breast.

Strange place for such activity, Rhia thought, with all the sooty dust. In fact, the young woman looked fairly well grimed from kerchief to boots, and the ash on her face appeared tracked through with tears.

Rhia dared walk closer. "If you're in distress, may I help?"

The woman looked up. "Help? What could ye do?" she asked bluntly.

Rhiannon shrugged. "I just thought, well, this seems a dismal place for resting. If you're stranger to Woethersly, I might show you greener space and water for drinking."

So quietly Rhia barely heard, the woman said, "Oh, I know Woethersly well enough."

There'd been bitterness in her voice, and she suddenly glared hard at Rhia, anger burning bright behind the tears in her eyes. "If you'd help, pray tell me how fair Woethersly's come to this," she whispered miserably. "Tell me how a daughter may wed and move but a three-day ride from her own birthplace, then return widowed two years later to find things tangled to a snarl! My father for certain is become dimwit, and my mother lies asleep in yon churchyard. All I'd dreamed of was her joy in seeing this babe, her grandson. Even our house has turned to ashes! *All* is ashes! How can this *be?*"

She clutched her child more tightly, her red cheek pressed against his head and her tears flowing freely into his downy orange hair. She stared at the sooty traces of what had been her homely neighborhood last she'd seen it, or imagined it.

Rhia watched helplessly. "I'm sorry for your loss," was all she could think to say. "I . . . I have a friend whose home, like yours, was burned when they cleared this lot. They told him nothing of it, either, and he had to arrive and find it gone, just as you have." She sighed. "At least he has no child to bear the shock of it as well." Though Jim had said if he *had* had a child to give week-work to the lord, his cottage might have stood.

"Rhiannon! Rhia, fine friend, I've found you at last! Don't move, I'm coming!"

Rhia winced and whirled round to see a girl running toward her down the path from town. Everyone Maddy passed seemed knocked off-kilter a bit by the sheer energy of such a lively runner. Rhia felt off-kilter at the sight of Maddy as well, especially at remembrance of the trap she'd set and sprung for her regarding Beltane Eve.

"I'm sorry," Rhia whispered to the weeping woman, who wasn't paying the slightest attention anyhow, so lost was she in her world of woe. "My friend comes and I fear when she reaches me I'll have no choice but to—"

"There, I've thrown a fine lasso around ye!" Maddy yipped. Indeed, she'd come up close and tossed a beautiful bandanna of blue silk over Rhia's head. It settled loose and glimmering around Rhia's neck, then Maddy pulled the center knot tight at Rhia's throat. Clutching the trailing ends of it, she made ready to playfully pull her friend toward town.

"Come along, then, captive!" Maddy sang with glee.

As Maddy laughingly jerked her along by the ends of that silk scarf, all Rhiannon could do was steal a last helpless glance over her shoulder at the woman and her babe.

Rhiannon liked not this means of journeying as captive toward market, and liked it less and less as Maddy sped them right recklessly through the narrow gamut of craftsmen's booths edging the green. Maddy tripped right over the glassmaker's bellows, in fact, keeping her own balance but very nearly tipping Rhia right onto the red-hot kiln! Rhiannon smelled the singe of some threads of her skirt and it made her some angry. She wished, after that, to become even *more* angry, as in such a state she might possibly have the moxie to go against headstrong Maddy about Beltane Eve.

Around the potter's wheel and the cartwright's shed Maddy zigged and zagged them, never letting that bandanna go slack. She maneuvered them close to a huge pig carcass hanging outside the butcher's stall. It swayed as Maddy gave it a hard sideways bounce with her muscled shoulder as they passed.

Hard to say how many ox took alarum as Maddy went lunging along past carts and stalls and around all manner of walkers, both on two feet and upon four. "Look sharp!" she'd yell if there was time for such crude warning, though there was usually not. Three small children sitting at innocent play together along the verge of the road bawled in fright as Maddy leapt clean over their heads, her skirts toppling two of them right over into the dust!

"Pay the piper!" Maddy demanded, stopping abruptly when they'd finally got past the houses and craftsmen and near to the center of the busy green.

She turned and teasingly jerked the lasso tighter so's Rhia near gagged.

"Maddy, have a care!" Rhia squeezed her fingers under the silken knot to jerk it some loose.

"Pay the piper, then!" Maddy smiled so the dimple in her left cheek deepened. "Pay for the ride with your solemn promise to join us in our revels on Beltane! You *must*!"

Why was it that with all the mischance Maddy had just then exposed Rhia to, still Rhia could not put her foot down to firmly naysay

Maddy? When faced by Maddy in such direct fashion, Rhia could not even summon that bright anger she'd planned would help her out when this very promise was required of her.

Alas, the will of a bold girl like Maddy will oft prove too much for a less audacious girl like Rhiannon. All flustered Rhia could think to do was to look down and stall for time by unknotting the bright scarf, but Maddy quickly stopped Rhia's fumbling fingers, catching them in her own.

"Don't loosen the scarf, but rather wear it always, Rhiannon! It's for you, a token sent from Leonard to tell how he longs to meet you as his partner on Beltane Eve! Now, quick, tell me your decision. Shall I meet you on the green at dusk and together we'll join Frederique's party at the dragon's chamber, or shall we come up to your private chapel for our romp? One or the other, say which!"

Rhia's ears rang. "I . . . I shall meet you down here, near the manor house."

Maddy hugged her right quick, then danced away backward, blowing a kiss. "Adieu until then, Rhia! That's what they say in Francia, you know. Adieu! Braid your hair all jaunty like that when you come, and don't forget to wear Leonard's scarf! A lady wears a knight's colors when she would show her true love! Isn't that romantic? My Fred's colors are red and gold."

With a giggle and a blush, Maddy pulled down one corner of her bodice to expose a bit of the red bandanna she safekept there. And then she turned round and was off at a run toward the manor, where she had doubtless been expected some time ago.

Rhiannon was left in her usual state upon being caught up in Maddy's whirlwind, then tossed from it without warning right back to the ground. On the one hand she felt gloomed by her own endless cowardice around her friend. On the other, she couldn't quit glancing down at the gorgeous scarf that now swathed her neck. She'd never thought to own such a glorious thing, and had never especially wanted to. But now she did, she found she couldn't regret its possession.

And wrongheaded though she knew it was, she also felt a strong prick of curiosity about this Leonard as she trekked back to the church-yard to reclaim the two valuable packs of goods she'd had no choice but to helplessly abandon there when Maddy snatched her into that cavort to town.

But when she reached the grassy lot this side of the churchyard, Rhia's usual flighty imaginings instantly gave way to a true and solid problem of the first order.

For where she'd left two packs upon the grass, now there was but one.

Chapter 15

Rhiannon sped to the single pack and dropped to her knees to dump its contents onto the grass, praying mightily that nothing was lost, though that was a foolish hope since certainly a pack's worth of contents had gone missing. There upon the grass spilled the seeds, the wax figures, some combs of the honey, most of the beeswax candles. She missed one of the loaves, a honeycomb, a single wax figure, and two or three candles. Was that all? Rhia could not think, and dropped to sit there upon the grass with her head in her hands, all shame and misery. She snatched at the blue scarf where it draped upon her chest and untied it in a fury, growling in frustration. That gaudy scarf seemed the very cause of her slipup, though a *thing* will not of itself cause a slipup, and that's that.

In truth only a *person* will be the fine cause of a dire slipup. Rhia remembered that in time to stash the scarf into her waist pouch, when she'd meant to tear it to pieces, or almost meant to. Though, honestly, she wouldn't have. She thought the scarf too fine, that's how vain and shameful she truly was. Shameful!

"I'm hopeless, and *shameful!*" She knocked at her forehead with her knuckles.

"How now, Rhia! Hold up!"

Thaddeus was approaching at a lope from the church. Her heart rose to her throat. How much of her churchyard hysterics had he witnessed *this* time? And how doubly shameful to worry about such a paltry thing as your own humiliation when you'd *best* worry that you'd just lost your mother's prized pack!

"I'm shameful and hopeless from all directions and that's the sum of it," she whispered again, shaking her head.

Thaddeus dropped to the grass beside her. "What's the sum of what, Rhia?"

She covered her eyes with her fingers and would not look at him. "I've lost my mother's pack to some sneakthief, Thaddeus. I'm certain Mam will never, ever trust me again, such a hopeless fool am I!"

He said nothing. She waited. He still said nothing.

"Such a fool as I ne'er walked the earth," she pointed out.

Still, Thaddeus didn't deny it. Finally, she'd had enough and took her hands from her face so that she might frown at him.

He was quietly fitting the spilled goods back into the single pack, looking some sheepish. "I'm afraid I witnessed the theft and knew it not for what it was, Rhia," he admitted. "I was at the window, filling the prior's inkhorn in the good light. I happened to glance outside and saw Jim's daughter picking it up. I assumed it was her own."

Rhiannon's eyes got wide and she shook her head quite firmly. "Jim's daughter? Thaddeus, Jim *has* no daughter. On that awful day he came to town with us, Jim said straight out that he should have expected his cot to be taken by Lord Claredemont since his wife was dead and he had no child to take over the week-work he owed as rent."

Thaddeus narrowed his eyes. "Well, but it seems—"

"And a daughter would surely have come up the trail with him when he was so hurt by that cart! No, you must be mistaken, Thaddeus."

Thaddeus shrugged. "I'm sure I'm *not* mistaken, Rhia. Since she arrived yesterday, Jim's daughter has spent all her time here in the yard, near where their cot used to stand. She may not speak with Jim under his rules of sanctuary, yet she feels that from within the church Jim might catch a glimpse of her and his little grandson and find comfort in the sight. I doubt she knew of his injury last year. She lives at a distance and knew nothing of her mother's death, which, I'm told, happened some months before Jim was hurt. And for his part, Jim knew not of his grandson, nor that his son-in-law had got a fever last winter and left his young wife widowed. Jim and his family are just now reunited, though the terms are hard and the circumstances sad."

Rhia concentrated, thinking back to the morning before Jim's arrest. "I suppose Jim may have said he had no *son*," she murmured. "No son to give the lord his week-work! Yes, that *is* what he said, Thaddeus!"

Thaddeus looked nervously over his shoulder. He put a finger to his lips and whispered, "The church has ears, Rhia. Later we'll speak more of this. When will you finish at the market, d'you think?"

"I must reach home before twilight or Mam'll skin me alive."

He nodded. "I'll wait for you on the beach when the afternoon wanes, near where the trail begins. Now, if you will, wave to Jim as you stand. He may well see you from his station upon the frid stool near the altar, where he must stay most hours of his days."

Rhia cringed imagining the awful cramp a person was bound to get from all those hours sitting upon the church's short and squat three-legged frid stool. It was purposely made that way for thinking of the Scriptures and your own immortal soul, as you'd never get comfortable enough to go to sleep or otherwise lollygag the time away.

She stood, shouldered the remaining pack, then turned toward the church and waved sadly to Jim, wherever inside those fine but fearsome walls he might be.

Granna's friends at the ale booth always found a space on their sales table for Rhia or Mam to display the things they had to sell at market, and the only rent those dames required was the gossip from atop the bluff.

"How does that dear little Daisy?" one after another of them asked Rhia that day, and she was glad to report on Daisy's quick and sunny smile, which clearly showed her soul to be intact, though she'd suffered so very much.

Three or four asked if Daisy's sister and mother had indeed gone along to God, and Rhia answered with a simple nod, then crossed herself as Granna's friends did likewise.

Then, without preamble, a right hefty barrel of a lady named Hilda Mopp sat down next to her on the makeshift wood bench behind the table, sagging it but not quite splitting it. "Here's a message for your granna," she told Rhia. "Tell Moira that her bunions will be mightily eased if'n she swallows five spiders both morn and eve. That's five morning and five evening, don't forget, and it's to be done for three days running. That's six dose of spiders altogether. It worked like magic for my cousin Freeda."

Rhia bit her lip at the thought of spiders eaten alive, though she'd heard of it before. They'd tickle their way down to Granna's feet and then the easing would come up through the hide of her toes. That's how spiders were rumored to work, anyhow.

"I'll tell her for certain, Mistress Mopp," Rhia said. Then, as Hilda Mopp was known to have her ear always cocked to the business of others, Rhia leaned closer to ask, "And mistress, have you heard tell of how our friend Jim Gatt came to escape to sanctuary?"

Hilda Mopp looked in all directions with her hands clasped beneath her large bosom, then she spoke all stealthy and shifty-eyed, though not so quiet as she might have.

"Well, Guy Dryer's a simple man. As bailiff that goes some in his favor, and some not. When Jim confessed, Guy had no stomach for a quick execution and let him slip. Now that Jim's got sanctuary within the church, by law no one can touch him for forty days, though that time will flee quick enough and then Jim'll hang anyhow, of course."

Rhiannon's stomach fell at that last blunt pronouncement, and she was glad to have a band of customers walk up so's her mind could be put for a bit on her honey and seeds.

When those folk had made their purchases and walked on, Rhia whispered to Mistress Mopp, "Granna would have me find out exactly what was said by the vicar and bailiff at Jim's confession, and who witnessed it besides those two. She'd also have me find who profits, though none could surely profit by Jim's confession but the true murderer."

Hilda Mopp heaved a great, disgusted *humph* and pulled her chins down so's they dwelt upon her bosom. She leaned some sideways and said from the corner of her mouth, "Oh, *one* other profits well enough, and that's Beornia Gatt, the selfish little hussy. Never a thought for other than herself when she was growing up here, and still never, so far as I can see. Poor Jim always gave her everything she wanted, that little brat. She pretends such grief over that dead husband of her'n. *Humph!* If grief well-acted is liable to buy her sympathy from the town, then she'll *act* grieved, and further I've heard that . . ."

Rhiannon had gaped at Mistress Mopp throughout this talk, trying to separate out the tangled threads of Mistress Mopp's information and opinions. So she was some abashed when something landed with a padded thunk on the table in front of her. Rhia turned around straight, ready to apologize to the customer who'd been neglected, and faced the tall young woman who'd been weeping in the burned lot next to the church!

Her baby was balanced upon her hip. He sucked two sticky fingers, and along the front of his smock were drippings of honey. In one chubby hand he clutched a small mass of what looked like Granna's sweet rye bread, and under the other arm he held the missing wax effigy, cuddling it as though it were a playtoy.

"I brought your carrier back to you," the woman said in a flat, unfriendly voice. Her chin was atremble, though she had a proud lift to it. "You'll find three pence inside it. I've got cabbages, and if they sell, I'll pay most of the rest of what I owe you today. If they don't sell, I'll pay the first moment I ever can."

Rhia looked down and saw her lost pack upon the table, flat and empty. When she looked back up, the woman was already striding away, her shoulders high and her long hair swinging. She called back over her shoulder, "You asked if you could help me, but I mighta known your offer would prove as hollow as all else seems now in Woethersly!"

Mistress Mopp clucked her tongue. "Did I not tell you? All sass, that Beornia Gatt. You should not lend to her, Rhiannon dear, as she says she'll repay but is not to be . . ."

Rhiannon's forehead fell to her hands. "I fear she heard what you said about her," she told Mistress Mopp with a great sigh of regret. "I *did* offer her help, and meant it."

"And for *my* part, I hope she did *indeed* hear my words," the mistress replied quite huffily. "And I also wager she'll hear more good earfuls e'er she walks the crowd! For it wasn't just my boy, Arnold, had his heart broke by her, but many another as well. Arnold might not be a

176

looker, but he's not so dull-headed as some hereabouts, and further I believe that—"

"Mistress?" Rhia interrupted, having heard as much of this as she could stand. "I still don't understand why you'd say Beornia Gatt profits from Jim's confession."

Hilda Mopp snorted. "Well, if a murderer dies denying his guilt, he loses all right to what's been his in life, now, don't he? Yet if he dies having confessed, he may at the vicar's pleasure keep what's his and so pass it to his children. Beornia will inherit all Jim owns, now that he's confessed to the crime."

Rhia knew that was the law, yet since Jim owned nothing, it didn't seem to apply. She might have asked Mistress Mopp for a bit of clarification on that score, but Mistress Mopp was hefting herself up off the bench, surely eager to discuss with more important folk than Rhia this chance encounter she'd had with the infamous hussy, Beornia Gatt.

And Rhia, to be honest, had no wish to slow her in her leaving.

Besides, a great commotion had just begun at the edge of the green, and now was progressing down the street that fronted the ale booth. All chatter and dealings stopped cold as folk turned to see what caused the ruckus.

A gang of running boys, it was, fair barreling along, careening like drunkards, kicking up the dust, scattering the geese and confounding the nearby folk as well.

"Make way! Make way and be quick about it!" those six gangly lads demanded of all, waving their long arms as if they were stuffed dolls come alive to scare the crows. They even whacked some folk in the face with their gawky, flapping hands. "Make way for Lord Claredemont's party to pass! Clear this street, you common lot, so's your betters may ride through unhindered!"

Paid way-clearers these boys were, then, and doing a fabulous job of it, as when else might they make such a nuisance of themselves and not be given over to the bailiff?

And then came the riders. Rhia recognized those same young squires that she, Granna, Jim, and Daisy had watched taking the creek. The galloping mounts brushed by and upset one of the market tables so the potter's wares were toppled. Dust and broken shards flew everywhere. Small children screamed and clutched their mothers' skirts, yet the horsemen rode the harder, heedless as mounted demons bringing on the apocalypse.

A little girl, confounded by the dust and noise, walked right into the path of a horse, and the rider of it, never swerving, instead used his whip to flick her away. The small girl's mother snatched her up in the very nick of time or she'd have surely been trampled, but her arm flamed red from the bite of the whip.

Then, in the time it might take for a jug to be filled with ale from the barrel tap, the gang had passed on. The crowd was quiet in their wake, somewhat stupefied. After a few moments, the small girl bawled with her pain and several women came unfrozen and hurried close to see to her hurt. The roiling sounds of market slowly started up again.

Rhia found her remaining two small rye loaves to be so filthed with dust that they'd not be edible by humans. Furious, she stood and threw them, hard, to the geese.

All the wares she'd brought were now sold, ruined, or stolen. She bought what she could with the paltry coin she'd made from her two meager sales, stuffed that and her emptied pack into one light pack, and gladly left the green. Good riddance of it, as all had been mischance in her market dealings this day. Thaddeus could tell her what she needed to know of Jim, and without market gossip muddying the news just as surely as those horsemen had so muddied the market green.

She was surprised to find Thaddeus already standing where they'd agreed to meet at the beach, since she herself had arrived some early. He stood facing the wide water, and something about the set of his shoulders made Rhiannon reluctant to disturb him. He was clearly involved in thinking his thoughts, and the holy brothers' thoughts were always deep, surely never simple. Or indeed, he might be praying.

While she stood hesitating, Thaddeus bent and picked up a rock, then skimmed it hard across the water so it jumped four, five, six times.

"Thaddeus!" she called at that sign, and ran to join him.

He turned to her, but the stricken expression upon his face made her come to a halt while still some yards away. Her heart felt turned to ice.

"Has . . . something happened to Jim?" she whispered. Things could go horribly awry in sanctuary, as they sometimes did in gaol. Suicides, or escapes that ended bloodily.

Thaddeus dropped his head without making her an answer, then bent to take another rock. And when he threw this one, he hurled it so viciously it ricocheted hard several times against the cold sea before finally sinking within the waters.

He was angry, then. Rhia could not have been more shocked if he'd turned to a lizard or a dog. She'd not thought anger could find any corner in him, so mild did he seem. But there it was—in the white of his face, the blaze of his eyes, and in the ferocity with which he'd fight the very sea with his small stones.

David he'd become, but against what Goliath did he rage so fierce?

Then Thaddeus suddenly reached and grabbed her by the hand. He began running, and with her free arm she hefted her pack more securely, then held her skirt above her ankles and struggled to keep up. He veered from the sand, where folk walked and idled the time in conversation, and sped across the rough rocks, right toward the wilderness. He then veered into the narrow passageway where the bluff met the water, a place too rough for common use, ventured into only by pirates who would hide from other folk.

The boulders here were slick with sea brine. The path was a ledge of tumbled rock where, Granna claimed, mermen and mermaids basked in the light of each full moon.

Finally, when no trace of Woethersly or the castle or the quay was visible behind them, Thaddeus slowed and let go her hand. She dropped to her knees, out of breath and dizzy with the run. He bent with his hands on his own knees, winded as well.

Presently, he got his breath back enough to wheeze out, "I beg you forgive me, Rhia, but I *had* to put Woethersly at my back! I could not *breathe* in its surrounds." He sat down hard, put his chin into his hands, and stared at the sea. "I *am* sorry to have brought you along so roughly," he murmured. "What a fool you must think me."

Rhia murmured, "Well, you didn't rush to deny *my* foolishness earlier today, so I think neither shall I deny yours now."

She smiled and he looked at her and smiled back. But his smile was forced and lasted only a moment. He looked down and rubbed at a paint stain upon his palm.

"We're fools both, then," he murmured. "Yet to be a fool may indeed be the wise course in a topsy-turvy world like ours is become of late. These days princes think they can buy heaven and priests sell the truth as fast and cheap as two-day-old fish."

She was shocked at the bitterness of his words when he was never bitter. "What on earth are you talking about, Thaddeus?"

He stared out at the endless chop, still rubbing his palm. When he finally spoke, his voice was so hollow and flat that she almost wished his earlier bright anger would return.

"Jim's *sold* his life to the local priest, Rhiannon. I've heard it with my own ears, just this past hour."

Chapter 16

"Sold . . . his life? Oh, Thaddeus, whatever can you mean by such a thing?"

He closed his eyes and took a deep breath, then turned to her.

"I was a fly upon the wall, unnoticed as I painted high up in the west corner of the nave this afternoon," he began. "The scaffolding was still in place from the recent plastering, you see, and I thought I'd climb up, test my colors, and maybe, if the plaster seemed set enough, start a bit of rough sketching upon it with my brush.

"At first I was alone and glad to be, but then I heard conversation below. I looked down through the ribs of the scaffold and saw the vicar walking down the aisle, speaking with a man sent from the earl. I knew the man as such because he wore the earl's livery, beribboned here and there in mourning black. I might have called down to alert those two of my presence, but I guess I was hesitant because I thought the vicar would be angry, seeing me perched where I was without his prior knowledge or permission. And soon enough it would no longer have been wise to call out, as I'd heard too much.

"Rhiannon, the earl's man had come with gold for the vicar to give to Jim's daughter after Jim's death! They said it out clear enough. 'I've brought what the poor wretch has asked as the cost of his full confession,' the earl's man said, pouring out coin into his own hand. The vicar leaned to count it, then nodded, saying, 'God will be pleased. The daughter will have it at the father's burial.' Then, as the vicar stood waiting for the earl's man to repouch the coin and to hand *him* the pouch, he added, 'And by the way, my son, I must correct you. This is not the cost of his confession, as his guilt was clear and the confession a mere formality. This is merely alms given in Christian charity to the convicted man's orphaned daughter. God will note the earl's largesse in this matter.' The vicar then took the pouched coin from the other and tucked it into his sleeve."

Thaddeus looked harder at Rhia, his hands out before him. "You see, don't you, Rhia, that your vicar has surely *bribed* Jim into confession with the promise of this money for his daughter and grandson?"

She nodded, tapping her chin with the cross Mam had given her. "Jim was already broken of spirit when he was arrested, and I doubt he'd bother to defend himself much," she murmured, figuring as she went. "Everyone knows the manor court practically never finds a prisoner innocent when the vicar's ordeal of laid hands has pointed to guilt. If the vicar came to the gaol yesterday morn to offer 'charity' for Jim's daughter, Jim would know that the offer would stand only upon his confession, as nothing can be given to the family of those dying unconfessed. He'd probably figure he had nothing to lose by confessing and suddenly would have much to gain."

She looked quizzically at Thaddeus. "Granna saw a robed brother knocking upon the church door in her firewatch yestermorn. Does that bear on this thing at all?"

Thaddeus looked some sheepish. "I left a robe behind in the gaol when I visited Jim the evening before the vicar's visit to him. I'd heard that Guy sometimes lets a condemned murderer slip to sanctuary, and I hoped that if the manor court found Jim guilty, Guy would let Jim robe himself to better reach the church door unhindered." He covered his eyes with his hands and added, "Little did I think the need for it would arise the very next morning! I'd hoped for the delay a scheduled trial would provide so's we could somehow prove Jim innocent, but with this ill-gained confession, he will have the forty days of sanctuary and then his fate's sealed, with no trial or possible reprieve."

The young monk shuddered and looked again to the choppy waters, clenching and unclenching the muscles of his jaws. For her part, Rhiannon was tapping her chin with that cross again, trying to work out in her head some pattern to the earl's recent unpredictable doings.

"The earl first gives coin to have the church here made grand, which I guess is to the good," she mused. "Though it displaces peasants such as Jim, which is to the ill. He also endows your outpost monastery, which is good. But he has a band of lepers brought to the woods he owns, which I'd say is ill, since he appears to care not one fig what happens to them now they've come. And here's this new and . . . and *hideous* gesture that the earl thinks God should find praiseworthy. Thaddeus, it's as though the earl would please God, but has no sense at all about it. He flails like a fish thrown upon the beach."

Thaddeus nodded. "These are strange times, Rhiannon," he said quietly. "Since the *White Ship* went down last November, many gentlefolk who are normally too well fed and comfortable to worry one whit about the Great Hereafter have suddenly developed extreme concern for the condition of their souls. At Glastonbury we saw constant evidence of this newfound and oft misthought piety last winter. Noble parties would arrive at our gates daily, demanding that God immediately forgive their sins as they'd taken the time and expense to make such a pilgrimage. Or many nights a band of gentry would awake the abbot from his sleep, ordering him to tell them where they could join a quick Crusade to the Holy Lands, as they knew for a certain fact God forgave Crusaders of all sin. When the royal ship carrying Prince William and his party went down so suddenly last winter, I believe the elders of those young gentry, lords and ladies throughout the realm, were shocked into awareness of their own bleak chances for eternal survival. And exactly as you say, they now flail like grounded fish. Most would *buy* heaven, as the buying of lands and people is what they understand. Others excel at warfare, which explains their preference for bloody Crusading. Few indeed comprehend compassion as being heaven's true route, as that trait is not useful when acquiring a knightly portion of manors and titles. In fact, most rulers think it a trait of fools."

They were both silent for a moment, then Rhiannon murmured, "All this jives with something mentioned by one of Granna's friends today. She said Jim's daughter, Beornia, will profit from Jim's confession as she'll inherit if he hangs confessed. It rings true that, as you've said, Beornia *is* the true reason for Jim's false confession, now there's inheritance involved. But do you think she knows of the earl's coin she'll have? She called Jim dimwit, though she said not whether she believed he'd murdered. Did she mean dimwit for murdering, or dimwit for confessing to a crime he did not do?"

Thaddeus sounded miserable as he said, "I doubt if she knows the twisted schemes that have led to her father's dilemma. And even if she *did* know Jim had been bribed to confess, I doubt she could reverse what the vicar has set upon simply by renouncing a claim to Jim's inheritance. Vicar Pecksley *will* have his hanging, though I still know not who is being protected by it. I only know the coin the earl's given as a gesture to God can only have been needed so that a murderer may walk free."

Rhiannon's ears rang. "Thaddeus, has it really not occurred to you that the earl himself may indeed be the one being *protected* by Lord Claredemont and the vicar?"

Thaddeus looked quickly over at her. Was he puzzled, or thinking a similar thing?

She shrugged, suddenly exhausted. "I don't know what I meant by that. Truly, I don't. I'm just angry at the earl's false piety in bringing the lepers to the bluff, as it's caused Mam a fine dilemma. And the earl's son and his cronies lately ride like demons through the woods and the town, careless of all. But I suppose they don't exactly *sin* with their brash ways when all's said and done."

Thaddeus smiled, but his smile held no mirth. "Their *brash* ways. So might have said those who watched the dockside revels before the *White Ship* set sail last November. Youth will have its fun, those fond watchers surely thought, those parents and sisters and doting aunts."

"I've never really heard what happened," Rhiannon whispered, her exhaustion instantly gone. A grand curiosity had just perked her like a week's dose of Mam's most potent tonic. "I merely know that the prince and others drowned when that ill-constructed ship hit a rock coming back to England from the wars in Francia."

Everyone knew that much, but until now, Rhia'd not met anyone who might know more—an aristocrat, that is. She held her breath, though she wouldn't hound Thaddeus for details, as his day had already been so fraught. Unusual restraint, for Rhia.

"You say the *White Ship* was ill-constructed, Rhia, but you've got that wrong," Thaddeus said quietly. "It was the most worthy of all ships, newly fitted out, and offered by its proud captain for the king's transport back from Francia after his great victory there last winter. King Henry thanked the captain and then gave over the sleek ship to his son William, who'd fought valiantly at his side, though barely seventeen. William invited one hundred forty young knights and some young ladies of the highest rank to sail back to England in victory with him aboard the fine

White Ship. Those privileged youth danced in the moonlight and made merry with many casks of wine before they finally boarded. It's said a group of priests traveled from Rouen to bless the ship, but were thrown into the water by the laughing crowd. All were in high spirits at the midnight of their departure, dressed in brilliant mantles of festive color, as for a grand occasion. The other vessels of Henry's fleet had long since departed, and as William's party sped through the dark waves, the prince laughingly cajoled the fifty strong oarsmen to row faster and faster so they might overtake the slower craft of their elders."

He stopped. Rhiannon swallowed. "And they . . . wrecked?" she asked.

The young monk shrugged. "The rock was there beneath the waves. Going so fast with a drunken crew, they hit it hard and square. All aboard are said to be drowned."

Rhiannon crossed herself. "But . . . who told of it, if all died?"

"A stowaway butcher from Francia survived to swim to land. They say he'd snuck aboard the ship to collect a bill owed him by one of the revelers aboard. He told of the prince's attempt to save his half-sister's life. Prince William, it seems, was quickly taken by his bodyguards to the small cockboat that was pulled behind, and he would have been rowed safely to land had he not, upon hearing Adela's screams, ordered the rower to return to the sinking ship. There, so many jumped into his lifeboat that it was swamped, and he perished with the rest."

Rhiannon had stopped listening—indeed, had stopped hearing altogether. She sat as one turned to stone. She hardly drew breath.

Thaddeus took her arm. "Rhiannon?" Alarmed, he shook her. "Rhia!"

She looked at him. "Not Adela," she breathed. "Prince William's sister was never called Adela."

Thaddeus nodded. "Adela, Countess of Perche." He leaned around to search her face. "Rhiannon, you've lost your color. Have a care upon the rocks, and let's hasten to get you something to eat before you start for home. Here, let me help you stand."

But Rhia got herself to her feet, swaying a bit. "It waxes late," she said shortly, adjusting her pack. "I must start up the trail right *now*, Thaddeus."

She snatched her skirt to her knees and well nigh ran back along the slimed rocks of the narrow beach, and not until she'd reached the place where the bluff trail merged from the sand and started its steep climb upward did she turn around to bid Thaddeus a courteous farewell.

He was behind her some paces, looking confused, as well he might. She was some sorry for that, but she'd have to confuse him more. There was no help for it.

"The butcher, Thaddeus?" she called to him. "The one who swam to shore and told the story? Do you . . . know what he looks like? I mean, might he be young and well-formed, with slender bearing and a certain pirate-like elegance?"

"I heard he was barrel-chested, bald, and of some fifty years," Thaddeus called back.

"And he the only survivor? Are they so sure of that? That he *was* the only?"

Thaddeus was growing used to Rhia's mode of thinking, which seemed some helter-skelter, but honestly was only so in the way of a spider's webweave. Her thoughts came from all directions but would eventually yield a pattern—most times, at least.

"Of such a thing there *can* be no certainty, Rhiannon, can there?" he said gently, walking closer. "Bodies have washed up weekly ever since it happened, all of them in tatters of fine raiment and with jew eled bones where ringed fingers once were. Mothers watched the beach for their lost children for days and days after the catastrophe, and watch these late days for their children's corpses. None swam ashore to arms yearning for embrace. None walked ashore seeking home. All that came ashore were brought in the icy arms of the merciless waves, and so it's said there were no survivors save the butcher, and that's the best end that can be given it. Five months have now passed. There needs *must* be an end, you know? False hope is surely much heavier to bear in the long run than lost hope."

Rhiannon dropped her head. "Yes. Those grieving mothers must go on, even if their comfort is chilly. There must be an end to it, as you've said."

Thaddeus cleared his throat. "Uhm, Rhiannon? I . . . would now ask a large favor of you. But before I do, will you stay right here? I'll be back in but a moment."

Without waiting for answer he turned and ran along the beach to the place where several drifted logs made a tangled heap. He knelt in the sand and reached into that snarl, then, with a jerk, pulled forth a damp woolen bundle. He carried that sand-shrouded pack in both arms as he ran back to where Rhiannon waited, puzzled.

"Rhia, I've decided I can't go back to your vicar's church right now," he told her in a rush. "I can't chance meeting him, looking him in the eye. Instead, I'm going on retreat for some days, or longer if needs be. That is, until my mind clears and God gives me grace to see the situation more clearly."

She swallowed. "Your brother monks would let you . . . do that? Just . . . leave?"

And what of Jim? His situation wouldn't wait for Thaddeus's mind to clear!

He nodded, then thought again and shrugged. "Retreat was encouraged at Glastonbury when a brother was troubled in mind. But here? I really don't know. I've told Brother Silas that when I'm missed he's to tell the prior I'm on retreat, and if our prior likes it not and calls me to account, Silas is to say he knows not my location."

Thaddeus looked down and solemnly brushed sand from the bundle he held. "Not a lie, as I don't know myself where I'm going, Rhia. But I don't think anyone here will miss me much. I've become a thorn in the vicar's side with my questions about Jim. It's obvious he finds me annoying, though I doubt he considers me a real threat, young as I am. My brother monks will surely welcome a break from me as well. The vicar's annoyance with me has begun to stir the waters, as he is ofttimes testy with all."

He then knelt, put the woolen pack upon the ground, and concentrated on carefully unrolling it as he spoke in a voice that was much changed, quieter and hoarse. "It's been six years since my father gave me as oblate, and now I'm seventeen. I love God, and the good abbot at Glastonbury was in all things His servant. I saw in him that a brother might attain great wisdom and peace of heart through serving others in Christ's name, but is that in me to do? On retreat, I *must* decide whether to take my final vows."

Rhia's throat ached, so much did Thaddeus's dilemma suddenly remind her of her own. Mam, too, was a great servant of God, but Rhia often doubted her own ability to be such a selfless healer as Mam. To tell it true, Rhia oft doubted her own willingness to stay forever upon the bluff doing such hard work, *that* was the thing.

"I hope you fare well with this, Thaddeus," she forced out. "And if the favor you seek is that I tell no one of seeing you, rest assured my lips are sealed." She then made the rash decision to quickly spill her real thoughts, though he might think her a meddlesome scold. "But Mam and the rest of us upon the bluff *will* miss you sorely! We call you true friend, and would have cherished your considered advice and ready help right now. With the lepers, that is. And, of course, with Jim."

The young monk blew out a long, relieved breath, then looked up at her and smiled.

"Your words have made my request much easier, Rhiannon, as I wondered if you and your family would grant me use of one of the hospice cottages for my retreat from the brotherhood? I'd pay my way with chores, and as well, I'd ask leave to paint inside the little church. It's some dark the way it is, and paintings of Our Lord's life here on earth would be fitting treatment for those walls. I would pray as I worked, for my work *is* my truest form of prayer."

He'd reached the final fold in the cloth and displayed for her his well-loved paints and brushes. "As you see, I'm set to go with you right now, if you give me leave."

She crouched beside him to reach and touch the bristles of a brush, then lifted two or three of the small pots of paints. Her quiet gestures might have seemed to the young monk like sincere appreciation of the tools of his work.

But in truth she noticed not what she was doing, whether it was brushes she was touching or the quills of a living porcupine. For to touch those brushes and paintpots was the only ready way she had of grounding herself, elsewise she feared she might spin right up into the air, buoyed by the pure joy she felt upon hearing Thaddeus's plans.

"You'd be most welcome among us, Thaddeus," she finally found breath to say.

"Brother Thaddeus. That's indeed what I will call you now." She smiled over her shoulder at him, then turned round treacherously so she walked backward as they climbed single file up the trail. "You're to be my brother upon the bluff, and a welcome son for Mam. So *brother*, Thaddeus. How's that?"

He smiled back, then reached forward to yank one of the many small braids Rhia'd made in her hair that morn. "How's *that* for a brotherly action, *sister* Rhia? Now, as elder brother, I'd order you to turn back around and face forward e'er you step wrong!"

"Aye, aye, wise brother!" She turned, giggling and obedient, but muttering, "Daisy as small tag-along sister and now you as *bossy* brother. My *dream* family, for sure. A small pest and a lordly tyrant!"

Suddenly, a black shadow soared 'twixt the bluff and the sun, racing across the moss and stone so that Rhia stopped all her teases and shivered with real foreboding.

"Creeee-*awwwk*. Cra-ra-ra-awwkk!"

"Oh, Gramp!" Rhia let her breath out in a giddy, relieved laugh, feeling her knees atremble. "Good winged sire, the sight of you is most welcome, but I need no more jolts today, if it please!"

Gramp came in for a landing upon a slender willow tree that grew from a small fissure in the steep trail, bending it nigh to the ground with his cumbrous weight. He made a right silly sight, bobbing on his tiny branch just feet from the two of them.

But woe to anyone who took as fool that large and crusty bird upon his tiny, bouncing perch. For Gramp had not flown clear to meet them for no small reason. Indeed, he was now staring hard into the woods and had begun a throaty growl with his neck feathers spiked and his eye feathers gathered to a menacing squint.

Rhia reluctantly followed his gaze, then yanked on Thaddeus's sleeve and pointed.

There, deep inside the twisted vines and dense shadows of the forest, stood the riderless horse she'd seen first on Ona's funeral morn! It looked straight at them with large wet eyes that seemed so filled with loneliness and yearning that Rhiannon's breath caught in her throat.

"What would the beast have us know?" Thaddeus whispered, as though he'd read her thoughts. "Is it a mount from Lord Claredemont's stables, gone missing?"

"It must be," she breathed, "as no one else upon the manor rides. The vicar's acolytes use donkeys sometimes, but never would mount a horse."

Gramp, reassured now the other two had seen the threat, hunched down into his neck feathers and surveyed the horse with cooler eyes, giving up his growl.

"We'll tell Almund Clap about this lost steed as soon as we may," Rhia decided. "He'll take it back to where it belongs. Though it's strange it hasn't returned on its own, or been searched for and found by the lord's groomsmen."

Thaddeus nodded agreement. And still they stood quietly watching for a while, as it was impossible to pull one's gaze away from the beast's great, beseeching eyes.

It was the horse that finally broke the spell. He shook his head, sending his long mane spinning, then cantered away through the thick trees.

By then the trail had grown treacherous with twilight. They hastened their step, and Rhia felt a niggling dread, as the sun had most certainly gone to the nether side of the steeple tower ages ago. Mam would be fit to be tied.

Chapter 17

In fact, the sun had clean finished his nightly sink into the choppy waters of the bay when they reached the top of the trail. The sky was swirled with vivid hues of orange and woad. A hush hung over the woods as all creatures made tracks for home, and the rough see-saw of the crickets and peepers and other night chirpers was just starting up.

"I hope I'll be welcomed." Thaddeus sounded worried. "I lack true invitation—from your mother, I mean. I'd not be a burden to her, nor to your grandmother, either."

At that, Rhia laughed. "Thaddeus, you'll be the great and good surprise that makes Mam forget to chide me for this close-cut return." Too close, really, and she added, some nervously, "I *would* say it's almost still twilight, wouldn't you?"

"Well," he said, giving a shrug. Rhia decided to take that as a yes.

The settlement now loomed in the clearing just ahead. Something seemed odd, though. The door to their cottage was closed, unusual on a warm spring night, and the window remained uncandled, though light from the firepit danced upon the walls.

That firelight was not cut by the usual shadows of people moving inside the house, though. Where *was* everyone? She cast her eyes over the other cots.

Sal's window was candlelit, but no candle burned in the window of the French pirate. The door of *his* cot, which Rhia had most times pushed hard upon and with reluctance, now hung wide open, thudding back against the wattle in the rising wind!

"Hark," Thaddeus whispered. "Someone weeps at Sally's place."

Rhia nodded. "It must be Sal herself," she whispered back. "It's not Mam nor Granna, nor could such a low voice be Daisy. Whatever's wrong has surely brought the others to her side, though. I've *never* heard Sally cry before. She's too damaged to know how much she's lost, so never goes to whining nor wailing about it."

A sudden and quite terrifying sound then issued from the open door of the pirate's dark cottage, a cry much resembling the muffled shriek of a forest creature beside itself with the pain of a greater creature's toothed attack.

Rhia's hands went to her mouth but she was too frozen of brain to speak or act.

"Whoever is in that cottage needs immediate help!" Thaddeus asserted, heading toward the open door from which issued the pitiful keening.

"Wait, wait!" Rhiannon grabbed his sleeve and spoke in a frantic rush. "I wanted to tell you something of this earlier, but hadn't the chance! Thaddeus, remember when I told you of the Man Who Sleeps, that he was past knowing anything at all? Well, I was mistaken, for he has indeed come awake these past days! The moaning we hear is certainly his, yet things are never as they seem with him. He may be dangerous!"

"But he needs quick attendance!"

Thaddeus strained to proceed, but Rhiannon dug in her heels and detained him, grasping his arm with both hands.

"If there was quick help to give him, do you not think Mam would have given it? The fact that his door is left wide open tells me that Mam has had some encounter with him, mayhaps involving Sally, causing her to weep so pitifully! Some encounter less than gentle, for certain, as he is a great deal addled, also shaded, and unknowable. And . . . he has a dark wish."

That did the trick. The young monk was now all ears. "A dark wish?"

Rhia nodded and released her hold. "He says he would sleep forever. He sees terrible things in his head—hellish visions, nightmare scenes. You may do him harm, or he may harm *you*, as he may mistake you for some shade come from his dreaming world. He ofttimes calls *me* a dream name, the name of some phantom sister of his . . . Adela."

Thaddeus's eyes widened with that. "Adela? Like the countess who perished aboard the *White Ship*, the half-sister of . . ."

She quickly nodded.

He paused a moment. "So *that's* why you insisted upon knowing for certain if there were survivors of that tragedy." He took a breath and let it out. "Though, of course, Adela is a common enough name, in the Norman tongue."

For an instant their eyes met, and they acknowledged the slenderest possibility of the impossible. Much like the impossibility of dragons held within an artfully decorated chamber, deep within marshy ground. Impossible, but . . . just possible.

"We must go first to Sal's," Rhiannon stated firmly, leading the way.

All were in the cottage—Granna and Daisy, Mam and poor distressed Sal, who sat upon the pallet with her head upon Mam's shoulder and her pale face blotched from hard weeping. Daisy sat close on Sally's other side with Queen Matilda held fast against her chest in mimic of the embrace given Sal by Mam. Granna stood on her two feet near the pallet like a tree grown up through the floor, watching it all and clucking her tongue.

Sally was the first to spot Rhiannon standing in the doorway. The weeping girl sat up rigid, reaching her arms toward Rhia and trying to say her saying, though she hiccupped through it, which was right pathetic. "Three . . . huck, huck . . . *three* . . . huck! Huck *fish!*"

Rhiannon ran and knelt at Sal's knees. "Oh, Sal, whatever's happened to grieve you so?" She took Sally's hands into her own, searching Sal's empty eyes. "Oh, Sally, nothing should ever, ever intrude upon your peace again, nor pain you!"

It was a mark of their worry over Sal that when Thaddeus walked silently over the threshold to stand beside Granna, all merely nodded as though he'd been expected.

Mam whispered to Rhiannon, "Daughter, I ask your forgiveness. I should have considered that you wouldn't tell me the sleeper had come awake unless you'd seen it. Had I taken you at your word, Sally might have been spared this ordeal."

Rhiannon looked Sally over. There was neither blood nor bruise upon her, not that Rhia could see. The cloth of her nightshift was some ripped at the neckline, though.

Granna meanwhile leaned to speak from the side of her mouth to Thaddeus. "You are most welcome, young monk," she told him, gruffly and quietly. "Whatever the reason for the climb up, it was well-timed, as we have ne'er before dealt with such a lunatic. Why, the one next door may be devil possessed, and if so we'll have certain need of a monkish priest such as yourself!"

Thaddeus whispered back to her, "Will you walk outside with me, to fill me in?"

As they exited Sal's cottage, Granna stepped quite spritely and kept Thaddeus between her and the cot wherein crouched the man she'd decided was most certainly a lunatic. She slowed to a hobble, though, when they were some way past that danger, and she took the young monk's arm as they neared the hives. There, she sat heavily down upon the work stump and took a big heave of breath, shaking her head. The bees stopped their drone to get a good listen to what she'd say.

"Well then, young monk, here's what happened," she set in. "Rhiannon had told us the sleeper was awake sometimes, but we discounted that, as none of us had seen him so much as move a muscle. Until this afternoon, that is, when, as Aigy noted, we found the hard way that we ne'er should have doubted our Rhia. Aigneis was taking Sally for a short walk in the nice weather, and she thought to stop and check the sleeper whilst she was about it. She had Sally by the hand when she came up to the pallet where he lay. We now believe he's watched with slitted eye our comings and goings for some time, as when he glimpsed poor Sal he sat smack up and reached to put rough hands upon her afore Aigy could think what was happening!"

The bees got even quieter, as though they'd been shocked and now held their breaths.

Thaddeus quietly asked, "Rough hands?"

Granna pushed out her bottom lip and nodded. "She'd a little charm upon her bodice, see? Rhia'd given it to her this morning, and Sally seemed to think it quite the thing, kept touching it and looking down at it. It was silver and shaped like a clamshell. Well, *he* wanted that charm, was it. He reached and tore it right off Sally's shift as rough as you please, and that put Sally to screaming fierce. Those screams is what brought *me* to the scene of the crime. By then the lunatic had pilfered that charm and was hunkered down upon his haunches in the corner of his cot with it. Aigneis had hustled Sally back to her own cot by then, and Daisy'd joined them. I and those two has been there since, comforting Sal as best we could while the other one hunkered and howled next door."

Granna sighed and took her pipe from its pouch. "Sally is not hurt, that's a blessing. She's mostly afeared because the loony what took her charm put her in mind of her bad brother what cracked her noggin, that's my take on it. Poor helpless little thing."

Thaddeus had stood silent through this account. Now he asked, "Did the sleeper who's now woken say anything at all when he acted so rudely? Drop some word that might tell us why he became so agitated about that charm?"

The moon was now high in the sky, and the courtyard lustrous, though the door of the man they talked of yawned open and black as the mouth of a cavern.

Granna hard-eyed Thaddeus. "Interesting you ask it that way, monk," she muttered. "He *did* drop a single word. Aigy says that he pronounced that one word right clear when he lunged at Sal, and he says it o'er and o'er even now. Can you not hear it woven within his moans? *Aleron*, that's the word, if word it be."

Though they were at some distance, the man's pitiful keening still reached their ears. And within that formless sound there floated those three syllables: *A—le—ron*. He moaned them as a child may moan its mother's name, enclosed in blubbers and boohoos.

"*Ayyyy . . . ahhhyyy . . . ahyyeeeeleron!*" the wretched man wailed.

"Yes, I do hear! Aleron is a Norman name, mistress. A name given males."

"Norman, you say?" Granna spat upon the ground. "I mighta *thunk* they'd be the root of such trouble."

"And here's something else," the young monk continued excitedly. "The silver shell? I believe it's a pilgrimage token. In fact, I think it's a badge from the church where the bones of Saint James are said to lie, in far Espania. Do you know where Rhia got it?"

Granna slapped her knees. "Well, not in Espania, monk! Unless she grew back the birdy wings of her great-granddames and flew there unbeknownst to us one fine night! You'll have to ask her yerself where it came from."

Granna pulled upon Thaddeus's arm and rose.

"I'll go on home to see what the fire may have to say of all this," she said. "Take me there, please, then hasten back to be with the others, if you will."

When Thaddeus had seen her safely situated beside her fire, he hurried back to Sal's, resisting the strong temptation to enter the cot of the mysterious man instead.

They sat much as before, with Rhia now finger-combing Sally's hair and with Daisy upon Aigy's lap, her eyes nearly closed and her thumb in her mouth. "I'm hungry," she mentioned, yawning large. "Did we ever eat?"

"We did not, and we should," Mam answered gently, putting Daisy to her feet, then standing herself. She turned to Thaddeus. "I'll be glad of your escort, sir, as we take Sally home with us. It's been a hard afternoon and all, I think, are nigh exhausted."

As they shared bread and soup that night, they spoke of light things, talk suitable for Sally and young Daisy, leaving matters of more import to be discussed later. Thaddeus timidly asked if he might stay with them a few days and was given wholehearted welcome by all. Rhia told the news of market, and of the rough riders through it, making the story seem a bit funny, honking geese, that sort of thing. She passed along to Granna the spidery bunion cure given her by Hilda Mopp, then turned to Daisy. "Everyone at the ale booth asked about you. They were overjoyed that you've healed so well."

It was decided Sal and Daisy would go along to bed in the sleep loft, with Rhia joining them up there later. Mam gently braced Sal from beneath and Rhia held her arms from above, and in this way Sal made it slowly up the six rungs of the ladder, step-together-*step*, step-together-*step*. Rhia washed their hands and faces with the rose water kept in a wooden trencher on the stool beneath the clothes pegs, then put them both in clean sleepshifts. She settled Sal in bed and let Daisy kneel and say the bedtime prayer Mam had taught her. When Daisy finished and climbed to the pallet, she snuggled close to Sal and embraced her as she'd embraced her own sister Primrose in sleep, and Sal smiled at that and closed her eyes. Rhia, smiling herself, crept back down the ladder.

Her smile faded as she heard Thaddeus just then breaking the news to Mam and Granna of the gold brought from the earl's man to buy Jim's false confession. That cast a gloom over the entire house, of course.

"It's why I've left," Thaddeus told them. "I couldn't dwell within walls that held such treachery. Though God may think my judgment is uninformed and hasty, so I'll take back those words, for now. It's what retreat is for, to question one's own thinking."

"Hmmph." Granna closed one eye and leaned toward him, gesturing hard with her pipe stem. "Too much of that sort of second thinking can garble up your brains! You saw what you saw, young monk, and that's an end to it. The vicar is as crooked as a humpbacked snake. It's no grand surprise, not to me."

201

Mam sighed and rubbed her neck. "Thaddeus, you will have Jim's old cottage, if that suits. The pallet has been made up anew and the place swept out since Jim's left. Take a jug of water with you, and a candle. Upon the morrow we'll see what else may be needed, but I think you'll find it sufficient for tonight."

She stood to get the water jug, and whilst her back was turned, Rhia shot Thaddeus a look, then cleared her throat. "Mam, should I not at least close the door of the cot next to Sal's? Or . . . maybe take the man a bowl of gruel? Thaddeus could go with me."

Mam stopped in her work and turned back around with her hands upon her hips.

"Rhia, don't even think about it. Understand me?"

There's a way a mother says a thing with each syllable separate and grim, and that's how Mam said this, thus leaving no chance whatsoever for Rhiannon to think she could change her mother's mind. Nevertheless, Rhia took a try at it.

"Hark, he no longer howls! I'm sure he's grown peaceable again, and likely regrets the events of the afternoon. This morning I *told* him I'd be back by evening! He said he needed a friend, and I said I'd come! I *must*, with Thaddeus. Would you have me lie?"

Rhia glanced at Thaddeus and saw his lips pressed tight and his eyes lifted skyward.

"Hee, hee," Granna snickered from her place beside the fire.

Mam wagged her finger at Rhia. "A false question, that. For his own actions have made us *all* fearful of him this night. I would rather you lie, daughter, than *lie* broken and bruised, a second victim of this man's unpredictable nature."

"She's right, you know," Thaddeus whispered, and that made Rhia right angry.

In fact, she could have just *spit* at all present, that's how angry she was at being treated like some . . . some *child!* Why, she'd seen the French pirate like this before, twice in fact, and had handled him just fine! A pity she couldn't mention those two events, as Mam would be all the *more* stubbornly afeared. If anyone was to get to the bottom of this outrage against poor Sal, why, *she* was the one who could do it, she and she alone! With Thaddeus as backup, of course, since it *was* right dark.

But there they were, all three of them ranged stubbornly against her well-considered plan, though she was fourteen, *fifteen* in three months!

She flounced across the room. "I go to bed then, since you have so little trust in me!" She hoped her words made them all ashamed and sorry. When no one rushed to repent, she pounded her feet upon the six rungs of the loft ladder so they'd have a second chance to consider their rude and misthought treatment of her.

Only when she stood upon the floor of the loft did she recall that since she slept downstairs these days, her sleepshift was hanging on the kitchen hook, not up here where it had used to be. Well, who cared? She kicked off her shoes and loosed the cord about her waist, then flopped in her skirt and blouse upon the pallet, pushing Daisy forward a bit with her hip to make herself some room.

As she ofttimes did, Rhiannon dreamt that she was winged. Over the wide water she flew, with dolphins far below, racing her shadow as they jumped through the green waves. But how came dolphins to make the low growl that suddenly gave a sense of menace to this peaceful dream? "Crrrrrr. Crrrrrrrrrrr. Rrrrrrrrrrr-ruh. *Ruh!*"

Gramp! She came wide awake and pushed up to one elbow. Gramp seldom gave that particular sinister sound, and when he did you'd best pay attention, as it signaled something extremely dire! She slipped from the pallet and raced to the gap in the twigs.

Upon the chapel roof she saw the frowsy clot of darker darkness that was Gramp engaged in his usual vigilant nightwatch. His wings were spread in a threatening way, and he looked straight down betwixt his rough old feet.

Something went on *within* the church, then! But what, at this midnight hour?

The moon was lined up so that it shone through the nether windows of the small sanctuary and then through the two windows on this side, as well. She squinted and pushed her forehead right against the twigs, trying to see what she might of any movement inside. She could perceive nothing—no shadows, no disturbance.

And yet, Gramp stood highly alerted and gave that most urgent gruntish growl deep in his throat that was never false alarm, not ever in Rhiannon's lifelong experience.

She jerked her skirt cord tight, then took her shoes and went silent as she was able down the ladder. She tiptoed to light a taper from their candle, then opened the door slowly, slowly, so its creaking might not waken the two who slept beside the fire. Neither stirred, as Granna snored full, obscuring the small sounds of Rhia's escape and the sounds of Gramp's concerned growls, as well. To tell it true, the Devil Dogs of Clodagh might escape their hidden cave tonight and fight each other upon Mam's table, and neither Granna nor Mam would likely hear above Granna's present broadcasts.

Outside Rhia knotted her hair and put on her shoes, then scurried around the side of the cot so she could get a clear look at the church. Gramp had not moved and still gave that throaty rumble of a growl, though nothing about the churchyard seemed changed at all. She took a deep breath, and ran across to the chapel door. She paused there to look up at Gramp. Girl and bird looked hard at each other.

"Is someone inside?" Rhia whispered.

"Crrrrruk," warned the bird.

Chapter 18

Then Rhia figured out who the intruder to the chapel must be, and slapped her forehead. "Oh, Gramp, it's only Thaddeus! Monks must arise in the darkest part of the night to pray, and I'm sure he'd seek the church for it!"

Much fortified by this certainty, Rhia put her shoulder to the door and shoved hard.

Still, any visitor to an ancient chapel at midnight must keep company with its usual resident phantoms and saintly spirits. Rhia stepped inside and let the door creak closed behind her. The moonlight shone off the ancient stones of the walls and the floor, exposing mists that danced through the breeze she'd let in.

Mists and ghostly vapors, most certainly both.

"Thaddeus?" she whispered, and heard that little sound absorbed by the gloom.

The hermit who'd built the chapel was certainly buried down a short stairway behind a stone of granite set into the east wall. Rhia'd been shown his grave by Granna long ago, and the two of them now took flowers down to his bones each year on his name day. What was less certain was if there were other folk buried beneath the large, smooth stones that she was now walking upon. Granna's opinion was that it seemed likely, as why else would those stones be cut long as a man was tall?

Monks were buried in this floor, was Granna's guess. The ancient stories had it that monks had hidden within the chapel upon the bluff when the Northmen arrived in their fiercesome dragonboats and burned the great monasteries, seeking the golden chalices and other precious treasures kept there. Trouble was, the Northmen worked their way clear across England and eventually pillaged even this bluff. Two of Granna's great-grandmother's little sisters were killed by those bloodthirsty raiders, so wouldn't any churchmen hiding out up here have lost their lives as well? Certainly, Granna reasoned.

Sad, if the monks had indeed sought safety upon the high bluff and been killed instead. Well, any death was sad, and that was the truth of it. Though all die, of course.

Rhia shivered and clutched Mam's little cross, tapping it upon her chin and wishing she could think of something besides death and spirits, though that's never easy in an ancient church at midnight.

The candleflame flickered with some wind that came in through the wide-ledged windows. The flame did not go out, thanks be to God. Rhia wet her lips, and asked again, "Thaddeus, are you here?" Receiving no answer, she turned to go, the flesh along the back of her neck acreep with the caressing fingers of unseen things.

Her hand was upon the iron ring that would open the door and give her release, when far behind her she heard the unmistakable sound of heavy stone scraping slowly against heavy stone. Her heart went quivery so she could not get a good breath, nor could she gather the wit to pull upon the iron ring and exit. She could do naught but turn back around, hoping to find that her ears had somehow deceived her.

But they had not. The granite stone sealing the hermit's crypt was being pushed aside from within! And when it yawned wide, a bent figure slowly emerged from the ancient tomb and began to hobble toward her with one hand extended. "Rhiannon . . ."

Without a breath to protest, all she could do was hold the candle in the phantom's direction and stare wide-eyed, though soon enough she perceived with vast relief that it was *not* the ancient hermit arisen from his grave. It was rather the French pirate! He fell to his knees and knelt there swaying a bit, his hand still held out toward her.

If his keening earlier in the night had been a wild tempest, now she saw in his bearing the devastation such a storm may well leave in its wake. And yet in spite of the ragged exhaustion that showed upon his face and in his bowed shoulders, he somehow seemed more solid, more *real* than he'd been before.

She took cautious steps toward him. He was very still, the blinking of his eyes the only thing that showed he lived and breathed.

When she was but the length of a floor stone from him, she stopped and held the candle up between them to better see his face. For certain, he was much changed from the blustering play actor he'd been. He was no longer pale effigy nor frightened invalid, either one. He certainly was no berserker pirate, nor flighty scamp of any kind.

In point of fact, as she perceived up close the bottomless sadness upon his face, she gasped and covered her mouth with her hand, stricken to the core.

"Yes, as you see, I've remembered," he said quietly. "I know precisely who I am."

And though later she could never explain to herself exactly why, she dropped to her own knees and bent her head before him as one naturally does before high royalty.

"Don't," he whispered, reaching to clutch her hand. "Rhiannon, never do that, and never say you saw me here upon your bluff. Will you grant this boon for the sake of friendship? I'll leave directly, before the new day breaks. Within the hermit's tomb I'll pray for my soul this night, and then I will take a penitent's garb anew and follow the pilgrim's road again. Many months ago I pledged myself to follow that path forever until, upon my knees, I died and found Divine forgiveness. Or damnation, as God wills."

She shook her head. "How . . . come you to be hid within the hermit's tomb?" It wasn't the most important of the many things she needed to know, just the first to form itself so that she could speak it.

"Your friend, the monk, stopped by my cottage earlier this night. I believe he thought to find me lunatic, but after a hellish afternoon I was finally come to myself, as you see me now. He suggested we pray together within this chapel, and as we entered he pointed out the hermit's tomb. Later, I returned alone to pray there." He took a breath and looked down. "My good friend Aleron and I sought out the tombs of saints, you see. We took the pilgrim road together as penitents, seeking peace. Now, I must travel alone, as Aleron is . . . is gone. I have recovered his token from our pilgrimage to Saint James's tomb. He would never have parted with that sacred memento while he lived, and so I know that my only friend in the world is most certainly . . . most surely . . . dead."

Rhia swallowed. "If you wayfared together, how came you to be separated from him?"

"In Wales, upon the road to Saint Winifred's holy shrine, we were overtaken by thieves. I was hit upon the head and some Samaritan must have found me lying thus beside the road and brought me up to your bluff. I know not what became of Aleron when we were set upon, but I know he surely died looking for me. I *know* he did."

In the set of his jaw, Rhiannon saw the grief he felt. He spoke no further, but raised one fisted hand, then opened it. The flesh of his palm was torn by the clasp of the little clamshell. For a moment she didn't recognize the shell itself, so bloodied was it. She reached her fingers to explore his wound, worried that his hand badly needed dressing. But he flinched and brought his fingers closed over the shell again, then raised that bloodied fist and pressed it hard upon his chest, over his heart.

Shaking her head, she whispered, "I don't even know what name to call you."

At first he made her no answer. Then, "Call me Jonah," he said.

She nodded, then seized every bit of nerve she had. "Sir Jonah, you say you will be gone before the morrow, but that will not sit well with my mother, who has nursed you all these past days. I feel you could surely tarry one day longer, to reveal yourself as healed at last. It'll give her mind's ease."

She bit her lip and watched him pondering how to answer.

"Another thing you should consider is the maiden who wore the shell," she pressed. "She's dimwit, and you gave her a fright that may take long recovery."

"I was beside myself and owe her sincere apology," he answered quickly enough. But he stopped at that and looked down, thinking. Finally, he confided, "Indeed I owe a great debt to you and your kin, and amends to the girl. But I cannot lose another day. I must hasten to find the trail of Aleron's murderers before it has gone colder."

So *that* was it. She squinted her eyes. "Well, by that I know you are not *all* meek pilgrim, Sir Jonah, for surely such a one would turn the other cheek and leave justice for the bailiffs of the world! No, you reveal yourself to be still a soldier, as you claimed to be while you were still fogged in your mind from your injury."

His eyes widened at that, but then he had the grace to own up to it.

"Truly, I am not perfected yet in the gentle ways of holiness.

Indeed, I once soldiered, though no more. And I *will* return to my pledged calling of pilgrimage as soon as my friend's murderers have found comeuppance at my hand."

Rhia's heart beat fast and her eyes shone as she leaned closer. "Then, sir, you are in luck. For it was I who found the token Dull Sal wore, and quite nearby! I propose a deal to you. Tarry for just one more day and I promise to show you exactly where I picked that token from the stream. Surely that's the place your quest for vengeance must begin."

Why, she'd just discovered within herself the moxie to spring a trap as well as ever Maddy could! Rhia was some surprised at herself— and pleased, she'd admit it.

Her astonished quarry was not so pleased. "I beg of you, show me tonight! Right *now*! To make me wait longer is sheer torture!"

She shook her head firmly, crossing her arms. "Tomorrow. Stay only one day. That's all I ask." She then used his own earlier words to press her advantage. "Will you grant this boon for the sake of friendship?"

After a moment he sighed, and then even smiled a bit at being so cornered. She took that as agreement to her plan, and stood to go before he could change his mind.

"I leave you now to get whatever rest you may with our holy hermit. Upon the morrow, my mother will rejoice to see you journeyed back to yourself, Sir Jonah."

She nodded him a farewell and hastened from the church, giving Gramp a similar nod while she pulled the church door closed behind her.

Gramp folded his wings and yawned a wide and beaky yawn at this sign from Rhia that all was now well, or at least well enough. Mayhaps he thought to catch a nap, as much had been aslant upon the bluff of late. Yes, there'd been constant need for his vigilance day and night, which naturally took its toll, though seldom was he thanked.

Rhiannon hurried across the churchyard and rounded the back corner of her cottage with a thousand new questions careening in her head like bats in dark rafters.

Which is why, when the mysterious woodland horse galloped past along the rim of the forest, carrying upon his back the will-o'-wisp spirit of young Primrose, it took her a long moment to realize the right wondrous sight her eyes had just by chance beheld.

Double wonder it was, in fact! The horse and the phantom child, both!

"Wait!" she called out, to no avail. She now perceived only the moonlit silvery tail of the horse disappearing as he and his ghostly rider veered through the tree line, heading back into the heart of the midnight woods.

Rhiannon stood transfixed, her eyes on the place where the silent horse and rider had parted the dense thicket. She dared not so much as breathe or twitch in the close wake of such an enchantment, for fear the faery world would take offense.

"Rhia? Did you see what I saw?"

Rhiannon whirled to face Thaddeus, who'd just stepped from the shadows she herself had come through along the nether side of their cot.

She placed her hand upon her hip and glowered at him.

"I *guess* you mean did I perceive the horse and rider. But you *may* well mean did I perceive the man who slept and now kneels within our church! How *dare* you not side with me as I begged Mam to go check on him, Thaddeus! Then, alone, *you* checked on him! I take that very, very hard! He's *my* sometime lunatic invalid. Mine!"

Her voice had risen above the whisper required by the place and the hour. She recovered herself and leaned an ear toward the house, nervously listening for ill effects. But within the cot, Granna still snored her finest, which was a good mask for any sound less than typhoon. Thus Rhia felt free to continue her complaint in a strident whisper.

"Thaddeus, you've treated me as a *child* with this!"

Thaddeus had his hands tucked into his sleeves. He looked nervously down at the knobs of his wrists and cleared his throat. "You're mistaken, Rhiannon," he said simply, "My fear was not that you were too much child, but that you were too much . . . grown. I would worry for your safety in any man's night chamber."

She blinked.

"Besides, folk oft regard a monk as safe confessor, if he comes alone." He dared a glance at her from under his brows. "It's embarrassing, really, to be trusted as we are. For where gossip's concerned, all the holy brothers I've e'er met could hold their own with your granna's cronies at the ale booth, and that's a fact."

Rhia bit her lips. "Will you joke me from my just anger, *Brother* Thaddeus?"

"If I can," Thaddeus admitted with a shrug. "For as you've said, you *are* my sister whilst I'm here, and I'd not have you stay upset with me."

She sighed and gave him a begrudging smile, then grew somber.

"Thaddeus," she whispered, "did Jonah tell you that he ripped the clamshell off Sally's shift because it had belonged to his bosom friend?"

"Jonah?" Thaddeus looked surprised. "Forgive me. I did not know his name, and now you tell it, I find it intriguing. Jonah, as you've called him, only talked with me of spiritual things. He said he'd wrestled with demons and was wearied to the bone by it. I could see he told

213

that true. He asked me to accompany him to the chapel, and we prayed awhile, then parted ways. I was not made privy to any details of his life."

Rhia nodded. "Even now he prays within the hermit's tomb. He says the shell is a pilgrimage token, and that he and his friend Aleron prayed ofttimes at such shrines. He believes his friend is dead, Thaddeus. Murdered! He says if Aleron still drew breath, he wouldn't have surrendered that token. That's what set him to wailing when he saw the shell on Sally. Though the wailing was a boon, really, as his extreme misery seems to have burned away the foggy threads of his confusion. He's remembered himself at last."

Thaddeus murmured, "Jonah is a very unusual name in these times. Though if you were lost at sea, then cast upon the shore in a rough state, it might suit you to take such a name for yourself."

They looked at each other for a long moment, then Thaddeus shrugged and smiled. "I believe I can now find sleep, as you must, too. Just tell me one more thing, Rhia. Your granna says you gave the shell to Sally, so where exactly did *you* find it?"

She thought. "Well, I found it at the crossing of the river just where you come out of the ashy trees at the trail's end, then a little ways toward the edge of the barley field. It gleamed in the water near the nut tree, the one with gnarled roots. Why do you ask?"

Thaddeus frowned. "No special reason. Just curious is all. I bid you a good night, Rhia, what's left of it. Sleep well."

He turned to walk back to Jim's cot, but Rhiannon hastened after him. "Oh no you don't! Brother dear, I will right now strangle you with the rope around your waist if you don't spill your thoughts!"

Over his shoulder, he said, "You'll sleep better not knowing them till the morrow."

She reached and grabbed one dangling end of his waist rope, making to wrap it round and round his neck.

He turned, his hands raised in submission. "Well, then, Rhiannon, since you'd throttle your dear brother merely to assuage your flaming curiosity, here it is. Almund has shown me the exact place where he discovered the body of the man Jim stands accused of killing. He asked me not to reveal it to your family, in respect for your peace of mind when you pass that way. But as you plan to rough me up, I'll save my neck by telling you that it was right exactly at the gnarled roots of the large nut tree."

She dropped the end of the waist rope and they stood staring at each other.

"Just where I found the clamshell," she whispered.

Thaddeus nodded solemnly. "Rhia, I believe we may now call our murdered stranger by his Christian name. I'm most certain it must be . . ."

"Aleron," she finished quietly.

Chapter 19

Thaddeus had been right and Rhia *would* have slept better without knowing his thoughts until the morrow. A dead man with a name and a grieving friend is a different thing entirely from a gray stranger upon the butcher slab, touched by all but loved by none. He'd hardly seemed a person, then. Now, he did. *Aleron.* The name swam through her half-formed dreams, sometimes as an echo, other times as a banshee screech.

She snuggled closer to Daisy's sharp little back, buried her face in Daisy's tree-smelling tangled hair, and then fell into deeper slumber and dreamt she was wandering down a lonely trail in dense fog, searching for her drowned father. *Aleron,* sang voices in the fog. *Your da is long gone—like Aleron,* sang the gloomy fog.

She woke from that awful dream shivering, and to warm herself she named in her mind the folk she loved, living *and* dead. For Rhia well knew that death cannot fend against love, and even the grave could not steal her father from her heart. Picturing his face, she drifted off again, this time to a short dreamless rest that ended when Daisy turned and jabbed a knee to her ribs so sharp, Rhia flinched backward, teetered for an instant on the edge of the sleep pallet, then lost that hold and landed upon the hard floor.

She came to a sit and stayed there for a few moments, rubbing her hurts. Then she remembered the intrigues of the night and forgot all the slight pains of her thump in her eagerness to start the new day. She sped to the gap in the roof twigs, but found it still very dark outside. Gramp slept on the chapel roof with his beak in his wing. And what of

Sir Jonah—did he still stay cramped among the hermit's bones, or had he found it too rough and damp and made his way back to his cot? Thaddeus at least might be up and praying, as monks are said to rise before dawn for that purpose. She'd find him.

But she might sleep one moment longer first. She sank to her side on the floor there in the corner and did not wake until the sun was full up, splattering the loft with patches of buttery light. Daisy and Sal were gone from the pallet, and those two never rose early!

Down the ladder Rhia sped, her heart thumping at all she'd likely missed.

"Granna, what's gone on?" she demanded, for Granna sat alone, watching the firepit.

"*All* are gone on, granddaughter," she teased. "The two young men are gone off with your mother to take food and drink to those quartered in the woods. Sally and Daisy play out near the hives. They dress up the tortoise for a wedding they plan. The bride be grasshopper and the vicar a beetle they've caught. No, wait—one be grasshopper, the other beetle, though I don't believe I was told which be which, whether the beetle be bride or vicar. Let me think on it and I should be able to—"

Rhia was sore impatient with this. "So Sir Jonah explained everything, then?" she asked in a rush and with a scowl she hoped might make Granna desist with her talk of buggy weddings. "And he is no longer feared but rather welcomed in this house?"

Granna took a breath, blew it out, and frowned at the fire. "Oh, he's given apology for taking Sally's clamshell, if *that's* what ye mean," she muttered, "though he's not offered to give it back. He says it belonged to his lost friend, the one he wailed about so when he went lunatic. He seems well recovered for one who'd put up such a powerful fuss, and polite enough, if you can *trust* such quick-found manners from one

217

who'd lately raised such a howl some might have thunk him a true hellish demon. A handsome lad, now he's come to hisself. Your mother's much pleased that he's healed."

Something was wrong. "Why don't you like him, Granna?" Rhia dared ask.

Granna turned out her pipe and tamped the cold ashes into her hand. " 'Tis the *flames* don't like him, Rhia. No, as the fire tells it, he's not who he claims to be." She threw the ashes into the firepit. There was a sharp pop and blue sparks flew high. "There! Can you not see the man-shaped shadow that flickers brightly in the middle? You'll note that shadow has no face. This young man calls hisself Jonah, but the flames paint him faceless to say that is not his *true* identity."

Rhia fell to remembering how she'd dropped to her knees in the night upon first seeing Sir Jonah newly come to himself. Granna was suspicious of him, fearing him a danger, mayhaps even a demon. But Rhia's hunch was opposite. She feared him not, but felt boundless pity for him if the impossible proved true and he was who he certainly *seemed* to be. A mere man, young at that, with a princely load of guilt to somehow bear.

Hearty voices just outside showed Mam's party of three to be approaching. Rhia shivered off her thoughts and hurried to the door, throwing it open to them.

"It's about time you showed your face," Thaddeus teased, shaking his head.

Mam smiled in a harried way and dumped the empty baskets into Rhia's arms so she herself could loose the tie of her cloak. "Daughter, Jonah and Thaddeus wish you to show them where you found that little shell the other day. So be off, and when you've all returned from your endeavors, we'll be ready to eat."

Rhia stood much surprised, as she had, of course, promised Sir Jonah at their midnight meeting to do that very thing, but was set for a good resistance to it from Mam. It was, after all, a long way down the trail, and she'd not done her chores what with the late rising. And there was further need for her to help with the cooking, and then . . .

Mam grabbed her elbow and pulled her to a turn, then whispered harshly into her ear, "This young Jonah will not let the matter rest a single moment! He tires me out with his pestering so that I'd take a stick and knock him back asleep with it! Please, daughter, take him from under my feet e'er I lose my composure and go to howling!"

Mam then covered her mouth with her hand and giggled with shock at herself, and Rhia, much surprised, laughed along.

The day had started bright and clear, but the sky gradually clouded over as the three took the trail downward. Then thunder rumbled. Every so often a stiff breeze came up and tossed the budded treetops. It was Rhiannon's favorite kind of weather, as it seemed unpredictable and kept each hair alert upon her neck, each bit of skin feeling well alive.

Thaddeus led, with Rhia in the middle, then Jonah bringing up the rear. They daren't go too fast, as the recovered invalid surely had not fully regained his strength after so many days of near fasting. In fact, both Rhia and Thaddeus cast many watchful glances back at him, ready to rest if he seemed in need. But his will to learn the fate of his friend was indeed powerful, and it lent him amazing stamina. Rhia thought his iron will was mayhaps the most striking thing about him, when nearly everything about him *was* right striking in some way or other. His eyes blazed blue and his gaze was forthright. His hair was not the burnished red of Mam's, but rather the orange of maple leaves in autumn. It grew straight out from his head in all directions, as though it too were willful and would go where it pleased.

She decided *willful* was indeed a good word for everything about him. His way of walking, his quick reach, the way he kicked the undergrowth aside and thrust with his arms to clear the brambles from his way. His wrists and forearms became scratched raw from that in no time, though he didn't seem to mind.

Thaddeus went his usual sure way down the trail, moving swiftly but with care, dodging what might be dodged and easing aside all else that blocked his way. Whereas Jonah, by contrast, *trampled* his way forward. The natural world could take care of itself or perish, for all he seemed to care. Rhia wondered—had soldiering made him so? Or had a certain boldness in his makeup been what had led him to soldiering in the first place? Either way, unless he learned more patience, Rhia suspected he'd have a hard time sticking it out for very long in his new vocation as penitential pilgrim.

"Rhiannon? Earlier this morn I told Jonah our suspicions."

"What suspicions?" she asked Thaddeus, though she really meant *which*. It seemed to her that these days since Jim's arrest, dire suspicions swam everywhere around, plenteous as eel in the miller's pond.

"I've told him of the murdered man found just where you found the token," Thaddeus answered. He stopped his measured tread and turned to face them, bowing his head to show Jonah his respect.

Rhia likewise stopped and faced Jonah. "I'm right sorry for your loss," she said quietly. "If it *was* your friend who was murdered on our shores, I mean."

For a moment, Jonah looked at the ground and was silent. Then he said, "Things point that way, and now I *will* know the murderer.

Thaddeus says there were pirates docked here that night, and that your reeve saw fit to let them go along their way."

"I'm sure Thaddeus has told you as well that Almund determined they were too sick to move about on the night of the crime," Rhia explained. "Our reeve and the bailiff searched their boat and found nothing that pointed toward local mischief."

"And what's your take on this Arnold Mopp fellow?" Jonah demanded. "Thaddeus says he, too, was interviewed as a suspect several times, but never arrested."

Rhia shrugged. "He lives in the cottage nearest the ford, but his mother swears he was at home with her that night." She sighed. "Everyone knows Arnold thieves what little things he easily may, but to tell it true, I believe he lacks the . . . well, the *ambition* to commit and conceal a blood crime. He's a laughingstock in town, as he pilfers only the goods of old widows who cannot easily chase him down and punch his ears for it."

"Aye," Jonah said grimly, "a murder *would* indeed take effort. Though Thaddeus tells me your one-legged friend Jim is accused, and surely he, too, would have little ability for such brutal work. Though Jim *did* live upon the bluff, not so far from the scene of this crime. That might cast especial suspicion upon him, might it not?"

Something inside Rhia flamed. "Jim would not swat a flea though it were in the act of biting him!" she insisted hotly. She closed her eyes and took a breath. "But you have a right to know that in truth, Jim happened to walk the woods that night. He surely was nowhere near the crime or would have told what he saw of it! He surely stayed nearby the settlement, and he certainly is as innocent as any of us upon the bluff!"

"Jim walked the woods?" Thaddeus echoed softly.

"It seems many were stirring that fateful night," Jonah murmured. "Who else?"

"Well," Thaddeus told him, "I saw no reason to mention the lepers when we spoke of this earlier, but they were certainly brought to these shores and left that night. But as you've seen this morning, Jonah, they stay apart and do not speak. In fact, they were asked by our reeve if they'd witnessed anything amiss upon the beach or in the wood, and they merely dropped their eyes and made him no reply, which surely means they'd not. They are thought to oft be vague of mind with their disease, though I myself believe that's more prejudiced opinion than true fact. Their silence has more to do, in *my* thinking, with their own deep feeling that they are not worthy to voice their thoughts aloud. It's hard to overstate the damage done to their sense of worthiness by those who would set them apart as unclean, or sinners, or worse."

Thaddeus had gotten wound up in this spiel, and he covered his lips with his fingertips, bidding himself leave the subject at that juncture.

Jonah stood dejected. "Poisoned pirates, a lazy petty thief, the gimp Rhia defends so strongly, and these diseased folk. All were in the woods that night, yet none seems a right likely murderer and none saw a thing. And what of their *ears*? You'd think someone would have heard the scuffle, or the sound of Aleron's desperate screams as he took such grievous wounds. You've told me, Thaddeus, the murdered man was stabbed seven times. Seven knife wounds cannot be had by anyone silently."

"Yes, you're right," Thaddeus said thoughtfully, jabbing the air with a finger. "I hadn't considered that. It would not have been an instant death, and his calls for help *should* have been heard." He pinched his chin, puzzling over this new element as he turned and led them in silent procession downward again.

The grumbling thunder joined them as a fourth, not-so-silent companion.

It was raining steadily by the time they reached the ford. Rhia pulled her soaked hair into a dripping knot, then crouched in the shallows to show the other two the exact spot where the little clamshell had shone in the water on that other, sunnier day.

"False sunshine it was, though, since Jim did not come home with us that afternoon," she mentioned sadly. Then she added in an even quieter voice, "And your loyal friend Aleron, Sir Jonah, had given his soul to God just the day before."

Thaddeus nodded toward the nut tree that rose straight and tall just feet from where they crouched. "The spot Almund showed me was right there, near the submerged roots. The murdered man wore nothing but a flaxen tunic and had no possessions upon him. Almund figures his outer clothing was taken as booty, along with whatever coin he had, and that thievery was the motive for the crime. I saw no reason to disagree with the reeve's thoughts on it, though now . . ."

Rhia awaited the rest of that sentence, and at the same time watched Jonah, who was engaged in returning the little clamshell to the spot where Rhia'd found it, leaving it as fit token to mark the place his friend had breathed his last. He'd pulled his hands from the frigid waters, and Rhia caught her breath and winced at what she saw.

"Sir Jonah, you've right maimed yourself, squeezing onto that jabbing pin all through the night!" she scolded. "Your fingers are swollen as can be, and I'll be much surprised if that wound in your palm does not fester and make you ill. I must bind it with something right now, while it's cleaned from the water."

She looked about for some ready stuff that would make him a bandage, and then remembered the blue scarf tucked handily enough in her waist pouch yesterday. She right quick withdrew it as a wrinkled mass and turned to stretch it taut across a rock.

And then, things happened fast, all in a matter of moments, and behind her back. She heard a sort of growl from Jonah, then she heard the splash and scrape of some scuffle in the water. Then Thaddeus called out, quite sharply, "Desist, right now!"

She'd turned by then to see what was happening, and was astounded. For Jonah was straining toward her with his teeth bared and his eyes abulge! Thaddeus had his arms restrained behind his back, elsewise it looked like he would have lunged right at her as a serpent may lunge and strike the life from a hapless toad!

"Where did you get his scarf?" the pilgrim demanded, writhing in Thaddeus's grip.

Rhia regained her wits enough to realize that Jonah was not straining toward *her*, but rather toward the blue cloth.

"This?" She hastened to him with the scarf held out so's he might have it. Thaddeus carefully let go his arms, and instantly Jonah snatched the cloth with trembling hands, then fell to his knees in the rocky waters and buried his face in it.

The other two stood watching, not for the first time stymied by his actions.

"I . . . I was told that scarf belongs to Leonard, a friend of the earl's son," Rhiannon ventured. "Several young men came with the earl's son to squire this spring with our Lord Claredemont. My friend

Maddy knows them, and she brought the scarf to me from Leonard, in token of, well, some . . . some interest he seems to have in me."

Thaddeus looked surprised and frowned.

The pilgrim shook his head. "As I have breath, 'tis Aleron's," he pushed out.

He got to his feet, struggling for balance upon the slick rocks. He fumed—you could see it in the bright color of his face. "Where do I find this . . . this *Leonard*?" he demanded. He wrapped the scarf around both hands and held it taut in front of him as if it were a garrote. "I'll see him painfully throttled ere I sleep another night!"

Thaddeus, slip-sliding, hastened around to meet him face-to-face. "Listen to me," the monk said firmly, taking his shoulders. "You *must* learn to practice restraint. This Leonard may simply have found the scarf, or he may have borrowed it from someone who had found it. You *must* remain far calmer than you are right now if you're to do justice to the memory of your friend. Otherwise, you'll only wreak havoc."

At first, Jonah just looked at him with glazed eyes, not comprehending anything beyond his own raw pain. But Thaddeus met the pilgrim's eyes with a steadfast gaze of his own, and finally Jonah took a deep breath and put his own hands upon Thaddeus's shoulders.

"Brother, you remind me of Aleron," he said. "I swear to God, you do. He was squire to me, though we were much the same age. He'd turned eighteen not long ago, and I will be that age in some few months. We'd been together since my father bade him serve me our thirteenth year, and his was ever the cool head, while I blundered on, liable to pick any fight, quick to draw my sword against any perceived insult. Aleron stayed my arm time and again, you see. And then last winter he saved my life, though oft it has seemed to me that this was a blow, not a boon."

He closed his eyes and dropped his head to his hands.

Rhia dared put her hand upon his shoulder. "I beg you listen. This dark wish you carry does Aleron no honor. Your loyal friend would surely tell you that each day you live in the sunny world *is* a great boon. Each breath you take is a gift from God."

He looked up, but his eyes, meeting hers, were hot and troubled.

"I hear what you say, Rhiannon, but now hear *me*. I dare not reveal myself to my family or friends. My rumored death was at least honorable, whereas my survival is not. And so I travel incognito, hoping, *yearning* for forgiveness from God that I cannot expect and do not deserve. I've been responsible for the deaths of many others, you see. First upon the battlefield, and then . . . well, then in a much, much worse circumstance."

He fell to his knees again so the icy river waters flowed around him. He raised the blue scarf over his head, held taut between his fists whilst the rain diverted down his arms and dripped from his elbows. Water, water—all was rushing water.

Rhia knew that he wished to become a part of all that water, to dissolve and cease to be. Yet the longer she was around him, the more she somehow sensed he wouldn't easily yield to that impulse. He was too alive, too stubbornly impatient and strong.

Suddenly, he threw back his head and shouted to the skies, "Aleron, help me! Adela, my dear sister, forgive me!"

Just then, Thaddeus grabbed Rhia's arm and pointed into the woods. "Look!"

Rhia gasped, for the mysterious white horse was walking slowly from the trees, entering the clearing that edged the river. It pawed the ground and whinnied, then fixed Sir Jonah with its luminous dark eyes.

"Charlemagne?" Sir Jonah rose cautiously. The steed reared and pawed the air with its front hooves, then walked directly to him, shaking its silver mane so it shattered the rain in all directions. Sir Jonah lay hands upon its noble forehead for a moment, then the horse dipped its head and turned to canter gracefully back into the dense woods.

Jonah stood frozen there astride the rushing water. "Charlemagne, it *was* you," he breathed.

Chapter 20

There could be only one conclusion, and Thaddeus was the one to voice it. "The steed belonged to your missing friend," he said quietly.

The pilgrim nodded, his eyes still upon the opening in the trees where the stallion had disappeared. "Charlemagne was ever loyal to his master, and so I know for certain now that Aleron is . . ."

He stopped and lowered his head, swallowing, unable to say the final word.

Rhiannon felt tears press behind her eyes as Thaddeus splashed through the water to grip Jonah's shoulder. "God's will be done," he said.

And though none in Lord Claredemont's manner of Woethersly had properly mourned the man found murdered there, they three mourned him well that afternoon as they took the trail homeward with slow step and private thoughts of friendship and loss.

When they'd set foot upon the blufftop again, they looked at each other and by unspoken agreement tarried some ways from the settlement, making a circle of three under the bent and scraggly little stand of orchard trees. In truth, they were reluctant to be questioned by their elders until they'd made some private plans for proceeding on what they'd learned at the river ford.

"So, this Leonard fellow held the scarf belonging to Aleron," Thaddeus said. "He would certainly not have killed for such a thing, being wealthy himself. But . . ."

He paused, never willing to speak rashly when so much was at stake.

Rhiannon was meanwhile picturing those racing horsemen with their flying cloaks and tall boots, their glinting weapons and the bright vestments of their horses. One had certainly *been* Leonard, but *which* in that pack of heedless riders?

"But *what*?" Jonah shifted from foot to foot. "If you've thought of some other reason for Aleron's scarf to be in his wretched hands, spill it, good monk!"

Thaddeus tapped his lip with one paint-stained finger and proceeded carefully. "My line of thought was merely this. Jonah, you brought up the fact that there were many in the woods that night, and none reported hearing the screams that might portend a bloody crime. Well, what if the death were too sudden for the victim to call out, and the stab wounds done later, to mask that fact? What if, in fact, Aleron was not stabbed to death at all, but instead died some other, quicker way, maybe even by accident."

"By accident?" Jonah said hotly. "Sir Monk, you misjudge my friend's skill and horsemanship if you think he might have fallen from his own steed! And why, pray tell, would someone stab him afterward in that case? What purpose would it serve?"

"What if he was . . . was run down, *knocked* from his horse?" Rhiannon whispered.

Jonah's face went white. At first he seemed to be considering that, but then he threw up his arms. "We waste time on pointless speculation whilst the bloody murderers flee beyond our grip!" He strode to a nearby tree and began pummeling it with his fists.

Thaddeus started toward him, but Rhia put her hand on the

monk's arm. "Mayhaps he wrestles just now with his *own* demons," she whispered. "I say we let him, though his knuckles fester from it later. He may eventually learn restraint from such ordeals."

Thaddeus looked surprised, but stayed. As they watched, grimacing, Rhiannon felt a great helplessness flood through her.

"Truly, Aleron is dead and nothing will change that," she murmured sadly. "What matters now is Jim, and there's nothing to be done on his behalf. Nothing! Even if we were to find that Leonard came to possess Aleron's scarf through the worst possible mischief, he will doubtless manage to stay beyond the law. No one in the realm can stand against the earl's own household. We will *never* see Jim's name cleared."

"The king's household can stand against the earl," Thaddeus mentioned.

Rhia's breath caught in her throat and she jerked her attention from Jonah to him. She dared not imagine what Thaddeus meant by that, and though she searched his face, he said nothing more, and his calm expression gave nothing away.

Jonah meanwhile skulked back to them with his bruised and bloodied fists hugged in his armpits. "I'm my own worst enemy," he mumbled. "You might as well say it."

"You're your own worst enemy." Rhia wagged a finger in his face. "And oft enough a waste of good nursing, to boot!"

Thaddeus sternly eyed first one and then the other. "All right, *children,* may we leave your important squabbles and get back to the small fact of this bloody murder? It's occurred to me that if the young nobles squiring here came by Aleron's scarf in a criminal way, they may well speak of such an exploit among themselves, or even boast about it. If we could somehow *hear* what they say when they think themselves alone, we might get to the truth of the matter."

Jonah nodded eagerly. "Good thinking, monk! Is there somewhere we may go concealed and hear their private brags? The lord's stables, perhaps? They will be speaking freely while they ready their mounts, as that's the way of all young men."

"The horses are stabled within the castle walls, and a guard posted," Thaddeus replied in a thoughtful murmur. "I did not mean to make it sound a cinch, my friend. I can think of no place or occasion where we might get sufficiently close to them to not risk quick discovery as spies."

They talked more of this, but Rhiannon's ears rang so that she could not tell what indeed they said. The fact was, *she* could certainly think of a place and occasion with plenty sufficient closeness, and in fact could think of naught else. Why, tomorrow night she was to meet that bunch for the Beltane Eve revels at Wythicopse Ring!

When they were eating their meal that afternoon, Rhia glanced toward the boys, then asked in a whisper, "Granna? Would you tell right quick what you know of Wythicopse Ring?" By *right quick* she meant before Mam came back from fetching more bread.

Predictably, Jonah and Thaddeus frowned, unfamiliar with the local reference.

"Ah, Wythicopse. That walled grove is ancient and then some," Granna began, nodding with satisfaction. "It's come through the mists of time, just as our bluff has. To start with, it was a fine gathering place for all in the faery realm, see? This was when our first dames were as yet circling birds. There was a right grand castle built upon that site, large by faery standards, though mostly invisible, as faery things usually be. It had spiral passageways within its walls that spun together the world we walk and the deep underworld beneath, the spirit realm.

231

Bridged the two up and down, did those spiral stairs, but they was made from the flimsy stuff of spiderwebs. Not made to take the weight of us humans is what I'm saying, since humans be big and coarse. So that was the problem and the ruination of the thing, see?"

Granna had spoken freely to that point, but now Mam slid back onto the bench and Granna went to slurping her soup as though she'd never set in upon this telling.

Jonah pressed her. "Would you leave us there, madame, without our knowing the outcome of this Wythicopse faery castle?"

"Wythicopse Ring?" Mam asked. "That overgrown walled garden back beyond the manor house?" She pursed her lips and shook her head, tearing the bread, then handing the basket to Thaddeus to pass along. "I believe Lord Claredemont's gardeners pronounce it haunted so's not to have to care for it. The thing should be plowed over."

Granna solemnly clucked her tongue. "Ye dasn't do a thing like that, Aigneis dear. No, no, ye dasn't so much as *touch* with a plowhead that which lies hidden beneath the place." She leaned closer to Jonah. "The truth of it is this. A young maid who'd lost her love to a pestilence was right desperate to see him again, and for that she braved the faeries' anger and snuck right into that place so's she could travel those gossamer stairs down to the spirit realm. Well, she was a slender girl and shimmied right dandy along the spiral turns. But one small strand of that fine thread snapped apart behind her. And when she'd kissed her dead lover and was bound up the return way, she found she could not go it, nor could she go back, as that single broken filament tripped her feet, then wrapped her tight as a fly in a spider's web. This happened way back long centuries ago, but far under that walled grove she dangles to this day, guarded by a dragon set by the ancient faery king to block any who would venture down to save her."

Rhiannon gulped. That would have been the dragon she'd heard, sure enough.

"Oh, Mother." Aigneis shook her head. "It's a good thing Daisy is already napping, as she'd believe your nonsense and have bad dreams."

Granna ignored that, still wrapped in her tale. "She'd chose All Hallow's Eve to see her dead love, thinking that on *that* night things would stand wide open between the realms of life and death. But she neglected to think how on that night all is dark mischief in the faery world, as it brings in winter, which faeries dread. Now on *Beltane* she mighta had better luck, as the faeries love the spring and let most stupidities of mortal folk be. As I always tell Rhiannon, timing's the thing with much in life. Remember that, children, as it may come in handy."

"Timing's the thing," Jonah repeated, nodding. He stood abruptly, as he did most things, and bowed to Granna. "You have told an instructive story, and I thank you, wise woman, for the telling of it." He then bowed to Mam. "And again I thank you for your hospitality, and beg you say what I may do this afternoon to earn my keep."

Mam gave him chores to do, the gathering of firewood and the plowing of a new space to expand the vegetable garden. He left to begin, joined by Thaddeus.

Granna moved to the pallet for her nap. "I say the fire was wrong about that young man," she murmured to Rhiannon as she closed her eyes. "I believe he's better than most his age, faceless in the flames or no, and indeed I'll stick with that opinion."

"You yield to his flattery, Granna," Rhia teased, "as he called you wise."

"So be it," Granna allowed, then set to snoring.

Rhia's mind raced as she quickly cleaned up from the meal, and the moment she could she ran to join Thaddeus and Jonah where they worked behind the nether cottage. Jonah was sharpening the ax blade at their grindstone, whilst Thaddeus was harnessing the cow to their garden plow. Rhia leaned against a tree, tapping her chin with Mam's cross, wondering how to approach them with what preyed so heavily on her mind.

"So, now you both have heard of Wythicopse Ring," she finally called out to them. "And many believe a fiercesome dragon does indeed guard the spot, as Granna told. Though certainly, I believe dragons do *not* exist, as to believe elsewise would be ignorant and never Christian, would you say? Still, there's that rumor of a dragon ever afoot among plenty of people. Good people, too, and many of them Christians."

Why could she not come to the point and speak of the chance she'd soon have to be spy within that place? Instead she talked of dragons, a simpler thing in many ways.

Thaddeus looked over at her and smiled, stroking the neck of the harnessed cow to ease its nerves. "You've lost me, Rhia."

Jonah wiped his streaming forehead with his arm and slid his thumb along the ax blade. "Sharp enough," he pronounced as though he'd not so much as heard her. He shouldered the ax and headed toward the woods.

Thaddeus took the handle of the plow and eased the cow to a pull with a cluck and a small touch of the withy limb he'd cut for the job.

"Stop!" Rhia called out, pulling her hair, frustrated with the both of them beyond endurance. "Would you two have me toasted to a crust by the fiercesome Dragon of Brynourth whilst I spy upon those un-predictable squires and never so much as protest it whilst you still have the chance?"

The cow had decided to put on some speed, and Thaddeus had no recourse but to come along fast behind it. He struggled to guide the plow as it bit into the ground with its single sharp tooth, but he looked at her with wide and startled eyes as he stumbled past.

Jonah, meanwhile, turned on his heel to face her.

"Rhiannon, stop your riddles and say exactly what you mean, else Brother Thaddeus and I may well decide to toast you to a crisp ourselves!"

Rhia planted her knuckles upon her hips. "How's *this*, then? I have a plan for hearing the boasts the squires may make about Aleron's scarf! I am to meet Sir Leonard and his friends to celebrate Beltane Eve at Wythicopse Ring, though there be dragons about, or might well be! Or *one*, anyhow," she rambled. "I've heard its fiercesome sighs with my own ears! It's held in an underground chamber, the roof of which is made of tiny flat stones that make up magical pictures—a brown hare, and a fine lady with large dark eyes! Though I figure you won't believe me, I nevertheless say to you that my friend Maddy has also seen the very same—"

"And has the hare a pink nose?" Jonah called back. "The lady holds a red flower, I'll wager. Look further and you may see an ancient man upon a donkey, as well."

She stood stunned for a moment, then drew in a sharp breath. "How'd . . . how'd you know?"

Thaddeus, meanwhile, had cornered with the plow and now was staggering back in their direction. He noted the expression on Rhia's face and pulled the reins taut, throwing his full weight backward to bring the stubborn cow to a reluctant, mooing halt.

"I said, how'd you *know*?" Rhiannon again called to Jonah, stomping her foot. As he'd chosen to ignore her the first time, this time she was outright bellowing.

Jonah calmly replied, "Rhiannon, how I know of that chamber can be of little importance to you, as you'll not be joining their party on Beltane Eve or at any other time. I don't know how you could consider it with what we suspect of that bunch."

He turned again toward the woods.

"He's right, Rhia," Thaddeus said, quietly and firmly. "We won't hear of it. I too am shocked you would consider such a thing, if you want the truth."

Well, it was the worst course the two of them could have taken, as Rhia now would not have been dissuaded from attending had a band of angels come to order her to desist.

"When did you two become the lords and I your vassal?" she fumed. "For your information, good sirs, I go where I choose to go and do what I choose to do, and I've been much looking forward to attending this party! I suppose I can spy upon a private conversation as well as anyone else, including the two of you!"

And then, her anger made her do a thing she might elsewise never have done.

"As for you, Sir Jonah?" she called at the top of her lungs, her heart beating fast. "Would you be so reckless with the feelings of your own true sister, Adela? For her sake, heed my distress and come tell me what you know of that chamber! I must needs know *everything* of it in advance, as I *will* go there on Beltane to confront those we figure to be Aleron and Jim's dire enemies, and there's naught in the wide world you can do to stop me!"

Lifting her trembling chin, and in a more courteous voice, she added, "In particular, if it please you, I'd know if there be a dragon."

Sir Jonah again stopped walking, but this time he stood frozen in the bracken at wood's edge. He slowly turned in her direction, then took the ax from his shoulder and drove it easily into the nearest oak. An oak is a very hard tree, Rhia thought. She gulped, somewhat regretting that she'd opened her mouth.

He meanwhile trod with measured step and downcast eyes to where she waited with Thaddeus. "Tell how you knew of my sister," he demanded, staring at the ground.

"You mentioned her yourself this morn, remember?" Rhiannon answered. She cleared her throat and forced air into her lungs. "And, well . . . you mistook me for her, several times, when you were ill and not yourself."

He lifted his eyes and looked at her. "I loved my sister," he whispered raggedly. "I tried to save her. Her *screams!*" He pressed his hands to his ears. "I took the oars from Aleron and rowed back for her—I *did! Naturally* I did! But the small craft was meant for only a few, and it capsized and quickly sank when so many jumped inside."

His anguished eyes suddenly filled with tears that he made no move to conceal.

"Why, why, why could I not have perished with the rest?" he whispered. "Why did God give Aleron strength to pull me to shore and revive me from my drown? In His mercy, why would He not let me sleep eternal with the others?"

"But it could not have been your fault that . . . ," Rhia began.

But Sir Jonah did not want to hear, and indeed had already turned from them to run blindly toward the forest, stumbling across the rough ground, punching and kicking the brambles aside as he went. This time it was Rhia who started after him, and Thaddeus who reached to stop her.

"He needs to be alone," he said simply.

Rhiannon whirled to Thaddeus, some exasperated. "Say it, Thaddeus, won't you, finally? Just put words to what we both know."

Thaddeus stared at the place in the tree line where Jonah had just disappeared. The leaves and rushes there still quaked as from a typhoon.

"Yes," Thaddeus said with a small smile. "I believe he is."

Chapter 21

Now that they'd decided Jonah's hidden identity must indeed be fact, not vague imagining and far-fetched conjecture, Rhia felt dizzy with the knowledge of it. "I bent my knee to him in the chapel last night," she whispered. "He asked me for friendship's sake never to do that again, nor to tell anyone he'd been seen here upon our bluff."

Thaddeus nodded. "You heard him say that he and Aleron traveled incognito to those shrines, and that his only wish is to die seeking Divine pardon. He cannot bear the shame of owning up to his rightful station, nor the turmoil it will bring. I truly fear he would end his life rather than resume it as Prince William Aethling. We have to respect his honorable decision. Even to you and me he must always remain Sir Jonah."

"Of course, Thaddeus," she whispered. "As a pilgrim, he may eventually find some measure of peace. With the world watching and judging him, how could he ever?"

They stood together in silence for a while, marveling at the secret they shared.

Then Thaddeus cleared his throat. "Rhia? I can understand that you now wish to overhear what you may at Wythicopse Ring on Beltane Eve. But, well, why did you consent to be a part of the Beltane revels there to begin with? Forgive me if I presume too much, but it seems unlike you to join such a dangerous and . . . well, *frivolous* party."

Her neck felt aflame at this unexpected query. "I would never have said yes to such a thing, except that I was . . . *trapped* by my friend Maddy."

Thaddeus gave her the slightest frown. "Trapped? *How* trapped?"

Rhia closed her eyes. "What she tells me to do, I *must*. I cannot naysay her, as when I try, she comes up with a different road to the same thing, and I am hoodwinked before I know it! Ever since we were little girls, Maddy's begged to be brought to our chapel at some midnight. See, she likes a scare, and she likes a frolic, as well. Her new boyfriend is one of the squires, and she wanted to impress him and his mates this Beltane with a scare *and* a party, at our sacred chapel! Which is ridiculous, of course. I *had* to say I'd join them at Wythicopse Ring so she'd drop her insistence on coming up to our bluff!" She put her face in her hands and shook her head. "I know, I know. It sounds right daft. But . . . if you *knew* Maddy. I must please her or . . . or *else*."

Thaddeus looked glassy-eyed. "I confess, I've little experience with such things."

She sighed and nodded. "Being an oblate for holy brotherhood, you mean."

He shook his head and gave a laugh. "Nay, I mean I've had little experience with such complications because I'm *male*. Our friendships be true and simple, thank God!"

He strode toward the treed ax, still shaking his head and laughing.

"Well, *sir*!" Rhia called after him. "I thank God that I am *female*, and therefore do not traipse through life unaware of friendship's necessary *complications*. I marvel that boys have friends at all, as careless as they treat each other, what with their constant rough brags and crude jokes and punches to the arm and . . . and *so* forth."

She could not resist a bit of laughing pantomime, swaggering with her arms held from her body in rude imitation of a boy, her mouth gone slack and her features pulled stupid.

Thaddeus watched, amused, as he meanwhile struggled to free the ax. "Fair trade, then, lady. I'll stay simple and sleep nights, whilst you brood about your girlish entanglements." With a final smile, he yanked the ax free and turned to begin cutting the wood for Mam.

As she headed back to the cot for her seed bag, Rhia thought how she might have added that her girlfriends did not run so abruptly to the woods when they were upset, either, leaving their mates to do their afternoon work for them.

Mam was not about when Rhiannon reached the cottage, and Granna still dozed beside the fire. Rhia grabbed the seed sack from its peg. She was tiptoeing back toward the door when from above her came a plea. "Sister Rhia! Take us *with* you!"

She looked up to see Daisy grinning hopefully down at her from the loft with Sal doing likewise over Daisy's shoulder. Sal had spent the day with them as they observed her reactions to Sir Jonah. At mealtime she'd seemed unfazed by him, so mayhaps she was no longer spooked and might soon go back to her own dwelling.

Rhia put her finger to her lips. "Come along, then, but quickly and quietly!" she whispered. "Have a care you don't wake Granna, or she may have *inside* jobs for us!"

On such a bright and warm afternoon, that would truly rankle.

Daisy came clomping down the ladder, made clumsy by dragging her tortoise along. Rhiannon hurried to lift her down the last two rungs, then climbed up to the top and steadied Sally from behind as she climbed slowly step-together down. Rhia then grabbed the hands of both girls and hustled them outside.

241

"Three fish, three fish!" Sally cried when they were standing upon the violet-studded new grass. She clapped her hands, squinting up at the sun, heedless of its dazzle.

"What's that noise?" Daisy asked. "Sounds exactly like thunder, only different."

" 'Tis merely Thaddeus, cutting wood," Rhia answered, staring at the lumpish bundle the young girl carried. "Daisy, why is your pet wrapped to resemble a sausage?"

Queen Matilda was wearing a red stocking of Granna's. It was pulled taut over her shell's wide girth, then had been cinched closed around her scrawny neck and stringy tail with dandelion chains.

"Tildy is dressed for a wedding," Daisy proudly explained, holding her up.

"Or someone's funeral, if Granna misses that sock," Rhia murmured, shaking her head. "And how may she walk, as you've trapped her feet within her gown?"

"She's to be pulled to the wedding in a fine carriage," Daisy answered with a dignified air. "Meanwhile, I shall carry her majesty where'er she pleases to go."

The animal had perceived that she was now outside and batted within the woolen sock so furiously that she slipped from Daisy's hands. She fell the short distance to the ground and, though she'd doubtless expected freedom, was panicked by finding herself still stranded within her woolen dress. She opened and closed her beak several times, still struggling and squirming, then stretched her neck to its entire amazing length as her eyes bulged with distress.

Sally covered her own eyes with her hands at this pitiful sight and crouched down, crying, "No! Stop!"

Rhia immediately bent to pull apart the flower chains that bound the animal. "Queen Tildy's now free, Sal," she said quickly. "And Daisy, *hear* me—Granna's best red stocking must *not* be shredded by a rampaging . . ."

But Daisy was staring at Sal. "She said new words!" the child whispered.

Rhia's heart raced, for indeed she had! She dropped to crouch knee-to-knee with Sal and took Sal's hands from her face. "Oh, Sally, you spoke a different speech!"

But Sally looked back at her with empty eyes. "Three . . . fish," she whispered.

Rhiannon kept tight hold of Sal's hands, as over her shoulder she gave quick orders to Daisy. "Take Queen Matilda right this minute and leave her in the large bucket beside the beehives, hear? Elsewise she may meet with mischance at bluff's edge. We'll put Granna's stocking in the seed sack so's not to wake her by returning it to the cottage just now, but hurry with the other, so's we may go on along!"

Daisy did not argue but grabbed her pet and ran quickly, not wanting to miss anything.

"Now, Sally, while we are alone, say it again," Rhiannon ordered in a fierce whisper. "Say your new saying. 'No, stop!' *Say* those words for me, Sally, please? *Please?*"

Sally would not. But she now looked at Rhia direct, and drew her brows into a frown.

Rhiannon had never seen Sally frown. She let go Sal's hands and noted that her own hands were suddenly shaking a bit, though Sally was smiling her simple smile again, waiting for Rhiannon to pull her to her feet and lead her where she would.

Rhia stuffed Granna's stocking into the seed sack, then pulled Sally to a stand. At that, Gramp, who'd kept one eye upon them from his roost in the yew tree, opened the other eye as well, stretched from his off-and-on doze, and flew to join them.

"I'm back!" Daisy announced as she thrust herself between Rhia and Sally, taking a hand from each. "Sally's hand is dry and warm," she sang out as she skipped along. "Rhiannon, *your* hand is damp. Eee-euw."

"Well, if you like not holding my hand, go home right now," Rhia told her peevishly. "As at the bluff's edge you must hold my hand at all times, or if not my hand, then the hem of my skirt. And if not my hem, then the cord at my waist. I must *feel* you at all times, Daisy, and know you are on the clearing side of me, never the bluff side."

In the air, Gramp may well have rolled his eyes to hear Rhia of all people become instructress regarding safe behavior at bluff's edge.

There were few seeds left to gather that late in the day. The birds and the wind had snatched the better part of the night's scatterings. Still, Rhiannon was glad to have some time to think out the developments from the morning with female company, and that on the young side, so Rhia herself could be the boss of them. She was boss to very few in this world, and it oft seemed a great many were boss of her.

She quick gave up her order that Daisy hold on to her garment. Daisy and Sal sat upon the ground near the opening from the trail, playing at Daisy's favorite patty-cake game. Sal's hands were palm up where they rested on Sal's lap, and Daisy happily patted them as though Sal patted back. As long as Rhia could hear the gentle pat of Daisy's hands on Sal's and the singsong of Daisy's high voice, she knew where they were and could safely work with her back to them.

Besides, Gramp sat upon his faery rock, watching the girls' every move.

It made a pleasant harmony—the gentle pat of the girls' four hands and the sharp and rhythmic resound of Thaddeus's ax in the distance. For the first time since Sir Jonah had come fully awake, Rhia relaxed. She breathed a deep sigh, having found more air in the world when Thaddeus and Jonah were not nearby to absorb it all. She'd missed voicing her thoughts aloud as she worked, too—letting them progress from her lips all willy-nilly, as she oft did when alone with Gramp, or Sally. With Jonah and Thaddeus, she'd had to consider before she spoke, always on guard lest she offend Thaddeus, or upset Jonah, or sound ridiculous to one or the other or both. That *last*, being ridiculous, had been her great concern, to tell it true. Was it always so when boys were around?

Anyhow, now she eagerly picked up her habit of gabbing without regard.

"Gramp, here's the thing. As you well know, Mam must let me go where I will on Beltane Eve, as that's the custom. Last year I went with some other girls to the bonfire on the green and didn't come back till morn." She squinted at an unfamiliar seed, then tossed it aside, as it was not seed at all but merely some ragged pod of milkweed. "Some nerve Thaddeus and Jonah have, naysaying a thing even a mother would not dare forbid. Can you *believe* their nerve, saying I may not go to Maddy's party, Gramp?"

"Come, come, lollywaggle, slap, slap, slap," sang Daisy from a ways behind her. Rhia heard the soft slap of the girls' hands just as the monk's sharp ax bit into oak.

"It *would* be a relief to yield to their nags and stay home, I'll admit it. But what of Jim, then, Gramp? His days of sanctuary wane, and soon he'll face the gallows. The true murderer *must* be flushed out and made to confess. And so I *will* go to Wythicopse, though there *is* a dragon beneath that rocky picture seal, I'm certain of it at this point."

245

"Go ye wiggle-woggle, off with thine *cap!*" Rhia waited for the girls' squeals, as here was the point in the game where Daisy reached to ruffle Sal's hair, a thing they considered hilarious, no matter how often they did it. They squealed, right on time.

"Grrrrrahhhhh," complained Gramp, hard-eyeing them.

"It's just a game, Gramp," Rhia murmured, intent on separating a few tiny seeds from a large handful of briars. "They only play. Pay them no mind. You must give your attention instead to *my* dilemma. I *should* join that bunch tomorrow eve, wouldn't you think? Or not? Give me a peck upon the rock for yes, two pecks for no."

But Gramp kept his eyes tight upon the girls, who'd now started over on their game.

"Come, come, here's a woggle, there's a woggle, lilly-lolly *slap!*"

"Grah-*raaaahhh!*" Gramp, very perturbed now, stretched up tall on his birdy toes, lifting his wings so high above his frowsy ear feathers that Rhia feared he'd lose his balance on the holed rock and fall backward into thin air. "Graaaahhhck-ack!"

Rhiannon stopped her work, surprised by his folly. "Gramp, settle yourself, please! Do you not recall how the last time you fell backward from that rock, you nearly collided with the water e'er you got your wings outspread enough to fetch air and get flying? The girls are only *playing* at slapping! Daisy is not hitting Sal, and would never!"

She shook her head, smiling in amusement as she resumed scooping her little piles of seed onto the wide sycamore leaves she'd use as wrappers. When each leaf was neatly folded and stored within her sack, she stood and tightened the string, calling over her shoulder as she turned toward them, "Girls, I've finished and it's time . . ."

By then she'd turned round far enough to see not two but *three* players sitting cross-legged upon the ground! Three girls, but only *two* of them human. The third, close between the other two, had the whitest of knees, the whitest of thin girlish arms, and long white hair that blew across her face in the breeze. She pushed it back with bone-white hands, then smiled with white lips. The eyes in her white face were the lightest of colors. Bluish, they were, but only as milk may be said to be bluish, though it is truly white. She wore a thin garment. It was indeed her shroud, for Rhiannon recognized with dread the phantom from the night of the wake, the will-o'-wisp ghost she thought was Primrose!

Rhia advanced slowly, one arm out toward the girls in a semblance of calm, though beneath her skirt her knees were knocking. "Daisy, that is *not* your sister," she said. Then she took a breath and said more firmly, "Take Sally's arm and let us go home."

Daisy put out her hands, palms up. "Of *course* she is not my sister, Rhia! Primrose lives in heaven now, remember? Ingrid lives right here, within our woods! She doesn't even *look* like Primrose."

And then, Daisy began to giggle at Rhia's foolishness, and Sally joined her in it, their knees bobbing upon the ground, their skinny shoulders hunched as though they would laugh forever at such a silly mistake. Only the third abstained, looking down at her lap as though with guilt at being caught among the living.

Rhia turned to Gramp, who turned his head away. If she would not believe *him* when he'd given dire alarm, why should *he* respond to her conundrum now?

But without his counsel, what to do, what to *think*? It was well known that ghostly spirits were tricksters. What better way could Primrose find to lure her sister to an eternal wander in limbo than to change her aspect so's not to frighten Daisy, and then to sit on a spring afternoon and join in her earthly games?

This new child *did* look made of solid flesh, not ghostly mist. But children were *not* white-haired and did *not* possess the snowy skin of doves! Further, this child did not resemble the folk in the woods. She was without color, whilst *their* color was grayish, or ofttimes yellow. She was so smooth she seemed made all of glass, whilst their skin flaked and was oft scaly, except where it flamed red with soreness.

While Rhiannon stood fearful and perplexed, the girl jumped up and took to her heels. At wood's edge she turned to blow a kiss, first to Sally, then to Daisy. Daisy blew a kiss back, then bent across and raised Sally's hand to Sally's lips. The deathly pale stranger pretended to catch Sally's clumsy kiss upon her cheek, then to take it in her fist, then to clasp it gently as a precious treasure between her two white hands.

Rhiannon felt all her dire certainty dissolve in the warmth of that small gesture.

"Ingrid, then," Rhia whispered, and burned with shame for the poor welcome she'd given the strange woodland child. For it was certain that no trickster spirit would do such a graceful thing simply for the heart's peace of an invalid like Sally.

"I *still* don't understand how your new friend came to be in our woods," Rhia declared as they three walked home under Gramp's circling shadow. "Is her mother there?"

Daisy shrugged. "How should *I* know? Ingrid never speaks of her."

Rhia frowned. "Does she talk of how she fares in the woods, whether she needs anything? Does she speak of whether she'd like to come from the trees and live inside?"

Daisy shook her head. "She never says."

"I saw her on horseback, galloping at midnight on Aleron's steed,"

Rhiannon mused. "Do you know how she learned to ride so well? Was she born an aristocrat, then?"

Daisy sighed. "Maybe. What *is* one of those?"

Rhia thought. "Well, an aristocrat is . . . hmmm. Put it this way. Most aristocrats speak the language of Francia. Does Ingrid speak the language of Francia?"

"Ingrid speaks no language of anywheres," Daisy said.

Rhia grew exasperated. "Oh, Daisy, everyone speaks *some* language."

Sally leaned around Rhia. "Three fish!" she said cheerfully to Daisy, as if to demonstrate Rhia's point. "I'll have three. Three!" Then, in the blink of an eye, Sally stopped walking and pressed her palms to her ears, crying, "No, stop, *stop!*"

She began to tremble head to foot. Rhia and Daisy hastened to put their arms around her—Rhia's around her shoulders, Daisy's around her hips. But still, Sally shuddered.

Something terrible played in her brain, but who might know what it was?

In another moment, as quickly as the sun may slide from behind a roiling thundercloud, Sally took her hands from her ears, seemed confused, and then smiled bright again, looking to Rhia with nothing in her eyes except the reflected late-afternoon sky. The three of them walked on along, though more slowly, Daisy and Rhiannon holding fast to Sally's arms from either side. Though Sally now seemed recovered from her fit, it had left small Daisy shaken, and Rhia well nigh in tears. No one spoke until the cottages were in sight, then Daisy said quietly, "Rhiannon? Ingrid does not talk."

Rhiannon frowned, her thoughts still with Sally. "What do you speak of, Daisy?"

"Ingrid, my new friend! She does not talk is why she speaks no language!"

With this mysterious saying, Daisy hugged Sally good-bye and ran toward Granna, who kneaded bread on the stump beside the hives with the bucketed tortoise near her feet.

"Rhiannon!"

Rhia recognized the pilgrim's voice and turned quick toward it. Sir Jonah stood alone back beside the nether cot, giving her a wide-armed wave with the ax in his hand. Nearby was a goodly pile of oakwood. A log was balanced upon the splitting stump.

She noted that Sal, too, saw Jonah but had no especial reaction. She did not fear him, though the fright she'd had at his hands might still live somewhere within her.

"I see you have come home from your forest sojourn!" she called to him. "I'm sure Brother Thaddeus is gladdened to have *some* relief from the chore you left him!"

She'd meant to sound witty, but instead had sounded gruff, she knew.

He drew his arm across his face so that his orange hair, newly gilded with sweat, seemed like an ornate, ragged mane. His eyes blazed, even from this long distance.

"Thaddeus has gone looking for you!" he called to her.

Again, like the midnight before in the chapel, when she'd raised her candle and perceived him newly become himself, she was seized with the impulse to drop to her knees. She held Sally's arm tighter and tapped Mam's cross upon her chin, seeking her own balance.

"He'll find me at home in a moment!" she answered Sir Jonah.

A quick glance told her that Granna was paying no mind to this exchange. She and Daisy were fully occupied retrieving the thrashing tortoise from the overturned bucket.

"He'd speak to you in private, and there's some urgency to it," Jonah called. "You may find him in the chapel, as he expressed a need to catch up his prayers. Go straightaway, if you can."

Rhia started walking Sally again. Something inside her was too stubborn to quiz Sir Jonah about this *urgent* matter. "I've no wish to disturb anyone's prayers!" she called back, feeling a little thrill at having the last word.

Though once past his line of sight, had she not had Sally with her, she would certainly have hitched her skirt to her knees and run full speed to the chapel.

Chapter 22

Rhiannon and Sally soon enough reached the cottage. Mam looked up and smiled at them from where she stirred their second-largest kettle over the firepit, making a quantity of barley soup that smelled rich and delicious.

Rhia sat Sally upon the bench and tossed the seed sack onto its peg, then hustled to her mother and spoke near her ear. "Mam? Sally used a different saying today. She has said it twice now that I've heard. 'No, stop, stop!' I wonder, did she utter it first yesterday, when Sir Jonah grabbed her clamshell?"

Mam stopped stirring and looked at her. After a moment, she shook her head. "No, I didn't hear her say that. Her only words were her usual ones, and those not uttered often, miserable as she was. She cried until she was all hiccoughs, poor Sally."

Mam and Rhiannon both looked at Sally then. Seeing that she rocked calmly there upon the bench, they turned back to speak more, their heads together over the kettle.

"Well, I am afraid the shock yesterday made her remember her horrible brother cuffing her when he'd got no fish," Rhia whispered. "The first time Sally said her new words today, Daisy's pet was trapped within her fancy clothes and fighting to get free. I fear Sal saw in that struggle her *own* hapless struggle to stop her brother hurting her, and that she may now remember anew *whenever* she sees such things."

Rhia's throat had grown too filled with anger to let further words through.

But though Rhia fumed, Mam fumed hotter. She stirred the soup as though she'd like to beat the turnips into runny liquid and whip the rabbit meat until it hopped away. When she finally spewed out words, they were as blistering as the fire itself.

"Violence is like a poison arrow shot from a tight bow, so why will you not provide some hard target to take that arrow's hit and stop its travel? The heart and memory are wispy things, never fashioned to fend against the brutal force that flies unchecked throughout this world! Why, why, why have you designed things so uneven? The hurt to Sal now travels well past the skull-crack that tore her mind asunder. It presently sails right through the heart of her, taking away her innocent peace, damaging over and over again with no stop to it! How . . . how *dare* you construct things so lopsided, the brutal things so endless in their flight and the gentle things in brutality's path so *breakable!*"

By the end of this tirade, Rhiannon realized to whom Mam spoke and was truly shocked, as who would blaspheme so, calling God to account as Mam just had? The large vein in Mam's thin neck pulsed as though it would burst. Rhia was afraid *of* Mam and *for* Mam, both. God Himself may well have shuddered, had He been here.

Knowing not what else to do, Rhia fetched a bowl and reached far around Mam to quick ladle soup into it, then escaped to sit beside Sal upon the bench and feed her. Sally opened her mouth wide for each mouthful. She looked into Rhia's eyes with her usual candor, innocent as a babe, though near as grown as Rhia herself.

Rhia tucked Sal's light hair behind her left ear and gently ran her fingers across the filigree of shattered bone beneath her clear skin. She closed her eyes and prayed with all her might that God might right quick heal Sally and redeem Himself in the eyes of Mam, His faithful handmaiden in all things.

Rhia kept her eyes tightly closed for so long that lights danced be-hind her lids and her ears roared as with the ocean's voice. She would give God plenty of time, as healing bone must be especially hard work.

But Sally's head was *not* healed when Rhiannon finally opened her eyes. Sally indeed thought Rhia was playing some game with her, and laughed with delight.

Mam was now crouched upon her haunches nearby the bubbling kettle. She stared into the fire with her elbows upon her knees and her cloud of shining hair held back from her face by the slim fingers of both hands. Rhia thought she looked much like a young girl, crouched like that. She'd given God a tongue-lashing, and now she was for cer-tain waiting for Him to make an answer to it, just as Rhia had waited for her own answer, and received it not. Did Mam indeed expect Him to speak from the flames, as to Moses?

Rhia stood. "Mam? Shall I take Sally along to her own cot, now she's eaten? She appears over her fear of Jonah. Just now she was calm when we passed him, and she was not afeared when he came in with you this morn, or to eat the midday meal."

After a moment, still staring at the fire, Mam said listlessly, "Yes, Rhia, if you please. And daughter, you'd best go find Thaddeus when you've taken Sally home. I'd forgotten. He would speak with you."

And then, Mam turned to give the barest glance to Rhia and Sal, where the two stood hand-in-hand near the doorway. But strangely, her eyes arrested on them, and then bore into them, as though they were a wonder and not the daily thing they certainly were.

Mam then covered her mouth with her hands and stood, yet still she stared at them.

Finally, she wiped her eyes right quick with the heel of one hand, then took to stirring the soup again.

"We go, then, Mam," Rhia said, a bit uneasily. "If indeed you are . . . all right?"

"Yes, daughter." Mam gave her a small smile. "I'm fine."

"Did God make you an answer to your complaints?" Rhia asked in a rush. She feared Mam would think she pried, but she needed to know! "Did He show you in the flames how the brutal of the world will burn eternal when they die?"

Mam still smiled, but wrinkled her nose. "That is cold comfort here on earth, Rhiannon, don't you think? And such eternal punishments are best left to God, His business, never ours. Come close here, daughter. Bring Sally."

They went close. Mam leaned to kiss Sal upon the cheek, then Rhia. She grasped their linked hands within the two of her own. "God reminded me that one thing *can* fend. The care we take of each other comes from His own loving heart and will *not* be broken." She squeezed their hands, then released them and waggled her fingers at them as one will to shoo chickens. "Now off with you two, as it soon grows dark!"

Rhia was a bit surprised to see the sky already painted with glowing streaks of orange and pink and yellow as she and Sal left the stoop to walk to Sal's cottage. The day had been overfilled with events, and had gone racing by so that already it was twilight.

"Sally?" Rhiannon confessed in a whisper. "I did not expect your shattered skull to be knit back when I opened my eyes. I saw what I expected, a beautiful girl with a dent aside her head. My lack of faith may well have stayed God's hand from healing you. If that is the case, I give you heartfelt apology." Rhiannon sighed.

They'd got to Sally's stoop, and clearly Sal was glad to be home. When Rhia opened her door, the young girl rushed to her pallet and lay upon it, curling into her sleep shape with a smile upon her face. Rhia pulled the flaxen blanket over her and said good night.

"I shall bring a candle when it gets full dark," she whispered, pushing Sally's tangled hair back from her eyes. "But first, I should find Thaddeus."

And then Rhia could finally run full-tilt to the chapel. As it was not yet time for Gramp to assume his nightly sentinel duties upon the roof, she threw her weight against the chapel door without seeking his go-ahead, then suddenly felt uneasy entering without it. It was an eery time of day. The moon floated above the trees, and yet the sun had not handed over the world to that silvery dame quite as yet. It was that brief time when things hang suspended—not day, not night. Caught in that hairline crack between past and future, the present is not well formed and can be dreamy and unreal.

In fact, Rhia'd heard rumors of sudden disappearances of both animals and humans, all gone missing in those uneasy moments when the sun keeps his mighty hold, yet haughty Mistress Moon spreads her dark cloak anyhow.

She decided not to enter the part-opened door until she'd peeked around it first. And indeed, she saw that the shadows were grown long upon the walls, and the light was chilly and dim. The large floorstones had grown dampish, as soon the mists would rise from them to float where once those monks had surely walked, chanting their songs, hiding from fierce Northern slayers in their dragonboats. Hiding for a while, that is, but not for long, as their own days were numbered had they but known it.

Rhia wet her dried lips and took a step inside, though still she kept the heavy door cracked open with her heel. "Thaddeus?" she whispered, her voice echoing the single word. "Are you about? It's . . . Rhiannon."

Indeed, she now made out Thaddeus near the altar up front, but he was not alone in that gloomed place. A small, bright figure had been nearby him, and it came hurtling toward the door, bent upon escape now that Rhia had spoke and startled it.

Rhiannon dodged aside, her heart in her throat, intent on giving the spook freedom to take its hasty leave, as who would contain a ghostly haunt against its wishes? But as the one who sought to flee came close, Rhia recognized her and jumped back to bar the door, her hands out imploringly. "Child, please don't go! I'd give you sincere apology first, as I hope to be your friend!"

Ingrid had no choice but to stop, though she right out trembled.

"If it please you," Rhiannon pleaded in a rush, "forgive my earlier . . . well, bad manners." *Stupidity,* she might have said. "I *will* be a good friend to you, if allowed."

Still Ingrid stood atremble, saying nary a word, frozen as a hare gone helpless in a net. Thaddeus had come gently up behind her, and when he put his hand upon her shoulder, Ingrid did not flinch but looked up at him, awaiting his direction.

"Thaddeus, tell her!" Rhia begged. "Say that I would *never* do her harm."

Thaddeus smiled at the girl. "It's true, Ingrid. Rhiannon will be a friend always."

Hard to say what the child thought then, as who may know the thoughts of the hare upon seeing the net opened? Whether to *trust* is the question, for an open pathway may lead to freedom, but may instead lead only to the hunter's well-sharpened knife.

And so Rhiannon could only move aside, and the child dove through the open door and into the murky dusk. Thaddeus and Rhia watched her dart to the woods as though she were a wisp of cloud tatter blown along by a raging gale.

"What was she *doing* here?" Rhia breathed. "Did *you* bring her hence?"

Thaddeus shook his head. "She was here when I came in. Rhia, I believe she hides in here when the sun is brightest, as her skin and eyes are harmed by its rays. At night, then, she goes about in the woods. We saw her on Charlemagne last night, remember? And on the foggy evening I first came up here, she was at Sally's window."

Rhia nodded, though still puzzled. "But she was at bluff's edge when I gathered seeds with Daisy and Sally. Though she stayed within the deep shade, now I think of it. Was she lured from here by the sight of Daisy as we progressed along the trail, do you think?"

"I'd imagine so," Thaddeus allowed. "I'm sure she longs for the lighthearted company of girls her own age, as any child will."

Rhiannon frowned and put her hand upon her hip. "Wait. How do *you* know so much about her, even her name? She's mute and could not tell it." She tapped her chin and murmured, "For that matter, how does *Daisy* know the child's name?"

Thaddeus wearily shook his head. "She's not mute, though she will not often talk. We might not either if our words had brought us the misery hers have brought her." He looked at Rhia with great sadness in his eyes. "I've met her before, you see—in Glastonbury. I'd not seen her close enough to know it until I saw her upon the altar bench when I entered this place earlier this evening."

He sat heavily upon the wall bench by the baptismal font and leaned forward with his elbows upon his knees. "She was born to peasants in Coventry just as you see her now, without a speck of color anywhere about her, even her eyes the faintest pinkish blue. The local gentry there bought her from her mother, believing she could tell the future, which is a common superstition with children such as she. They installed her in their manor house, taught her to ride when she could sit the saddle, kept her like a prized pet and asked her the meaning of their dreams. She answered well enough to please them in her childish way, I imagine. It's not hard to tell folk what they want to hear. But there came a time that . . ."

Rhia went to sit next to him, as Thaddeus had spoken more and more quietly as he'd proceeded. Indeed, he'd mumbled the last sentence so she'd barely heard, and now it seemed he might stop his account altogether.

"Thaddeus?" she nudged, elbowing him lightly in the ribs. "A time that *what?*"

He covered his face with his long fingers.

"There came a time that hardship arrived at the manor, as there *will* be hard years at any house," he murmured. "A fire ravaged the lord's barns, and then his ships were sunk that might have filled his coffers. Both mishaps coming so close together were thought to be witchcraft and blamed upon the child. She was put out of the place, left on her own to fend in the streets of Coventry at the age of six. She was starved and kicked, and lay dying in the mud of the common pigsty when one of my brothers at Glastonbury came upon her. Brother Gyles secreted her to our infirmary, where we kept her for a year."

Thaddeus abruptly stood and began pacing in great agitation, his hands tucked within his sleeves. He paused beneath the window with the Devil Dogs of Clodagh painted above it, and Rhia saw opportunity to ask what she could no longer wait to know.

"But Thaddeus, how came she to be in *our* woods?"

Thaddeus looked upward and appeared to address the gruesome hounds. "At Glastonbury we nursed her as well as we were able," he said, in a hollow way. "But one night as we slept, she disappeared, walked away from her bed without a word, as oft happens with those in our care. We were able to strengthen her limbs a little, but I fear her spirit was too damaged for our skills. I can only think that she lived wild then, helped by the lepers who dwelt in the countryside. When they were gathered by the earl's men for removal to this bluff, she must have been taken in the same net. She is now about eight years old, or nine. Though she's the size of Daisy at six, from rough treatment."

Thaddeus could not have known how sick Rhiannon felt upon hearing all this, seeing as how at the bluff today, with her actions and demeanor, she'd echoed the witchy accusations those vile folk in Coventry had made.

She had indeed shunned a child who'd nearly died from just such shuns . . . *that is* not *your sister . . . let us go home. . . .*

She stood. "Thaddeus, I feel unwell and must bid you a good evening."

"Please, Rhia, wait." Thaddeus hurried over to her. "Jonah will not rest until I speak to you of his plan for Beltane Eve. That is, *our* plan. I confess I went along when he proposed it. Though now I've had time to ponder, I'm not so sure. You know how Jonah is. Blinding in his enthusiasm. Anyhow, I will tell you and judge by your reaction if his ideas be lamebrained, or not. For there will be dangers and pitfalls that—"

Rhia grasped his arm. "Thaddeus, I don't want to hear of this just now!"

She ran from the chapel, sure she would be sick from the sourness that churned within her. But it didn't happen, and when she reached the nether side of the beehives, she fell upon her knees and fisted her hands in her laps.

"I am *bitterly* ashamed of the way I acted toward a young girl today!" she wailed to the bees, who stood silent jury as Mistress Moon above sat judge. "Could I do it over, I would *never* let vile superstition cloud my sight and turn my heart all stony cold."

Whether Rhia'd known it or not, her regret had been a prayer, and the sort God is wont to answer much quicker than a prayer for flashy tricks, a healed skull or some such. The bees held their silence when she'd finished, and so she was able to hear the soft clop-clop of slow-stepping hooves coming up behind her.

Hardly daring to breathe, she stood and turned toward the sound.

It was Sir Jonah who trod in her direction, leading Charlemagne by a cord thrown loose about his neck! And upon that tall steed's bare back and holding his reins sat young Ingrid! The horse and child glowed with the moonlight as though they'd drifted down from heaven, whilst Jonah seemed a hardier, earthbound thing, made of dense shadows and smelling strong of sawdust and sweat.

He grinned, proud of himself. "Rhia! See what I've caught in the woods tonight?"

But Rhiannon's eyes were only for the child. She walked as close as she dared.

"Earlier I asked your forgiveness for my bad manners, but indeed I need forgiveness for a much weightier thing," she whispered up to her. "My own nervous fears kept me from feeling what you were feeling. I believe fear of what we do not know may be the devil's best tool, meant to keep us back from those we long to approach."

At this, Ingrid gave her the slightest of smiles.

Then, with the air of a child engaged in a grand game, she pulled the reins taut so that the steed pranced upon his back legs and pawed the air. Then the two of them turned with a flourish and were off for the sheltering woods from whence they'd come.

Sir Jonah let the lead rope be pulled from his hands and roared with laughter as they galloped away. "They will come close to you when they wish, but indeed *won't* be caught," he said admiringly. He then turned to Rhia with his knuckles upon his hips. "Well, did you speak with Thaddeus? What say you to our brilliant plan?"

Rhia lifted her chin. "Indeed, I have not heard it, though I confess I think it no plan at all unless I have had a large hand in it. After all, Beltane Eve is *my* affair, never yours."

Jonah played at being confused. "You say you've not heard our plan," he said teasingly, "and yet you know it to be a plan for Beltane, and so I think you *have*."

Rhia felt her neck burn and was glad of the darkness. "I need to candle Sally's window," she said, and hurried to leave him. "As for your plan," she threw back over her shoulder, "I only know you made one, but I've little desire to know more."

A brazen mistruth, of course, and so transparent Sir Jonah right out laughed.

"When you hear the great bird squawk tonight, you'll know Thaddeus and I wait in the chapel for your attendance so we may talk more!" he shouted after her, still laughing.

Chapter 23

Rhiannon lay sleepless that night, listening for Gramp's midnight signal.

Daisy breathed beside her, the child's rosebud mouth moving as though she would speak to the shades that lived in her dreams. Lucy the cat snored at Daisy's feet, and the tortoise Queen Matilda clicked about upon the floor. Mayhaps she believed she traveled far, though she only went in a small circle, round and round and round.

Rhia lifted one hand and placed it between her face and the sparrow's gaping hole in the roof weave. She noted how her fingers cut the starry sky into wedges, as though the sky was a half round of cheese and her fingers the lines the cheesemonger's knife had made. She might close her hand into a fist and crush a handful of stars, if she liked.

She yawned. "Hurry up, boys," she whispered. And then, she was suddenly asleep.

Gramp's alarm brought her round a little later, but she was then so fuzzy-headed she slid down the ladder, thumping her rear with every rung, and staggered nearly into the firepit before she made it out the door. She stopped still upon the threshold, waiting for Granna or Mam to call and ask her business leaving the house at this unheard-of hour. If Mam had, she'd have pled that she'd been sleepwalking, and it would have been so nearly true that God would forgive the lie, she reckoned.

But neither one awoke and called out. Her luck was holding, then. She ran straightaway to the brook and slapped water on her face, gasping at its icy chill, then turned on her heel and sped to the chapel.

Gramp sat upon the roof, growling, so Rhiannon hushed him with a finger to her lips as she approached. "All's well, Gramp. We three meet here tonight to make a plan."

Gramp raised one eyebrow, but hunkered his head into his neck feathers, relaxing his guard. He'd been halfhearted in his warning this time anyhow, mayhaps from his own overwork, or mayhaps because he now recognized the two who'd sneaked into the place. He'd kept up a *grrrrrrr* in his throat that sounded more like annoyance than a true squawk of alarm, but it'd been enough to penetrate Rhia's deep dreams, that's the main thing. "Thanks, Gramp, for your vigilant protection," she whispered, for courtesy's sake, as she threw her weight against the heavy door.

She'd forgot a tallow. "Piddle!" she whispered, stubbing her toe as she went up the stoop and into the ancient church. The door creaked closed behind her as she jumped around the ancient flagstones upon one foot, calling out, "Thaddeus and Jonah! You've got me here from a deep sleep and I've nearly torn my toe off, so *show* yourselves without delay!"

In the far shadows, stone squealed against stone as the ancient hermit's tomb was slowly opened from the inside. Rhiannon rolled her eyes and went in that direction, feeling slowly along lest she stub her hurt toe *again* upon a lip of floor stone.

"I've seen this before, remember, Jonah? This time, I shall *not* take you for . . ."

But there was eery light coming from deep within the vault, so that the figure now looming in the entrance to it was framed with back-glow. Each bone in his face was sharp and skeletal, each finger threw a long and dancing shadow, and his head was capped with mossy things that squirmed and slithered. He groaned as he advanced.

In spite of herself, Rhia took quick steps backward, her hands at her throat.

Thaddeus then appeared behind the phantom, lunging from within the vault to slap the spirit upon the back so that cobwebs puffed from its filthed jacket. "We *got* her, Jonah!" he raved, then turned eagerly to Rhiannon. "Admit to being frightened, Rhia! We got you with the worms and the lamplight, even though you had every reason to think it was Jonah, having seen him similarly emerge last night. We *got* you!"

Jonah pulled off the hideous headdress and the two of them stood there slapping hands and laughing. They reminded Rhiannon of nothing so much as the little girls at their game that afternoon. More to the point, her feelings were hurt at their laughter.

"I *thought* we were to speak of saving Jim tonight," she scolded, "but instead you would . . . you would do *horse*play!" She turned to leave them to their boyish antics.

But ere she reached the door, they rushed to her, took an elbow apiece, and turned her back around with nothing she could do about it, even had she truly wanted to.

"You misunderstood our little play, Rhia," said Sir Jonah, his eyes glistening. "You took it for performance, when it was but practice. Forgive us."

"Practice?" Rhia asked, though her question was ignored in their excitement.

"And the glee I showed was surprise, never ridicule," Thaddeus added happily. "I ask your pardon for our coarseness, but in my contemplations this afternoon I truly had decided Jonah's plan was harebrain, whereas now I can see that it just might work!"

Rhia could not get in a word to ask the questions that now swirled within her head, as Sir Jonah had objected to the word *harebrain* and he and Thaddeus bickered rapidly back and forth as they walked with her between them, still held by the elbows. And then quick enough she realized they were not headed for the main part of the room at all, but were headed right back to the dampish and nearly airless crypt!

She dug in her heels. "Wait! Wherefore go we, to the hermit's vault? We can talk up here in the wide part of the church *much* better."

She'd never visited the hermit's bones after dark, so why start now?

The boys stopped walking and let go her arms. Thaddeus tucked his hands into his sleeves. Though before he'd been mirthful, now he looked as solemn as she'd seen him.

"Rhia, again I beg you pardon us," he implored. "Sir Jonah and I have had the same thought, which is that we should seek the hermit's blessing before embarking on this course. We will need help from all sides if this is to work."

Jonah nodded. "I've told you, Rhia, how these past months my friend Aleron and I have sought the tombs of saints upon our journeys. And so your ancient hermit's resting place seems the natural spot, and a goodly one, to pray that we be pure of heart and worthy of this quest. Things may go without a hitch, but again, there is always the chance of . . . disaster."

Rhiannon's eyes widened. "Disaster?" she whispered.

Jonah shrugged quite cheerfully. "I might better have merely said danger."

Still, dangers are only a smidgeon less worrisome than disasters.

Rhiannon threw up her hands. "I confess I think you *enjoy* danger, Sir Jonah! Though I cannot see what dangers *you* may encounter during *my* meeting at Beltane Eve!"

With that and a vexed shake of her head, she led the way through the stone door and into the ancient Irish hermit's crypt.

There were four stone steps down from the crypt's entrance to the vault itself, and one had to crouch, as the ceiling was low. There was not much space within the stone vault, either. Only a child of Daisy's years might have stood upright there, and with three of them gathered round the scooped-out slab where the hermit lay, elbows met and knees thumped. The scant air smelled of chilly stone and the lamp's dwindling supply of oil.

The saintly Irish hermit lay staring up at heaven as they three stared down at him. His bony jaws gaped and his finger bones had come some undone, as Granna reckoned he'd been there three hundred years or more. His woolen robe had stayed mostly intact, with his iron cross upon its leather thong over his heart, or what remained of it within his robed chest. The last flowers Rhia and Granna had brought on his name day and placed nearby his head were shriveled to crispy weeds. Rhiannon took them between her hands and crushed them to pleasant-smelling shreds, which she sprinkled gently down upon the hermit, as Granna had taught her to do.

Thaddeus made the sign of the cross, and the other two followed him in it. The monk knelt, Rhiannon sat upon her heels with bowed head, and Jonah crouched.

"We pray you, sir, intercede so that our actions may be well planned and bravely done as we set out to save our innocent friend, James Gatt," Thaddeus whispered to the hermit.

The other two said amen to it, then all but the hermit opened their eyes.

Rhiannon turned to Jonah, tapping her chin with Mam's cross. "Let's hear your plan then," she said flatly. "The good hermit may give his blessing, though I warn you, *I* know of your rash nature and may be harder to please."

Jonah squinted his eyes, taking that in. "Yes, my nature is indeed rash," he mused. "In the past that often served me well, though in more recent times it's been my undoing. You're good to remind me, friend Rhiannon. I'll let you hear and judge, then."

"Tell her first of the stone pictures at Wythicopse," Thaddeus urged in a whisper.

"Yes!" Rhia nodded eagerly. "How *did* you know of those ceiling pictures?"

Jonah took a breath. "Those small stones are *not* a ceiling as you suppose, Rhia. They rather make up the floor of an ancient palace, fallen to ruin, or burned, many centuries ago. Conquerors from near the time of Christ built such palaces throughout the world, including in this land. Romans, they were, and though they were chief among pagans, their capital is now capital of all Christendom. I've seen floors like the one you described when I've been traveling with Aleron in Italia, and indeed have glimpsed bits of two or three of them even here in England. Beneath those elegant picture floors are open spaces run through with large pipes. Once, slaves stoked fires that breathed hot air into those pipes, thus heating the floors in winter. The building skills of the ancient Romans were formidable, though their grand kingdom is long since fallen and their opulent buildings now lie ruined even in the city from which they took their name."

Thaddeus cleared his throat and added, "In truth, once Jonah had spoken of those stone pictures, I, too, recognized what your ceiling must be, Rhia. I saw Rome with my father, as a child, and marveled at the fine mosaic floors left in ruins from those ancient times. The artistry is incredible, though the subject matter is pagan, gods and goddesses and the like. Of course, there are natural things, too, such as the hare you saw, and—"

Jonah grew impatient. "Yes, yes, they're pretty enough. But for *our* purposes, the interesting thing is the space left for those pipes to run beneath that stone floor. The moans and huffings you've heard, Rhia, must mean that air still goes through those ancient pipes. And since the pipes are still intact, one *should* be able to crawl beneath that floor from some ancient fireplace that surely lies hidden somewhere in the overgrowth. Thaddeus and I will search for an opening in the morning."

"You'll do *what?*" Rhia was completely lost. "Search for an opening? But *why?*"

Ignoring her question, Jonah leaned toward her across the hermit, his eyes flashing. "Rhiannon, Thaddeus has told me that the earl's son and his friends desire to come up to the bluff, to visit the chapel some dark evening to see if it may hold haunts. Is this true?"

Rhia's breath came faster. "Well, yes, it's an outrageous wish of Maddy's, and now it seems the new friends she's made at the manor are taken with the idea as well. She gave me a choice of celebrating Beltane Eve at Wythicopse or here upon the bluff, and I of course told her that I'd meet her at Wythicopse. The day Mam allowed such a thing as a party in this sanctified chapel would be the day it rained down frogs upon us all."

Jonah nodded, grinning ear to ear. "But they *want* to come here, is the thing. And if something fearsome should happen at Wythicopse to spoil the party, they'd welcome your suggestion that the festivities simply be moved to the bluff, am I right?"

Rhia tore at her hair. "I've just *told* you—Mam would never *hear* of it! And nothing fearsome *will* spoil things at Wythicopse. The boys squiring here have heard the moans and hisses that Maddy and I heard and do not fear dragons one whit!"

"They do not fear air pipes one whit is more like it, Rhia,"

Thaddeus told her. "Likely they have traveled and seen the same type of Roman ruins Jonah and I have seen. As they have decided to use this secret knowledge to their own advantage, we might be forgiven for playing a similar game."

"They'd use it for their own advantage?" Rhia whispered, puzzled.

"To lure young girls, Rhiannon," Jonah was bold to explain, snickering. "It's one of the oldest tricks in the book. Invite a young lady upon a dangerous adventure, then wait for the ooglie-wooglies you've contrived to frighten her into your protective arms!"

Rhiannon, embarrassed nigh to tears, thought of protesting that Maddy would never be so innocently susceptible to such low tricks, nor would she herself. But the truth was, Maddy had probably hoped just that *would* happen, and she herself had been too innocent to expect it. Maddy, then, was willing victim. But worse—she, Rhia, was gullible dupe!

She put her face in her hands, but Thaddeus took her arm and lightly shook it. "Rhia, though we've painted an honest picture of the company you'll be keeping, do you still have the nerve to meet them at this Wythicopse place? Our plan allows for Jonah and me to be nearby when things come to a boil, but no matter how we try to contrive it otherwise, you must still be at the center if our plan's to work."

She drew a breath and held out her open hand to Jonah. "Give me Leonard's scarf."

Jonah drew up his knee and quickly pulled the silken fabric from within one side of his tall boot. He held it toward Rhia, but kept it within his own tightly clenched fingers. He looked her solemnly in the eye for a long moment, as if trying to see the depth of her bravery. Then he yielded the silk, let it drop softly across Rhiannon's sweating palm.

She tucked it quickly away into her waist pouch, murmuring, "One of you must now tell me our plan, and do it stepwise, for this willy-nilly accounting makes my head reel."

"All right, then," Thaddeus pronounced. "You will go with your friend as you'd planned tomorrow eve, Rhia, and meet this Leonard and his mates at Wythicopse Ring. If you can, you'll wheedle or tease them into speaking of their recent, uh . . . exploits."

Jonah interrupted darkly, "Get them speaking of their *crimes*, he means."

Thaddeus sighed. "All right, their crimes. Meanwhile, my good friend Brother Silas and I will be hidden just beneath your feet, under the mosaic floor. After we've heard what we *expect* we'll hear, we will proceed to give them a scare they certainly *won't* be expecting. After that you will suggest that the party move away from such wretched turf and up to the, well, the romantic privacy of the bluff." Thaddeus said this last quickly, then dropped his eyes.

"You're *blushing*, Brother!" Rhia teased.

Thaddeus looked straight ahead and cleared his throat. "So be it. Now, continuing, if I may, I'd tell you that even if the company of young men makes no brag and confesses no misdeed, still Brother Silas and I will raise a commotion, as neither Jonah nor I want you lingering in that place with them for long. Upon the bluff, you'll be on home turf, and better protected. I shall follow at a distance, providing some guard from behind as you make your way up the bluff pathway with them. Should there be any mischief on their part, I would not be a match for them physically, of course, but the authority of my robe oft puts an end to unseemly and, well, *lewd* behaviors."

Jonah raised his eyebrows. "Now you *do* blush, Thaddeus." Grinning, he turned to Rhia. "Then comes my part in the thing. When you've got them to this chapel, Thaddeus will lock the door from out-

271

side, and I will then proceed to compound their fear in the way you've already witnessed tonight. In the moldering guise of this venerable hermit, I will demand a full confession from them as the price of a live exit from this church, which will have gone mysteriously sealed tight at my unearthly bidding."

Caught up in the thing, he pulled on the worm-woven headdress and pointed a quivering finger first at Thaddeus, then at Rhia. "Murderous villains!" he intoned in a macabre voice holding great and awful power. "Fall now to your wretched knees and seek full confession, else I'll see you spun down into fiery damnation this very midnight! *Now,* I say, get upon your knees, ere with my own knuckle bones I break your foul necks so as to *make* you bend them low!"

Thaddeus and Rhia, impressed, gave him a small applause.

Rhiannon then took a deep breath. "So my part is to get them bragging. Jonah's is to bring their brags to full confession when they've come to this chapel. And in the middle, your part, Thaddeus, is to scare them witless from beneath the mosaic floor so they're eager to flee Wythicopse for the bluff. But how may you bring about such a scare?"

Thaddeus looked at her. "I mentioned that Brother Silas will be with me, did I not? That is, I hope to speak with him in secret when Jonah and I go down to Woethersly tomorrow morn, and he will doubtless join me, once he's asked. Did I mention he plays bagpipe? Quite badly, too. When he begins it, the dormitory instantly clears. Some brothers have been known to jump into rough waters and swim quite some ways to get clear of Brother Silas's talents. Others that he's asked to listen have hidden in high trees for entire days until he's given them up as audience." He cleared his throat. "I confess, I've done my share of hiding, too. Rhia, you might want to be well braced when it begins, if you startle easily. Or even if you don't. Have some cover for your ears, as well."

Jonah began to chuckle, and Rhia could not keep back a smile. "Poor Silas," she mused, "to love his music so much he'd creep upon his stomach beneath the mossy ground to find ears above for it. Will you confess to him that you want him not for the beauty he may bring to the evening but only for a fright, Thaddeus?"

Thaddeus shrugged, looking both amused and some shamefaced. "Indeed. He's a good-spirited fellow and will not mind. I'm sure he'll think that to be a fright is better than to be shunned completely. He'll be thrilled to play in any circumstances, and will gladly take whatever compliment he may get, including that he's frightful."

It had been in Rhia's mind that one sky-high obstacle towered above all the many other little obstacles inherent in this daring, though helter-skelter, plan. She hated to bring it up again, as it would spoil things, but it was high time, before this went further.

"You've both ignored the thing I told you that will certainly break this, and that is, Mam will *not* hear of it! I'm sorry to foil your designs, but that's just how it is. You may find your hidden passages and fill them with dreadful noise, Thaddeus. And you, Jonah, may become a saintly hermit. But indeed, if you bring any of this up with Mam tomorrow, she will refuse to let me take any part in Beltane Eve at all! And if you try to go ahead with it without letting her know, she'll come raging when she sees that troupe entering the clearing, as she will not allow the chapel to be used for a Beltane party, ever. And don't hope she will not notice, because *nothing* gets past her up here. Nothing."

Jonah and Thaddeus were quiet for a bit, though Jonah murmured, "You said it will rain frogs when she allows it."

Rhia gave a sharp nod. "Exactly. You *do* remember, then."

Thaddeus cleared his throat. "With all due respect, Rhia, there may be someone who could talk to your mother about this more persuasively than you yourself are able to. I speak of Reeve Clap, and we have reason to think he may throw in with our plan when we tell him of it tomorrow."

Rhia's eyes widened but she waited to hear more.

"Rhiannon, today we learned there was indeed a witness to Aleron's bloody murder," Jonah said gravely, and the sudden grit in his voice sent a chill up Rhia's spine.

Thaddeus whispered, "The poor child Ingrid. I fear she saw it all."

Rhiannon gasped, then froze with her hands over her mouth.

"Something she heard you saying as you gathered seeds this afternoon made her know that Jim stood accused, Rhia," Thaddeus continued. "When I came upon her here in the chapel, it was much on her mind, enough so that she came to me straightaway, took my hand, and said, 'I saw it done.' It took me a while to realize *what* she'd seen done, though by her trembling and her fearful aspect I might have figured it out quicker. And then I ran our suspects past her—Arnold Mopp, Jim himself, the pirate gang, the others that make the woods their present home. To all of these she solemnly shook her head."

Jonah covered his face with his hands, as this was opening his grief anew. "She must have linked with Charlemagne that awful night," he whispered. "It comforts me to imagine her giving Aleron's steed solace after he had witnessed such . . . butchery."

"And then I asked if the murder was done by horsed riders," Thaddeus went on, squinting with the effort of remembering each detail precisely. "Ingrid nodded! I asked if the riders were nobility. Now, most children might not know of what I spoke, of course, but I thought she would, having lived in a noble house. Again, without a moment's hesitation, she nodded. Finally, I asked if she would recognize them if she saw them again. A third time, she answered me with a firm nod."

Rhiannon closed her eyes. "And so our strong hunch is proved with a witness."

"And you see now why we must let the reeve know straightaway, and tell him also of the plans we've got in place!" Jonah interjected, pounding one fist repeatedly into the other hand as he spoke. "The eyewitness testimony of a simple woodland child will never be enough to bring accusation against the earl's house. Since no one of higher rank was witness to the thing being done, the murderers themselves must make confession within hearing of the law."

"We think Reeve Clap will endorse our plan and will conceal himself nearby when the party of suspects comes to your chapel," Thaddeus concluded, more mildly. "We also believe your mother will wish to help him, now that a witness has given us true hope."

Jonah had a tease in his eye. "In other words, get set, Rhia, as it may soon rain frogs."

Rhiannon swallowed, and she must have looked some shaky because Thaddeus leaned close and took her shoulders in his hands, as though to steady her.

"Rhia?" he said, speaking near her face. "You are at the heart of this, and there are dangers at every turn. If Leonard and the others sense our suspicions and feel a trap closing, well, the blade of a concealed knife is quicker than any of us may be able to move to stop it. If this doesn't sit well, you must now say it."

Rhia looked back at Thaddeus, but she was thinking of Jim, of his brave smile and laughing eyes, and of the downy hair of his unmet little grandson.

"I can do it," she whispered, extending her hand above the hermit's concealed heart.

Jonah and Thaddeus reached to place their hands upon hers and they bobbed them once, twice, thrice to set a seal upon the thing.

Chapter 24

Beltane Eve is a time of no time, when the earth holds its breath and the seven sister stars called Pleiades rise just before dawn to dance on the red horizon. Things shimmer in the distance and dissolve when you run close. Things call to you from behind your back, and when you whirl around quick to hear, they turn out to be memory voices of those long gone. The veils are thin at Beltane between the world of men and the world of faeries, and the faeries oft bend human things *their* way.

After she'd left Jonah and Thaddeus the night before, Rhia had crept exhausted to her bed and immediately begun dreaming a deep and birdy dream. In it she flew above churning waters and was blown about by the updrafts of spouting whales. Her feathers were shiny black and her wingspan was wide. She was free and happy, but right before dawn, as the Pleiades began their Beltane dance, Rhia's dream took a sudden dark turn. For then her birdy self looked down upon the green sea just as a boat capsized and went under with its crew. She heard screams melt away to the fearful silence of still water. She saw the bubbles of those last breaths rise into the air, and when they burst they splattered salt water that burned her feathers.

Rhia woke at that and sat straight up, her breath coming fast. She pushed her damp hair from her face, for she'd found that in her sleep she'd been weeping tears that only humans, never birds, may weep.

With more effort she pushed the haunting shreds of the dream back as well, trying not to dwell upon it as she hurried into her clothes to gather seeds. She bent to kiss Daisy as she left, noting how Daisy snored a miniature version of the hardy snores of Granna's, then moved the sleeping tortoise aside with her foot and slipped down the ladder.

The pallet Granna and Mam shared was still lumpy with shapes, so Rhia grabbed the seed pouch and hustled quietly outside to splash her face. She then awaited Gramp, though after some moments, there was still no sign of him. Strange, his tardiness.

"Will you come along, Gramp?" she groused, tapping Mam's cross upon her chin. "I am nervous enough without a game of hide-and-seek to begin this fraught day!"

No Gramp, though, so her best course was to go on, leaving him to catch up.

There was dewy mist, a strange and flickering sort that comes when flowers open themselves wide and let their essences, their flowery souls, fly out to change places with another's for the day. Granna said that on dawn of Beltane Eve a lily might fly to a peach blossom and trade essentials with it, and the lowly dandelion may become essentially a red rose for a day, with the rose essence clothed in humble dandelion garb. By May Day, all would have swapped back, ready for the picking, having learned a thing or two from living in another's skin. *If* flowers may learn, or remember *what* they learn. Granna didn't claim to know, and Rhiannon certainly wouldn't claim to know, either.

"I don't know much about *anything*, in fact," she mused as she walked to bluff's edge.

For years she'd longed to be grown and treated as such. But this morning she was homesick for her childhood days, when Beltane was a time of watching costumed revelers dance the streets, led by the town's massive, rollicking hobbyhorse with his yellow corn teeth. That hobbyhorse was merely a costume for three folk to wear, but she'd believed he was real and enchanted, then. And she'd looked forward for weeks to seeing the beautiful white-clothed Queen of the May ride upon her snowy horse from the faery kingdom, and to watching the glowing bonfires grow higher and higher and wondering if they'd eat up the very sky.

She'd wanted to be grown, and got her wish. And now she knew the Queen of the May was a local girl with a glittering white wig upon her head. What knowledge was that? What *use* was there for it?

She knew as well about the tricks boys will play upon girls at Beltane, or knew it as hearsay anyhow, from Thaddeus and Jonah. She supposed girls might play tricks upon boys just as readily when they got a chance, but she wasn't thinking of that as she walked to the bluff to gather seeds. She was stewing the evening's plans through her head, wishing she might be that saggy hobbyhorse, or Lucy the cat. Wishing she might be a child again, with only light, childish thoughts.

She would avoid Mam today, that was one thing for sure. Let the reeve come up and handle Mam if he could, but Rhia herself would just lie low ere Mam sensed what was afoot and confronted her with it. She'd get the seeds now, then stay with Sally until time to go down. She gulped hard at that thought, for the time to go through with this thing approached so very quickly!

Then all of a sudden, something shifted. Whether of light or whether of sound she couldn't quite tell, but it was enough to make Rhia stop in her tracks near the windbent and scrawny orchard trees, holding her breath. "Gramp?" she dared to whisper.

The mist flickered, the little white buds of the scrawny trees quivered. The rising sun went loop-de-loop with cloud so that shadows chased across the pathway. The grasses crackled as small animals awoke, or mayhaps it was faeries running rampant.

Then Rhia heard someone singing with the sad and haunting voice of a mermaid. The sound came from the very edge of the bluff, or mayhaps from the sea beach far below it. That sweet voice was filled with such longing that it drew Rhia nearer, against her better judgment. She'd all her life longed to see a mermaid, and Beltane *was* the likely time for one to come ashore, but she felt the strings of her nerves might plain snap today if this most enchanted of voices issued from some unheard-of monster. Who'd truly seen a mermaid to know? Not even Granna.

And so she crept along the last of the pathway on tiptoe, holding her breath. The song was in an olden language Rhiannon did not know, or elsewise a mermaid language. Her hands felt numb as she pushed aside the branches of willow that hung low over the pathway's end.

But it was *Mam* that stood at the very edge of the lip of high stone that overhung the bluff! The sea wind made a sail of her green cloak. Her arms were filled with woodland flowers, which she threw, one by one, to the waters. The wind tossed each of them for a while, then let them fall to the waves, abandoned playthings.

Rhia, scarcely breathing, would have gladly watched forever without a sound to break the spell. But Gramp sat upon his holed rock, squinting and all puffed up, and presently he noticed Rhia and craned his neck in her direction. Mam turned then. The hood of her green cloak framed her face, and her eyes, meeting Rhia's, were red with crying.

"Rhiannon?" she said in a breathy, windy way. "Did you know that your da and your grandfather died on Beltane Eve? I don't believe we ever thought to tell you that."

She turned back to the sea and threw another red poppy to the careless wind. Dozens of birds circled silently above the place in the water where Rhia's da had drowned when the whirlpool had opened twelve years before. Rhiannon walked quietly over to stand beside Mam, closer to the edge than she would have dared to go without her. She lifted a corner of Mam's cloak to shield her own shoulders from the wind, and Mam shrugged so that more of the cloak went to Rhia.

"Coln was of the water," Mam whispered, handing Rhia a flower to throw. "Like my father, he could not sleep unless he heard the sound of the sea nearby." She looked at Rhia. "You were so young, not yet three. How well do you remember him, daughter?"

Rhia's throat ached. "I remember his black hair, and the way he picked me up and whirled me around, then held me to the sky so that I laughed myself breathless."

Mam smiled and looked again to the sea, nodding.

"He marveled that you were not afraid of that, that you laughed when you might have cried. He took you out in the coracle every fine day. He would have made you a fisherman, with my da's willing help. You'd have grown up with thumbs all fin-pricked and your own black hair smelling of brine and being yourself afeared of nothing in the world, just as he was. But instead we've kept you airborne up here, your granna and I. We've likely been selfish, keeping you so close. I was just so very afraid . . ."

Rhia gasped. "Mam! I believe this morn I *dreamed* of my father's death, and awoke crying seawater tears." She frowned then, fully realizing what Mam had just said. "But you're the bravest of *any*one and *never* afeared, Mam," Rhia said quietly. "Everyone who knows you says it."

Mam didn't answer at first. "Afraid of but one thing," she finally whispered.

She took Rhia's arm and turned them away from the treacherous lip of rock, walking them back from the edge a bit so the wind was lessened, then wrapping the cloak closer around them both.

"You were singing the old songs, weren't you, Mam?" Rhia got the nerve to ask. "The songs of enchants and lost loves Granna has kept, the ones you say are not fit for Christian ears and right out blasphemous in these modern Christian times?"

Mam blushed. "Coln loved to hear me sing them, and this once a year I sing them to him," she admitted. "God may forgive me for such a thing, as He's a just God, and a forgiving one as well."

"Your song brought the birds this dawn, didn't it, Mam? Which might show that—"

Mam cut her off, stepping in front of Rhia and taking Rhia's shoulders in her hands.

"Daughter, we have other things to speak of. I know all about your plans for this night, Rhia. The monk and Sir Jonah skulked away to town some time ago, and I glimpsed their departure as I gathered blossoms for your da. When they saw me watching from the woods, Thaddeus came running, his face all contorted by his conscience at work. He confessed every word of your plans to me, Rhia. You mighta known he would not wait for Almund to come and do it for him."

Rhia slapped her forehead with her palm and heard herself make a little squeal like a mouse caught in Lucy's claws. "*Please*, Mam! Don't bid me stop!" she begged. "If you had but seen Jim's baby grandson! If you'd felt his downy hair! I *must* do this, and do it well, though to do it well I need your blessing upon it. Please!"

Mam pulled Rhiannon close and wrapped her arms tight about her, pressing her cheek against Rhia's wild hair. She stared over Rhia's shoulder to where the birds still circled above the waters, then Rhia heard her whisper, "You see your girl, Coln? Do you see the strong-willed daughter you've left me with?"

Presently Mam stepped back a little ways and reached to touch the little cross about Rhia's neck. "I must hear what Almund has to say about it," she said, quietly but firmly. "And I've told Thaddeus that some trusted deputy must come up with the reeve to escort you down the trail, then he must stay at a distance behind you even when you've met Maddy. You will *not* proceed one step without him following behind as guard, do you understand, daughter?" She raised her eyes to Rhia's and demanded, "*Do* you, Rhiannon?"

Rhia nodded, though privately she had doubts about this part of the thing. She'd never yet seen anyone keep up with Maddy, deputy or housemaid, friend or jilted foe.

Without another word, Mam raised and kissed the cross that now hung on Rhia, then kissed Rhia on both cheeks. "Stay and gather your seeds, and have a thought and a prayer for your da and grandda," she said simply. She turned to walk home with bowed head and slow step.

Rhia stayed. As she'd been told to, she gathered her seeds and thought her thoughts.

Sir Jonah, Almund Clap, and his best deputy, Holt Yeoman, arrived upon the bluff shortly after midday. Rhia noted that Jonah had costumed himself for the trip he'd made to town that morn in bits and rags left atop the bluff by previous tenants. He'd tied a yellow bandanna about his face as some field workers will do, and his hair he'd gathered under a black woolen watch cap, where it bulged, doubtless wishing to break free in all its glory. All in all, this conglomeration of clothing made him a good disguise.

Granna, Mam, and Rhia had been nervously awaiting their arrival, trying to stay busy stringing herbs for drying. Young Daisy hovered just outside the house, sensing from the tight silence within that something big was afoot, though she knew not what.

"Three men come!" Daisy piped from the doorway when the reeve and his party entered the clearing. Rhia and Mam jumped instantly to their feet and bustled to get drink and cheese for them, all thumbs in the doing of it so that Rhia cut her knuckle and Mam spilled some ale upon her skirt. Only Granna sat and calmly chewed her pipe.

The three settled themselves around the firepit and without delay reported that indeed in the wild brush of Wythicopse they had found the old fireplace opening, where Roman slaves had once bent to stoke the pipes that ran beneath the floor of that ancient palace. Almund, who himself was needed in a thousand places the morn of Beltane Eve, had commandeered two of the languishing pirates to help Jonah, and they had spent the morning breaking through that fireplace with axes, opening an entrance to the crawlspace beneath the floor, then covering the entrance with overgrowth again.

While they did this, Thaddeus had managed to signal his friend, Brother Silas, and the two of them were even now positioning themselves and Brother Silas's instrument within that shallow crawlspace.

"Everything over there is now in order, Aigy, as safe as we can make it," Almund concluded. "Holt will be but steps behind Rhiannon all the way to the place and all the way back. He's skilled in concealment, and you could find no better bodyguard than he'll make." Almund put his hand upon Holt's shoulder.

Holt looked embarrassed but pleased by the praise. "Aigneis, you know I'll guard her with my life," he said simply.

"Silas gave me a short concert on his bagpipe before we left, and indeed, I was much impressed by the sheer wretchedness of it," Jonah interjected, pulling off his bandanna and cap in one impatient move. "It would frighten the devil himself and turn him to righteousness. So, madame, all is well-done. The plan is tight as Noah's ark."

Sir Jonah obviously expected Mam to be charmed and won over by his wit, but the others knew that wit would likely not sit well with her in this particular circumstance.

You could have heard a bird breathe as Mam stood.

"You ask of me the hardest thing anyone has ever asked," she said, quite icily. "And Almund, though I know Holt to be true and capable, you yourself must stand ready to interfere within the church at the slightest hint of anything amiss over there."

Almund looked troubled and did not answer her at first. And then he stood and walked some steps closer to speak with her more direct.

"Aigy, though Holt and I will watch that holy chapel from here within your cottage, we have to stay clear. There is nowhere in its court-yard to conceal ourselves, and we will only dare approach when we have our signal that a confession is very near to being made by them. Understand that. Rhiannon will make sure that a candle is lit in the southwest window of the church when they've first arrived there, and she will move it to the southeast window to signal us to come close beneath the windows to hear what transpires. To storm the place too early would greatly endanger those inside. These young folk will be largely on their own. It's how it must be."

Without a word of answer, Mam walked to her medicinal corner and got busy. She'd spoke nothing nor done anything to scuttle the plan, but indeed she held her lips in a tight line and her hair was a moving blaze that Rhia could feel scorching the place.

The others felt it, too. "We'll to the chapel now to make it ready," Almund mumbled.

Holt and Jonah, looking greatly relieved for the excuse to escape, jumped readily to their feet, and the three of them left.

Daisy frowned, confused by all this. "Well, *I'm* going to *Sally's*," she told them, and flounced out as one who's frustrated beyond endurance by the present company.

Rhiannon, scarcely daring to move, nevertheless crept around the edge of the room to sit close beside Granna, who had stared deep into the firepit for some time, frowning.

"Do you . . . see anything?" Rhia whispered, first glancing nervously in Mam's direction. "Does the fire speak of tonight's goings-on?"

Granna would not answer at first. Rhia watched her eyes, and saw a spark in them she hoped was concentration, though it might have been dread, or even fear.

"I've watched these flames all day, since your mother told me of your risky plans, Rhiannon," Granna finally murmured. "In the fire I've seen a shadow procession of folk coming up our bluff, and I've seen as well a procession of shadow folk going back down." She reached for Rhia's hand. "But looky there, child." She pointed with her pipe stem. "Can you na see the space of circling black there between the glowing ashes? There to the nether side, amidst the bluish sparks. See?"

Rhia bent and squinted, but could not, as usual, see any such thing.

"It's death," Granna whispered in a weak crackle of sound like a quick-burning leaf. She kept tight hold of Rhia's hand, but would say nothing more.

Chapter 25

Reeve Clap's deputy Holt Yeoman was not much of a talker, and Rhiannon was glad of that going down the trail that early evening. All the better to practice in her head the coy conversation she was expected to use upon the earl's son's sophisticated friends. Not that she hadn't already been trying out various ways to get them blabbing about their exploits. Ever since she'd heard Jonah's plan, a big part of her brain had been working on it all the time.

She might widen her eyes and say, "Tell me, Sir Leonard, of the bravest things you've done, as I long to hear of your most outrageous exploits!" Or, "How fast I've seen you ride! Surely you've had escapades at such speeds?" Would Leonard, or one of his mates, then brag of doing reckless mischief in the woods the night Aleron was murdered?

Oh, but *why* would Thaddeus and Jonah *ever* think her capable of such a thing as flirtatiousness? Why, she'd never so much as said two sentences to a boy near her age until she'd met the two of them! The earl's friends, courtiers that they were, would surely spot right away her country ways and lumpish speech. She tapped her chin with Mam's cross and bit her lip, trying to be consoled with the thought that at least she looked her best tonight. She'd gone to a fine lot of trouble for that.

She'd washed her hair in the brook and rinsed it twice in rose water this afternoon, and now it swung free and slippery along the length of her green woolen tunic to below her waist. She'd braided her waist rope with honeysuckle, and cinched that belt so tight her small waist showed, then she'd put sprigs of morning glory and wild rose in amongst a few tiny braids she'd made in her tresses and through the laces of her boots.

"Hear that?" Holt suddenly spoke, startling her from her thoughts. "The party's well begun in the streets of Woethersly, though night has yet to fall."

Indeed, above the lapping of the sea, they could now hear the distant thrum of tambourines, the high swirl of dance music played upon flutes, and the squeal of raucous laughter. In another hour, when the bonfires were lit and Beltane Eve had wound up to its heights, that thrum would become a roar with little chance of anyone hearing what was said or being heard themselves when they tried to call above the racket.

Only Wythicopse's remote location might make it quiet enough for coy conversation.

Rhia reached in her pouch for Leonard's scarf. She draped it round her neck and, with fingers made clumsy by the afternoon's nervous imaginings, tied it in what she hoped was a fashionable and jaunty way.

It was fully dark by the time Rhia, with Holt some steps behind, came to the far edges of Woethersly. Once past the holy grounds of the church, they were caught up in the roiling and rambunctious crowd that surged willy-nilly through the streets. All were by now either drunk or feigned being, as drunkenness brought with it the giddy heedlessness the evening allowed. Some were costumed and many wore masks.

Bonfire wood was stacked high in several places, and would be lit when the Queen of the May arrived at the center of the green to give the signal. After the flames had burned a little and got some low, the young maids and lads of the town would go to jumping the fires, as this would help free the summer sun from the wintry grasp that held him still. Winter *must* loose the sun by the end of tonight, else the May warmth could not come in upon the morrow.

Thinking of that, Rhia mused that more than a few of those fire jumpers would wake in the streets at dawn to find themselves with burns they'd naught felt when they'd got them, drunk and loony as they'd been. Maddy last year had burnt her ankle, but now wore that scar with pride. Rhia'd not jumped. Typically, she'd wished she had Maddy's nerve and could just *do* it without thinking it ten times first. But she *had* thought it ten times, then had withdrawn into the shadows to meekly watch the others.

No bonfires to jump or *not* to jump this year was the one comforting thing about this Wythicopse plan, she decided, as a howl of general delight turned her attention to the left. The Queen of the May was riding sidesaddle toward the green. The torches set in the ground showed her near-nakedness, for she wore but a short tunic, as a boy would do, and her legs from above her knees to her toes were completely and shockingly bare, though glistening with faery dust. Her white hair flowed to her waist, glistening as well, and her steed's snowy mane was strung with bells and sparkles.

"Come, ye lads—share the delights of the faery realms!" she sang as she rode so provocatively, touching some handsome young man gently upon the head with her wand, whilst next giving that boy's girlfriend a sharp hit with it. All of this brought laughter and lewd comments from the boisterous crowd.

Everyone in the White Queen's path pretended great temptation, though none would consent to jump upon her horse and ride pillion behind her. To return with the Queen of the May to faeryland's pleasures brought certain doom when Beltane was over and the faery gates closed again.

The horsehair wig had tipped a little from the Queen's white brow and Rhia noted a bit of the actress's dark hair showing beneath, a thing she would have ignored two Beltanes ago, when she still believed in all magics. And then someone yelled, "Make way!" and there came the shabby hobbyhorse careening through the crowd, the three performers hidden in his skin running blindly along so that all had to move or be collided with. A cheap trick he was, like the Queen herself, yet Rhia smiled at his clumsy, helter-skelter trot.

Then suddenly— *Whoof!* A dozen high fires sprang from the wicker wood that had been brought and piled high. A dozen orange blazes waved spiky arms against the dark sky, casting dancing shadows upon all below so that cheekbones were picked out and skin hollowed and all present became something more delightfully patterned and strangely formed than they were in normal times.

Here was the true magic, then, in the firelight's transforming touch. The musicians pranced all the more gaily with their lutes and pipes, the sweating revelers wove in delirious snake-lines behind that music, and innocent children gaped from the shoulders of their elders, their eyes wide with the spectacle of it all.

Rhiannon looked quick behind her, and after a moment located Holt. His eyes were fastened upon her in the way a hunter is said to fix his prey, so she let herself relax a bit as she searched through the flickering light for the sort of off-kilter movement in the crowd that would signal Maddy's careless approach.

But the folk in the green were already off-kilter to such an extent that Rhia had no inkling of her friend's close arrival until a hand clamped shut upon her wrist and she felt her shoulder jerked nigh clean of its socket. And then she was taken through the roil and press of bodies as if she were a rag dragged along by some mongrel. Indeed, Maddy moved them as the hobbyhorse moved, heedless of all knocked asunder by their passing!

"Maddy!" Rhia screamed. "Slow down, won't you? My feet barely touch ground!"

But Rhia could not hear her own entreaties, and so it's sure Maddy could not, either.

Indeed, Holt might be left far behind, though Rhia could not spare a worry for being unguarded, as a greater conundrum loomed large. Maddy had *two* wrists in her two strong hands, and she pulled along *two*, Rhia and another! The galloping glimpses Rhia could have of her twinned captive showed the long skirt of a female, but all else of that person was concealed beneath a cloak and mask.

While it would not have been past Maddy to snatch a good-looking stranger from the crowd, this girl appeared to be a willing tag-along. But *why* was she here, and what dire effect might it have upon the evening's proceedings?

Past the left turn at the manor gates they sailed, then on along the line of yew trees. When they'd nearly got to the nether ford of the river, Maddy finally decided to loose her grip, and they all three collapsed to the ground. The clamor and noise of the festival was reduced so much that Rhia could hear the gurgle of the river, along with the sound of blood rushing within her ears. The fires poked up into the sky far behind them so that they all three turned to face that way as they got their breath. Everything nearer to them was shrouded in the absolute darkness of a moonless night.

"I . . . I thought it was to be only you and me from town, Maddy— you to be with Frederique and me for Leonard, with the other squires too young for, well, feminine company," Rhiannon found the spunk to say. She'd no wish to offend this other, but she dreaded what this new complication might do to the plan they'd made, which already, to say it true, was hung together by the flimsiest of threads.

"Yes, I did say that," Maddy admitted. "But last year you said you'd jump the fires, Rhia, and then you didn't, see? So how could I know for sure you'd come? And without a good-looking girl for himself, Leonard would be so angry, who knows what he might do? I mentioned he has a temper, did I not? Anyhow, two girls will not offend him, so never worry about it." She shrugged. "In fact, once Roderick sees this other, *he* will likely want her for *his* own companion and will wave away his lady cousin."

Rhiannon gulped. "Lady . . . cousin? You said nothing about *her*, either."

Maddy laughed gaily. "Some of their lady cousins have arrived today from Francia for the party. Let's along then, as the boys await!" Maddy jumped to her feet. She leaned and quickly whispered into Rhia's ear, "This other's older than us, and quite beautiful."

If she'd had time, Rhia might have wept from despair. How *could* their plan proceed with all these girls come from Francia? Yet there was no going back now. It was set.

Maddy ran on, and moments later Rhia heard splashing that showed her to be crossing the river. Rhia and the other quickly stood and followed then, never wishing to be lost out here with it so dark and Maddy gone too far ahead to see.

The other girl outpaced Rhia, being longer legged. But at the water, she waited and the two of them made the dark crossing together hand-in-hand, as it's courteous to do when night makes even the shallow crossing of a river ford difficult. Neither spoke.

Then, following a flicker in the darkness that was Maddy's bright hair far ahead, they ran up the steep rise beyond the ford, and presently arrived atop Gallux Hump.

The black oak that crowned that execution spot spread wide arms against the night sky, as though it would snatch all comers and hold them to its woody breast forever.

Rhia wanted to hurry on past it, but the other girl suddenly halted beneath those dark branches and put her hand out to clutch Rhia's arm, hard, stopping her as well.

The moon had finally appeared a little above the tree line, and the girl stepped solemnly into its silver light, faced Rhia, and removed her mask.

"We stand upon the wretched hill where my father will soon hang," said Beornia Gatt.

Rhiannon gasped and covered her mouth with her hands, but Beornia seemed not to care that she'd given such a shock. Indeed, she seemed not to notice.

"The obnoxious son of your friend Hilda Mopp is the *true* murderer," Beornia leaned close to declare, quite heatedly. "And yet they will hang my father for it!"

"Come on, you two!" Maddy called from a distance.

Startled, Rhia jerked her gaze toward Maddy's voice and saw a spiral of murky light circling in the night sky. The brambly walls of Wythicopse Ring were completely invisible in the darkness, but servants from the manor must have been sent ahead to light the place, and the smoke and fireglow from torches set inside the stone walls formed a ghostly outline that hovered above the place. "We come!" Rhiannon called to Maddy.

Turning back to Beornia, she whispered urgently, "Just so you know, Hilda Mopp's *not* my friend. Mistress Mopp throws her gossip like a net over anyone nearby. I was stupidly entangled in her talk when you saw us at market the other day, though I'd have chewed my foot off to escape, had I been a hare or a red fox."

At this, Beornia snorted a quick laugh, then smiled. "I believe you," she said simply, then started to traipse forward again.

"Wait!" Rhiannon pleaded. "You've not told me why you're here!"

Beornia's eyes flashed. "The silly girls who work as maids for Lord Claredemont have spoke all week of this party. Oh, they whisper and giggle of how they've got such a great secret, but anyone who sidles up when they're at the water well can't help but get an earful. I sought invitation from the maid-of-all-poultry so that tonight I could appeal to the young squires attendant at the manor. They *must* hear my evidence and agree that the real murderer *is* Arnold Mopp, never my father! Then they will surely tell Lord Claredemont of it with all haste, and Father will go free." She narrowed her eyes, then added, "It would be a most welcome thing to be paired with the earl's own son tonight, as he's bound to have the most direct influence. I can put my evidence right into his hands to pass along to his godsire, Lord Claredemont!"

"Evidence?" Rhia cleared her throat and struggled to get a good breath, for indeed, this was staggering information. *Arnold* the killer, and never the gang of reckless lords?

"Look!" Beornia pointed to where the darkness boiled as a party of riders rounded the manor walls at a full gallop. The young squires shouted to each other with high spirits and much laughter, reaching the confines of Wythicopse Ring, then riding around it at an unheard-of speed. Rhia tried to count the torches they carried and thereby determine their number, but there were too many, and there was too much movement.

A small scream followed immediately by a louder shriek of high laughter told that Maddy had been snatched up as she got near the brambly walls to ride with that gang. And then they swerved and were barreling toward Beornia and Rhiannon, who only had time to exchange a wide-eyed look of panic before they, too, felt strong gloved hands beneath their arms and were painfully swung up to sit pillion behind their kidnappers.

"Stop!" Rhia screamed, for they still went at a gallop and had barely slowed to fetch her and Beornia. "I can't hold on!" Already she'd slid dangerously to one side, and would soon fall completely and be trampled by the beasts that followed close behind!

"Grab round my waist!" her horseman yelled impatiently back to her.

She had no choice, and once she'd done it, she felt stable, though distressed at holding this stranger so. The pack took a fast circle around Gallux Hump, then headed straight back toward Wythicopse Ring again. Surely they'd slow, but nay, her horseman spurred them faster as they drew near!

There was one small breech where tumbled rock had shortened the height of the tall circular wall, and when they'd reached that spot, "Heigh ho, up and over!" the lead rider called, and all the steeds took to the air, nose to tail. Once those sailing steeds had landed one after the other inside Wythicopse Ring, they fell into a circle of the torchlit walls, gradually slowing.

Her horse had come down with a jolt like Rhia'd never felt in her life, and as all her insides settled back into some order or other, she wondered if she'd permanently scrambled them up. What would be the outcome if her heart had settled itself where, say, her gullet had dwelt? She looked for Beornia, and by the torchlight presently spotted her slumped behind her own kidnapper, holding his horse fast with her knees. She was wild-eyed, and Rhia knew from that how wild-eyed she herself must be.

"Some fun!" Maddy called out, but her laughter seemed hysterical. Presently, she slid from the horse she rode and signaled for the other girls to do the same, though none of the young squires had brought those steeds to a complete standstill.

Rhia watched Beornia slide from her moving horse. She stumbled a bit, but then regained her footing and stood whipping dust from her skirt. Well, Beornia had ridden before, no doubt, but Rhia had certainly not! To jump from such a distance to the ground seemed impossible, and twice impossible with the movement of the steed!

"Will . . . will you not please stop your horse?" she found nerve to lean forward and ask the squire she rode behind. "I'm . . . new at this."

Without a word he brought the horse up short. "Dismount," he told her abruptly.

Though Rhia wondered why he would not do her the small courtesy of dismounting himself and helping her to the ground, she felt all eyes upon her and wished the ordeal over at any cost, even that of a broken bone. She took a deep breath and dropped clumsily from the high steed, then staggered and fell to her knees before standing.

Meanwhile, the squire she'd ridden behind had clucked to his horse, and it walked again in a circle with the others. From their exalted position above, all the horsemen were now doing a ride-around to openly scrutinize the three girls who had moved to the center of the ring and stood huddled there, back to back to back. Rhia counted and found there were seven riders upon seven horses. Where were the other ladies, the cousins come from Francia for this party?

"This is humiliating," Beornia grumbled. "I like not being gawked at as though we be hens."

"Don't take it serious," Maddy hissed back. "It's just part of the game." To the rider she'd sat behind, Maddy then called, quite gaily, "Frederique, are your lady friends from Francia to join us here presently, then?"

There was laughter from some of the squires, then one of them called down a rude quip of an answer. "Why would such as they come to *these* rough fields? We will divert ourselves here, then heigh home to greet those ladies after they've rested from their journey here and had supper."

"*Divert* themselves?" Beornia murmured, staring at Maddy as though she'd like to melt her with the gaze. "And are we three, then, to be this . . . *diversion?*"

Maddy looked some shamefaced, but only whispered, "Pray, hold your voice down. I said I'd try to bring a date for each, but the other girls I spoke with were all too afeared to come to this place. And so I believe the younger four of these boys will ride home presently, though disappointed."

"By the way, my cousin Blanche awaits you, Frederique," one of the squires suddenly called across. "She tells me she nigh swooned with love when she got your letter."

The tall and slouch-shouldered squire with the sharp black mustache that Maddy had rode behind was indeed her Frederique, then. Rhia noted the downward turn of his large, moony eyes, and the snide way he produced a slow smile from one side of his mouth at this tease from his mate. She noted as well that he did not bother to cast an apologetic eye toward Maddy, who had certainly heard this reference to another lady.

The squires on each side of Frederique snickered.

Then the one across the circle that Rhia'd ridden behind threw back his glossy curls and laughed, drawing all eyes his way. "Back to the here and now, boys," he called out, stroking his yellow beard to a point just beneath his sharp chin. "Let's choose. I'll gladly have the drunken one. Though young, she'll yield her kisses easily in such a state."

Rhia was mortified, for it was clear that his eyes were fastened upon *her*!

"I assure you, sir, I am not drunken, nor have I ever been!" she called to him, made bold by her chagrin. "I stumbled in my dismount because I'd never attempted it before. I dislike the idea of kissing, as well, having never before attempted *that* in my life, either."

All seven of the squires laughed robustly at that, even the four so young they had no beard upon their faces.

"Never fear your clumsiness in that arena, pretty wench," this brazen squire called right back, "as I stand ready and able to teach you kisses and *more*!"

Rhia was near tears and wished with all her heart she'd never consented to this come-along. Misery was her name, twice misery. Once because of her shame, and again because of her dread. This was not going at all like she'd imagined it, and could only end in disaster with no good done on Jim's behalf. Even Maddy was distressed at the rude turn of things. You could see it in her harrowed eyes and in her shrill laugh. For all her bluffing ways, Maddy was certainly in over her head and near as frightened as Rhia.

And still those riders circled, circled with firelight glinting in their eyes, grinning as though they were indeed hunters and Maddy, Beornia, and Rhia were quarried foxes with all hope gone of mercy or escape.

Chapter 26

Suddenly, Beornia muttered, "Well, I guess I've heard plenty." Before Rhia could so much as turn her direction, Beornia had run to stand right in the path of the circling horses, waving her arms!

"Sirs, desist!" she called up to the boys, who looked down at her with expressions of some amusement. They left their reins slack, letting their horses decide whether to take the trouble of swerving round her. "Sirs, I say!" she called again. *"Listen to me!"*

As they showed no signs of doing that, Beornia then pulled back the hood that had contained her bright hair and obscured her face. She crossed her fair arms and stood straight-backed and firm upon her two long legs, glaring at the lot of them.

Probably more from surprise at her exceeding good looks than concern lest she'd be trampled, the riders halted their horses and looked down at her with lidded eyes and smirks upon their faces.

"Are you daft?"

The sullen and nasal inquiry had come from a squire with greasy hair and pocky skin whose wide girth set him apart from his well-formed mates. The others laughed as though that small, dry question had been some great witticism.

"Methinks she merely grows impatient for your touch, Roderick," one drawled.

Roderick the Paunchy Whiner, Frederique the Handsome, Leonard the Rough and Tumble. Rhia now knew them apart, though that little knowledge was small comfort.

Beornia's hair blew wild in the breeze. "I'm a widow, no young girl," she called up to them. "And I inform you that these games are childish, and unworthy! Now, I believe Lord Claredemont will welcome some information on the recent murder in these parts, and I've come here for the one reason of giving it to you so's that you may give it to him with all haste! Listen closely, if you please, so that Rhiannon and I may get this done with and be on our way home."

Maddy dropped her head to her hands, but no one else moved a twitch, though some of the squires now sat slack-mouthed, squinting with confusion at this development.

"Here it is, then," Beornia continued heartily. "The man found knifed to death at the foot of Clodaghcombe Forest last week was killed by a local boy named Arnold Mopp! I carry the purse that Arnold took from the body. He bragged to me of the coin he had!" Beornia threw open her cloak and pulled forth a leather purse she'd folded into her waistband. "Arnold spent the coin, but I took this empty purse direct from the pig shed, where Arnold had hid it amongst some acorns kept for feed. Now you may take it to Lord Claredemont and tell him what I've told you. He'll doubtless be grateful to you for putting the *true* murderer in reach of the capable hands of his gaoler, Guy Dryer."

In spite of her own near crazed state, Rhiannon noted with admiration how Beornia stood like some tall and forthright warrior queen, staring down her fears, if she had any.

The squire Frederique lazily opened his long-fingered hands, and Beornia threw the purse to him. While his mates guffawed, he pantomimed stroking it against his cheek as though it were precious, then took it by its strings and twirled it above his head. "Here might have been a better prize than the scarf you took as memento of your escapade that night, Leonard!" he drawled.

He let go the purse and it sailed toward the rider who'd transported Rhia.

Leonard snatched it from the air. "I felt it to be lean as the pilgrim himself and not worth the bother! It served us well left behind where this local fool could pick it up!" Laughing, Leonard twirled the purse and made ready to throw it to another of the riders.

But Roderick suddenly stood in his stirrups and loudly commanded, "I've told you, speak French if you will speak of this, Leo!"

The others offered no comment but merely dipped their heads, and presently, the empty purse went sailing toward Roderick himself. He snatched it, ready enough to join in this impromptu game of catch now that he'd had his say. In fact, he jested loudly in the language of Francia whilst he twirled it above his head, and all the squires were laughing heartily when he let it go to the waiting hands of another across the circle.

Meanwhile, the three women helplessly grouped themselves together again beneath this childish game, ducking quick when the hard-thrown purse sailed too close above their heads.

"What can he mean, he felt the purse and found it lean?" whispered Beornia.

"I don't believe Frederique will meet this French lady cousin of Roderick's at all," sniffled Maddy. "They talk of it only to make me jealous!"

"But what could he *mean*, unless . . ."

"We've suspected that some of *these* have done the murder, Beornia Gatt," Rhia whispered through closed teeth. "They've nearly admitted it tonight, but alas, have stopped short and assumed this foreign speech. Arnold Mopp must have come upon the corpse afterward and thereby got the purse."

"Hey, you girls down there!" Leonard called out. "Will you not quit your yapping and lift your eyes to the sport we provide you as preface to romance this evening?"

Then, before Rhia knew what was happening, he'd trotted his horse right up to her and leaned to unwind the scarf from around her neck. He draped it over his left shoulder and bent down to her with a snide smile upon his sharp-boned, handsome face.

"I see you've worn my colors, lady, so now I claim them back as your champion for this night of revelry!"

With that, he reached under her arm to again lift her to his horse. Rhia looked frantically around the circle and saw Maddy run eagerly to Frederique. Meanwhile Roderick, smirking, walked his horse to Beornia.

"Well? Climb aboard, then, wench," he told her. "Can you do else than talk? If so, let's see it, for your blather proves tiresome, and yet you are comely when silent."

Rhia hung suspended against the side of Leo's panting horse, kicking at the air beneath her feet and slapping at Leonard's arm where he still clutched her beneath the arm. "Let me *go!*" she howled.

Then suddenly, as though summoned from the netherworld by her distress, there issued from the ground an unearthly wail of agony, a yelping screech of such unutterable horror that it might only have been made by demons, and *those* hundreds in number.

The seven horses whinnied and reared and staggered against each other in fear, their eyes widened and rolling. For through their hooves they indeed *felt* the ground quiver with the roil of that heathenish sound.

The riders struggled to control their mounts. Leonard released Rhia and she fell to the ground, off-footed. Maddy, too, had only partly completed her mount behind Frederique, and she found herself tumbled so she sat down hard upon the mossy earth.

" 'Tis the end of the world!" Maddy screamed, though it's doubtful she could have been heard, for the racket of all those offended demons still shook the black night as though the whole of Wythicopse Ring would indeed open up and collapse into hell itself.

"We ride for home!" one of the younger squires yelled, and he with three others turned their horses and jumped the tumbled part of the wall, as all the mounts had strained to do.

Leonard, Frederique, and Roderick were left, and they three tried their best to gain control of their steeds, though hard reins and threat of whips would not settle them in the least. Indeed, such efforts only served to make them rear all the higher, so as to throw off their masters and rid themselves of encumbrance.

"Dismount!" Leonard finally yelled, and following his lead, Frederique and Roderick swung off their horses. The steeds immediately jumped the wall and galloped into the night, so that now six stood inside that ancient ring of brambly stone, the three young maids and the three haughty sires, with none sitting high and mighty upon a horse.

The heathen shriek from below stopped so suddenly that the new silence made a ringing in all their ears. They stood frozen, awaiting what might come next.

"No leaky Roman pipe ever gave such a blasting," Roderick murmured after a while. "Our mounts will have reached the stables, and I suppose we'll needs go home afoot," he further grumbled.

Leonard laughed and slapped him on the back. "Buck up, friend Roderick. Don't you see that these frightened girls need the comfort of our strong arms?" He gave him a wink and a sideways nod of his head, then strode toward Rhia.

She stepped backward from him until she was pressed against the dampish stone of the wall. "We'd best hurry home our separate ways, afore that demon's riled again!" she protested in a rush. "If it be but one, and in truth it *sounds* like more."

She was too harried to remember the rest of the plan, what it was she was to do or say. It took all her attention to dodge Leonard's clutches!

"Wait! I *know* that sound!" Beornia suddenly exclaimed.

All looked at her. Even Leonard, holding fast Rhia's arms, looked over his shoulder.

"Yes!" Beornia continued eagerly. "I've heard it not so loud but just as mawkish, not this shrill but shrill enough. It's the sound of an instrument played by one of the monks here resident at the church! The others send him to the outside courtyard when he feels he must play, and I've languished there of late and marveled at the, well, the *bawl* of it."

Rhia bit her lip and shook her head with all her might, hoping to signal Beornia to just *stop* in her description before she doomed Thaddeus and Silas to whatever dire consequences would await their unfortunate discovery!

But it was no use. Beornia herself was certainly playing for time with this, hoping to delay the night's progression with a bit of small talk, as smarmy Roderick had his arm draped across her slim shoulders and stroked her cheek with his porcine hand.

Leonard released Rhia and drew his sword. "Come, Fred, it won't take long to poke some lost monk. We'll rout him from the pipes and send him squealing home to the vicar, then be left without further threat of interruption."

"No!" Rhia grabbed Leonard's sleeve.

He turned back to her, blinked, then smiled. "I'm surprised and well pleased by your complaint at the delay, lady. Don't fret, we'll make this fast."

But she would not release his sleeve. "Let me go with you," she pleaded.

He frowned. "To stab a monk? The hole that contains him is dark, and it may be a bloody business. Stay here, I say, and I'll return momentarily."

"If we're going, let's *go*, Leo," Frederique groused, leaning upon the hilt of his sword and adjusting his mustache with the thumb and finger of the other hand.

Leonard tried to pry Rhia's fingers from his arm, but Rhia would not unhinge them.

"But . . . but . . . !" She shook her head fiercely. But, but, but . . . *what?* "But, sir, I fear this monk is one who . . . who is idiot resident of our hospice upon the bluff! Yes, yes, I'm sure that's him! He escapes sometimes, makes foray down to the town, and steals the robes of a monk! Dressed in this way, he plays his irksome instrument until he's taken into custody and brought up the trail to us again! He has . . . he has a friend, also a simpleton, who goes missing as well. They were last seen by us some days ago, and I have no doubt he, also, hunkers in this hole you speak of. They mean no harm, and I would be so much in your debt if you would let me call them out and escort them home."

Leonard stared at her with his brows knit, flummoxed. Then he assumed a grin that showed his deep dimple and flipped back his light hair, murmuring, "In my debt, you say, fair Rhiannon? And how do you propose to *repay* this debt, then, hmmm?"

She released his sleeve and forced a coy smile. "If you three will come as escorts up our trail, sir, you will *not* be disappointed. The trail itself is bound to be enchanted upon this night, and an old church stands atop the bluff and would afford romantic shelter. It's haunted, you see, and so can only add to the excitement of this moonlit night." She looked down and took a breath, then raised her eyes. "Besides, sir, my mother and her mother will be gone to Roodmas. The blufftop will be completely our own, with none other upon it but the sleeping invalids and these two heedless idiots."

His eyebrows shot up. "Yes, Maddy's spoke to us of the place!" He spun round to the others, sheathing his sword. "Roderick? Fred? Let's away to this blufftop, as we've a willing guide to the secrets of the place. Now, *this* promises to be an adventure!"

Frederique tilted his head and shrugged. Roderick raised one eyebrow.

"It's a long hike," the earl's son stated. Then he sighed. "But I suppose *anything's* better than going back to the house and dancing all night with those ugly, goose-necked cousins of mine who have arrived this day from Francia."

Thaddeus and Silas were so covered with ancient slime from the Roman pipes that they seemed more glutinous, miry reptiles than men. Silas's bagpipes, too, were slimed, so that his instrument was a third preposterous clammy thing drifting between the two of them. They were ordered by Roderick to walk the distance of one hundred paces behind as Rhiannon led their troop on a shortcut skirt around the town and toward the bluff trail.

When they all traipsed on a straight course across a patch of stubblefield, though, Rhia managed to drop back to join the two slimed monks for a few moments upon the ruse of giving them a good scold for their escape.

"You smell awful," she whispered to Thaddeus, though it's surprising she wasted time on this observation, given how little chance for talk they'd have.

"Rhia, they made a full confession!" Thaddeus whispered eagerly back. "When they spoke French, they joked of the murder in full detail!"

She gasped. "Was Roderick the killer?"

"No, Leonard. He knocked Aleron from his horse purposely, just for sport. They saw he breathed no longer, and also discovered from his possessions that he was Norman. As all Norman murders are by law thoroughly investigated, these others then assisted in disrobing Aleron so his aristocratic background would not be evident from his boots or papers or horse. I suppose they left his money pouch in hopes someone would pick it up and thereby bring guilt upon himself. They added stab wounds so it would look like a murder for loot done by a local peasant or some vagabond. They *joked* of all this!"

"Rhiannon!" Leonard turned to call harshly across the distance and the darkness. "Leave those halfwits to stumble along as they may and come back to us up here, I say!"

The three squires held torches, and by that light Rhia could see their shapes far ahead, and also the shapes of the close-held girls they hiked with.

"I come," she called back, then swallowed. To Thaddeus, she whispered, "I like this not. They will *never* fear Jonah's disguise. They easily and quickly take whatever they want. Did you not hear them say they would poke the monk that played beneath our feet? They'll easily kill Jonah if they think he comes in the way of their . . . their lewd intentions!"

Thaddeus whispered back, "When you've escorted me to my simpleton cot, I'll double back and hide just under the window of the church that's nearest the hermit's tomb!"

Wiping tears from her eyes, she whispered, "But Thaddeus, you *can't* do that! Almund himself only dares watch from our cot, as there's no hiding spot outside the church and Gramp sounds the alarm when anyone's about! We were *fools* to attempt this! How did we ever expect to get them to repeat their confession within hearing of the reeve to begin with? It will be your word against theirs, and so *yours* will count for nothing, and all this approaching mayhem will have been for naught."

"Rhiannon, I said *come!*"

She squeezed Thaddeus's arm and ran to join the group ahead. She would not have hurt Thaddeus's feelings for the world, but she wondered at his innocent saintliness sometimes. Oh, he would jump through that window and give his life gladly in defense of his friends, she had no doubt of that. But truthfully, it would be such a waste, for against three ruthless and well-trained swordsmen such as these, Thaddeus could be no help at all. Why, he didn't so much as own a weapon!

What would he do, flail at the squires with his paint box? This while Jonah batted at them with the false headpiece he wore? What had they all been *thinking* last night?

And now Holt was given the slip, and no one respected the monks' robes, certainly, as they were slimed and the monks thought to be idiots. Besides which, this lot poked monks and thought it good fun when they squealed!

This was no plan whatsoever, but sure catastrophe.

Chapter 27

Rhia's shortcut kept them at a distance from the town, which from their vantage resembled a garish painting daubed with a rough brush upon the black canvas of the night. The fires burned high and the revelers shouted and shrieked, each sound reaching the ears of the eight walkers a moment or two after it had been let forth. Each giddy laugh was over before their group so much as heard it, then, Rhia mused. A shriek of pain was not perceived by her ears until the throb that had caused it was ended. In fact, the one who'd laughed might well be crying by now—who knew? Laughter and tears, pleasure and pain, each of the four was but a passing and phantom thing, yet who did not desire the first of each couple and tremble at its linked second?

Such were Rhia's fevered thoughts as they trudged, for she'd never felt such turmoil in her life, traveling beside these unpredictable squires, forcing laughter at their crude jokes, though her stomach turned and her head pounded. This false laughter was surely twinned with real pain to follow, yet they had no choice but to walk straight toward it!

The earl's paunchy son began to pant and blow by the time they'd gone halfway through the barley field. On the bank of the river (in fact, quite near where doomed Aleron had been tumbled from his horse), he dropped to a sudden sit upon the ground.

"My knees dislike the pounding they take!" he fumed, fanning his face, which streamed with sweat. "How much more of this?"

"We near the trail," Rhiannon said meekly, afraid to tell how grueling it would be.

"And what adventure going up it!" Leonard quipped, surely seeking to lighten Roderick's foul mood. He sat down near his friend and yanked Rhia down beside him.

"How extraordinarily savage these locals indeed are," Roderick said after a bit, looking toward bright Woethersly with his elbows upon his knees. He seemed completely fascinated by the sight of the merry, drunken town.

The others had now stopped and seated themselves upon the mossy ground as well, and all watched the fires and the fire-leapers, awaiting Roderick's signal that he was rested and ready to proceed. Rhia stole a glance over her shoulder and saw Silas and Thaddeus standing in the far shadows, trying not to draw notice.

"Indeed, what debauchery," Frederique murmured. "These *pagan* ways!"

"Beltane Eve is a holdover, is all," Beornia said tartly. "We are most of us Christian here, as you yourselves claim to be."

"*Claim* to be, you say?" Roderick drew back and glared at her as if she were some speaking rodent.

Beornia shrugged and sighed. "Sir, excuse my ignorance, as I have never known the exact beliefs of nobility and was some surprised that your friends would plan to poke a monk with a sword and never fear God's displeasure with that."

Rhia felt herself go rigid with nerves as she looked over at fearless Beornia. Did this bodacious girl indeed have some plan in opening this box of snakes?

Beornia looked back at her, all innocence. "Rhiannon, I've meant to ask you. Are there presently hospice beds unoccupied upon your bluff? A young girl in town—just a babe, really—was injured at market this week. Her arm grows putrified where it was caught by the whip of some careless rider. Anyhow, it's clear she will soon die. It would be a mercy if the girl could be brought within your mother's care, as her pain's a dreadful thing to behold and her mother grows insane with the horror of the child's constant cries."

Beornia's speech was met by deep silence, *black* silence it was, as dark as the night.

Rhia finally found breath to whisper, "Yes, we have room."

As though adding its own brooding comment, the sky grumbled with muted thunder in that empty moment, and Rhia saw the flick of a bright skeletal finger of lightning in the eastern sky. She felt she should point out the coming storm and urge some haste upon them, but she could not find the nerve to do it.

Leonard, meanwhile, had turned to Beornia, his face grown tight with anger.

"Lady *Chatter,* as I shall call you," he addressed her, "you might better look for God's *displeasure* in the idle disobedience of peasants who gaggle about the streets and yield not to their betters as they ride by. King Henry rules by God's will, and we who are his knights *display* the king's will—that is, *God's* will—for all in the realm to see. The mother might have moved this child from our route. As she didn't, I had to."

"One less peasant to grow up and breed," Frederique added with a yawn.

To Rhia's surprise, this comment drew Leo's ire as well.

"And what would *you* know about it, Fred, as I am the one who has to assume the follow-through for all such things?" he snapped. "Your mind is on the trysts you plan or your next wager at the games table, whilst *I* am generally left to be champion for us all!"

They all sat without talk for a bit longer, then Roderick, with a sigh that was more a groan, got to his feet, which signaled the others to stand as well.

Beornia's bold move and Leo's anger in response had stifled conversation, and they proceeded to cross the river and take the trail in uneasy silence. Maddy led, having been up the path before, so that Rhiannon could bring up the rear with Silas and Thaddeus following.

Rhia'd worried a little that she would be expected to lead, and thereby would not see Thaddeus and Silas at all. But no one wanted the job of traveling so near those two, because of the unpredictable nature of the witless, and because of their smell. Besides, with all the hazards of the woods, those last in line were quickest to be picked off, just as those who led were most likely to come upon any treacherous landshifts in the trail. The squires obviously preferred to travel in the middle with their lessers taking the chances.

"This Leonard has shown murderous disregard not once but *twice*," Thaddeus hissed to Rhia from close behind her. "He's caused one death and if this girl dies will soon cause a second, and that's just what we *know* of."

Rhiannon could make no reply, and she wished Thaddeus would not speak of it, as her heart seized so she could barely breathe when she thought of a child suffering so. The fire that had caused such awful misery to Primrose was bad enough, but this seemed worse, as a fire has no power to reason out its actions, and a man does, or *should* have.

"Say, can't you stop that idiot's blathering?" Roderick complained. "It lowers my vigilance as I pick my way."

"Doodle doodle *doooo!*" Thaddeus crowed in response.

In spite of the feeling of black foreboding that dogged her, Rhia had to smile. Then she turned to shush Thaddeus sternly enough for the others to hear.

Constant lightning flickered the darkness by then and thunder boomed close and closer, so that all the walkers looked up at the sky whenever they might take their eyes from their feet for a step. Phosphorescence leapt upon the swirling waters of the bay as the wind grew blustery, pushing waves that crashed against the beachfront with some force. A moaning wail set up as well, the sound of mermaids keening, Granna might have said, though more likely the rising wind howled through the many crevasses and small caves that pocked the bluff's rough limestone skin.

And if the sky and the waters grew fearsome, the woods grew more so. For the oaks had begun to thrash from side to side, as if they meant to pull their gnarled roots from the ground and stride away. Lights danced amongst the leaves as well, the same phosphorescence to be seen upon the waters, purplish and sizzling. Rhia'd seen this before in other storms, though it was rare. The sailors hereabouts talked of such light playing about their masts in especially murderous weathers.

But though the howling wind and thrashing, loose-rooted trees were disturbing, the small lulls when the wind died down were truly terrifying, for then could be heard the clickety-clack that had so concerned Granna the day they'd gone down this trail to lay hands upon the corpse. The lepers within the trees had ganged in a chorus, it seemed, intent on climbing along with these midnight travelers and harrying them in this way.

"What *is* that?" Roderick finally demanded, pushing his hands against his ears. "It sounds like the devil himself, playing upon the rib bones of the damned!"

313

"Doodle do, doodle *dooo!*" Thaddeus crowed from the rear. "The devil plays upon the rib bones of those left to die within the woods, doodle-doodle-*doooo!*"

Roderick whirled angrily to Rhia. "Stop the mouth of that idiot right *now!*" he demanded, unsheathing his sword. "Another word and I run my blade through his and his brainless friend's worthless hearts and shove their stinking hides into the sea!"

Rhiannon froze with horror. Then she stepped back, shaking her head, her arms spread wide, as though she could protect Thaddeus and Silas with that limp gesture.

Roderick meanwhile took a step toward her with his eyes wide and frenzied. A small, hard smile now played upon his lips. "Stop his babbling, lady," he said quietly, slowly placing the tip of his sword right against Rhia's throat. "See, I find that I care not how I skewer them. Whether I slice them each alone, or the two together, or reach through *you* to skewer *three* upon my sword. No, it simply, alas, matters not to me one whit how many meet their doom."

"Roderick, leave it!" Leonard called with a nervous-sounding laugh. "It's of no importance. We *must* beat this storm and claim our rewards for this fraught hike!"

Lightning gave Rhia a look at Leo's face, and from his expression she suspected that Roderick was bullying by nature, and that though he was too lazy for swordplay, he might savor just this chance to feel mighty by "skewering" those who had no way to fend. He might be quite daft, in fact. Who would dare tell the earl's son so?

Leonard and the others were grouped and watching from ahead on the trail. The two girls looked about to swoon, and even Frederique seemed alarmed. "Er, Roderick? Best bear in mind there will be *witnesses* to this thing you contemplate," he warned.

Rhiannon was suddenly shoved off her feet and into the writhing trees. She looked up to see Thaddeus advancing upon Roderick, swinging Silas's bagpipe above his head! He managed to bring the thing down so as to knock Roderick's sword from his hand. It went spinning into the air and over the side of the bluff.

Roderick lunged for the spinning blade and found himself treading thin air. Thaddeus grabbed his cloak and held on tight as Leonard and Frederique rushed over. With lots of hefting and grunting from all three, the earl's son was finally pulled up and dragged back from the edge to sit shaking and sputtering upon the solid ground of the path.

He scrambled clumsily to his feet, put out a quavering hand, and howled, "Your *sword*, Leo! Give it to me this instant, for mine is gone and I needs must kill this idiot with the rooster crow who parted me from it!"

Rhiannon saw Leonard and Frederique exchange a hooded look. Then Leonard sighed and moved close to throw a comradely arm around Roderick's shoulders.

"Well, here's the thing, good friend. We stand in a small calm before a storm, and we're close to adventure with three good-looking maids inside a tight-roofed chapel bound to hold some pretty thrills. Let's get where we're going without further ado and have our fun, then afterward I will lend my sword for this killing. Your revenge will be a capstone to the evening's promised entertainment. How's that sound?"

No one will ever know how that sounded to the earl's son, because the storm right then gave up its ample warnings and dropped down upon them with a banshee screech. Everything in all directions became a swirl of wind and water and biting sleet that knocked the torchlight out and took all thought from their heads except to somehow keep from being blown to kingdom come. They each of them clawed their way and slip-slid, partly on two feet and partly on all fours, sometimes sliding downward but gradually moving upward until they'd finally managed to travel the last quarter mile of the path.

But upon the blufftop's slippery rock floor, there was small relief awaiting them, for they staggered in murky darkness, unsteady on their feet, their outer garments so caked and heavy with mud that they all matched the slimed pair Thaddeus and Silas had presented before. Indeed, it seemed that by some outrageous fluke of fashion, those two had recruited the others to their way of dress.

Rhiannon pushed her hair from her face and stood with her teeth achatter, straining to see through the downpour. She was hoping with all her heart to perceive a tiny spot of light glowing in the direction of her well-loved settlement of cottages. Any small glowing ember or candleflame would be so welcome to her eyes, as it would show where Mam and the others waited and watched, ready to rush from hiding at any signal from her or Jonah or Thaddeus. She needed such assurance!

But there was not so much as a spark atop the bluff that night, as Mam and Granna were supposed to be at Roodmas. This afternoon, all had agreed that candles in the cots and even the large flame in their firepit had to be extinguished to make the ruse work, as such an extinguishing would normally be in order when an entire family had ventured from a forested place for the evening, leaving no one behind to tend the fires.

Rhia knew this, and yet she hadn't been prepared for how dark darkness truly is when all we love is hidden within its black grip. For death is darkness, and darkness death.

"I have never seen all lights gone from atop this bluff," she whispered, then shivered.

At that moment came an unequaled collision of fire and sound that brought light aplenty, though for but a moment. The storm extended one finger of lightning to mockingly flick the iron cross affixed to the tip-top of the chapel steeple! A nerve-shattering crash arrived with that and shook the ground beneath their feet.

"Lord preserve us!" Beornia exclaimed, dropping to her knees.

Mayhaps only Rhia noted the frowsy and feathered guard that took off squawking from that place to seek better shelter.

"A fortunate target for lightning, as we would not have easily located the church upon this blasted dark rock had it not been so illuminated," Leonard observed. He added with a laugh, "Indeed, it looks like it may hold haunts aplenty, as you've promised, ladies!"

"But wait!" Beornia insisted. "Just *look* at the place, will you?"

Rhia had been trying to follow Gramp's dark flight with her eyes, but at Beornia's insistent words she turned again to the chapel. Indeed, it was strangely changed. Fire the color of lavender flower now crept along the roofline, sizzling and popping, though if it were real flames it would have set the wooden shingles ablaze by now. It had not, which showed this to be the same eery phosphorescence that danced elsewhere this night, now traveled on a lightning bolt to embellish this highest of places in all the countryside.

Those false flames jumped down to the windowsills even while she watched, lining the stone archways with that phantasmagorial light, a glow that gave but little illumination.

"I've seen that stuff at sea," Frederique murmured in a bored way, pulling Maddy closer against his side. "Get too close and it makes your hair stand on end."

"The sailors hereabouts say it's the souls of saints, giving protection," Rhia said quietly. "There *is* a saint buried within this stone church. He may . . . show himself on such a fraught night, demanding confession of all sinners."

Thump, thump, thump! Rhiannon's heart took note of her outrageous move.

"Well, apart from these two witless, surely damned by God, there are no sinners here, so we're well come," Roderick said with a snide guffaw. "There are only we three of God's obedient knights and three innocent maids under our protection." He looked slantwise at Beornia and asked in a sarcastic voice, "You *are* innocent, are you not, saucy wench?"

Beornia stood from her kneel and looked at him as though she desired to melt him with her gaze. "Sir, you forget that I've told you I'm a widow, and devout in all my practices." With that she threw back her hair and flounced toward the church.

The three squires shared a smile and a whispered comment or two about that, then all proceeded to the church as well, though Rhiannon tarried.

"You two idiots run along to your cottage now!" she called back to Thaddeus and Silas, hoping her voice did not give away her nerves. "Go straightaway to your pallets and then to sleep, and my mother will bring you gruel in the morning, when she's returned from Roodmas."

Silas bowed and scampered into the darkness, but Thaddeus grinned wide and came trotting up to her! Nay, with only a glance and a wink he went right *past* her, straight toward Leonard, who waited some ways closer along the path to the church.

"I am to be killed later by Sir Leonard's sword, do you not remember?" the young monk called out gaily as he twirled and spun his way past Leonard and the others and then arrived to stand upon the threshold of the chapel door. "I *must* come with you, as I provide the capstone entertainment to an evening of frights and Beltane revelries, cock-a-doodle-dooo! Cock-a-doodle-doodle-*doooo!*" He pushed open the door a little way, bowed comically, and disappeared inside before the vicious wind slammed it shut again.

Well, if he hadn't been on the menu for killing, right then Rhia would have killed him herself! Such an easy out she'd provided, with no one showing a sign of stopping his exit to safety! And now *this,* as if Thaddeus *desired* to die, *longed* for such an end!

She was so furious with him that she burned all over as she stomped along the dark and stony pathway to the chapel herself. Leonard caught her arm as she neared him.

"You are so changeably mooded," he mused. "This idiot has angered you, I see that in your movements. Would his early and bloody killing win your favor for me tonight?"

She jerked her eyes up to his, but managed to stifle the hot words on her tongue. "I . . . I am not angered, but afeared. Much afeared, sir, of the hermit entombed within this place. He . . . he may well require confession from all of us, and woe to any who withhold it! Oh, I *wish* we'd never come here on such a night as Beltane, but as we have, we must do as he bids . . . or . . . or *else!* Please, sir, search your heart and prepare to tell all, else you're sure to be sent to hell tonight! Prepare, and I'll do the same!"

She threw her arms about his neck and wept upon his bosom, or pretended to. She was learning it was easy to fool a boy who wished to be fooled. She only wished she might live to practice this knowledge some other time, and that Thaddeus might live, too.

"I knew the other girls would think this place was haunted, and that it would add to the thrill of the thing," he murmured, stroking her back. "But I confess, I'm surprised to find you similarly superstitious, Rhiannon, as you've seemed so cool upon the trail."

With that, he gave the heavy door a shove with his bootheel and it crashed wide open.

Rhia had but time to glance over her shoulder as she was led inside, brought along helplessly by Leonard's embrace, just as a hen is brought beneath a farmer's arm to the chopping block that precedes the stewpot. Indeed, she felt she was climbing Gallux Hump, approaching the hangman's loop that swung in the breeze.

And so over her shoulder she grabbed a last look at the blufftop, though little could be seen in the swirling rain and darkness. No cottages, no orchard trees nor hives.

Just the eery, bedraggled shadow of a lone night flyer against the forest's edge, and the plaintive note of his solitary call: "*Crrrrawwwwwk!*"

Chapter 28

When all were inside the chapel, the thick oaken door slammed closed, as though some ghostly porter had held it. The storm still raged without, but within there was a silence that rivaled the tomb. The mists slowly rose straight up from the floor stones, though a mere fog should certainly have been wafted about by the draft that blew across the place, window to window. Mayhaps those mists *were* spirits, Rhia thought.

Two candles burned upon the altar, too far from the windows to show outside. Leonard strode over and snatched them up. "How considerate of your family to leave us light for our revels," he quipped to Rhiannon, handing off a candle to Roderick.

Frederique and Maddy strolled to the deeper shadows in the nether corner.

Roderick held his light aloft and traveled it along the dampish stones of the wall nearby him, wrinkling his nose. "What an ancient place this truly is, and a shabby one at that." He turned to Beornia and clutched a handful of her cloak, making to pull it from her shoulders. "This will serve us as a cushion. These floor stones are rough, and surely dampish as well."

Beornia stepped back, yanking her cloak from his grip. "I'll keep it, sir, if it please you," she snapped. Rhia heard her add, in a mutter, "Or even if it does *not*."

Leonard handed his flame to Rhia, and sat upon the floor to pull off his boots.

"Roderick, have patience, friend," he chuckled, shaking his head.

321

"Can't you see these girls are worn-out from the long hike? Let's all get comfortable, then Rhia can tell us the story of the dead hermit that haunts this place. We'll play a game, shall we? As she tells the story, at each fearsome part we boys shall be your protectors, girls. You may seek your safety within our arms. *That* should revive you quickly enough."

Rhiannon saw her chance and moved quickly to light the window candle that she'd later move to signal the reeve.

"Is there no wine kept in this place?" Roderick inquired. "None for the sacraments?"

Rhia found herself mute, but she shook her head as she walked reluctantly back to Leonard.

"Barbarous," he pronounced, sulking. "No wine, and damp floors."

Leonard ignored his friend and pulled Rhia by the wrist to sit beside him. After a few moments, Beornia sat down near them, yanking her cloak string tight at the throat and pulling her woolen wrap close as a bundling blanket about her. Roderick presently sidled over and carefully eased down next to Beornia, watching her sidelong, as one watches a snake in the nearby grass. She, meanwhile, kept her face turned away.

"Now, isn't this cozy?" Leonard asked.

Where was Thaddeus? Rhia roamed her eyes across the shadowy nooks of the place, trying to be casual about it. The others had luckily not noted his absence yet, but why would he not show himself? What was up his sleeve?

Then suddenly, she spotted him, crouched in perfect camouflage behind the small bench and nearby the window where he'd stood so fascinated by the painting of the Devil Dogs the other day. When she widened her eyes, he put one finger to his lips.

And then, well, he reached to *pull* at some invisible thing, a thread or some such, and a cloth drifted silently to the floor. The painted Devil Dogs had been covered by that black cloth, and now that they were freed from behind it, Rhia drew in a breath, so near to screaming that Leonard turned to her in amused puzzlement.

"You've not *started* your grisly tale as yet, Rhiannon, but it must be good if mere contemplation of it makes you look so pale and frighted! Tell us it!"

Rhia closed her eyes, swallowed hard, and nodded, willing herself to speak.

"In truth, sir, I know little about the hermit, just that he arrived upon the bluff when there were no folk here and it was tangled with birdy nests and the habitat of deer." Her voice was a quavery whisper, weak as the candleflame in the damp hall. "The hermit built this church, but not the cottages that ring it round. They were already here when he came, and it is the tragic tale of *their* builders I'd tell of, if it please."

Roderick nodded brusquely. "Tell on."

Rhia focused her eyes on the candleflame as Granna would have while storying.

"My tale is set in the winter when King Arthur was killed by Sir Mordred's evil treachery. That ancient winter dragged on for three years, so hopeless and sad a time it was. Arthur's knights scattered, assuming their separate griefs like heavy loads to carry throughout the world. And then two of them rejoined by chance upon the road one day and somehow ended up upon this blufftop. It was they who built the cots. I suppose they found this place good respite and hoped their brother knights might someday join them here. In Clodaghcombe Forest you'll see ancient trees with the mark of the Holy Rood upon their highest branches. Sir Gawaine and Sir Gareth slashed those marks

323

with their noble swords when those trees were but frozen saplings. I expect they marked them thus for protection against the enchantments known to hide hereabouts, but alas, those holy markings were in vain. On some dark night, or mayhaps in the gloom of an icy day, those two good knights were torn limb from limb by the Devil Dogs of Clodagh. Their bodies were discovered by a woodsman in the spring, and they are buried beneath this church, within the circle of cottages they built with their grief for their king that winter."

"Arthur Pendragon's knights buried upon this soil?" Roderick whispered, impressed in spite of himself. He recovered his scorn. "It can't be. Not here—we're *nowhere!*"

At that moment, Thaddeus came charging toward them, waving his arms and screaming, *"Don't let them get me!* Please, the Devil Dogs of Clodagh are come alive! Don't let them drag me down to hell, there to gnaw eternally upon my nitwit spleen!"

Rhia jumped to her feet. "Look!" She pointed. "The ancient painting, there above the window! It . . . it *burns* as though with hellfire! I have *never* seen it thus! I fear the story I've told has . . . has somehow *summoned* the demonic spirits of those ancient beasts!"

The others rose to their feet, staring in frightened bewilderment at the painting Rhia'd pointed out. Even Maddy and Frederique stepped from the nether shadows where they'd sought privacy and peered fearfully in that direction.

"What the devil?" Roderick whispered, his eyes gone abulge.

"Yes, yes—indeed!" Thaddeus blathered, pulling his hair. "The devil has sent his hellhounds to avenge some crime! They come! Don't let them take me, for I am but dimwit and crimeless since my birth!" Thaddeus chased in circles, wringing his hands.

"Be quiet, fool!" Leonard demanded, unsheathing his sword as he proceeded toward the painting that had caused such a scene.

If he crept slow and seemed rattled, who could blame him? For those two Devil Dogs painted above the window had suddenly begun to shine bright as the full moon. They had been so pale in their ancientness as to be invisible to all before, but now looked forged by some hellish smithy from brimstone and flames. They glowed and strobed in every part of them—their fangs, their claws, their serpent tails, their hideous eyes.

"What magic is this?" Beornia whispered, crossing herself.

"Fred!" Maddy wailed. "There *are* enchantments here, and evil ones!"

Frederique tore her arms from about his neck. "Quit choking me, wench!" He looked to Roderick, muttering, "This is strange stuff. We should just freeboot out of here, you know? I mean, look at those *fangs*. This *can't* be good."

Leonard grunted and wiped his face on his sleeve as he manhandled the heavy stone bench, moving it under the window. "Fred, you stand as usual useless as some toad. For God's sake *help* me with this, man!"

"They'll tear my gizzard from me and eat my kidneys whilst I watch!" Thaddeus moaned, trotting tiptoe amidst the others assembled there.

Leonard now looked angrily over at Frederique. "Fred, I can't do *everything* around here! If you won't move the bench, at *least* kill the babbling idiot!"

Rolling his eyes at being thus put upon, Frederique drew his sword and slouched toward Thaddeus.

"No, no!" Rhia pleaded, running to kneel between Thaddeus and

Fred. For a moment she wondered what to do now that she was positioned so strategically, then she bent and wrapped her arms hard around Frederique's legs. He swayed like that, nearly tottering to a fall, and she held all the harder. "We here are witnesses, remember?"

Leonard, meanwhile, had climbed upon the moved bench, and now he carefully reached one gloved hand toward the glowing pair of hounds.

"As I cannot move my legs to walk, come closer here, nitwit, so I may kill you," Frederique requested of Thaddeus. To Rhia he said, "*Your* death, lady, might have gone down hard were it witnessed. This *fool* will not be missed. We do the world a favor."

And at that moment, with Rhia kneeling and Leo reaching and Fred requesting and Thaddeus trotting, there came the sound of massive stone scraping against massive stone.

Everyone froze in place, then all eyes turned in the direction of that solemn reverberation. For the scrape and crunch of an old tomb being slowly opened is a distinctive and very unsettling sound. And when a tomb is opened from the *inside* . . . well, more so, of course.

About time, Jonah! With the tiniest sigh of relief, Rhia let go Frederique's legs and stood to feign horror at the black hole that now yawned wide in the corner of the wall.

" 'Tis the tomb of the ancient hermit!" she uttered in a rush. "He's broken the seal put upon it long centuries ago!"

By then all could hear the clatter and scrape of old bones pulling themselves together to drag through that stony threshold. The dim glow of their candles began to reveal the hoary outline of something no longer human, yet almost certainly once inclined that way. It shuffled along, groaning as it came, dripping grave cloths turned to putrid rags.

"Whose transgressions have aroused me from my just sleep?" the thing moaned.

Beornia covered her mouth with her hands, and Maddy made a low squealing sound.

Rhia dared to glance sideways and saw Roderick and Frederique huddled together, openmouthed. "This isn't happening," Roderick pronounced, but his chin quivered. Indeed, he looked close to tears.

And still the hermit progressed in his moldering way, shedding worms from his loathsome head and leaving slime and ashes as he moved clear of his sepulcher.

He then stopped, held up one finger bone, and pointed separately to each of those six who stood in a loose arc before him, none of them daring to move from their spot.

His ancient eyes sparked with righteous indignation as he asked, "Who *dares* bring the smell of unconfessed blood crime into these holy chambers?" His loathsome voice gurgled and sucked like swampy quicksand. "Who stands here unconfessed of black deeds? For there will be no exit from this place for those unshriven. Repent, I say! Fall to your knees and tell of your murderous sins!"

"Yip, yip, yip!" Thaddeus pranced about on his toes. " 'Tis a good night to be witless, as *some* crimes must confound all who are witted! Who may have the wit to understand it when a child dies of a whip purposely mishandled by a rider? Why? asks the fool."

Rhia saw something new and hard enter the hermit's eyes. "A child?" he whispered.

Roderick dropped to his knees, then reached a shaking hand to pull Frederique down as well. They folded their hands and bowed their heads in attitudes of earnest piety.

"Sir," Roderick meekly addressed the sainted hermit, "I make *full* confession in the sight of God that it was not *I* who thought of running down children to teach their parents to better clear the road, but that indeed—"

"Shut up, Roderick, you *fool!*" Leonard called out.

All gasped and turned toward the stone-cold voice.

Leonard jumped to the floor from the bench where he'd stood. He came toward the hermit while the others parted for him. The knuckles of one hand he had planted on his hip, and the other gloved hand he held up for the inspection of all present. He smirked as he came, and swaggered.

With a sinking heart, Rhia saw that the fingers of his extended glove were glowing.

Leonard stood in front of the group with the hermit at his back, giving all a chance for closer inspection of the glove. "It's paint, never fire and brimstone!"

He whirled around then and with three great strides came eye to eye with the hermit.

"And so I conclude this holy man is but a sham as well! I'll grant it's a good costume, friend. You even *smell* the part."

With a flourish of his glove, Leonard swept the elaborate worm-ridden headdress from Jonah's head. It lay a squirming mass upon the floor, and Jonah stood with but a woolen hood pulled taut around his living skull. He dropped his head and wordlessly stared at the floor.

Thaddeus gave up his fool's act then and fell to his knees, his face in his hands.

"And why would you have us confess to things we had no part in, eh?" Leonard queried, pacing before Jonah. "You've heard rumors, no doubt, and wished to entrap us." He walked quickly to Rhia and took her chin in his hand. "You make a third in this conspiracy, don't you, sweet girl? You, the fool, and the actor over there. Bad acting it was, though the *fool* acted well, since I doubt he acted. He *was* a great fool to be involved in such a dangerous game against the king's own men."

Roderick and Frederique laughed with relief, and Leo walked to them and threw his arms around their shoulders. "Draw your swords, men. For once, you'll join me in cleaning up a mess. Who'll take care of the girls? After they're neatly run through, we'll throw them from the cliff and none will be the wiser. Beltane revels surely yield drunken missteps on a regular basis."

Rhia saw there was no way to move the candle from window to window, as those three blocked the way and held all in the room frozen with their swordblades. Besides, by the time Almund saw that signal and charged here with his men, they'd only find them all run through. It would go that quick now, for certain.

"Kill me first, then!" Beornia called out. She strode to stand face-to-face with Leonard, her arms crossed and her chin high. "Upon my son's beating heart, I will *not* see murderers go free to kill again, especially when your freedom is purchased by my own dear father's life. So make a beginning to your further damnation with *me*!"

The three squires looked at her oddly, then shrugged.

"Suit yourself," Leonard said. "I'll honor your courage by making you the first."

Beornia closed her eyes and he drew his sword. Maddy screamed. Thunder crashed. The mists rose thicker, as if the resident gang of monkish souls were outraged, though helpless.

Rhiannon moved closer to Thaddeus and put her head upon his shoulder, and he reached to cover her face with his large hand.

Rhia mused that her last thought would be how much he smelled of paint.

329

Chapter 29

Time can be dreamlike when it's running out. Upon the bluff they'd had plenty of experience with dying folk, of course, and many claimed each moment seemed to them now to be a day. In those last dreamy moments some even told that they had time to see their life performed before their eyes, the whole of it in a swish of color and sound.

Yes, Rhia knew that time played shifty tricks near the end, but *this* seemed ridiculous. She feared that if they didn't kill her soon she'd have to change position, as her left leg had gone asleep. She didn't *want* to, though, as Thaddeus might then move his comforting hand. And another weird thing—the place had gone so *still*. *Too* still. Even Maddy'd quit her carrying on. And if Beornia had been killed, wouldn't they have heard her fall? And what of the squires, their brags and shuffles and swaggering talk? *No* one was talking or moving one whit, which sent a shiver up Rhia's spine.

She could think of but one explanation. "Thaddeus?" she finally dared to whisper. "Are we . . . dead?"

After a moment, he whispered back, "I dare not open my eyes to find out."

She took a breath. "We'll open our eyes together when I count three. One . . . two . . ."

But before she reached three, there was a large clanking and clattering, and she and Thaddeus both looked up in time to see the last two swords of the three squires thrown down upon the floor. They gleamed by the nether candle, though the squires were some ways back from there, grouped in much the same place they'd been when Thaddeus had closed Rhia's eyes with his hand, except that now instead of standing with drawn swords and murder in their eyes, they knelt. They also looked as if they'd seen a ghost—a *real* ghost, that is.

Even Leonard had lost his brash expression and wore a strained and baffled look upon his face. A sweat had broken across his brow—the candleflame caught the beads of it.

Thaddeus nudged her with his elbow. "Look at Jonah," he breathed, nodding toward the hermit's crypt.

She took her eyes from Leonard to check where Jonah'd stood last she'd seen him. Then he'd been bowed in defeat. He'd looked humiliated and smallish after Leonard's saucy dispatch of his wormed hat. She'd assumed he waited humbly for death, and that of the five of them, counting brave Beornia and silly Maddy, he'd be the only one who'd welcome it with wide arms, as death had been his wish all along

But now he was so utterly changed it took her breath away. In truth, he'd advanced only a step or two from the stony threshold and had pulled off the rough hood that somewhat had contained his bright and shocking hair. He'd picked up the nearby candle, too, which showed his strong bones, all the angles of his face.

But mostly, he'd taken on some new spirit, absorbed it with his breath.

"I *knew* he'd dare it, once we'd told him of the whipped child," Thaddeus whispered from the side of his mouth.

Dare *what*? And how'd the poor child figure in?

Roderick then cleared his throat and spoke, though his voice trembled. "Are you . . . ? Uh, that is, your majesty, forgive me, but are you . . . ?"

Jonah placed the candle upon the floor and folded his arms as though he'd converse in a leisurely mode. "Speak freely, cousin, for we're all friends here, and you and I are distant family, are we not? Do you wonder if I live?" He opened out his arms and turned once round. "Well, what do you say? Am I rough flesh or refined spirit? And which do you fear the most in me, cousin? Man, or ghost?"

Jonah then took a teasing quickstep toward the three, clenching his hands to claws and uttering a small "Boo!" The squires shuffled backward upon their knees.

Beornia Gatt laughed. Jonah looked at her and grinned, then instantly got solemn again. He moved in eight long strides to stand before the kneeling squires, fastening his bright and piercing eyes upon each of them in turn.

"I have but two questions, then I'll leave you forever and you may consider me a phantom," he said quietly and grimly. "First, which of you killed my squire and boon companion Aleron of Chartres upon the water's edge? The second question goes with the first. Why . . . why was it done?"

This last sentence came from him in a rush of grief and longing. He dropped his head and Rhia knew he struggled with the overwhelming anger that was ever his nemesis. Presently, he turned and strode to the swords, snatching one up.

Frederick put a foot upon the floor and made as if to rise. "Sire, I know not who you can mean, as I have never been privileged to meet your squire, but I can explain every—"

"On your *knees*!" Jonah bellowed, rushing toward him with the shining sword directed at his throat. "How *dare* you stand in my presence without my consent! You're certain to have some weapon concealed upon you, and indeed may be up to *any* sort of vile treachery! I'll tell you this—I trust *none* of you to behave honorably, not after what I've heard, and . . . and *seen*, this night!"

Rhia took Thaddeus's arm, trembling at Jonah's shifty mood. He would ever be their friend, and he would ever scare her, both. If the squires noted his unbalance, would they rush for the remaining sword and finish what they'd planned? How *would* this play?

Jonah caught himself, breathed deep several times to bank the flames inside him, then lowered the sword, though he kept it at the ready. "Roderick, as you have the high status within this group, I'd have my questions answered first by you," he said sternly.

Roderick jerked, startled and dismayed. He patted his streaming forehead with the lace sleeve of his shirt, then bowed. "Sire, you must believe that I have never killed the slightest flea! This thing was done *completely* without my participation, I swear it upon my dear mother's soul! We rode merely for pleasure that night, to take the air on a spring eve. And, well, your friend was apparently thrown from his steed. With all respect, it's likely he was not paying attention, and—"

"And he fell upon seven sharp knives?" Jonah boomed.

Roderick pressed his sleeve to his mouth, and Jonah turned to Frederique.

"Let's hear *your* version," Jonah commanded. "And if you value your life, you will not again insult me with the phrase 'I can explain.' I seek confession only, as there can be no explanation under heaven for such a vile thing."

Frederique squinted and chewed his lip, then bowed. "Uh, we were riding really fast, see? And Leonard slammed into the fellow in the dark, like he ofttimes does collide with those who will not yield. Pow! The fellow died, so Leo made us stab him."

Rhia swallowed down bile at this flat answer, but Jonah sadly nodded.

"This has the ring of truth," he murmured, taking a small step over so that he now stood glowering down at the central squire.

Leonard raised his own hot and angry eyes to meet Jonah's. The sweated curls of his yellow hair fell back so that Rhia could see his jaw-bones were set hard as well, and he ground his teeth. When Jonah did not speak, Leonard put a foot upon the floor to stand, and Jonah did not stop him. The two presently stood eye-to-eye, facing each other in silence so fraught, Rhia thought the air between them must ignite and burn them all.

After some moments, Jonah said, quietly and coldly, "Bow your head."

Leonard smiled a small, snide smile, then bowed his head, though there was no respect in this token stance. His every look and movement held outrage and scorn—she could even *hear* it in the hard breaths he breathed.

Jonah shifted the sword to his nether hand, then slowly reached for the end of Aleron's blue scarf and began unwinding it inch by inch from Leonard's bowed neck.

"After you'd killed him, why take his scarf?" Jonah asked, his voice little more than a ragged whisper. "Your father is rich enough to buy you your own colors. So why?"

Leonard snickered. "Why *not?*" he murmured coldly. And then, he dared to raise his head so he looked eye-to-eye with Jonah again. "I have now had time to untangle this thing in my mind, though at first you gave me a shock, I'll admit it. I have seen Prince William Aethling at court, and you bear a striking resemblance. But the prince is dead. And so you are either his ghost or an impersonator. I think impersonator, given the trickery we've already witnessed this night. But if you *are* indeed his spirit, I'd say to you that you are no better than I, sir. Yes, I rode too fast the night of your squire's death. Yet all in the realm know of *your* enormous folly. If I was selfish, how much more were you, to lose so many at the price of showing off with a drunken party and a fast race upon the waters? You *killed* a boatload of your friends with your recklessness, have you *forgot?*"

Rhia heard herself gasp, and felt Thaddeus's arm go stiff. Indeed, Roderick made a whimper and Frederique put his long and moony-eyed face into his hands. All despaired of what was to come, and braced themselves for Jonah's final, violent response.

Jonah swayed where he stood and his breath came in a fast pant. A sheen of sweat had broken out upon him, and his eyes bored even harder into Leonard's own until Leonard dropped his gaze, overcome with the intensity.

Jonah slowly wound Aleron's scarf around the hilt of the sword, then took a firm two-handed grip upon that hilt. His eyes were glazed so that Rhia wondered if he even knew what he was doing as he raised the weapon above his head.

Thaddeus jumped to his feet, but could find no way to intervene. Rhiannon looked down at her lap, weeping and praying a single word: *No, no, no!*

"I would give my very soul for a second chance," Jonah whispered. "Yet *you* already kill again since my friend's recent death, just from blind selfishness! How *many* chances have you been granted to show repentance, and how many have you *squandered* thus?"

Panting and shaking, he stood poised to bring down the sword upon Leonard's head. It seemed to Rhia an eternity crawled by as he prepared that fatal strike. Most others in the room now wept, and had turned their faces from the bloodbath to come. Leonard could do naught but close his eyes and wait for his deathblow to fall.

Then Thaddeus spoke in a clear, bell-like voice. "Second chances come in many forms, good friend. A chance to show mercy is surely one of them, else why did Christ advise to turn the other cheek?"

Jonah glanced toward Thaddeus, and Rhia held her breath and changed her prayer to *please, please, please* as she frantically tapped Mam's cross against her chin.

Though Jonah instantly focused again on his revenge, raising the sword a bit higher and gritting his teeth, Rhia saw the white fury gradually retreating from his face as a tide leaves the beach. Finally his sharp features were shed of that completely, and assumed instead an expression of sad wonderment, as though now in Leonard he inspected a monstrous fish with a murderous nature, hardly man at all.

Jonah finally stepped backward and brought the sword down with all his strength upon the floor, grunting with the effort. It made a bright sound when the tip sparked upon the stone, but Aleron's soft scarf stopped its further clatter when he let it drop completely from his hands.

"I pity you, Leonard," he muttered as he turned his back and strode to the door. He jerked it open and stepped outside. The wailing storm then took the occasion to elbow its way inside, like a nervy guest.

All was instantly chaos. The squires found their feet and Leonard and Frederick rushed for their swords. The others in the room bundled against the gale and moved closer together, wondering what would happen next. Thaddeus pulled Rhia behind him, as it was unclear if there would be more swordplay. It seemed likely the three would simply take to their heels, but then again, they might first seek to silence all who had heard them confess to causing Aleron's death, and to its subsequent concealment.

Indeed, when he'd retrieved his sword, Leonard turned to run wild eyes across the group of fearful witnesses huddled in the shadows. He gripped the hilt of his weapon, set his teeth, and half turned toward them, but Roderick caught his arm.

"Leo, we *must* get out of this wretched place!" he urged.

Leonard snarled, "Let *go* of me and leave me to my work, you spineless snitch! You *bragged* that you have never killed, yet you did not bother to add that it's because you faint at the sight of blood and *I* must do the dirty work on your behalf and lazy Fred's! Unhand me, or you'll regret it, Rod, I swear!"

"Leo, let's just *go!*" Roderick screamed, pulling him along against the wind and toward the door. "My father will stitch this up when we may reach him, but don't make it more a mess for him than it presently lies! He grows much *weary* of this sort of trouble!"

"Frederique?" Rhia heard Maddy whimper.

But Frederique was well gone, the first of the three to scramble.

"*Crrrrrrrrrawwwwk!*"

"Gramp!" Rhia cried, for indeed that perturbed groshawke had flown in on the wind at this first chance, squeezing just beneath the stone top sill of the oaken door and above the heads of the two quarreling squires. He was flapping his wings with much ado and upset, insulted at his perch being shifted by the eery light and *further* insulted that all these had taken advantage of his absence to sneak inside the place.

Leo flinched and looked upward, unnerved at Gramp's theatrical behavior. In fact, Gramp may well have been the factor that tilted Leo toward leaving the witnesses unkilled and yielding to Roderick's hysterical urgings. He was still peering uneasily at the rafters when he finally gave up his plan and fled with Roderick from the place.

The four inside hastened to watch from the windows.

"Jonah left to bring the reeve," Thaddeus said in a rush. "I hope Almund's arrived."

The wind and rain swirled everywhere, yet they could see the three squires met up in front of the church, arguing with many wide and angry gestures about where the path might start that would take them down to safety. And then three others approached along the very path the squires sought—Jonah between Almund and Holt. They carried no swords, but held the large fighting sticks known along the frontier to pack quite a wallop.

Those three halted and stood glowering in the rain. Almund called, "In the name of King Henry, you three stand accused by your own confession of manslaughter and complicity, and are placed under arrest by my authority as reeve."

Rhia could see from the haughty way they stood that the squires had no intention of submitting.

"No frontier reeve can arrest the earl's own son and his retinue!" Leonard called. "Better luck next time, dunderheads! I compliment the middle yokel on his acting as he is a ringer for Prince William and *nearly* took me in. In fact, only his cowardice in sparing my life showed him to be an actor, not our hotheaded dead prince. Now, you must *part* for us immediately!" He drew his sword and Frederick drew his.

Within the church, Thaddeus sadly murmured, "What Leonard's said may be true and the reeve lacks the authority we'd thought he'd have in this. Who can say for sure, given the unsettled nature of the law these days."

Almund raised his stick to a defensive position and the others did likewise. They would not yield the path but would fight it out, though Rhia thought sticks could surely not prevail against blades. She put her head in her hands.

But Beornia grabbed her shoulder. "Look! There, at the edge of the woods!"

Rhia squinted and saw a line of folk coming from the trees! They were hooded and masked, and clacked upon their clacking bowls so that the closer they walked, the louder became the bone-rattle of their freakish advance.

The squires by then had also taken notice of this army of the ragged dead. Leonard stood speechless, his brash talk dried up at the sight and his sword dropped to his side.

"The gang of three at their left blocking the pathway down, the lepers at their front blocking escape through the wood," Thaddeus observed quietly. "We are at their backs. Yet methinks they have *most* to fear, if they knew it, from trying an escape to the right!"

Rhia looked that way and saw Mam, Granna, and Daisy approaching their fastest. Granna brandished the large oaken paddle she used for the bread, and Daisy had her pet in its sling and seemed ready to sacrifice her for catapult against the enemy if need be.

Without knowing what she was doing, Rhia ran through the door. She would join her kin! They offered flimsy resistance, and if the squires were smart they'd charge that way. She would be *with* them! Her kin—*hers!*

Thaddeus grabbed round her waist and hoisted her back, and they might have had a battle about it if just then Maddy hadn't let out a squeal.

"May all God's angels preserve and keep us!" she yelped. "It's most certainly the Queen of the May, come from the faery realm!"

Beornia Gatt for once stood openmouthed and gaping. "It *is*," she breathed.

The lepers had parted their line in the middle so that Ingrid, seated upon Charlemagne, could slowly advance from concealment in the woods. The glowing horse and rider seemed an enchant that might dissolve at any moment, made up of the moonlight and wispy curls of mist.

Rhia's breath came fast as she watched Ingrid walk Charlemagne nearer to the flabbergasted squires. The girl dismounted lightly as a snowflake, but not until she and Aleron's steed were the mere length of their shadows from the three.

Ingrid's eyes stayed fast on Leonard, though she uttered no word and made no further movement. Charlemagne nuzzled her shoulder and she bent her head to his muzzle.

Then Leonard suddenly lunged forward to grab the reins that hung lightly in Ingrid's hand. He swung himself up to sit upon Charlemagne's back, and the steed whinnied and circled in a tight little dance but offered no challenge nor resistance to Leonard's sit.

"This place, this land of phantoms and freakish weathers, I *leave* it to you!" he cried down to all of them. "Fred, Roderick—you two may better slip this pack alone. As you've so graciously pointed out to them, 'twas *I* who did the dirty deed, and as usual, you barely helped. When I reach the manor house, *I'll* send help *your* way, *if* I decide I've the energy and nerves for it, that is!"

With a bitter laugh, he dug his heels into Charlemagne's sides, then spotted the pathway down and turned him toward it, veering wide around the three who stood blocking that route. They gave chase, but he quickly far outdistanced them. Then, seeing they'd given up, he pulled the reins to correct his veer. But those watching saw the steed ignore this direction. Instead, with a rear of his hooves and a brave toss of his fine head, Charlemagne proceeded to run at a full gallop straight through the orchard, ignoring Leo's pull and proceeding in a perfect line toward the bluff's rim.

Rhia knew they galloped too fast to stop at the edge or to make the turn.

Indeed, Rhiannon and the others all heard the triumphant whinny Aleron's steed gave to the wind when he took his leap over the edge.

The Pilgrim Resumes His Journey

May Day was but ten days gone, and already the trees were so thickly leafed that one might not catch so much as a glimpse of the forest's ancient contents. Beautiful Clodaghcombe would now hide her face behind green hands until the breathy wind of September notched her deep canopy and let snoopers have another peep at her wonders—her rood marks, her standing rocks and faery circles, her enchanted caves. But what *good* was that peep, really? Even when winter had completely bared the trees, you might look at it all, take in every sacred stone, but no matter how you tried, you could *not* see the layers of mystery and meaning that dwelt deep inside those ancient things. So truly, you saw nothing, and you *knew* nothing!

And the worst thing was, Clodaghcombe Forest was but one of a long *list* of things Rhia feared she'd never so much as *begin* to understand!

Well, but she was gloomed this afternoon, heartsick to say it true.

"I don't see why he could not wait to go for but a few days more," she murmured, tapping her chin with Mam's small cross. "He should at *least* have let us walk him down the trail. And Thaddeus, don't you *dare* tell me not to cry!"

Thaddeus stood with his arms in his sleeves, watching Jonah and Beornia walk hand in hand past the hives. "He wanted privacy to tell Beornia good-bye," he explained.

Rhia rolled her eyes. "Don't you think I *know* that?" She sat upon the cool grass and bounced her knees, squinting at the pair. Beornia herself would only get to go with Jonah to the edge of the orchard. He wanted to descend the bluff alone. "Will . . . we see him again, ever?"

Thaddeus thought that over. "Yes, I believe we will," he answered, and then he settled himself on the grass nearby Rhia. "Don't cry," he pled softly.

She sniffed. "I can't help it," she moaned, and wiped her eyes upon her apron just as Jonah took Beornia's face in his hands and leaned to kiss her lips.

Rhia sighed large. "I shall *never* be kissed!" she cried, and then she feigned swatting at a hornet with her apron, as she'd not meant to utter that at *all*.

Now Jonah and Beornia had let go each other's hands, and Beornia wiped her own more justified tears as Jonah shifted his pilgrim pack and walked on.

"In a moment, he'll pass through the first apricot trees, then we won't have another glimpse of him!" Rhia's heart was breaking. "*Everyone* leaves us! You, too!"

Thaddeus shook back his hair. "I've told you, Rhia, I *must* take this sea ride that the pirates have graciously offered so's I may quickly reach the road leading to Glastonbury. It's a chance to bring back the workers who can help the lepers."

"I know, I know," she cut him off. "But I mean, you'll *leave*. Not upon this trip to bring back the workers your prior has promised, but . . . soon you'll surely *leave* leave. Return to your brothers, to your work in the church, or in a monastery somewhere."

She pulled up her knees, hugged them to her, and tried to ease the tightness in her chest by looking round the settlement. Whilst Sal watched smiling, the three little girls played at their patting games, though Mary played with but one hand. Still, it looked like someday she'd use her arm again, and now 'twas certain she would not die. Mam was proud of that. Though she rarely showed pride, this time she had.

Beornia was running toward her father and son, who waited with Granna upon a cloth spread by the brook. She reached them and hefted Jamesy toward the sky. Rhia could hear his chortles, that sweetest of all baby sounds, which meant it was likely the sweetest of *all* sounds. Beornia's tears would be eased by it, for certain.

Some few of the folk from the woods were hoeing at the garden. When Thaddeus got back from Glastonbury with his brother monks from the infirmary there, all the lepers could settle into the spacious nether cottage and be cared for properly by hands that knew well how to perform the tasks required.

There was Mam, humming as she spread her new washed bandage rags upon the willow tree to dry. Gramp watched her from the yew tree, or he slept—hard to tell.

Rhia's eyes had now reached round the circle to return to Thaddeus, who shredded a dandelion stem, his brows knit as he concentrated on the job.

"Rhiannon, do you ever think about what would have happened if Jonah had indeed killed Leonard that night? He might be hanged for it by now, as I'm certain he would not have revealed his true identity even to save his life. And the other squires would certainly have been outraged by Jonah killing Leonard, so they would probably have publicly denied the confessions we heard, which means Jim, too, would now be hanged. As Leonard lived on exactly long enough to leave them in the lurch, they were shaken and angry enough to blather the whole thing to Almund and Holt, so now Jim's saved."

Rhia nodded. "I *do* think about it. I just wish Roderick and Frederique had been punished a little. But the earl's boat snatches them up and carries them to another castle. A new start, just like that—poof! Though, of course, Leonard . . ." She shivered, then smiled. "You saved things that night, Thaddeus. You always have just the right words."

He frowned at her, puzzled. "Me? Rhia, you did that *thing* you do."

"*What* thing?" She tapped the cross upon her chin, waiting for him to explain.

"*That* thing! Since your mother gave that neckpiece to you, when things get tense, you tap the cross upon your chin! You were doing it when Jonah looked over at us, and it was *that* got through to him. My words may have done a little, I'll grant. But no, Rhia. It was definitely that little thing you do with your mother's cross that broke the lock his anger had upon his mind. Maybe it was the cross. Maybe it was, well, the *Rhia*-ness of it, reminding him of friendship and its power to heal. Probably both."

She sat there blinking. She had never been more stunned.

Thaddeus jumped to his feet. "I've got an idea. Let's follow him a little! C'mon, from the edge of the bluff we may be able to spot him as he makes that jagged turn on the trail where the trees are bent back!"

"Yes!" Rhia's heart leapt at the prospect of another glimpse of Jonah.

They raced along the path, and arrived at the rim winded and panting. They dropped upon their stomachs side by side and eased over the edge as far as they dared, holding with their fingertips so as not to slide too far.

"Do you see him?"

"Not yet, but . . . yes! Yes, yes!" Thaddeus raised one arm to wave it. "Jonah! Pilgrim, we spy you, we spy you! Hey, up here! Look, look! Up *here*! It's us!"

"Jonah! Jonah, Jonah, Jonah! We can seeeeee you! We can seeeeee you!"

The pilgrim turned and looked, then grinned so wide that Rhiannon knew for a fact the previous leave-taking had been as unsatisfactory for him as it had been for them. He pushed back his penitent's hood and let his wild hair salute them as he waved his staff in the air. "Godspeed, you both!" he called.

"And you as well! Godspeed, and we will hope to meet again!" Thaddeus yelled.

And then the pilgrim raised his hood and turned his back and was gone.

"We must never talk of him in town, or even with your family," Thaddeus said. "To us, he's Sir Jonah ever, a pilgrim who's merely detoured through our lives as he took the road to Saint Winifred's shrine. He wants and needs to be incognito."

"Still," Rhia breathed, "to think the Prince of England helped my granna soothe her bunions with a barley water soak."

They sat up, laughing, the wind from the sea blowing their hair.

"I will not leave you, Rhia. When I return from Glastonbury, I must decorate your church, and this time I promise not to use my recipe for glow paint!" He grinned. "It may take some time to do that work, and to help my brothers settle into their nursing."

She nodded. "And then you'll work at painting the church in Woethersly, yes? It's near enough to see you sometimes."

He frowned a little and looked to the sea. "I'm still oblate, but as I said when I came up here, I'm not certain at all about the church, less so all the time. The world seems so large, and God's work may be done in so many different ways."

She took a breath, so filled with hope and relief that she felt she'd burst with it. She'd longed all her life to believe the pagan enchants that Granna told of, and yet look at how the cross she had from Mam had been the mysterious agent of so much! And they *would* see Jonah again. Of *course* they would! And also, Mary's arm was almost healed!

She threw out her arms. "Mysteries! The world *swirls* with them, Thaddeus! Not just the ancient ones, but new ones as well. Everywhere we walk, we walk amongst mysteries and wonders!"

He was turned toward her, looking at her, she felt it.

"I fear I shall never be kissed, either," he said quietly.

And somehow, mysteriously, she knew he waited to see what she'd say back.

So taking a cue from fearless Beornia, she turned to meet his eyes and let her own eyes say that he need have no fear of that.